Epic of Ahiram

ಬಾಡ಼

Book One

Age of the Seer

Michael Joseph Murano

Oct 25 2014

Epic of Ahiram

ഌ൧ഝ

Book One

Age of the Seer

Michael Joseph Murano
CandleBright Books
EpicOfAhiram.Com/AgeOfTheSeer

Printed in the United States of America.
Text set in Adobe Jenson.

Book cover by Maria Bowman
Weapon on cover crafted by Josh Bowman

Murano, Michael (Michael Joseph) The Games of the Mines / Michael J. Murano. – 1st American ed.
p. cm. – (The Epic of Ahiram; bk. 1)
Summary: Ahiram, a slave in the Kingdom of Tanniin, seeks to regain his freedom by winning the Games of the Mines. Little does he know the Temple of Baal would level the entire kingdom to kill him.

ISBN: 978-0-9913200-1-1

0 1 1 2 3 5 8 13 21 34

To Anouk and the Gang
May the flame of Truth burn true
Always
In your hearts and hearth

CONTENTS

ACKNOWLEDGMENTS

To friends and early fans who kept me going.
To the strangers who told me not to give up.
To the shore of my homeland and my mother's elfish gaze.
To the league of editors, herders of the wild comma and grand masters of English grammar.

Thank you.

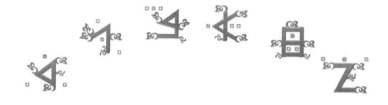

Twenty-two uncreated Letters of supernal power
To free from the Bottomless Pit the Lords of Darkness.
Their sleepless malice stirs beneath the mighty fallen tower,
Yearning to fill the hearts of men with madness.

In the raging Pit of Fire and everlasting darkness.

Standing before the dawn of the second Age of Blood,
Facing the terror of the Pit at the final hour,
A Seer alone will rise to stem the raging flood,
Commanding the twenty-two Letters of supernal power.

In the raging Pit of Fire and everlasting darkness.

Maps

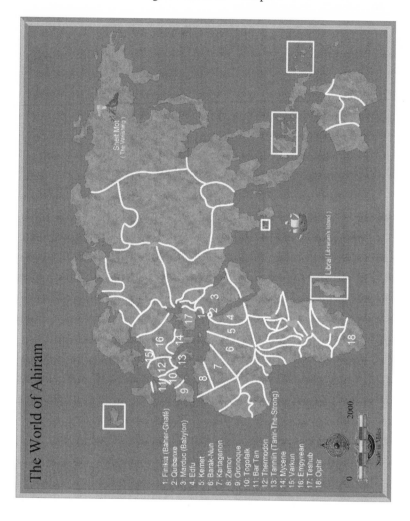

The World of Ahiram

1: Finikia (Baher-Ghafé)
2: Quibanxe
3: Marduc (Babylon)
4: Edfu
5: Kemet
6: Barak-Nun
7: Kartagenon
8: Zemor
9: Oronoque
10: Togofalk
11: Bar Tan
12: Thermodon
13: Tannin (Tanir-The-Strong)
14: Mycene
15: Varkun
16: Empyrean
17: Teshub
18: Ophir

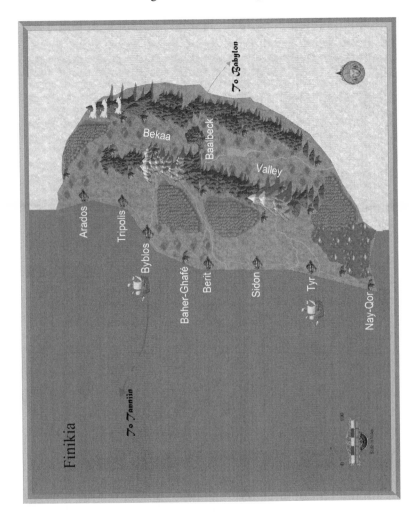

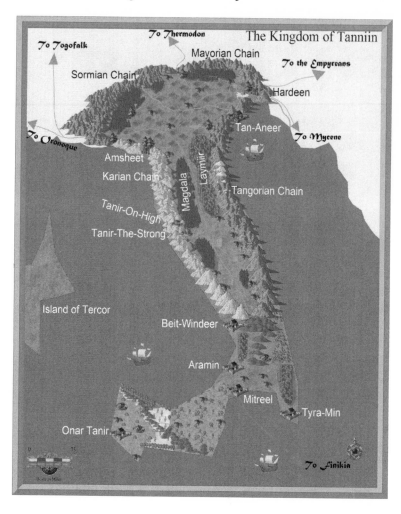

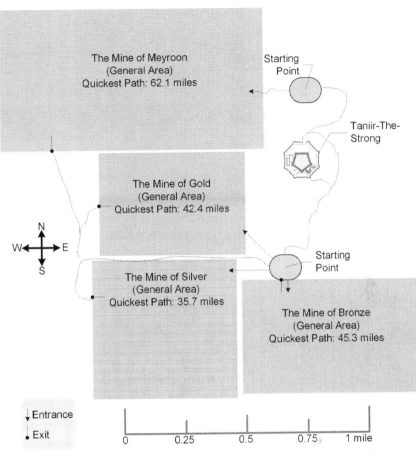

The Mine of Meyroon
(General Area)
Quickest Path: 62.1 miles

Starting
Point

Taniir-The-
Strong

The Mine of Gold
(General Area)
Quickest Path: 42.4 miles

N
W◄———►E
S

Starting
Point

The Mine of Silver
(General Area)
Quickest Path: 35.7 miles

The Mine of Bronze
(General Area)
Quickest Path: 45.3 miles

Entrance

Exit

| 0 | 0.25 | 0.5 | 0.75 | 1 mile |

TANIIR-THE-STRONG AND THE MINES

Age of the Seer – Maps

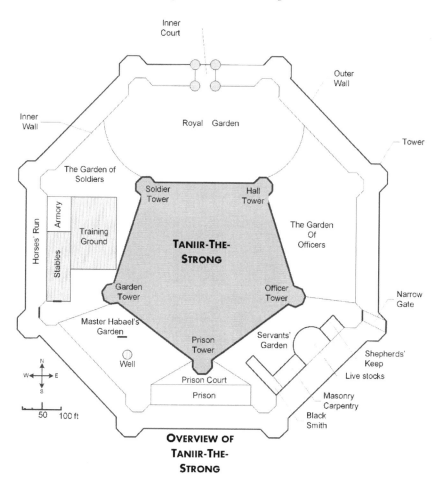

Inner Court

Outer Wall

Inner Wall

Royal   Garden

Tower

The Garden of Soldiers

Soldier Tower

Hall Tower

Horses' Run

Armory

Training Ground

Stables

TANIIR-THE-STRONG

The Garden Of Officers

Garden Tower

Officer Tower

Narrow Gate

Master Habael's Garden

Servants' Garden

Prison Tower

Well

Shepherds' Keep

Live stocks

N
W ← → E
S

Prison Court

Masonry

Prison

Carpentry

50   100 ft

Black Smith

OVERVIEW OF TANIIR-THE-STRONG

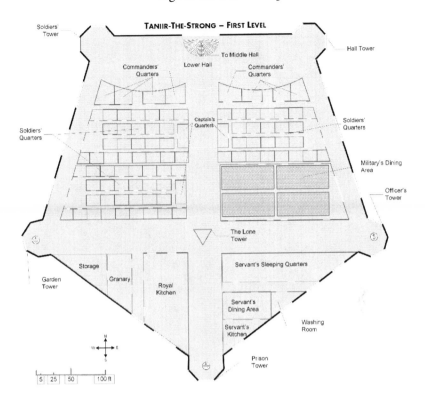

TANIIR-THE-STRONG – FIRST LEVEL

Soldiers' Tower

Hall Tower

To Middle Hall

Lower Hall

Commanders' Quarters

Commanders' Quarters

Captain's Quarters

Soldiers' Quarters

Soldiers' Quarters

Military's Dining Area

Officer's Tower

The Lone Tower

Storage

Servant's Sleeping Quarters

Garden Tower

Granary

Royal Kitchen

Servant's Dining Area

Washing Room

Servant's Kitchen

Prison Tower

5 25 50 100 ft

Age of the Seer – Maps

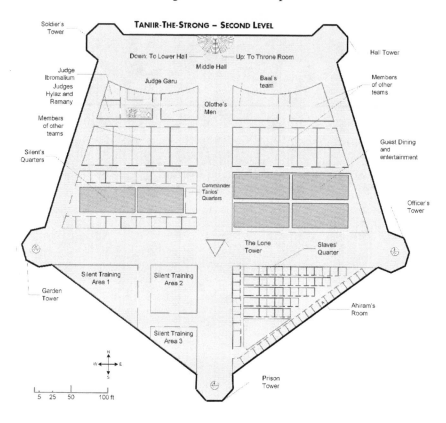

TANIIR-THE-STRONG – SECOND LEVEL

Soldier's Tower

Hall Tower

Down: To Lower Hall — Up: To Throne Room

Middle Hall

Judge Ibromalium
Judges Hylaz and Ramany

Judge Garu

Baal's team

Members of other teams

Olothe's Men

Members of other teams

Silent's Quarters

Guest Dining and entertainment

Commander Tanios' Quarters

Officer's Tower

The Lone Tower

Slaves' Quarter

Silent Training Area 1

Silent Training Area 2

Garden Tower

Ahiram's Room

Silent Training Area 3

Prison Tower

N
W — E
S

5 25 50 100 ft

Part One

ഇ‌ൻ

Festival of Light

1. TWELVE PIECES OF GOLD

"Baher-Ghafé, O slumbering giant, watchful day and night. Waiting. You who brought us glad tidings; a Seer, to see what we may not. How I wish I could gaze on your blessed shores again."
—**Memoirs of Shalimar the Poet**

Behind a crumbling pillar, deep within the ruins of the temple to the unknown god, stood a man with an assassin's dagger. His left hand toyed incessantly with two glass orbs. His eyes, steely and impatient, were locked on a brother and sister selling shark meat across the main plaza in the ancient city of Byblos. The young woman had a fair complexion with jet-black, curly hair which fell down in richly cascading locks, framing a serene face with two black eyes as tender as the dew, yet as strong as a tempest wind. Her brother's auburn, curly hair was longer than customary for a fisherman's child. The boy kept shifting his weight from one leg to another, while running his fingers on a wooden table.

"Imagine that. A wiry child from Baher-Ghafé is the recipient of a Merilian medallion," muttered the man. "How did my master find you, my young friend? How did he know you are a Merilian bearer?"

He took a red medallion out of a small pouch and slid it between the two glass orbs, which snapped against the metallic surface like iron to magnet. A flickering, red line shone inside the round objects, mist swirled from their surface, slithered like a snake and turned into a new, larger orb. A distorted face appeared on its hazy surface.

"Have you found it?" a disembodied voice whispered.

"You were right: it's with the boy," replied the man.

"Do not come back without it. If they take gold, then all is well, otherwise, do what you must."

"Understood," said the man, laughing sardonically. He waited for the face to fade before snatching the medallion from the grip of the glassy orbs. They shattered into a gray powder that fell heavily to his feet. Keeping his eyes on the young woman, he returned the red rondure to the pouch, grabbed two medallions—a silver and a rosewood—and hooked them to the gold chain under his shirt. *A Control Spell to break the boy's will, and a Rose Spell to enchant his companion and make her believe in love at first sight.* He chuckled inwardly, already savoring what was about to happen.

≻❋❋❋≺

Hoda did not believe in love at first sight. Naturally, girls her age were wont to mention the names of young men they fancied, and naturally, Hoda could not help but wonder what her future husband might look like and where she would end up meeting him. But to be spellbound by a man at first sight? This was the exclusive province of wicked sorcerers, maladjusted gods, or impossibly beautiful women who did not have a younger brother to care for and shark meat to sell.

"Ahiram," she called to her brother, "I forgot the sharpener in the boat. Run and fetch it for me."

The young boy bolted, always happy to run. "Be back in one hundred heartbeats," he yelled, before disappearing down Sunset Street, which led to the port.

2

"Three pounds, if you please, Miss Hoda," said Seamar, a shy slave from the Golden Oar, the main inn across the civilian section of the port of Byblos. He glanced at her and blushed. Seamar, a thirteen-year-old busboy, believed Jabbar's daughter to be a goddess come to put men to the test, and he was not about to fail this time. Hoda gave him a passing glance. He thought the sun, moon, and stars had turned into a beautiful light, hidden in the young woman's eyes.

"That'll be three silver pieces," she told him as she handed the young boy the cut of shark meat. One silver coin was a port worker's weekly wage, and only Tawr, the inn's owner, could afford to buy so much meat every week. Seamar gave Hoda his most dazzling smile, and the goddess fell instantly in love with him, whisking him up into her heavenly chariot, to the acclaim of the citizens of Byblos, who chanted his name...

"Seamar, Seamar?"

The young boy dropped abruptly from the chariot back into mundane reality. He saw the young woman handing him the meat, neatly packed inside a palm leaf. He took it from Hoda's hands and blushed.

"Do not lose it now, alright?" she added gently.

Seamar's complexion turned a bright red that would have awed the pack of lobsters gracing the Golden Oar's kitchen this morning. He muttered a quick thank you, and convinced he had failed the test, hurried away disheartened.

"Oh, was that Seamar?" asked Ahiram handing his sister the sharpener. "Did I just miss him? That's too bad. I wanted to ask him if we could run together tomorrow. He is a good runner, he helps me stay focused. I like him."

Hoda smiled. Her soon-to-be twelve-year-old brother had never managed to tell a straight lie. Ahiram was the fastest young runner in Fineekia, whereas Seamar might be able to outrun a turtle, if someone bribed him with sweets. To hear Ahiram, Seamar was doing him a favor, when in fact, it was the other way around, as usual. Hoda tousled his curly hair and kissed him. He looked at her and smiled. His earliest memories were of his sister singing a lullaby and rocking him gently in his bed. Hoda meant the world to him, and he could not refuse her anything.

"Oh, look at this boy," said a dainty tourist from the Kingdom of Ophir. "Isn't he a doll with that curly hair of his?"

Her two friends giggled with glee. Realizing they were talking about him, Ahiram opened wide his eyes, then frowned. Hoda felt a knot in her stomach. She turned around and casually steered the three tourists toward the shark meat their father had caught this morning.

"Fresh shark meat, m'ladies," she said with a beaming smile, "the best you will find anywhere in Byblos."

"Ta, ta, ta, young lady, we care not for your meat, but I would love to buy this young boy over here and get him in my employ; he is so daaarling," she said getting closer. "I'd love to pinch these ruddy cheeks."

Ahiram's face hardened instantly. His eyes blazed with an otherworldly glow, warning Hoda that her little brother was about to charge the three ladies with the strength of an enraged bear. A few weeks ago, while running on the beach, he saw five boys tormenting a little girl. One of them took her tiny wooden doll and snapped it. Their laughter had not yet died when Ahiram came down on them like a wrathful storm. Nearby, a group of fishermen were tending their nets and they jumped at once when they heard the screams of terror and despair. What they saw defied their understanding: a wiry boy moving through air like a shark through water, pummeling five boys with such speed and power, such single-minded purpose that the fishermen feared for the lives of his victims. It took the combined strength of four strong men to subdue Ahiram before he had permanently maimed the boys.

The tourists drew closer. Hoda nearly panicked. Bending down, she grasped him by the shoulders and forced her brother to face her. "Look at me, Ahiram," she said, ignoring the three ladies who perked up, ready to turn an event into a gossip. "Do not lose your temper, and breathe deeply, like I showed you. Come on Ahiram, listen to my voice: breathe, breathe..."

Ahiram closed his eyes and followed his sister's directions, then whispered, "Hoda, make them go away. I don't want to hurt them."

"M'ladies," said Hoda standing back up, "I am so glad to know that you want to buy my brother. You see," she added in a conspiratorial tone, "ten days ago, a shark-dog nipped him—"

"A shark-dog?" exclaimed the woman who had wanted to buy Ahiram. Her consorts shrieked in chorus

"A baby shark-dog," added Hoda hastily. "Yes, it did. My brother contracted rabies." Hoda barely managed to contain a smirk. Rich tourists from faraway kingdoms visited Fineekia with strange, preconceived ideas. Commonly, these tourists believed that Fineekians rode on sharks, kept them as pets, and they even believed that the god Yem had allowed Fineekian dogs to interbreed with sharks, and that the resulting animal was a formidable land-shark with four legs. This superstition was so strong that dogs were banned from Byblos to avoid scaring the rich visitors.

"Rabies?" came the dramatic refrain.

"Who?" asked one of the ladies confused.

"My brother, of course," replied Hoda quickly. "But you don't have to worry: The high priestess healed him—well, mostly."

"Oh?" responded the women in chorus.

"He confuses women's hair with chicken's feathers. My poor mother is now bald, I am wearing a wig, and our unfortunate neighbor Miss Mrad is convinced someone took her six girls away and left her with six balding boys."

"Well, daaarling," said the woman who spoke first, "I think we shall pass then. We are already *very* late..." The women backed away and their chatter was soon lost in the crowd.

Ahiram burst out laughing. Hoda relaxed; they had averted the storm. "Balding girls! The Mrad girls with no hair. Wait until I tell them. A bit of that solvent we use to clean the boats with, maybe..."

"Ahiram, son of Jabbar," chided his sister, "you'll do nothing of the sort. Do you hear me young man?"

"I was just kidding, Hoda," replied Ahiram smiling. "But I do admit, it is very, very tempting. A bit of solvent with soap—"

"Hoda; at last I found you."

Ahiram looked up and saw a young woman running toward them, and undisturbed by the smell of fish meat, she hugged his sister. *How different she looks from Hoda*, thought the young boy. The young woman had frizzy, dirty-blond hair, a freckled face with no visible cheek bones, and her light blue eyes contained the Great Sea in all its mysteries.

"Syreen, is that you? I barely recognized you."

Ahiram's eyes bulged like saucepans and his jaw dropped. Was this tall, young woman the scrawny, little, freckled girl he used to scare by getting spiders to crawl up her arms? *Perhaps she remembers*, he thought, guilty as a drunken sailor. *What am I to do?*

Hoda and Syreen engaged in animated conversation while Ahiram manned the booth. He kept glancing nervously at Syreen, wondering if she remembered the spiders. Whenever she had visited with Hoda, his sister would shoo him away gently, and sit with her friend on his favorite branch atop his favorite oak. Deprived of his sister's company, he would mope around, miserable and lonely; hence the spiders.

Speaking with a voice as polite as a shining pair of boots in the Temple's hall, he called out to Syreen, "Miss Syreen, please accept this morsel of shark meat in reparation for all the spiders I put on your arms." He held the meat the way his mother held an offering in the Temple of Baal, as though Syreen were a goddess, and he a humble supplicant.

Syreen looked at Ahiram, then at Hoda, and realizing who he was and what he had just said, burst out in laughter. "Is this Ahiram, Hoda?

My goodness, he is so grown and so cute." Before he could react, Syreen walked inside their booth, gave him a prolonged hug—she smelled of cinnamon and sweet oil—and a sonorous kiss.

Nobody does this but Hoda, he thought, offended. Kisses were the privileged province of his sister—and his mother, of course—but no one else. Syreen, seeing him pouting, burst out laughing and tousled his hair.

Why do they keep messing up my hair? he thought. *Mother will have a fit when she sees me.*

"Hoda, I was so jealous of you growing up," said Syreen. "I am an only child and your brother was so cuddly when he was a baby. I often imagined taking him home with me, you know."

Hoda smiled and winked at Ahiram. "Look at you now, Syreen, the second maid to the first priestess of the Temple of Baalbeck. I am so happy for you."

Syreen's eyes clouded for a brief moment. "We work on rotation," she replied evenly. "Three months in, three months out."

"That's odd, why don't they keep you all year round?"

Syreen sighed. "Let's just say that our load is unusually demanding."

Hoda gazed into her friend's eyes, and knew not to ask more questions. *What are you hiding from me, Syreen?* wondered the young woman. *You are so restrained right now, I feel I am talking to a shadow of you. What have they done to you at the Temple?*

"Morning of goodness," said a young man, utilizing the traditional Fineekian greeting. "Syreen, I hope I am not interrupting."

"Oh, Hoda," said Syreen with a twinkle in her eye, "I'd like you to meet my cousin, Karadon."

"Morning of light," said Hoda, giving the usual response. She looked at Karadon, and with no prior warning, fell in love... just like that. Or rather, fell into eternity. The world came to a stand-still, and Karadon's green eyes became the Great Sea carrying her to the ends of the earth. In that moment, Hoda knew all she needed to know about the world; it was passing away like grass, green today and burned tomorrow, but the surpassing power of love endures like an eternal river flowing from heart to heart. In that moment—that one perfect moment—Hoda found her center, the meaning of her life, and the purpose for which she was created: to love and be loved. Words, trivial and often destitute, shone with an everlasting light she had not known existed.

Karadon, awestruck, knew then that all he had lost would be restored to him: his village razed and burned to the ground by the High Riders of the Temple of Baal, his parents and all his friends massacred by the soldiers, and his shattered childhood. All of it, one day, would be healed and restored. Unexpectedly, the pain he had endured all these years began to lift. Karadon had just found his anchor, his strength, the woman of his life, and he knew, with the certainty of the heavens, that they were destined to be together.

On that bright, early morning of the month of Kislev, when the waning summer yearns to light up the forest with the mellifluous colors of fall, life in the eyes of Karadon and Hoda was a recollected lake beneath the heavens, and their gaze a fluttering sail tugging at a ship making ready for an unexpected journey to last a lifetime.

"How much for the medallion?"

The raspy voice hit them like a boulder shattering the calm of the lake. Hoda and Karadon exchanged a quick smile, then eyed the man who had just spoken. *Look at his clothes,* thought Hoda, *how outlandish. Most definitely a foreigner.* The stranger wore silk trousers, black boots reaching mid-thigh, a baggy red shirt, a white turban, and a thick, gray cloak. He had just addressed her brother, and his accent was so thick she could barely make out his words.

Seeing her react so calmly, the outsider staggered. *Impossible,* he thought. *The spell is not working.*

"Excuse me, sir," interjected Hoda. "May I help you?"

He looked Hoda in the eye and asked with a gentle voice if Ahiram was her brother. Confused, she nodded.

Good, the spell of enchantment is working after all, he thought.

"Your brother," he whispered, "is wearing a medallion." And with snakelike speed pulled it from under Ahiram's shirt.

"This medallion," he said with a quiver in his voice, "I would like to purchase it. Name your price."

"How did you know I had it on?" snapped Ahiram, his voice shaking with anger. "I haven't told anyone."

"I saw the chain on your neck," lied the stranger. "Besides, what does it matter? I want to buy it from you. Name your price."

Hoda felt a powerful surge of emotion engulf her like a crashing wave. Her will began to waver when Ahiram's voice, hard as steel, cut through the confusion:

"It is not for sale." The man's attention went back to the young boy.

"Come now, young man," he said softly, "I am prepared to offer you two pieces of gold." The emotional surge came back, and Hoda struggled to contain her feelings; feelings that did not capture her heart but seemed intent on forcing themselves upon her will.

Ahiram was speechless. The medallion had a dull, dark-gray appearance with a plain surface, and a thick, outer ring where a small, black peg protruded. It looked and felt like a trinket parents buy for their children. A shark fisherman might earn two gold coins after six months of hard work, and for a port worker two years.

"Thank you, sir," he replied calmly, "it is a generous offer, but I cannot sell it. It is a gift from my mother."

Impossible, how can this boy resist my spell? The stranger could not have known that the moment his powerful Control Spell reached Ahiram, it was met by the boy's temper. The two forces clashed and had quickly reached a stalemate; the spell became a soothing balm over Ahiram's fiery temper, leaving the young boy free to think clearly.

I can control my temper, Ahiram thought to himself. *Hoda was right.*

"I offer you twelve pieces of gold," said the stranger with mounting frustration.

"Thank you, sir," said Ahiram reveling in patience he never knew he had, "but a mother's gift cannot be sold for all the gold in the world."

"Incredible," muttered the man, "how are you..." He shook his head and yelled, "Are you slow? I am offering you twelve gold coins for a simple medallion."

"If it is so simple, why do you offer me this much money?" retorted Ahiram calmly.

Had their faces been any closer, their noses would have touched. "It is for my daughter. She likes medallions," countered the stranger.

"Well, this is one medallion your daughter will not have," cut in Ahiram sharply. "Would you like some shark meat instead?"

Karadon laughed. The enchantment was definitely broken.

Mortified, the man lifted his hand to strike the insolent boy, but Karadon stayed his arm, saying in a casual voice, "Careful, High Riders are behind you."

The man snatched his arm away. "I am not done with you," he snapped at Ahiram before disappearing into the crowd.

"What was all that about?" exclaimed Syreen, looking intently at the medallion. Quickly, Ahiram slid it back under his shirt.

"I don't know," replied Hoda. "Mother gave my brother this medallion at birth to ward off the evil eye."

"Well, no harm was done," replied Karadon smiling. Hoda met his gaze and felt her heart explode. Inwardly, she chided herself, *You're being silly, Hoda, focus.* She noticed her brother looking at her, and she knew instantly what his question was: "Did I do well?" She smiled, and that smile was all that he needed.

"Why don't you go run on the beach now?" she suggested. "You earned it."

"But the booth— I must help you clean up."

"Don't you worry about a thing. I'll take care of it."

"And Karadon and I will give your sister a hand," added Syreen, grinning. For a split second, Ahiram thought the grin meant she was about to take revenge because of the spiders.

"Go on now," said Hoda. "Don't worry, I will take care of the booth."

"I know how to scrub," said Karadon. "I am a very good scrubber. I mean, I can scrub this entire plaza and all the adjoining rooms. No wait— this is absurd, there are no adjoining rooms here. What I am trying to say is that I could scrub anything else that needs scrubbing: your house, if you'd like me to, or, well, actually, your house's door, or the entrance to your door, or..."

Syreen handed him a brush.

"Scrub, then. Hoda, do you realize that Karadon has uttered more words now than he has ever said to me since we were children?"

Hoda's heart skipped a beat, and she kissed her brother to hide her red cheeks. He sprinted toward the beach. "Don't be late for supper," she said, but he was already gone.

"Syreen, I am certain you're exaggerating," she said, glancing at Karadon who had rolled up his sleeves. *Good, not too hairy,* she thought, satisfied.

"Not at all," replied Syreen enjoying herself, "this is the plain truth."

"But I am sure you two must have had long conversations," protested Hoda, wishing she had been there.

Karadon did not reply, but his scrubbing accelerated.

"Oh no," said Syreen, "I had long monologues. He, on the other hand, had long grunts."

"Grunts?" replied Hoda "Really?"

If Karadon scrubbed any faster, he would have lit the table on fire.

"Isn't it so, Karadon?" asked Syreen with an innocent voice.

Involuntarily, he grunted. The two girls burst out laughing. Karadon stopped, wiped his brow and joined them.

The booth had three tables and a light, linen tarp to shade them from the sun. Having cleaned all the buckets, the tables, and the two chairs, they stowed the utensils in a wooden box under the main table and walked toward the shore.

"So, Ahiram has a hot temper?" asked Syreen casually.

"You noticed, didn't you?" replied Hoda. "You were always the perceptive one. My parents are at their wits' end, and I..." she stopped, and she, who was ordinarily so strong, could barely contain her tears. Syreen squeezed her shoulder. Karadon simply listened.

"I am scared, Syreen. I don't know what to do. I feel I am losing him. He is trying so hard, but it seems he is unable to contain this... dark rage. I don't know what it is... It scares me."

Karadon and Syreen exchanged a long glance but said nothing. Then Karadon lifted Hoda's spirits by recounting his voyage to the Land of the Marada. He spoke quickly, using short sentences punctuated by long grunts.

"Amazing," said Hoda, after he was done. "Traveling like that must have been expensive. How did you afford it, I wonder?" Inwardly, she was already expecting him to tell her that he was the son of a rich man, which would put an end to any romantic ideas she may have had.

"I was on the crew of a wealthy carpet merchant during the journey. He and his wife were very generous, and they took good care of us."

"I see," said Hoda, happy. She started to smile but thought it would be unbecoming and ended up with a smirk.

"We must be on our way, Hoda," said Syreen. She hugged her friend and whispered, "I will come and see you next week at the market. I promise." Hoda nodded but said nothing.

"Goodbye, Hoda, it was very nice to scrub the plaza with you... I mean, it was nice to meet you," said Karadon blushing.

She nodded, "You're definitely a good scrubber."

What am I saying? she thought, and quickly ran down Sunset Street.

A week later, Hoda was back at the market with a fresh batch of shark steak, a delicacy only the well-to-do could afford. To avoid angering Yem, the god of the sea, Bahiya, the high priestess, had commanded the fishermen not to exceed five hundred sharks each season. Even though Baal forbade the cult of Yem, the priestess showed her respects to Yem in order to protect the villagers from his wrath. According to the fishermen, Yem prowled the coast as a huge double-finned shark, a shark no one ever landed. Supposedly, shark meat granted those who ate it the strength of the beast and protection during travel. The cynics contended that the priestess used the meat as bait to exact favors from the wealthy. Others, more business minded, saw an opportunity, and an underground market quietly flourished in Byblos. There, eager travelers bought morsels of dried shark meat, paying fivefold the price for fresh meat.

The sale of shark meat in Byblos was strictly controlled, requiring express permission from the high priestess and Jabbar—Hoda and Ahiram's father—was one of the few chosen ones to receive Bahiya's approval. Still, he knew his fellow villagers very well, and, as such, contributed more than his fair share to the common purse. "You can get rich alone," he told his children, "or you can be rich with friends and family. Choose wisely."

"Hoda."

She had just finished setting up her booth, looked up and smiled when she saw Syreen, but her smile turned into veiled disappointment when she did not see Karadon.

"My cousin sends his greetings," said her friend with a sheepish smile. "He wanted to come with me, you know, for the shark meat, and just in case there was a bit more scrubbing to do, but he had to go out of town. He will be back next week." Hoda nodded. Her friend continued, "I can't stay for very long, and this is not the right place to talk. Could you come over after hours for a short visit?"

"I would love to, Syreen, but Ahiram is punished again. He got into a terrible fight and I am—"

"It is about your brother," cut in Syreen. "I have news. Please come." Hoda held her breath and looked at her friend who read her anguish. "I think we found a way to help him. I will tell you later."

"Who's *we?*" asked Hoda, confused.

Syreen cocked her head and gave her friend a reproachful gaze, "Karadon and I, silly. Who else?"

Hoda felt a wave of gratitude surge from within. She was relieved, relieved that she did not have to carry that weight alone. Ever since he was a baby, Ahiram had given Hoda his best smiles and his most tender coos, and when he became a toddler, she gave him a doll Syreen had made for her: a goat with two tiny bells. Immediately, he named it "Doda," and he and Doda became inseparable for years.

When Ahiram turned eight, the nightmares began, and he would run to Hoda crying. Then came the bad temper and the stormy rage and the brawls that became more frequent. It broke Hoda's heart to see him tormented, and she did everything in her power to ease his pain and protect him. Then, Arfaad, the captain of the High Riders, told her father that unless Ahiram learned to control his temper, he might end up dead in a dark alley one day. His words sent a chill to her heart.

Hoda could hardly wait for the market to close. Finally, after cleaning and closing the booth, she hastened to Syreen's house. Leaving the main thoroughfare, she went to Astarte Street, and just as she was about to cross Melkart Street, she saw the stranger who had wanted to buy Ahiram's medallion. He was leaning against the wall across the street. As soon as their eyes met, he started walking toward her. Entranced, she watched him get closer, unable to move, when a bucketful of cold water fell on the man, drenching him. They both looked up and saw only deserted balconies. Not waiting, Hoda ran. *What's wrong with me?* she wondered. *What is that man doing to me?*

Hoda sped through the busy roads of Byblos, zigzagging through a series of narrow streets until she reached the back alley behind Syreen's house. She knocked at a narrow, low door and was relieved to see her friend. This was the back door to Syreen's parents' expansive and expensive home, the door the two girls preferred to the ornate, marble front entrance.

"Hoda, are you alright? Did you run?"

"Yes," said the young woman breathlessly, "I ran into the man who wanted to buy Ahiram's medallion as I was crossing Melkart Street."

"How did he know you were coming this way?" asked Syreen after taking a quick peek into the alley; it was deserted.

"I don't know. And the way he looked at me..." she shivered.

"Come, I have hot tea steeping in my room. Let's sit and talk like we used to do when we were little."

Hoda smiled and followed her friend to her large bedroom, where they sat on a sea of brightly colored pillows surrounded by a cheerful collection of dolls.

"I love these," said Hoda, admiring her friend's handiwork. "They are beautiful, Syreen. You know, Ahiram had your Doda for two full years before he lost it in the sea. It was as if he had lost..."

"You?" completed Syreen. "Hoda, I know how much you care for him, and I am here to help."

"Thank you, Syreen," replied Hoda. "I really do think your dolls are amazing. You are so talented."

"Hoda, all that is mine is yours, but customers must purchase them from Master Kwadil. He is my exclusive distributor."

"Master Kwadil—wait, what? Kwadil? *The* Kwadil from the world famous 'Caravan from Beyond'? Are you serious?"

"Actually, I am. I needed silk cloth, and he had the best silk money could buy. He asked me what I would do with it, and I showed him my dolls. He told me to make as many as I could and that he would buy them all."

"Wonderful. It means you can retire from the Temple and run your own shop."

"It's a possibility," Syreen replied evasively. "Now listen, about that man—I felt it too."

"That weird feeling? Like someone roping your emotions and pulling you to him, even though you really don't want to go that way?"

"You are perceptive, Hoda. It is an Enchantment Spell," explained Syreen calmly.

Hoda gasped. "An Enchantment Spell? How did you find out?"

Syreen smiled. "Hoda, as a maid to the first priestess, I received basic training in the detection of simple spells. You would not believe the number of people willing to risk their lives to sway or charm the first priestess."

"Why the first priestess?" asked Hoda, whose curiosity got the better of her. "Why not the high priestess?"

Fear shot through Syreen's eyes. "Bahiya? No one would dare use an Enchantment Spell on her; she is too powerful."

"So this man, he was..."

"Yes, using a spell. He wants your brother's medallion at all cost."

Hoda looked at her, alarmed.

"What do you mean?"

"I mean," said Syreen, choosing her words carefully, "that he tried to buy it from your brother and failed. Next, he will try to enchant you into bringing him the medallion, and if all else fails, he will try to steal it by any means necessary."

"What?" said Hoda, scared. "But why? What is going on?"

"You're not going to like what I have to say. Still, I think it is good news... of sorts."

"Syreen, please tell me. What did you find out?"

"Promise me you will tell no one. You cannot share what I am about to tell you with anyone: not with Ahiram, not with your parents, nor anyone else."

"I promise," she said breathless. "Now, please tell me."

"Hoda, this medallion is... well, it may be a magical artifact."

"What?" exclaimed Hoda. Blood drained from her face. She stood up and backed away from her friend.

Syreen went to her, held her hand, and looked her in the eyes. "I know what you are thinking, Hoda, but I am your friend. If I wanted to alert the Temple, you and your family would be dead by now."

"Why didn't you?" asked Hoda, still panicked. "You work for the Temple, and we were all told, ever since we were little, that whenever we find someone with a magical artifact, we had to tell the Temple. You are risking your life and your family for us. Why?"

"I have my reasons, Hoda. You said it yourself; I work for the Temple and have access to the first priestess." Syreen repeated slowly, "If I wanted to let the Temple know, I would have done so already." At that, Hoda relaxed her stance somewhat.

"Hoda, please hear me, then decide whether you should trust me or not. As I said, Hoda, it is a possibility. We are not certain, but there is a very easy way to check. Tonight, when Ahiram is sleeping, take the medallion off of him. If the medallion is not magical, nothing will happen."

"And if it is, what would happen?"

"Well, we are not certain," continued Syreen. She hated this conversation and the pain she was causing her friend, but it could not be helped. "You might see improvement in Ahiram's behavior or..."

"Or what?"

"Well, we are not sure. Look, wait for Ahiram to fall asleep, then take the medallion from him."

"Why not ask him to let me have his medallion for the night? Ahiram would do anything for me."

"That's the thing. We need you to take it from him without his consent. If the medallion is a magical artifact, it will cause a reaction."

"Will Ahiram be harmed?"

"We don't think so because the medallion would still be close."

Hoda shivered. "So, if Ahiram consented to sell his medallion to that man yesterday..."

"Exactly. He must not, under any circumstance, lose this medallion until we find out more. Listen, Hoda, if the Temple catches wind of this, they will, at the very least, kill your entire family, or worse, destroy the whole village and everyone in it. We must act fast."

"But I don't understand," cut in Hoda. "Ahiram has had this medallion from birth. Mother said that she bought it from Master Kwadil, that it is a trinket to ward off the evil eye."

Syreen averted her eyes and did not answer.

"But why would my mother tell a lie?"

"Maybe your mother is telling the truth, and maybe this is a trinket. There is no sense worrying about this until we know more."

"How will I know that the first priestess did not ask you to do this, and once you find out, the High Riders, they..."

Syreen laughed a bitter, sarcastic laugh. "Hoda, Hoda, you do not know the Temple; they have their ways—terrible ways—to locate any source of magic. They don't need my help, believe you me."

They gazed at each other for a short moment. Hoda sighed and spoke first. "Well, our lives are in your hands. I wouldn't know what to do or whom to go to, even if I wanted to."

"And I ask you to trust me. I have not changed, Hoda, I am still Syreen. What I said about Ahiram last week is true, I wanted to take him home with me, he was so cute, and the way he wanted to give me the shark meat because of the spiders..." tears welled up in Syreen's eyes, "...such innocence, Hoda. It's so precious."

Hoda relaxed and smiled. "Thank you, Syreen. I will let you know as soon as I find out."

"Take the tunnel to the beach," advised Syreen.

"The tunnel we used to follow whenever we would sneak out of your house to go to the beach? Do you remember when your father caught us? The drubbing we got..."

Syreen smiled. "Yes, *that* passage. Follow it to the beach then go home that way."

"But what do I do about that man? Maybe I should go to the High Riders?"

"That would not be wise; they would find out about the medallion. Instead, why don't you tell your father that a man was following you? I know what your father is capable of when his anger flares."

"I'll think about it," said Hoda, as she turned and headed down the stairway to the tunnel below. She then stopped and looked at her friend. "I know this will sound crazy, but part of me hopes that it *is* magical."

"Because it would help explain your brother's temper?"

"Yes," confirmed Hoda. "It would give us something to work with."

"Be strong now," urged Syreen. "You are about to get some answers."

Hoda smiled. "It is easy to have strength when you are fighting for someone you love, and when you have a good friend to help you."

"And more than a friend," said Syreen, a twinkle in her eyes. "You know Karadon is itching for some scrubbing and..."

Hoda blushed and stepped into the dark corridor. Up ahead she could see the crashing waves of an agitated sea. She walked through the tunnel onto a secluded beach; seeing that it was deserted, she sprinted home.

Four men rose from the ground and watched her run.

2. A Second Medallion

"Three Merilians are known to the dwarfs. Three medallions whose power surpasses that of the Temple. Three objects of deep magic beyond our understanding, beyond our reach, beyond the Powers of the Pit."
—Philology of the Dwarfs, Anonymous

Four thousand miles southwest of Fineekia, on the remote Island of Libra, the warden of the Empty Seat of the Librarian stood alone in the main hall of the Library. He was contemplating  a medallion identical in every way to the medallion Ahiram was wearing, except for the position of the small black peg that was slightly off. This medallion was hanging by a simple nail above the ebony seat that no one had sat in since the days of Sureï the Sorcerer. Aside from the medallion and the seat, the building was completely empty, with the exception of an object floating up high in the main hall: a *libre* (a book) that no one had read for as long as anyone could remember. This was the *Libre Aharof* (the *Book of Power*) and whosoever could open and read it would control a magic so powerful it would make Baal's artifice look like child's play, a trick or even a mere trinket.

But no one had ever dared open that book, even though the Library doors were always open, and no one guarded the strange object. What was more, the Temple of Baal, which controlled the island, had not moved it to a secure location. The reason for this apparent lack of care was the powerful and intricate curse which Sureï the Sorcerer, the First Librarian, had cast on the building and its contents. A curse from Sureï was not empty words, for its effects would be disastrous if triggered. It would kill anyone who tried to break it with a very slow and painful death. In most cases, anyone present during the attempt shared the same fate; and in other rare instances, it led to the annihilation of the immediate vicinity. In short, no one in his right mind would ever defy the greatest sorcerer that ever lived.

Except, perhaps, Jethro. The warden was convinced he had the perfect plan to break the curse and open the book. This sordid affair began five years ago, when, after celebrating his thirtieth anniversary as the warden of the Empty Seat of the Librarian, Jethro heard a raspy voice whisper sweetly in his ear. It told him that he was the rightful owner of the medallion, that he should be the one to wield it, unlock the *Libre Aharof*, and break Baal's staff. So sweet and exhilarating was this voice, and so insistent in its tender plea, that the old man lost his senses and became obsessed with the medallion. His obsession was the worst kind; that of a man disgusted by his mediocrity who, having reached the twilight of his existence, believed with the strength of desperation, that he was given this one last chance to make a name for himself.

Still, his zeal did not overcome his pusillanimity—the fuel of his mediocrity—and he knew not to defy the curse with his own paltry means. He needed a partner, someone he could misdirect, abuse, and ultimately throw away once the deed was done; someone foolish enough to take the brunt of the curse, leaving him the luxury of plucking the libre without incurring Sureï's implacable wrath.

Every year, Baal sent a priest from the Inner Circle to conduct an inspection of the Library. This was then followed by a pleasurable tour of the island and its many stunning natural landmarks. Over the past four years, each consecutive priest had ignored him, acting as if he did not exist. *But then*, thought Jethro, *Rahaak noticed me*.

Ashod was the visiting priest the year he received his private revelation, as Jethro affectionately called the voice he had heard. Ashod led an ascetic life, refusing to taste beer or wine. He ate very little and slept even less. He was kind to the orphans on the island and avoided getting entangled in the daily disputes of the citizens. Before leaving, he warned Jethro not to touch the medallion.

"Your gaze tells me the medallion has captivated you. Beware, Jethro, the sweet song of magic; it will always deceive you. Do not forget that the greatest magic is in the gaze of a child. Spend more time with these orphans; they will heal you from this poisonous hunger."

But Jethro was too far gone to listen to the priest. Like a hungry spider, he waited and watched three more visiting priests come and go; priests who knew better than to tamper with magical artifacts cursed by Sureï the Sorcerer.

Jethro nearly despaired of ever reaching his goal until he met Rahaak six months ago. When he spoke to Jethro with great deference, the shrewd warden knew that this man, consumed by a secret ambition, would be the one to satisfy his raging hunger. Rahaak would help him break the curse.

Having completed his official visit, the priest lingered, and the two men spent much time talking about the Library. Jethro revealed to Rahaak that the wearer of the medallion would sit on the Seat of the Librarian and command every secret in the Library. In truth, Jethro had no idea what would happen if someone sat in that seat, and he carefully avoided mentioning the *Libre Aharof*. *Let the fool sit wherever he wants*, he thought. *Once the libre is in my hands, I will use the Letters of Power to break the rod of Baal and ride after the sun from its rising to its setting.*

"There you are, Your Excellency," said Rahaak, walking through the monumental door. "Amazing, isn't it?" he said admiring the walls and floors of the Library. "To think that this structure has been standing here for over eight hundred years, with neither scratches on its walls nor dents in its immaculate floors."

Elated, Rahaak raised his arms to the heavens; arms where sagging fat rippled and moved like slush. Jethro averted his eyes, for Rahaak's obesity, due to his insatiable appetite, verged on the obscene.

"Indeed, my Lord," replied the warden. "The Library is made of this unknown golden element which has proved indestructible." Rahaak's grin reminded Jethro of a shark. He nervously scratched his scalp—a scalp speckled with stiff locks of hair, resembling a desert peppered with clusters of cacti—and his scrawny arms looked like pointy twigs next to Rahaak's.

"Concerning the little matter of the medallion," continued the priest, "I stepped into Baal's circle of power, and it revealed to me how to break the curse."

Jethro's soul sucked these words like parched earth sucks water after a long drought. He was elated and so was Rahaak, but the two men misunderstood each other, and this misunderstanding was about to change the fate of the world.

Jethro believed Rahaak's words to be filled with power and divine authority. They confirmed the warden's secret desire: the voice he had heard five years ago, the voice commanding him to open the *Book of Power*—was Baal's. And now, the powerful and benevolent god had sent a priest to help him. Jethro saw himself as the new ruler of the Temple. He imagined the high priest and the entire priestly order of Baal bowing to him as he sat on the Seat of the Librarian and ruled the world.

Rahaak had heard a voice as well, but what he had heard was altogether different. The voice had ordered him to break Sureï's curse by lining twelve orbs of magic in front of him and fueling them with two concentrators; a task far more dangerous than ordering twelve tigers to stand in line before him to be hand-fed chunks of raw meat.

The Temple was merciless to the practitioners of magic who did not belong to its orders, but to its own, Baal provided magic aplenty in the form of orbs and concentrators. The orbs—dark glassy balls—were channels of magic that sourced from a single location; the Arayat, a world where every curse and every act of magic was grown and cultivated. To unleash this power, the orbs had to be activated and aligned in precise geometric configurations.

The concentrators were small, reddish, glass spheres. They held the energy required to activate the orbs—energy collected by the Kerta priests from their unsuspecting victims.

In its raw form, this energy turned the orbs that received it into explosive devices that could shatter reality and cause a spill-over from the Arayat. But when channeled through the priest's body—at great cost to the priest—it became suitable fuel for the orbs. The energy transfer had to happen quickly, before the priest would exhaust himself and die in the process. Some did. This is why a prudent priest would never use more than four orbs at one time.

Any other priest would have considered the idea of standing twelve orbs and fueling them with not one, but *two* concentrators, sheer madness. Had Rahaak conferred with his superiors, he would have been promptly locked up, and if not cured, quickly disposed of. But ambitious men nurse their desires in secret, the way a mother bear cares for her cubs—in a remote cave, with great love and deadly force.

"Has the Inner Power of the Temple indicated the auspicious hour of your glorification, my Lord?" whispered Jethro sweetly. "I hope you will remember me when you come to rule as the next Librarian."

"You have nothing to fear, Warden. I shall be generous. The best time to conclude this little affair is on the eve of the Feast of Light. Babylon celebrates it with great effusion, and no one will notice if I absent myself for a short hour. Meet me here, and you shall witness my greatest accomplishment. The medallion shall be mine."

Jethro gave a deep bow and smiled obsequiously. He would have licked the ground where Rahaak walked to keep him blind and motivated. Had he paid attention to the contemptuous gaze Rahaak had given him, he would have realized that the fat man had already consigned him to the cruel experiments of the Kerta priests. Indeed, to protect his power, a man with unbridled ambition could suffer a worthy enemy, but not a witness of his tarnished past. The two men nodded contentedly and left the Library sustained by incompatible dreams of glory.

"At last, it is decided." jubilated Jethro, walking outside the Library on this fine day of summer. "This Festival of Light will forever change the world. This quiet existence is coming to an end, and a new power shall rise to defy the Temple of Baal."

Being the warden of the Seat of the Librarian, he prophesied what would come to pass—but not as he had hoped.

>✪✪✪<

The sun was about to set when Hoda arrived home. The stranger was nowhere to be seen, but she nearly bumped into Captain Arfaad. *What is he doing here?* She looked around expecting to see the High Riders destroying her village, but the main plaza was empty.

"Evening of Blessings," she said, greeting the captain.

"Evening of Roses," replied the captain. "I am glad to see you in good health, Miss Hoda."

"Thank you, Captain," said Hoda, bowing.

She waited for him to leave before going back inside the house. Her father was beaming. "Hoda, Arfaad, the captain of the Lightning Division of the High Riders, just asked me for your hand in marriage."

She was stunned. Marrying a captain of the High Riders meant a life of comfort and security for her family. "What did you say, Father?"

"I told Arfaad I will give him an answer at the Feast of Light." Hoda sighed, relieved. "And judging by this reaction of yours, I should have told him you are not ready to abandon the life of a shark fisherman."

"You are right, Father. We need to give it serious thought," lied Hoda. "I was shocked, that's all."

Jabbar smiled again. "Well, my daughter, you are a true treasure, you know that. Blessed be the man who will be your husband. You are..."

Hoda kissed him, "Thank you, Father."

"Hoda," hollered her mother from the kitchen, "give me a hand."

"Coming, Mother," replied her daughter.

"Jabbar, you'd better be back in one hour, or we eat without you."

"Hayat, have I ever been late? No, the men and I sit down for a quick game of Salamander and..."

"What about the time when you lost your left shoe and came back three hours later?"

Jabbar threw his arms up, sighed deeply, and left the house muttering something about the gods, strong-willed women, and shoes.

"You know, Mother," said Hoda, rolling up her sleeves, "you do give Father a hard time."

"It's for his own good," replied her mother, sifting through a tray of lentils, inspecting them carefully, removing dirt and bits of grass. "Men need to be reminded who is running the house. Don't you ever forget that, my Daughter. Has the water boiled yet?"

Hoda inspected the steaming pot sitting atop the wood stove behind her. She threw two more logs inside the furnace and took a seat. Sliced carrots lay on a plate next to her, alongside chopped green onions and a cut of meat. Bulgur wheat, washed and dried, lay next to the meat.

"Preparing moujadra?" asked Hoda.

"That's for tomorrow. We're eating kibbeh tonight."

"That's Ahiram's favorite dish, and if you're preparing his favorite dish, it must be because you had pity on him. What did he do this time?"

Hoda longed to be with Karadon, spend time with him and come to know him better without this dark cloud hanging over her head. "Can't I be gone just once without Ahiram getting in trouble?"

"Careful, he will hear you," said her mother evenly. "He got in a brawl with six boys from Ghazir. You know, they don't want him to run in the next Festival of Light. With Ahiram out, they could win the race—"

"So, they threw insults at Father, and Ahiram charged them like a blind boar." exclaimed Hoda.

"Yes," sighed her mother, "and this time, he gave the six of them the beating of their lives. It took four men to pin him down and they could barely hold him until your poor father arrived." Hayat glanced furtively at her daughter. "I know he is a very heavy load for you, Hoda, but without you..."

Sitting side-by-side, the two looked alike from the back. Hoda had her mother's complexion and her long, curly hair, but her inner strength was that of her fisherman father who could battle a shark and a storm all night without giving up.

Hayat sighed twice. "I wish I had had another girl," she blurted after a while. "It would have been easier."

"Why do you say that now?" asked Hoda.

Hayat looked at her daughter with teary eyes. She opened her mouth to speak, then focused once more on the lentils. "I mean that Arfaad would be a great match for you, but the Temple will keep him busy, and you would live most of your life alone." Hoda was certain this was not what her mother meant. Hayat looked at her daughter. "Listen, Hoda, no matter what, do not marry a High Rider; your life will be miserable."

Hoda was dumbfounded. All along, she had been convinced her mother wanted her to marry a High Rider. *I guess I misjudged her*, she thought. "Why don't you give me the lentils, Mother? Father will be in very soon now."

"Oh no, he won't, he enjoys that game too much." Hayat handed her the dish and went to the sink where she pulled on a weighted rope and fresh water trickled from a stone conduit. She washed her hands and yanked the rope again. The flow of water stopped.

Hoda took a wooden pestle and beat the meat until it became pasty, added the bulgur wheat, green onions, and carrots, then sprinkled pine nuts and a mixture of seven spices, then kneaded the whole mix. She spread it into a pan, used a knife to create a crisscross pattern, drizzled the dish with a bit of oil, opened a cooking drawer from under the stove, and slid the dish into it. "It'll be ready in an hour," she said evenly.

When her father came back, Hoda was allowed to see Ahiram who had been locked up in his room. He was sleeping on the floor and had bruises on his arms and legs and a swollen, black eye.

Seeing him like this, a wave of anger filled her. *Why can't he behave just once! Must I be with him all the time?* She shook him. "Ahiram, come on, it's dinner time."

He woke up in a daze, saw his sister, smiled, and stretched. "Hoda, you're back," he said scratching his head. "So, did you see him again?"

"Who?"

"The fellow you saw last week."

"What fellow?" she said her heart beating faster. *You are a boy, you're not supposed to notice these things*, she thought.

"The man who came with Syreen," continued Ahiram yawning like a whale. "He seemed nice."

"No, I did not see him, why do you ask?"

"I've heard Mother and Father. They said you will be married soon, and you will be gone." He cocked his head and stared at his sister with his hazel eyes that could be so serious at times. "I am leaving, Hoda."

"What?" said his sister nearly panicking. Guilt and shame overwhelmed her. "What are you talking about?"

"I can't continue like this," he said seriously. "Father said I can't join him on his boat with my bad temper. He's right. I could harm someone, you know. You're the only one who can help me calm myself, but you can't keep doing it. I know you're upset with me, just like Mother and Father. I understand why you're all upset with me."

"Ahiram, stop it."

"It's true, Hoda. I heard you talking to Mother."

Hoda took him in her arms and held him tightly, nearly choking him. "Listen to me, Ahiram. Yes, at times I do get irritated with you, and yes, I wish you did not have this terrible temper. I wish I could spend time with Karadon, that's also true, but let me ask you this: if I were the one with the bad temper, and if it were you who had to take care of me, would you let me go?"

Ahiram looked into his sister's eyes and said quietly, calmly, and with a will that struck his sister like a fist, "Never. I would never let you go, no matter what. We will always be together."

"But would you not be irritated with me?"

"I can't be irritated with you, Hoda, you're the best."

She held him again and hugged him. "Ahiram, son of Jabbar, I will never let you go."

He held her tightly, and she knew he was crying.

>❄❄❄<

Late that night, Hoda went into Ahiram's bedroom. He was sleeping fitfully, and his breathing was irregular, as if he was still crying. She ran her finger down his cheek and kissed him. He smiled in his sleep. Quietly, she pulled the medallion from under his shirt, but just before slipping it over his head, she hesitated for fear of what may happen. Ahiram rolled onto his side. Hoda snatched the medallion and went back to her room where she hid it under her pillow. *If someone asks me, I can say I found it on the floor and planned to give it back to him in the morning.* Wanting to check on her brother in short order, she leaned her back against the wall, closed her eyes and waited in the dark.

"Hoda, wake up. Wake up, Hoda."

The young woman opened her eyes and saw her mother standing next to her bed. She sat up. "Mother, what is it? Is Father alright?"

"Your father is fine. He is home," replied her mother, her forehead creased with worry. "It's your brother. He is unwell. Go help your father while I get Aunt Samra. Perhaps she will know what to do."

Hoda bolted out of bed and ran to her brother's room. She could not remember the last time he had been sick. She found him drenched with a feverish sweat, and his breathing had become labored. Jabbar was by his bedside applying cold compresses to the boy's forehead.

Seeing Ahiram's uncovered chest, Hoda noticed that the medallion was missing. She was about to ask her father about it when she remembered. *I took it away, and I was supposed to check up on him.* Quickly, she ran to her room and brought back the medallion.

"Father," she said dipping her fingers into the water bowl, "the water is tepid." It was actually glacial. Discreetly, she spilled it out the window and handed the empty bowl to Jabbar. "Could you please fetch some more for me? I'll take care of Ahiram."

Silently, her father rose and went out to fetch a fresh bowl of water. Quickly, Hoda slid the medallion around her brother's neck. By the time her father was back, Ahiram's breathing had eased up, and by the time their mother walked in with Aunt Samra, Ahiram's fever had abated.

"Morning of goodness," said the gentle woman, greeting Jabbar. She had snow-white hair and skin as soft as a baby's.

"Morning of light," replied Jabbar.

Samra examined Ahiram and listened intently to his breathing. "Like I told you, Hayat," she said, rising slowly. "It's a passing fever. Maybe he ate a rotten fruit or maybe a spider bit him. Tomorrow, he should be fully recovered."

"Thank you, Samra," said Hayat. "We have grieved you," she added, employing the usual expression that meant "I am sorry for the inconvenience."

"*Wallaw*" (come now), replied Samra. "No grieving whatsoever; what are neighbors for? We look after each other in Baher-Ghafé. Do not hesitate to call me if his fever goes back up."

Hayat walked her to the door. "May your day be full of peace."

"And may you remain in peace," replied Samra.

"Hoda, we have a good catch ahead of us," said her father visibly relieved. "I need you to help on the boat this morning. Hayat, you'll be alright now?"

"Don't you worry about a thing, Jabbar. Go, and may El keep you."

"May he remain with you," said Jabbar. He kissed his wife. "Let's be on our way, Hoda. We are late."

"Coming, Father." Hoda rushed back into her brother's room. He was wide awake.

"Hoda," he said smiling weakly, "I dreamt of you."

"You did?" asked his sister, kissing his forehead to feel his temperature. It was back to normal. "What was I doing in your dream?"

"I was standing on a hill overlooking a wide plain. Creatures sprouted from the plain and formed a vast army that came after me. By the time they reached the hilltop, you were standing next to me, then you became a huge tower, and I stood on top of that tower. My medallion shot out a white beam, and they were all gone. You told me I should give you my medallion. I asked you why, then I woke up."

"What an imagination you have," said Hoda, breathless. "You should rest now, and I'll see you after I come back from helping Father."

Ahiram's features darkened. All he wanted was to be a shark fisherman like his father, but until he learned to control his temper, he was barred from their boats. "Don't you worry," she whispered. "You'll get to fish with Father. I promise."

He looked at her and smiled. "Thanks, Hoda."

Baher-Ghafé was the only village north of Baalbeck allowed to bait and fish shark. Half a mile south of the village, the sea bottom sloped gently for the first two hundred yards from shore and then dropped dramatically into an abyss beyond a steep cliff. Over the years, the salty water had managed to pierce through rocks that protruded from the cliff, turning them into natural anchor points for the fishing hooks that the men of Baher-Ghafé used to bait sharks. These anchors greatly increased the safety of their operation, but the nets the women weaved were the true hallmark of Baher-Ghafé. They were so strong a shark could not tear through them; and the making of their threads was the prized secret of the village, one that was protectively guarded with pride.

The fishermen would bait white or salmon sharks with pieces of pork or beef. Once a shark was hooked, the men dropped a net around it. While it attempted to free itself, the shark would rapidly become entangled in the net, and either suffocate or die of sheer exhaustion. The men carefully prodded the shark with long spears for fear that any bloodshed would attract other sharks and spoil the catch. They then hauled it to shore, where they prepared it following a local recipe.

When Jabbar and Hoda reached the coast, four small fishing boats were tussled by strong waves and Yonnan Sheraby and his son, Antoun, were waiting for them on the beach.

"How's the lad?" inquired Yonnan.

"Nothing to worry about. A simple fever; it'll pass. That boy is so strong he could swallow the sea for breakfast, the forest for lunch, and the mountains for dinner, and he would still be hungry."

Yonnan gave his friend a wide grin. "Good to know." He looked at Hoda and smiled. "You brought the princess, I see."

The Sherabys and the Jabbars had been neighbors, partners and friends for as long as Hoda could remember. Mr. Sheraby was as generous as he was gentle, and he had called her "princess" for the first time when she had scraped her knee. She was then ten years old. "A princess does not cry," he had told her, "not over a small thing like that. Come on, let's go see Mrs. Sheraby. She'll get you all cleaned up and she might still have some of that pomegranate drink you like so much."

It had stuck. So much so, that even Antoun, a reserved young man, her junior by a few years, had called her "princess" without giving it a second thought.

Jabbar placed his hand on Hoda's shoulder. "Yes, I did indeed bring the princess." he replied. "She loves fishing, remember? Let's head out now, it's going to be a good night."

"Are you trying to make a man out of her?" teased Yonnan as they stepped into the boat.

"Not at all," explained Jabbar, "I'm hoping the graceful sharks might teach her a thing or two about elegance, else no one will marry her."

Yonnan laughed. Antoun blushed and Hoda smiled and breathed deeply the air of the sea. The truth was that she loved shark fishing.

After several hours of toil on an angry sea, the villagers reached the shore with four sharks in their nets—a good catch by any measure.

Quickly, Hoda used razor sharp knives to carve the meat, then helped the women season it with a mixture of garlic, lemon juice, and spices. They smoked it slowly, letting the seasoning brine the meat before packing it in special wooden containers that two fishermen would later deliver to the Temple. The financial reward was split evenly among the families, while ten percent went into a common coffer for the needs of the village.

By the time she returned home, the sun was at its zenith. Hoda washed up and helped her mother with house chores. Hayat shared with her daughter the latest news of the village. Young Auline had asked Hayat if she could lend a hand in the wedding preparations, and Hoda's mother had accepted. Aunt Salma had brought some *namoorah* for Ahiram—his favorite sweet. Hoda laughed when her mother told her how Ahiram had tried to bribe the six girls of the Mrad family next door by promising them a piece of namoorah each if they gathered the wood for him. Instead, the girls had fought over who would get the biggest piece, and they had accused Ahiram of playing favorites.

"You know," added her mother, a twinkle in her eye, "he has a thing for Maha, their fourth daughter."

"He does?" exclaimed Hoda, surprised. "He never told me. Ahiram is keeping secrets from me now?"

"I'm not surprised," said her mother. "He is afraid that if he told you about his friendship with Maha, you would no longer be there for him."

"But why?"

"Because, my dear daughter, he is like a boy lost at sea, who survives by holding onto a raft, the only raft around. If he lets go, he will drown." Hayat looked at her daughter with great tenderness. "He doesn't know how to let go of you, Hoda."

Hoda felt a lump in her throat. *I should have known. Poor Ahiram.* Unable to hold back anymore, she held her mother's arm and asked,

"What about me, Mother? When will I be set free?"

Her mother sighed, held her daughter tightly and said nothing.

"So where is he now?" asked Hoda, after a while.

"In the woods, gathering fuel for the fire."

The young woman stared at Hayat, "You let him out? But he was so sick only a few hours ago."

"He is fully recovered," explained her mother. "Even Samra was surprised how quickly he recovered. It must be his temper; so you see, it's not all bad."

"Mother, do you mind if I go visit with Syreen?"

"Not at all, my dear." Smiling to herself, she continued, "What's his name? Is he of a good family?"

"Who?"

"The young man you met, of course."

"Ahiram told you about Karadon?"

"Karadon, that's a nice name. I like that. No, your brother would never betray your secrets."

"Then, how—"

"Hoda, I was a young woman once. I know you enjoy Syreen's company, but everyone has been talking about her dashing mysterious cousin. Then out of the blue, you want to visit her, and you're tense and impatient. So, off you go, but remember—"

"Yes, Mother, don't you worry. Father would have to meet him first. What am I saying? I just met him."

Hoda ran out of the house before her mother could reply. She crossed the short distance to Byblos by walking on the beach, constantly on the lookout for the mysterious stranger, but he was nowhere to be seen. Syreen opened the door and the two friends went into the expansive kitchen.

"No one is here now," said Syreen as they sat around a large table by a window that overlooked an enclosed garden. "My parents have gone to a function at the Temple with our three maids, so we can speak freely. Tell me what you found out while I prepare tea. Would you like a piece of namoorah? It's fresh from this morning."

Hoda could not help but smile at the mention of the treat. "No, thanks, Syreen. I'm not hungry."

"Did something happen with the medallion?" prompted her friend.

Hoda related how her brother had suddenly became so very sick and recovered just as quickly once she returned the medallion to him.

"Then I guess there is no time for tea," said Syreen, taking the pot of water off the stove. "Hoda, my source told me that if this were to happen, if Ahiram were to fall ill when you took the medallion away, then I must take you to him at once. Your entire village is in mortal danger. We must go now."

"Really?" whispered Hoda. "I didn't think it would be this serious."

"Come with me," said her friend.

They went back to the young woman's room, where she snatched a scarf and resolutely faced Hoda. "I need to blindfold you. I am sorry."

"What? What do you mean?"

"I cannot show you the way to my contact. He likes his privacy."

"But Syreen, I won't talk—you know me."

"Sorry, Hoda, his orders. You *need* to talk to him, and I will take you there, but I have to blindfold you first."

Hoda sighed and gave her consent. Expertly, Syreen tied the scarf around her eyes. As they left the room, Hoda felt that her life would never be the same. The echo of her footsteps on the marble reminded her of the sound of an anchor being lifted just before a ship leaves beloved shores for an unknown voyage.

3. THE FEAST OF LIGHT

"Some say Baher-Ghafé means 'the slumbering giant who keeps watch in his dreams.' The name is ancient, predating the Wars of Riharon and the coming of Tanniin. Sureï the Sorcerer told me the mighty Baal stood on the shores of this little village, after having subdued Yem, and ordered him to sleep."
—**Teachings of Oreg, High Priest of Baal**

 Syreen led her blindfolded friend down a corridor Hoda did not know existed, then down some stairs. The air was damp, and she heard water trickling all around her.

"Where is the water coming from?" asked Hoda, a tremor in her voice. "Are we walking under the sea?"

Syreen laughed, for she knew what her friend was thinking.

"The first time I took this passage, I was blindfolded too, and also thought I was below the Great Sea on my way to the eternal abode of the dead."

"Well, this is unnerving."

"To say the least, but it is a short passage, and we're coming to the end of it. Careful now, there's a step ahead of you."

They began walking onto a hard surface with hot air wafting about them. Hoda breathed a sigh of relief when she no longer heard the sound of water. Syreen led them through a maze of left and right turns. Throughout their journey, Syreen would direct her friend to bend down, lower her head, cross over a crevice, or climb onto a step. Eventually, they reached the top of a long flight of stairs. Hoda, judging by the echo of her feet on the stony floor, determined that they were inside a wide room. The air was fresh and dry. Syreen took Hoda's blindfold away, and she blinked a few times until her eyes grew accustomed to the dark. Across from her, a hooded figure sat cross-legged behind a low table with a simmering cup of tea. The silence in the room was complete.

"Hoda, welcome. Please, have a seat."

The voice was masculine, soft-spoken, strong but not threatening. *Most likely, a man my father's age,* thought the young woman as she slowly sat down.

"Please forgive the secrecy, but it cannot be helped. While we do not doubt your sincerity, let us just say that there are others, less scrupulous, who would like to find me by any means necessary, including torture."

Hoda winced and glanced at Syreen, as though saying, *What have you gotten yourself into, and why did you drag me into all this?*

"Indeed," continued the mysterious man, "by bringing you here, Syreen exposed you to danger. But this danger, I am afraid, is nothing compared to the dire situation your entire village is in as we speak. Once you understand the nature of your brother's medallion, you will better appreciate the great service your friend has rendered you and your loved ones."

"Sir, if as you assert, my brother, my family, and my entire village are in grave danger," replied Hoda with carefully chosen words, "I would want to know absolutely everything about this threat to help protect Baher-Ghafé."

"Spoken like Jabbar's true daughter," chuckled the hooded man. "Your heart is in the right place, Hoda, keep it that way."

"You know my father, then?" asked Hoda.

"Yes, indeed. He is a good man. Now tell me this, young one, have you ever heard of the Island of Libra or the Cave of Andaxil?"

Hoda shook her head.

"That's very good," continued the hooded man. "Most folks along these coasts would not have heard of them either; after all, why visit the wonders of the world when you live on El's footstool?"

Despite her anguish, Hoda smiled. As a daughter of Fineekia, she had a visceral attachment to her homeland. She believed, like the rest of her kin, that Fineekia, with its harmonious unity between snow-covered peaks, a fertile high plain, and an emerald seashore, was a miniature of what El—first among the gods—intended the world to be. Thus, the sons and daughters of Fineekia were content to live within these boundaries and leave the affairs of the world to mighty kingdoms and powerful temples.

"There are two other medallions identical to your brother's: one on the Island of Libra and the second in the depth of Andaxil. The former is protected by a deadly curse, while the latter is lost with the entire treasure of the dwarfs; for Andaxil is sealed and no one can open it."

Silence fell on the hall while Hoda tried to understand what her interlocutor had just told her. Libra and Andaxil seemed fantastical places, suited for dangerous quests. She was the daughter of a fisherman whose greatest adventure was measured by the size of their daily catch. The thought that strange objects hidden thousands of miles away could determine the fate of her entire village was revolting. Still, she could not deny that Ahiram fell ill when she took the medallion away from him and recovered quickly when she brought it back. If there was one thing she had learned from fishing with her father, it was to adapt to a changing situation.

Hoda remembered her father's words: *To catch a shark, my daughter, you must be fluid like a wave, nimble like a pelican, patient like a lion, and above all, be ready to lose the bait in order to save your life.'*

Hoda took a deep breath. *Alright,* she thought, *Andaxil, Shmandaxil, what do I care? Ahiram, my family, and my village that's what matters.*

"Three medallions then," she said. Determined to get some answers, she dared to ask the mysterious man: "Why three? What do they do? And how did Ahiram end up with one of them?"

"Excellent questions. These medallions are known as the Merilians—the origin of their name remains a mystery. They are thought to be powerful, beyond anyone's understanding. The source of their power is unknown, and they are very ancient."

"Mother said she bought this medallion from Master Kwadil. Why don't we just give it back to him? His caravan makes a stop in Byblos every Feast of Light."

The man chuckled dryly. "I highly doubt the famed dwarf merchant had such a piece in his possession, and if he did, he would not have sold it to your mother. Besides, the third medallion, the one in the possession of your brother, is supposed to be hanging on a wall deep within the temple of Babylon. The truth, my dear child, is that someone stole this third Merilian from the Temple of Baal."

"What? Stolen? From... who?" cut in Hoda, aghast. "Wait. If that's the case, the Temple would have been searching for it—"

"Unless the thief—cunning and highly capable—replaced the real medallion with a fake, which must still be hanging in the temple of Babylon as we speak."

"But why would anyone give this medallion to my brother? I mean, we are fishermen from a small town that no one outside of Fineekia has even heard of."

"That is the most troubling question of them all, is it not?" said the man pensively. "A very troubling question indeed."

He fell silent. Hoda glanced at Syreen, who shook her head, professing ignorance. Her eyes now fully accustomed to the light, Hoda glanced around and noticed four men dressed in black standing discreetly in the corners, their faces hidden beneath thick cowls.

"Leave us, everyone," ordered her interlocutor. His voice, now deep and commanding, shook Hoda. "Now."

Syreen got up and bowed. By the time Hoda glanced again at the figures in the shadows, they were already gone.

"Hoda, I am going to ask you two questions, and upon your answers rests the fate of your brother, your village, and so much more than your village. Are you ready?"

Hoda was confused. What could she possibly know that would affect anything or anyone beyond the boundaries of Baher-Ghafé?

"Here is my first question: did Ahiram ever scribble? Has he ever written anything?"

Hoda blanched. "How did you know?" she asked, dread seizing her.

"As I feared," sighed the man. "Do not worry, child, we are here to help you. Please answer my questions and do not omit any details."

For over a millennium now, the Temple of Baal had been the guiding, moral force for most kingdoms of the world. In this long span of time, the Temple had—for reasons all its own—outlawed writing, proclaiming it a capital crime. Further, if one member of a community lent assistance to a *Katiib* (a writer or scribbler) as the Temple called them—then the High Riders would mercilessly cut down the entire community, down to its last member.

As the years wore on, people forgot what "writer" meant, and accusing one of being a Katiib became an expedient means to be rid of a competitor or a family member. Depending on the magnanimity of the local high priest, the High Riders would either launch a proper investigation to determine if the accused was indeed a scribbler, or summarily abduct him. In the latter case, they would also turn a blind eye if the accuser wound up dead, a dagger between his shoulders. Therefore, the charges of writing were not brought up lightly.

"When Ahiram turned ten," started Hoda, with a shaky voice.

"On his birthday, or some time before or after?" clarified the man. "This is important, child, be specific."

Hoda nodded. "I will do my best. The incident happened at the end of the Festival of Light, so yes, it took place on my brother's birthday. I remember this because we were roasting chestnuts on the beach..."

"And chestnuts are out of season in the month of Tébêt," added Ashod pensively.

"Exactly. It was a surprise from Umnis. He brought them with him."

"The Zakiir?"

"Yes."

Since the written word was outlawed, people needed a different method to faithfully recall important events or transactions. A *Zakiir* (a memory man), consigns to memory every utterance entrusted to him, word for word. His league, the *Zakiruun*, was the indispensable intermediary in every commercial or sentimental dealing, remembering everything and forgetting nothing. Friends of all, and friends of none, they were the keepers of all secrets.

"Continue," said the man.

"Ahiram was sitting on the sand, playing with a stick, when Umnis jumped from his seat. He swept the sand with his feet, and pulled Ahiram's ear so hard he cried. Then Umnis sent him to his room."

"A friend of the family, I take it?"

"He is family, on my mother's side, but like all other relatives of a Zakiir, we're not supposed to mention that. Then, he told my parents that Ahiram had been scribbling. None of us understood what he meant, but we could see that he was scared. He told my father never to allow Ahiram do this again."

"Very wise counsel," commented the strange man, "Now, on to my second question: does your brother have a birthmark on the left side of his neck, just below the hairline?"

Hoda looked at him, aghast. She felt as if she had uncovered a complex web of intrigues that had been surrounding her brother since his birth. "How did you know?" she asked, "and how are these questions going to help my brother and save Baher-Ghafé?"

"What you just told me might change the face of the world."

"How? Why?"

"I am not yet certain," replied the man absentmindedly as if he was thinking out loud. "Now listen, child, if you wish to save your village, you must follow my command and do it quickly: tell your father that you shared your concern about Ahiram's explosive temper with Syreen, and that Syreen has asked Bahiya's advice."

"You are asking me to lie to my father," cut in Hoda.

"To save your village? Yes. The less anyone knows about this medallion, the safer they will be. Tell him the high priestess' advice is to find someone willing to train Ahiram—as if he were in the army—for three months. This is not a lie; your brother requires extensive training to subdue his temper. As you guessed, the medallion has probably exacerbated his boisterous nature, and after twelve years of continued exposure, the boy is no longer able to control it. Military training, suited for his age, will help."

"Training? Really?" replied Hoda, elated. "At last, one bit of good news. But who could train my brother in that way?"

"Why do we not ask Syreen then?"

He rang a small bell. They did not have long to wait. Syreen walked back in and settled next to Hoda.

"Syreen," asked Hoda, "Do we know anyone who could possibly train Ahiram? Someone we could trust?"

"Of course, Hoda," replied Syreen, "your great-uncle, Mil."

"My great uncle? Oh no! My father would have a fit; he and Uncle Mil are—"

"Mil?" cut in the man. "A retired commander of the High Riders? You are related?"

"Yes, he is my mother's uncle."

"And," continued Syreen, "he lives in Tanooreen."

"Excellent," said the hooded man, satisfied. "Tanooreen is secluded: a perfect training ground for your brother."

"But Uncle Mil is old. He may not have any desire to train my brother."

"He will not have to," replied the mystery man. "I will."

"You will go up to Tanooreen? Just to train my brother?"

"If your brother is who I think he is, then yes, I would go to the ends of the earth to train him."

Hoda shook her head in disbelief. She could see the same shock on Syreen's face.

"But never mind this now. What matters is to get Ahiram out of Baher-Ghafé as soon as possible."

"Mother has always wanted to visit Uncle Mil; she won't object."

"Perfect. Make it a family visit. That is even better," said the man. "Once your brother is settled in Tanooreen, I will take care of the rest, and after three months of intensive training, he will be able to return to Baher-Ghafé, without the medallion."

"That's not a bad solution," said Syreen. "You protect your village, you free Ahiram from the medallion, and he learns to control his temper. Think of what would happen if the Temple finds out that the medallion Ahiram is wearing is a magical artifact stolen from the Temple of Baal in Babylon. To find out who stole it, the High Riders will resort to torture."

"I suppose there is no harm in spending some time in Tanooreen," conceded Hoda. She looked at them and explained: "I have never lied to my father before. Ever. But..." she said with a deep sigh, "I can see why it would be a good thing not to share too much with him, or anyone else. Fine, I will speak to my father as soon as I go back home."

"Excellent," said the man, relieved. "Do it and do it quickly. Your family should be out of Baher-Ghafé no later than the Feast of Light."

"It will be difficult, but I will do my best," replied Hoda.

She rose to leave. The man grabbed her arm.

"One more thing: if the medallion activates—"

"Activates?" asked Hoda. "I don't understand."

"If the medallion's temperature changes, or if its surface lights-up—"

"It can do these things?" Hoda was positively frightened. If this magic was seen by Arfaad and his men, her village would be entirely destroyed.

"And then some," said the man, "and then some. Listen carefully to what I am about to tell you: If this medallion activates before you leave Baher-Ghafé, the High Riders will know it is a Merilian medallion they are searching for. They will come looking for your brother first. They will want him dead or alive. Save him, Hoda. He must not die, nor fall into the hands of the Temple. Find a safe place where Baal's soldiers will not look for him, and then hide with him there. If you have to choose between the entire village and Ahiram, save your brother."

"But sir," protested Syreen, "this is too hard. She can't..."

"She must!" cut in the man with a terrible voice that shocked them. He sighed and regained control. "She must," he added softly. "You know how much I hate the spilling of blood and the destruction the Temple leaves in its wake, but if the Temple lays its hands on Ahiram, destruction, the likes of which we have never seen, will be upon us. Now go. Time is of the essence."

The last image Hoda saw before Syreen blindfolded her was that of the cloaked man hunched over the small table, like a man hiding tears of sorrow.

After the departure of the two friends, one of the men, who had been standing in the shadows, walked briskly over and knelt.

"Forgive me for intruding," said Karadon to the former priest of Baal, his voice quivering with anger, "but when I agreed to bring Hoda to you,

I didn't expect you to treat her the way you just did, Ashod. You were supposed to help her, not terrify her."

Ashod pushed the hood off his face. His bald head glittered in the dim light, and his steel-blue eyes gazed at Karadon with a gentle determination.

"I am sorry, lad, but our choices are limited. Her brother may be far more dangerous than anyone imagined."

"Dangerous? He's a sweet kid with a bad temper."

"Yes, that he may be, but he may also be far more than that. Still, to allay my suspicions, I will need to travel to Babylon."

"Babylon?" exclaimed Karadon, surprised. "If they catch you..."

"It cannot be helped. I must be sure that the boy Ahiram is who I think he is. Now, what of the stranger who wanted to purchase the medallion?"

"We are trailing him discreetly," replied Karadon. "We are keeping an eye on Baher-Ghafé from a small observation post in the woods, in case he attempts to steal the medallion."

"He has access to some powerful spells," said Ashod, worried. "If he sees you before you see him, you and your men will be in grave danger."

"Understood, Ashod. If Baal has taught the Black Robes anything, it is to be careful. I can't wait for Hoda to be with us."

"Be careful, Karadon. We do what is best for the victims of Baal, not what is best for us. Otherwise, how different would we be from the Temple? Right now, she has a village to save and a brother to worry about. Be patient, lad."

"Understood," said Karadon, with a sheepish smile. "I guess I was getting a bit ahead of myself."

"No harm is done. After all, love has reasons that reason most often ignores. Now let me be, lad, I have much thinking to do."

"You say he was able to resist a Control Spell?" asked the disembodied voice. "Are you certain?"

"Yes, sir, that's what I said. Is it possible that the medallion came to his assistance?" asked the turbaned man.

"Highly unlikely, unless, of course, this child is the..." the face floating over the mist wavered, then came back steady and strong. "Change of plan; let no harm come to him or his family. Instead, bring them all to me safe and sound, and under no circumstances shall you harm his sister, to whom the young boy is very attached. Understood?"

"Yes, sir. Understood."

"Further, do not rely on any spells when you abduct them. Instead, use potions."

"This might prove difficult; this village of theirs functions like a close-knit tribe. Everyone knows everyone, and it will be nearly impossible to move four warm bodies without raising suspicions."

"Wait for the Festival of Light. The entire area will be in celebration and bustling with people. No one will be surprised to see drunkards helped by friends."

"This might work, but it will require—"

"Do not worry about the cost. Bring them to me safe and sound."

"Very well, sir. Consider it done."

After the mist dissipated, the turbaned man wondered what it was that his master saw in that boy. *No matter,* he thought pragmatically, *he wants the entire family alive; he will get them alive.*

>✿✿✿<

When Hoda reached Baher-Ghafé, she heard her father's voice and knew that, once more, Ahiram was in trouble. She stepped through the door just when Jabbar stood up, lifted his hands to the heavens, and exclaimed again, "What am I to do with this reckless son of mine? One more fight, and four more boys are injured. Ahiram, what am I to do with you?"

Ahiram was sitting in the kitchen with his mother, who was tending his light wounds, while his father towered over him. "They insulted your name, Father," protested Ahiram.

"You beat these boys badly and nearly caused an incident between the villagers of Ghazir and us," chided Jabbar, visibly upset. "Remember, son, a strong man is weighed in silver. A strong man who controls his temper is weighed in gold."

"You should listen to your father, my son," continued his mother. "I know those worthless boys insulted your father, but you conducted yourself shamefully. Do you think you can fish shark if you do not control your temper?"

Hoda walked in with a bag of apples she had picked up from Byblos on the way home, a good excuse in case her parents asked her why she was late.

"He got into another fight." Jabbar, whose anger was flaring again, told her. Hoda sighed, and gave an apple to her brother. "May you live until you see your great-great-grandchildren smiling upon your face," she told him.

"It's not my birthday yet," said Ahiram, setting the apple on the kitchen table. "My birthday is on the Feast of Light, which is in seven days. I will be twelve then, and Father still won't let me set up bait."

Hoda took it back and placed it gently in his lap. "I know," she said, kissing his forehead.

"It will be the Feast of Light, and I get to rest for once," replied Jabbar. "And, as I told you before, you won't set any bait with that temper of yours."

"Father, I would like to walk with you outside. I have something to ask you," said Hoda, as she slid her arm under the tall man's arm and led him out.

Unable to resist, Jabbar followed, and they stepped outside of their comfortable home into the sunlight. They strolled down the main avenue lined with two-story houses with smooth stone facades, sturdy wooden doors, and windows shaded by oak and pine trees. Rows of thyme, parsley, and coriander were interspersed with lavender bushes and rock roses. All the roads in the village were paved, for Baher-Ghafé was a prosperous town. Nestled in the foothills of the Lebanon Mountain Chain, the villagers fished—shark mostly—and farmed the narrow, fertile plain at the edge of the wood-covered hills. Over the years, they had learned the secrets of the vine and produced a clean, balanced wine with a fruity taste, which nicely complemented the shark meat they cooked over charcoal fires.

"See," said Jabbar, pointing at one of the houses. "The Sherabys are getting ready for Auline's wedding," he said with a tinge of envy. "You know, Arfaad is the captain of the Lightning Division of High Riders, and he and I have been talking about you..."

Hoda smiled. "Auline is a wonderful girl, and Meenar is a village boy. They will be happy together."

"But what about you, my daughter," asked Jabbar, gazing at her with all the tenderness of his generous heart.

Hoda laughed, "Hear, hear, the powerful and mighty Jabbar is anxious. This is a first, Father."

"Laugh all you want," replied Jabbar gruffly. "It doesn't—"

"Father," cut in Hoda nervously, "forgive me for interrupting, but I am worried about Ahiram."

"So am I," said Jabbar. "So is your mother."

Reaching the shore, they veered left and started walking toward the main beach where the boats lay. "Did you know his nightmares are becoming more frequent?" she asked.

"Yes, your mother and I are worried." He sighed. "Honestly Hoda, we do not know what to do."

"Father, you must listen to what I have to say now. You and I know how much Ahiram delights in anything that is good and true."

"I know, Hoda. That boy is without guile..."

"He is never jealous and..."

"...is generous to a fault," said her father. "We know how much the two of you love each other, and it warms our hearts. We wanted more children but were blessed with only two. But what does it all have to do with..."

"...his bad temper?" Jabbar and his daughter were accustomed to completing each other's sentences. "Father, you know that Syreen is the second maid to the first priestess of Baalbeck?" Jabbar nodded. "Well, she spoke to High Priestess Bahiya about Ahiram's temper."

"She did?" Jabbar was impressed. "Normally, it takes months to get an audience with the high priestess." He slapped Hoda gently on the back. "Ha! Who knew? My daughter has connections."

"Father..."

"So, what did the high priestess say?"

"She suggests we find someone who could give Ahiram military training—adapted to his age, of course—but rigorous. She believes the training will go a long way to help him control his temper. If that does not work, then Syreen might be able to grant us an audience with the high priestess..."

"Military training? I see. So the high priestess thinks that the discipline he's getting at home is not enough?" Hoda held her breath, waiting for her father to reach a conclusion. "It's not a bad idea, after all, but who? Wait, I know," he added triumphantly, and before she could reply, answered, "Arfaad, of course. He would be the perfect teacher."

"Captain Arfaad is certainly qualified," said Hoda. Inwardly, she shuddered at the idea. "But this training must be daily and needs to last three months."

"Three months? Three months?" Jabbar was visibly shocked.

"The high priestess said that for the training to form good habits, it must last at least three months and must be rigorous."

"That won't do; Arfaad can't be solely focused on Ahiram for that length of time."

Hoda sighed inwardly. "Exactly, Father, but I know the perfect man who can do just that, and here's the best part: he will gladly train Ahiram for free."

"Really? Who?" asked Jabbar, pleasantly surprised. Then his surprise turned into queasiness. "Oh no," he said, as the feeling of queasiness transformed into dread. "You cannot be serious," he added as an image, long repressed, popped in his head. "You don't mean going to Tanooreen?"

"But don't you see it, Father? Uncle Mil is a retired High Rider. He lives alone in Tanooreen, a remote village where Ahiram won't be taunted and provoked by kids who know him. We can all go there for a vacation. Uncle Mil will be delighted to see Mother. Then you and she can come back here, and I will stay with Ahiram for three months. When we come back, you will have a trained and mild-tempered son, ready to become a great shark fisherman like his father." Secretly, Hoda wished she could train with her brother, partly to be near him and partly to learn to defend herself.

"Ahiram will never be a fisherman," said Jabbar, his voice brimming with pride.

"What do you mean, Father?"

"Don't you see, Hoda? He has the makings of a king. Boys his age should already be imitating their elders: they pretend to set the bait, to lower a net, to prod a shark. These are the gestures they need to do over and over again to be good fishermen. Your brother, on the other hand, plays at diving in the water and riding a shark. He has turned more sticks into swords than the entire neighborhood. That boy has a deep sense of honor and virtue, and let us not say anything about his fighting skills. No, he will become a High Rider and will become a commander..."

"Like Uncle Mil," completed Hoda, smiling. Victory was close. She pushed forward. "All the more reason to ask Uncle Mil to train him."

"I know, Hoda, I know. Ahiram deserves the best, but me, go back and ask that curmudgeon cockalorum to help us? That cranky miserable smellfungus, that snollygoster? That's tough, Hoda, that's really tough."

"Think of Mother then," urged Hoda.

"Speaking of your mother, are you sure this whole thing is not a ruse of hers to get us to go see Uncle Mil?"

"Mother knows nothing of this. You can surprise her later," she added with a beaming smile. "Besides, Tanooreen is not all that bad at this time of the year."

"Not that bad?" cut in Jabbar. "How could it be 'not that bad' when your uncle lives there, watching every coming and goings like a vulture waiting for fresh carrions? That man told everyone at our wedding that I was born bald with a polka-dotted scalp and that my aim would miss a whale even if it were staring me in the eye. He humiliated me."

"Strictly speaking, we are all born bald, and furthermore, anyone would run away if a whale stared him in the eye."

"Hoda..."

"Father, it is to help Ahiram. Surely, you can put up with Uncle Mil for a few days?"

"Hoda, this," he said pointing at the sea and beach, "the village, the sea, fishing, these are my roots. It is hard to uproot an old tree."

"Thankfully, you are not a tree, and all that you need to do is set one foot after the next."

"So, now what?"

"In a week's time, at the close of the Feast of Light, you will let the villagers know that it is high time for you to visit Uncle Mil and make amends before his passing away..."

"Pass away? Pah! That mumpsimus will bury us all."

"Father—"

"Fine, fine, then what? You and Ahiram spend spring there and you are back before fall?"

"You mean summer," corrected Hoda.

"Exactly," replied Jabbar sighing. "You are right. Ahiram deserves the best." He sighed once more. "You know, we have never taken time off from fishing. Your mother has always wanted to rest for a week or two from the hustle and bustle here. She's a mountain girl, and by the name of all the gods, you are right. Your mother deserves a bit of a break. Let's do it."

"This will be a great occasion to renew your wedding vows while Uncle Mil is still alive..."

"Hoda, don't you push it."

"Alright, alright. Father, on the morning of the Feast of Light, I will help Ahiram set up bait for the first time. I am certain," she added over her father's objections, "that the prospect of setting up bait will keep him in a good mood and make the trip and the stay in Tanooreen much more bearable."

"Hmm... you are right. You know, if I didn't know you were my daughter, I would wonder if you were not secretly working with the merchant Kwadil because you could sell a whale to a man crossing the desert and make him believe it's a camel."

>❖❖❖<

Ahiram was doubly delighted when he found out that they would bait the shark on the morning of his twelfth birthday and that his sister would do it with him. His joy knew no bounds when he found out that she would not leave his side for the rest of the week; and for one full week, Ahiram was truly happy. He and Hoda spent most of their time on the beach swimming. They stayed up late watching the stars and enjoyed fresh, roasted fish over a small fire. Thus, the week went by peacefully, and it was the eve of the Feast of Light, the last day before their travel to Tanooreen. Hoda had told Ahiram the same story she had told her father, and he was eager to start his training if it meant that he would be able to join the fishermen on their boats.

"I love this beach," said Ahiram, yawning. "It is so quiet and secluded. We are about five miles from home, right?"

"Yes," said Hoda, "it's peaceful here."

"Yes, it is," said Ahiram, sighing. "I don't remember the last time I spent a day not being afraid," he added. He flopped onto the sand, his fingers entwined behind his head. "I sure hope this military training will help me so I can be with people and not hurt them, and you can get to spend more time with Karadon."

"Are you not happy with me?" asked his sister, teasing.

He set his gaze on her, and she saw how serious he was, far more than what would be expected of a child his age. "I don't really know what happy means, Hoda. All I know is that you're the only person I can be around without my temper flaring. There is this part of me I can't control, and it trusts you blindly. And when I am with you, I feel light, and life is not complicated."

"You can be with me as long as you want."

"No, I can't, and you know it. One day, you will go away..."

"Shush, Ahiram," she said. "I won't ever leave you, ever. I will always be by your side, at least until you have learned to control your temper. Then you will cross the seven seas and see the wonders of the world."

"I don't want to cross the sea," replied her brother. "All I want is to become a shark fisherman like my father and live next to you, Hoda. That's all I want."

She nearly cried, but decided to play tag instead. Their laughter echoed in the nearby forest, while four hooded figures, craftily hidden by the trees, followed their every move.

> ✦✦✦ ⤛

"Filthy piece of magic," screamed Rahaak. "Be still." Ignoring the command, the flying orb jittered so violently that the priest feared the worst. He willed for the dark sphere to stabilize. Instead, an ominous red light flashed beneath its glassy surface. The orb hung listlessly in the air.

Sweat rippled down the man's flaccid chin. Pain shot from his swollen joints, as if unseen hands were tearing him apart, and a long, mournful moan escaped his sealed, bluish lips.

"My Lord," pleaded Jethro, cowering in a corner behind him, "the red light, that's the *Shandirak*, the sign that Sureï's curse is about to be unleashed. It will level the entire island. Everyone who lives on Libra will die. The children," he pleaded, "the innocent children..."

The wave of pain receded. Rahaak, a member of the Inner Circle, was all too familiar with the rhythm of suffering that every act of magic begets. He straightened his posture and breathed deeply to clear his throbbing head.

"Shut your mouth, Jethro," he barked. Bending forward, he twisted his arms almost to the breaking point and spoke quickly in an abrasive, foreign tongue. He looked like a withered, bony tree about to snap. Slowly, the dangerous, reddish glow vanished, and the recalcitrant orb steadied its flight. It rose into the air to join the other eleven orbs already circling the priest, each along its own orbit.

"There," said the man of the Temple, breathless. He relaxed his stance, "There is nothing to worry about." He wiped his sweaty forehead with the sleeve hem of his priestly garment and eyed the old man angrily. "I know what I am doing, warden of the office of the Librarian." Jethro did not reply.

"And the next time you dare call the Light of Desolation by its Arayatian name, I will drag your miserable self into the Arayat and let the Nephral take you." Jethro recoiled and began crying like a child.

Ignoring the whimpering man, Rahaak gazed at the medallion hanging above the empty Seat of the Librarian. He grinned with anticipation.

"There is enough power in these twelve orbs to break any of Sureï's curses. Jethro, you shall witness my greatest victory: I will free the medallion, sit on the Seat, and the Library shall yield its secrets to me."

Furtively, Jethro glanced at a leather-bound book gently floating a few feet below the high, glittering ceiling of the Library. He tried to swallow, but his mouth was so dry he thought Sureï's curse had been unleashed and had turned his tongue into a pile of ashes and dust.

"My tongue, my tongue..." he stammered. "The curse, it's... it's upon us," and having realized what he had said, he nearly died of fright. His legs gave out, and he fell on his face, his jaw clattering so quickly a woodpecker would have been jealous.

"What are we doing?" he muttered, "No one has ever dared defy Sureï the Sorcerer before. Fool!" he yelled, unable to contain himself. "This is sheer madness. I command you to stop."

Ignoring the warden, Rahaak focused on the twelve orbs circling around him.

"Twelve orbs, Jethro," he said with glee. "No other priest of Baal, not even the great Sureï has done this." He glanced back at the warden curled behind a twisted column of the strange building, and laughed a wiry, maniacal laughter.

"Tonight, the medallion is mine," he roared. Not waiting any longer, he summoned Baal's power. Immediately, the twelve orbs formed a line from the priest to the medallion.

Jethro whimpered, covered his ears and shut his eyes.

The wave of pain came back with a vengeance. This time, Rahaak thought his veins had been filled with razor sharp nails. Still, his training prevailed, and slowly, carefully, he snapped open the cover of a small, silvery tube hanging by a thick chain around his neck. Two small blue spheres shot up and began circling the aligned orbs. Each time they passed by him, the priest shut his eyes and held his breath, for the stench of the concentrators was unbearable. Gradually, the fast moving objects drew closer to the orbs until their orbit brought them mere inches from the orb farthest from Rahaak.

"A little closer," croaked Rahaak.

Jethro wished the ground would open and swallow him, but he knew the Library was indestructible. No, there would be no hole to swallow him up. He would have to see this madness through.

"Steady now," said Rahaak, "steady..."

The concentrators were about to graze the farthest orb. Jethro had sufficient knowledge of Baal's magic to know that orbs were channels of power requiring energy to function: energy provided by the concentrators through the intermediary of the priest. It was the duty of the priest to release the lethal power locked within a concentrator and make it available to an orb by flowing it through his body. The pain he felt was excruciating, compounded by the number of orbs he was willing to use. The energy transfer must happen quickly, before the priest exhausts himself, loses control, and dies in sheer agony. Many did die. Worse still, if during this transfer, the priest allows a concentrator to touch an orb, reality would shatter and Arayatian creatures would materialize.

By now, Jethro realized that his strategy had turned Rahaak into an ambitious fool, a madman, willing to stand twelve revolving orbs in a straight line—the most potent formation for these objects—and let them be fed by not one, but two, concentrators.

"I am the fool," muttered Jethro, "an utter fool. What fit of madness led me to believe I could be the master of the Libre Aharof? What have I done? What have I done?" Jethro glanced at Rahaak and bit his lower lip so hard he tasted blood.

Rahaak willed for Sureï's formidable curse to be broken. Feverishly, Jethro entreated Baal to let him live through the night.

"Now," roared the priest.

The two concentrators stopped their flight in front of the farthest orb and sparked a thin, blue arc of intense heat that sizzled and crackled between them. Quickly, the arc broke into a multitude of tendrils resembling a miniature thunderstorm. One of the otherworldly stems licked the surface of the orb. The priest stammered as if hit in the stomach. He bent forward, cried out in a loud voice, and pushed against an invisible barrier.

Like an unstoppable wave, the blue light covered the surface of the orb and moved toward Rahaak in a straight line, turning the twelve orbs into an eerie, iridescent chain. When the strange light engulfed the orb closest to Rahaak, the priest flung his head back and screamed words that curdled Jethro's blood and made him wish he had never been born.

The concentrators shattered and the orb in front of the priest burst into a bubble of magma, nearly scalding him. The hot liquid seeped along the blue ray of light without harming it and swallowed the second orb, turning it into magma; it continued until it reached the farthest sphere. Slowly, the spheres of magma began to shrink while the eerie blue and red magma ray thickened until the spheres disappeared.

Rahaak, triumphant, let out a shout of joy. He had summoned the Okod—Baal's Staff of Power—a feat no other priest of the Inner Circle would have attempted alone. Filled with pride, Rahaak gazed upon the Okod like a mother over her newborn child. "Do you see this, Jethro," he cooed. "Now that I have the Okod, I am ready to launch a frontal attack on Sureï's curse."

Jethro watched with a sick fascination as Rahaak twisted his hands, weaving the red and blue rays into one thick strand. The priest's veins bulged under the strain, and Jethro thought he was about to explode. But with a fluid motion, he shaped the strand into a foot-wide, hollow circle, fused the two ends together and shrunk the circle into a blue and red, flat ornament. Arching his back and gritting his teeth, Rahaak moaned as he pushed the eerie, circular object forward.

The strange, object reached the medallion, their sizes matching perfectly. Without stopping, it sunk beneath the dark surface. The two men held their breath. The Okod reemerged a few seconds later, turning the ordinarily dull object into a dazzling display of brilliant light.

"Is it done?" asked Jethro.

Rahaak motioned for him to remain silent. "If the colors dissolve, the curse will be broken."

"Is it working?" asked Jethro, suddenly hopeful.

"I think... no. The medallion, it's—"

"What? What?" asked Jethro frantically.

He never knew what the priest was going to say. The two colors died out just as a terrifying, high-pitched scream pierced their ears. The medallion let out a white beam as thick as a man's fist. It lit the main room of the Library, as in bright daylight, and hit Rahaak in the chest, pulverizing him. Jethro screamed in terror. The beam struck the floor twenty feet behind him, and the warden thought he was dead.

He could not remember how long the beam had lasted, how long he had screamed, nor how long he had lain on his back with eyes wide open. Wearily, he stood up. Of the priest of Baal, there was nothing left. A shiver ran down the warden's spine as he limped out of the deserted Library, slipping into the thick night, grateful he had survived the ordeal.

Had he looked back, he would have seen a smoldering hole in the Library's floor. Beneath, a strange light began to throb, and an eerie sound filled the Library. Then the light and the sound vanished, and darkness fell once more.

High above ground, the *Libre Aharof* floated gently, and the Medallion of Power hung limply in place.

Moments before the white beam had struck Rahaak, Hoda and Ahiram stood on the beach watching a glorious sunrise, proclaiming the beginning of the Feast of Light—a day when the whole village rested from fishing and servile work.

"It's your birthday, Ahiram," said Hoda.

The young boy leaped for joy, held his sister's hands, and danced with her on the deserted beach. Hoda laughed and followed him.

"Are you ready to set bait, young fisherman?" she shouted.

"Absolutely," Ahiram shouted back.

Abruptly, his countenance fell, and Hoda saw he was in pain. He touched his chest and muffled a scream.

"Hot, hot, hot," he stammered, and frantic, he yanked the chain holding his medallion and threw it on the sand.

"Ahiram, what's wrong?" asked Hoda with a sickening feeling.

"The medallion," replied her brother, lifting his shirt to inspect his chest. "It nearly burned me."

Hoda quickly examined his torso and was relieved. "You are not burned," she said. "You are fine."

They stared anxiously at the small, round object expecting they knew not what. After a while, Ahiram laughed a nervous laugh

"Maybe I'm imagining things, Hoda." He bent to pick it up, but Hoda prevented him.

"Let's wait a little longer," she said with an altered voice.

A deafening shriek terrified them, while a powerful, white beam shot up from the medallion. The heat wave it produced hit them like a fist and threw them backward onto the sand. The shriek and the beam died as abruptly as they had started. Ahiram saw white symbols emerge from the medallion and fly away in a fast staccato. Drawn to them like a shark to blood, he leaped to his feet, and in a futile attempt, tried to catch them.

"Ahiram," asked Hoda, coughing, "what are you doing? What are you trying to grab?"

The symbols vanished before he could answer and seemed to take the rest of the beach and the mountains with them. Hoda shrieked. The boats were gone and so was the familiar landscape. All was replaced by rolling hills glittering with a green substance oozing from the ground. In the distance stood a massive pillar of flashing light surrounded by a cluster of giant dandelions. A dull, red light pulsed beneath the surface, and two shining stars behind the pillar mesmerized Ahiram.

Briskly, he walked toward the pillar, and had his sister not restrained him, would have crossed into that strange world. In a daze, she gazed at what she was seeing, wanting to disbelieve it, unable to make sense of the eerie landscape, when a young boy appeared before them.

Seeing Ahiram, he gasped. "You? What are you doing here? This is not your time."

"Who are you?" blurted Hoda, "What is happening to him?"

The boy saw the medallion on the sand. "Oh no, Rahaak, you fool, what have you done? You woke up the medallions and now they know."

The boy gazed at an object that was out of Hoda's sight and yelled, "Run! They are coming for him!"

He raised his right hand, formed a fist and snapped open his fingers. The hills and the pillar vanished, and the beach was back to normal.

"No," screamed Ahiram, "no, don't take them away from me..."

"What, Ahiram, what did you see?" asked his sister.

"I... I don't really know, but they were so beautiful. I heard them calling out to me."

"Who? Who is calling out to you?"

"I don't know."

Hoda held her brother, scanned the length of the beach, and breathed a sigh of relief. It was still deserted.

Think, Hoda, think. The strange boy said they were coming for him. The High Riders. They must know. What am I to do?

Protect Ahiram, came the answer. That's what the mysterious man told me. Protect Ahiram. She knelt down, placed her hands on Ahiram's shoulders. He was shivering, but time was of the essence.

"Listen to me, Ahiram, I want you to get into my boat and row as hard as you can..."

"In your boat?" exclaimed the young boy. "But Hoda, you told me never to get into your boat without you."

"And now I am telling you to get into my boat and row as hard as you can until you reach the spot where Father and the other men bait the sharks. I want you to lie in the boat until I come and get you. Can you do that for me?"

"I'd do anything for you, Hoda, but why do you want me to go there now? Hoda, what is happening to me? What is going on?"

She clasped his hands in hers: "There is no time to lose, Ahiram. Just do as I ask. I'll explain later."

"You will come, yes?" He just wanted to hear her say it.

"Do not worry. Everything I do, is for you. Now go."

Ahiram hugged his sister, and something told him he was seeing her for the last time. He held back his tears, kissed her, and after pushing his sister's small boat into the water, jumped in and rowed hard. Hoda waved and said, "Wait for me, Ahiram. I will be back to get you." She sprinted away in the direction of Baher-Ghafé.

Ahiram rowed as fast as he could and reached the submerged cliff in no time. He dropped the tiny anchor and lay in the boat. Dread hovered above him like a gathering storm. He felt like a hunted animal hiding from some unseen predator. A sense of deep loneliness gripped him, and the surrounding stillness compounded his oppression—as if he were lost, beyond the reach of mortal men. He closed his eyes, and when he opened them, he found himself standing at the bottom of a dead canyon hemmed by mountains of cold steel. A vengeful sun pummeled the ground with a suffocating heat wave, and in the rising haze, he saw shadows thundering toward him. Thousands upon thousands of filthy creatures he had never seen, or imagined, were growling, howling, nipping, and biting as they moved like a wave of black water in his direction. He heard an insidious voice whisper in his ear, "I see you. I am coming." Ahiram screamed and sat upright. He was back in the boat.

"This is all my fault," he said between sobs. "I couldn't control my temper and now all this happened, and Hoda is so scared. I really tried to control my temper, but I just couldn't."

"The covenant is broken," said a soft voice in his ears. "A life is given, and a life will be taken away; do not lose hope."

Ahiram sat straight up in the boat and looked around. This was not the first time he had heard this voice, the voice of an old man who spoke with power, yet his voice was laced with sadness. The young boy knew this was a friendly voice, for it had helped control his temper in the past.

Seeing no one, Ahiram was about to lie back down when the boat stirred furiously in foamy waters, as if a giant hand were toying with it. Ahiram gripped the edge of the vessel and peeked beneath the surface.

His hair stood up on end, and he quickly backed away. The shark was of monstrous proportions.

He took a second look, and his heart skipped a beat. Silver rays were on its back and it had a double fin. Ahiram immediately recognized the shark circling Hoda's boat; it was Yem. No one knew how old this shark was, and every generation of fishermen had stories to tell of their chance encounters with the shark of legends.

"Yem. It's Yem! I cannot believe it." Forgetting his sister's order to stay down, he peered at the shore and saw a small boat moving in his direction. Standing at the prow was the man who wanted to buy his medallion. *The medallion*, thought Ahiram, *I forgot it on the beach.*

"I am here to help, my friend," called the man across the water. "Hoda, your sister, sent me."

"What? Hoda?" said Ahiram, confused. "That's not possible. She said she would come for me."

"She is a bit delayed," answered the man. In the dim morning light, he had not noticed the foaming wavelets around the boy's tiny vessel, but now that his boat was a mere twenty yards away, he could clearly see the furious movements beneath the water. "What are you doing? Why is your boat moving so?" he asked, confused.

Before Ahiram could answer, Yem moved swiftly underwater, cut loose the rope attached to the small anchor, and hauled the boat away at great speed. The men in the other boat shrieked; they had not seen the shark.

"No," screamed Ahiram, "Hoda! Hoda!"

His scream was swallowed by the waves. The shark leaped forward faster than before, and Ahiram fell back, hit his head hard on the side of the small vessel, and lost consciousness. The shark pulled him rapidly away from home. Yem towed the boat for several miles until it reached a secluded, sandy area where the wooden vessel ran aground and came to an abrupt stop. Ahiram rolled over, hit the side of the boat, and ended up face down, motionless, and still unconscious.

>❂❂❂<

The sun rose on Baher-Ghafé. On this Day of Light, the *Feast of Adonis* (celebrating spring), the villagers enjoyed a good night of rest and slept late into the morning. None of them saw the High Riders surging through the forest, swords drawn, ready for the kill.

4. KWADIL'S DECISION

"The Malikuun are the guardians of light and servants of El. No mortal has ever seen them—not since the close of the Age of the Second Covenant—and lived. They are immortal."
—Lost discourse of Ramael, son of Shatumael, son of Hanayel, son of Zarubael, son of Lamatael and great-grandson of Habael the Wise

"Great are the deeds of the dwarfs and greater still, their heroes. Alone and unaided, Kwadil the Redeemed, shouldered the weight of the two realms when it was on the verge of collapse. He is the modern founder of the dwarfish nations, its unsung hero."
—Philology of the Dwarfs, Anonymous

Wearily, the sun reached its setting point, leaving behind a trail of bloodied clouds scattered in the sky like dead men across a battlefield. A sickly, white moon crawled across the heavens like a giant spider on an invisible web. The sentries manning the walls  of the Temple of Baalbeck saw lightning flash atop Mount Sanniin, towering some eight thousand feet over the Temple. Thunder boomed angrily, and storm clouds poured ice-cold water with a vengeance on Baalbeck.

"Riders on approach," said one of the sentries. "Archers at the ready."

Two hundred archers flexed their bows. After a tense moment, the sentry raised his hand. "Relax bows." The archers complied. "High Riders of the Lightning Division are on approach. Open the gates."

The order was relayed down to the porters. Three trumpet blasts shattered the quiet of the night. A gong answered deep within the complex, and the twenty-foot-tall iron gates opened to welcome Arfaad, captain of the Lightning Division of High Riders, returning with one light guard—two hundred and eighty-eight horsemen, one-tenth of the full division that had left at the break of dawn.

After putting the villagers to the sword, Arfaad had ordered half of his division to impose the curfew in Byblos. The rowdy metropolis was a stone's throw away from Baher-Ghafé. Merchants were bound to protest the closure of their stores on the busiest day of the year, when tourists flocked from the world over to celebrate the Feast of Light and partake in the all-night carnival of Adonis.

Of the remaining half, one light guard had stayed at Baher-Ghafé to burn all that could be burned, leaving nothing but charred ruins of the once prosperous village. The other two light guards had been sent on a punitive mission to seek and destroy the renegade Black Robes, for the Temple found it expedient to blame any one of its many foes for these ghastly expeditions.

Arfaad dismounted and ordered his soldiers back to their quarters. "Remain there until someone calls for you."

He headed to the ablutions hall in the Temple precinct to perform the Rite of Purification. He took off his helmet, a conical cap with two jade horns bearing a thunderbolt—the mark of Baal—and carefully placed it on an adjoining table, undressed quickly, and went into the Pool of Purification where he washed three times as prescribed by the ritual. After drying himself with three different towels, he put on the robe of purification and clapped twice. The *lahi* (beard trimmer) in attendance hurried in to inspect Arfaad's beard for impurities.

The hair of his beard was arranged in five tight braids that ran from ear to ear, the mark of captainship in Baal's army. The lahi carefully inspected each braid with a specially made silver comb until he was certain it was not contaminated. His task completed, he bowed reverently and walked backward as required of one who was little more than a slave. On the way, he picked up the dirty towels and clothes, dropped them into a large, tin container for unclean linens, and left with the sullied boots. The ritual forbade the participants from talking for fear that the spirit of the dead may speak through the one who is unclean and thus contaminate the Temple.

Arfaad sat on a stool and waited. A servant brought him a clean uniform and a clean pair of boots, bowed, and left. The captain dressed but did not put on his jacket. He clapped twice. Two elderly maids walked in. They inspected the cuffs of his gray pants to ensure no impurity had transferred to his clean clothes. Then, dipping their fingers into an aromatic jar, they laced his neck with a soft gel that smelled of lemon and orange blossoms, and helped him put on his jacket. He straightened the black lapels and tied the green band around his neck, then he clasped the thick, red belt around his waist, snatched his helmet, and walked out.

On his way, he stopped by the barracks to inspect his men. They stood, each by his bunk, their silent faces filled with grief and anguish. "I know you are all ritually unclean, but rest assured, you will perform the Rite of Purification as soon as I have reported back to the high priestess."

A wave of relief washed over their faces, confirming Arfaad's hunch. "They must have thought I barred them from the ritual to deliver them into the hands of the Kerta priest," he muttered as he walked toward the first inner gate of the Temple.

The experiments he had personally witnessed while in the sixth and deepest underground level of the Temple flooded his memory with images of simple folks going insane, others screaming in utter despair, and the silent chuckle—the sickening chuckle—of the priest filling up the concentrators. Willfully, Arfaad suppressed these memories and fervently wished that Baal could be rid of that cruel order. He inhaled deeply and began climbing the spiraling staircase that lead to the high priestess. As he moved up, he crossed five consecutive gates protected by vulture-like creatures with shining, green eyes. These were the *watchers*, guardians of the Temple. As he went under each gate, he felt their incisive gaze burrow deeply into his mind, assessing his intent, deciding whether he was a friend or foe, whether to let him pass or declare him fodder for the concentrators. Arfaad shuddered involuntarily; the watchers, created by the Kerta priests, were neither dead nor alive.

He found the high priestess sitting on her preaching chair, her hands gripping the silver, lion-shaped handles. Despite his inner turmoil, he held his right fist with his left hand behind his back and briefly nodded, then joined his hands next to his heart and bowed deeply.

I ordered you to kill the woman you wanted to marry, your Hoda, and still your military and religious salutes are flawless, thought Bahiya, distraught. *What kind of a man are you?*

"It is done," he said evenly.

"Any survivors?"

"No, Your Honor."

"Are you sure?"

He looked at her with eyes that did not conceal his sorrow. "Yes, Your Honor, every man, woman, and child of Baher-Ghafé is no more."

"How many casualties?"

"Your Honor, the casualties are 1,283."

This is the correct count, thought Bahiya. "Have you given pursuit to the Black Robes?"

"Three light guards are camping in the foothills of the mountains northeast of Byblos as we speak."

"The curfew in Byblos?"

"Half of the Lightning Division is enforcing it."

"The Temple is proud of your services, Captain. You are to leave immediately for Byblos and report to Captain Sind aboard the Astarte. Once at sea, you will be told about your next assignment."

"What is to be done with my men?" he ventured to ask. He owed them this much.

Bahiya waved her hand impatiently, "I will see to it that they perform their ablutions before sunrise. You have my word."

Arfaad knelt, then kissed the floor. He stood back up and bowed. "The Temple prevails, Your Honor."

Absent-mindedly, Bahiya gave the expected response to the traditional closure of Baal: "Always."

The doorkeepers closed the heavy rosewood door behind the captain. The high priestess shut her eyes, heaved a deep sigh of relief, and whispered, "At last, I am alone."

She stood up and started walking towards the altar of incense. Uncontrollable sobs shook her frame, forcing her to lean against the cold stony wall. Nausea and dizziness assaulted her with a savagery she had never felt before. She crumpled onto the giant mosaic of the god Baal in his heavenly chariot bringing bountiful rain over fields of wheat to the acclaim of a multitude of farmers waving at him with smiling faces. She laid face down, crying over the smiling face of a young boy. Regrets pierced her heart, and she wished she had never joined the Temple.

"I should have been stronger," she whispered. "I should not have left him. We could be together, hiding somewhere, like Corintus and Layaléa did. If only he had listened to me."

The order to eradicate Baher-Ghafé had reached her at the close of the first watch. The night was still young, and she was looking forward to her annual dinner with the dwarf merchant Kwadil and to the Festival of Light when the high priest of Babylon summoned her and told her that the Temple had, at last, located the Seer.

Bahiya was dumbfounded. "The Seer? The one the Temple has been dreading for twelve hundred years? He is here? In Baher-Ghafé?"

"In Baher-Ghafé," confirmed the high priest, who did not mind Bahiya's breach of protocol. He understood her surprise and dismay. "It is, indeed, hard to believe that the Seer of Chaos has risen in our own age, but there can be no doubt. The Letters of Power made themselves known to him in a burst of energy."

"He knows of the Letters?" Bahiya was aghast. "This is terrible."

"I share your dismay, my dear Bahiya; the people of Baher-Ghafé are hardworking and loyal to the Temple, and their shark meat is exquisite, not to mention that ruby wine of theirs that graces the Temple's table. But yes, the Letters were seen by him. We must strike before he can put them to use. Kill everyone. Do not have pity. The Seer must not be allowed to open the Pit, or else..."

"An age of a darkness, the like of which we have never seen, will overtake us all," completed Bahiya. She was all too well aware of the risk the Seer of the Letters of Power brought with him. She bowed before the high priest, "Have no fear, my Lord. It will be done."

"I would expect nothing less of you, dear child."

"And now, it is over," she whispered. "They are all dead."

With a supreme effort, she regained her composure, wiped her tears, rose, and walked to the golden altar at the northern end of the hall. She unbuckled the emerald straps of her short, velvet cape and hung it on a gold hook at the base of the altar, and exchanged it for the shawl of the ritual. She pulled back her flowing, yellow sleeves, and using the silk brush, she collected the ashes and coals from the previous offering into a silver pail to the right side of the altar. Then she poured a fresh batch of coals, sprinkled them with a black powder from a green, velvet pouch, and brushed them with the flame of a nearby candle. At once the coals began to burn, crackling under the intense heat.

Mechanically, Bahiya scooped some amber incense with a tiny, golden spoon from the first of three gold cups hanging over the altar by silk threads. She dropped the amber into the palm of her hand and added a larger scoop of myrrh from the second cup. The third cup contained a bright, red resin from a plant called, strangely, dragon's blood. She took a generous amount, combined the three substances, and sprinkled the mixture concentrically over the coals. She took two steps back and bowed to the twelve-foot gold statue of the god Baal standing behind the altar, holding a stylized thunderbolt in his raised right hand. Staring into the statue's dull eyes, she silently recited the three parts of the Beynitar Ketoret, the customary prayer of purification to ward off the evil of bloodshed.

"Today, your yoke is heavy, my Lord. Innocent blood has been shed from souls so dear that it is tearing me to pieces. Was it worth it, my Lord?" The statue did not answer. "Yes, I know," continued Bahiya, "I have heard it before: we cannot afford the horrors the Seer would unleash on us, but why Baher-Ghafé? Why?"

A discreet knock on the side door reminded her that her assistant, Zarifa, the first priestess, was awaiting her orders. She removed the shawl of ritual, took her cape, lifted the golden hem of her long, flowing purple priestly garment, and entered the antechamber where Zarifa was waiting. The first priestess had a fair complexion with curly, gold locks framing her pretty face, where a pair of emerald-green eyes glittered over strawberry-red lips. Bahiya, in contrast, had a darker complexion, jet-black eyes, and wavy, red hair. Her smile could ravish any man's heart, while the high priestess' austere countenance exuded strength and authority. She raised her thin eyebrows and pursed her lips upon seeing her first priestess in a sleeveless scruffy, white gown with hanging green ribbons. A purple chlamys was casually tied to her neck by a gold scarab, which the young woman used as a substitute for the cape of authority that she was supposed to wear. Normally, Bahiya would have chided her apprentice for her levity, but not today. Bahiya's jaw tightened as she gripped the icy side of the altar. She willed herself to calm down and turned to face the young woman, who flinched.

"Let the High Riders proclaim a message to the citizens of Baalbeck condemning the shedding of innocent blood and the destruction of Baher-Ghafé. They are to blame the rebels known as the Black Robes."

"Is there anything else you would like them to say, my lady?" Zarifa asked, choosing her words carefully. She was confused and scared. Never before had she felt the power of Baal—cold and mesmerizing—flow so freely from her mistress.

What is wrong with her? she wondered with a tinge of disdain. *High Riders routinely cleanse entire villages to prevent greater destruction of life, but she is reacting as if someone plucked her eye.* She bit her lip and lowered her gaze, for she knew better than to question the high priestess.

"Let them say the Black Robes attacked the town of Baher-Ghafé and massacred everyone," replied Bahiya evenly.

"Yes, Your Honor."

"Command the High Riders to enforce the Curfew of the Dead for the night."

"Only one night, Your Honor?"

"Yes, just this one night. Let the festival resume as usual tomorrow."

Zarifa bowed to the ground, walked backward toward the door with a sigh of relief, and was about to leave when Bahiya called her back.

"Yes, Your Honor?"

"Command the men of the Lightning Division to do their ablutions and... Zarifa, give me one more disdainful look and I will let the Kerta priest teach you the full meaning of pain for three days. Do we understand each other?" Zarifa nodded frantically. "Now go. I do not wish to be disturbed until the morning ritual."

The curfew was already in full force when the famed caravan of Master Kwadil reached Byblos, a city he loved, for it was as cosmopolitan as Baalbeck was austere. Shady sailors of Quibanxe filled the coastal taverns in the southern part of the city, while delicate noblewomen of Atlant strolled the fashionable northern quarters over air-heated sidewalks. Byblos was comfortable for the gritty and the cultivated, the tawdry and the princely.

The High Riders manning the main gate of the city were familiar with Kwadil's caravan. They let the convoy enter the city for the customary bribe. "Every bribed soldier is a future customer," would say the shrewd dwarf, who was an expert at getting back every piece of silver he gave out.

Master Kwadil liked to camp in the southern part of the city, even though his customers were in the wealthy northern side. "Cheaper rent," he would say unapologetically, "is the root of good profit."

Kwadil hopped out of his richly decorated carriage and spoke with his second-in-command following the peculiar manner of the dwarf's speech.

"Azerowut, I must tend to an urgently urgent business and a business that is urgent most urgently. Watch over my tent with extreme care and care that is caring in the extreme, and do not, under any circumstantial circumstance, allow anyone and his brother to be within an uncomfortably uncomfortable distance of her door."

"But Master," replied the stocky, bearded dwarf, "the curfew is imposed imposingly and imposingly imposed. The patrolling patrols will not be inclined to any kindly kindness. You could be dead in the most deadly manner and deadly dead, to say the least and the most of this unsavory business."

"It cannot be helped, Azerowut. This business must be conclusively concluded and concluded most conclusively before dawn. Now, do as I say and say as I do: if the soldiering soldiers come to my tent, cover them with bribing bribery but do not open her door."

"As you wish, Master Kwadil. May Kerishal protect you protectively and may Xanthor grant you victorious victory in your warring war."

"Thank you thankfully, Azerowut. Now, use some of these fiery fireworks to create a diverting diversion so I may be on my unnoticeably unnoticed way."

He climbed back inside his spacious carriage and took a peek at the young boy sound asleep in the midst of silk pillows—fourteen of them—featherstitched with strands of white gold and laced with *erjwan*, the famous purple substance prized in all the land of Baal. Each pillow was worth one camel or two fast steeds. Fondly, he recalled how he had acquired these pillows far away in the kingdom of the mighty Marada. They were the fruit of a gamble he had won in the Race of Kyril, known as the Wretched Race, where one could just as easily win a fortune, fall into slavery, or lose his life.

"Kwadil, Kwadil," muttered the dwarf, "this is neither the timely time nor the appropriately appropriate occasional occasion to reminisce reminiscently about willowy pillows." He watched the young boy for a moment longer.

"Goodly goodness," whispered Kwadil, satisfied. "The young lad is sleepily sleeping with a sound soundness." He opened the door and asked a nearby crew member to fetch the doctor.

"Have you brought the lad back from the land of dreamy dreams?" he asked the doctor as soon as he had stepped inside the carriage.

"Yes, I have," replied Jendhi, the doctor. He was an Ophirian by birth who travelled the world. The two had met during the Wretched Race ten years ago and had been traveling together ever since.

To Kwadil's chagrin, Jendhi never managed to master the dwarfish speech, so he switched back to the Common Tongue. "Why is he still sleeping so?"

"He was, shall we say, very agitated and took to screaming."

"Anything in particular?"

"Mostly his sister's name, Hoda. He kept repeating it, and nothing I said would make him stop."

"What flawlessly flawless and flawless flawlessly clue, revealed to you in the most revealing of ways that Hoda is the boy's sister?"

"He said it himself: 'I want my sister, Hoda. Where is Hoda? She said she would come back,' and so on and so forth."

"I see," said Kwadil, smiling, "so you administered a mild sedative?"

"Yes. I figured you did not want to attract the High Riders' attention, seeing how you took this boy from his boat that had ended up on a deserted beach. They're bound to ask questions."

Kwadil grinned. "And did you instructively instruct the men not to say anything about the double-finned shark swimmingly swimming nearby?"

"I promised them an extra bonus."

Kwadil winced, then shrugged his shoulders. Jendhi was right. If this boy was a survivor from Baher-Ghafé, then the crew's silence was worth an extra bonus. "Very well, this will be all, but it would please me pleasingly and in the most pleasing of ways for you to be ready for anything and mostly for everything."

Jendhi smiled, bowed, and left. The Kingdom of Ophir was free from the Temple's meddling, and even though Jendhi was not a revolutionary, he was always glad to help in the silent and secret war Kwadil was waging against the Temple of Baal. *Freedom is worth a few sacrifices, especially when "sacrifices" mean pleasant travels and warm meals*, he thought, grinning.

Even though Master Kwadil was extremely wealthy, he dressed as a commoner with his sturdy, leather boots, white shirt, wool sweater, and a leather vest with silver buttons. His stocking, leather cap hung nearby beneath his cowl. His beard was trimmed short, and he wore his black, curly hair shoulder length, which was the minimum acceptable length by dwarfish standards. At five-foot-two, he was tall for a southerner dwarf.

The one hundred and twenty crew members were busy setting up camp when one air bomb barrage was curiously set on fire. Strident spirals of silvery flames streaked the night. The High Riders stationed near the camp came running, swords drawn. Azerowut met them and explained the situation.

"A horribly horrible mistaken mistake," he said, bowing to the ground. "This is an accidental accident, and I apologetically apologize and apologize in the most apologetically fashionable fashion."

"Fine," grumbled Essam, the light guard leader. "We'll let it go this time, but I want your camp set up and the lot of you in your tents in fifteen minutes. Is this clear?"

"Clearly clear and clear with utmost clarity," replied Azerowut, bowing again. "It shall be done immediately in the immediate, and not a moment later."

Essam grunted. This was the first time, ever, that the caravan of Master Kwadil had caused a serious incident. Besides, he was looking for an exotic gift to impress Syreen, the second maid of Zarifa, the first priestess, and Master Kwadil had the best exotic products, bar none.

Taking advantage of the commotion, Master Kwadil slipped through the night. At first, he walked down a wide street leading to the center square of the city and quickly went into a dark alleyway, where he knocked at a narrow door that the casual passerby would have missed. Syreen opened the door and greeted him.

"Master Kwadil," she said, quickly closing the door behind him, "I thought you would never come."

"I have been delayed, child," replied the dwarf, following her down a set of steep stairs that led to a damp passage.

In the dim light of the candle, Syreen's eyes shone brightly.

"Syreen, you are crying. What's the matter?"

She looked at him and smiled sadly. "My friend, Hoda, she's from

Baher-Ghafé," she said quietly.

"Oh, I see," he said with a grief-filled voice. "I am so sorrowfully sorry and sorry in the most sorrowful way."

"Karadon and three other companions were keeping watch over her and her family, so there is still a chance she may have survived."

"And why were the Black Robes keeping a watchful watch over a simple fishermen's daughter?"

"It's her brother. He has had a Merilian since birth. Judging by Ashod's reaction, this boy is very important. Ashod has all the Black Robes searching for him."

"All the Black... Ashod is willfully willing to risk everything we have built until now for one boyish boy?" asked Kwadil. "This is incredibly incredible and incredible in the most incredible manner. What else did he say?"

"About the boy? He said he needs military training to teach him how to control his temper. The Temple must have destroyed Baher-Ghafé to be rid of him."

"This boy is her brotherly brother, you say?"

"Yes. Hoda would have done anything for him."

"And how old is he?"

"He just turned twelve today. He is a wiry boy with curly, brown hair and big, hazel eyes. Why do you ask?"

"I will be traveling everywhere in Fineekia. If he managed to escape, I might be able to recognize him." Syreen nodded. "Well, let us hope your friend is well. Do not lose hope hopelessly. It is all the more urgent that I speak with Foosh then."

"The heating conduits are straight ahead," she said, handing him a candle. "You cannot miss them. Follow them in a straight line, and they will lead you to the ruins of the Temple to the unknown god. Balid's tent is standing in the main plaza, a few feet away from these ruins. You should have no difficulty whatsoever reaching it."

"Thank you most thankfully, dear child."

"By the way, Master Kwadil, Foosh's husband, Balid, he does not know..."

"No, he is blissfully blissful and blissful blissfully that his wife is a leader of the Black Robes. Balid is a friendly friend of mine, and his congenially congenial, innocently innocent personality opens some doors for Foosh and prevents others from being closed. Now child, if Karadon has managed to safely save your friend, he will go into hiding for four to six weeks or six to four weeks. You must bravely bear this timely time with patiently patience and strength. Otherwise, the Temple might find out, and our operational operation will be most compromisingly compromised."

"You have nothing to worry about, Master Kwadil," said Syreen. "You have trained me well."

Kwadil nodded and walked away. His great mind focused on the question at hand: should he have told Syreen about the boy he found on that deserted beach? Jendhi, the doctor, had told him the boy screamed the name of his sister, "*Hoda, Hoda.*" Clearly, the boy matched Syreen's description. *But,* Kwadil reasoned, *if Ashod is willingly willing to mount a full rescue mission, then the boy must be importantly important, so it stands to reason that the Temple would be willingly willing to destroy the Black Robes to get him back. Now, thus far, and not one day further, the surviving survival of the clandestine organization hinged on the Temple's need of a conveniently convenient scapegoat to hide its dirty deeds, and the Black Robes served this purpose admirably. Their purposeful purpose is to save lives and protect the innocently innocent, but we are not readily ready no readily in most readily fashion to face a full blown assault by the High Riders.*

Kwadil quickly made up his mind; the boy must be sent faraway from Fineekia, and he knew just the place to send him. *His sister, should she survive, will think him dead in the most deadly manner. It is regrettably regrettable and regrettable most regrettably, but cannot be helped.*

>✱✱✱<

"A hero, a hero," muttered Balid, inspecting the deserted plaza of Byblos for the umpteenth time. He held back his red turban, preventing it from falling. "I may be a carpet merchant, but I can tell a true hero from a fake one, like a silkworm smells a good apple from a rotten one. This Arfaad is a butcher, my dear Foosh. I have not forgotten what he did in Alep."

"Are you trying to have us arrested?" whispered his wife. "Hurry and get back in."

"Tell me something, my dearest Foosh," continued the expansive man, while adjusting the large turban on his head and pulling down the golden, silk caftan that stubbornly wedged itself in the ripples of his flesh. "Do you believe what we heard?"

"And what are you going to do about it?" replied Foosh, a petite woman with long, scruffy hair held in place by a web of hairpins so complex it defied the wisdom of the gods. She was svelte, fast on her feet, and always elegant, thanks to her husband who could afford a pair of expensive seamstresses from the fashionable city of Atlant. Foosh was five-feet two-inches tall, and he towered over her at six-feet two-inches, a difference others may have noticed, but not Balid. He was deeply in love with his wife, and knew he could always count on her to enliven their tent and their guests with her refined and simple taste. Balid looked at Foosh appreciatively. She wore a gray, buttoned blouse with a bow collar over a deep-blue, accordion-pleated, long skirt. Her narrow face with blue eyes, high cheekbones, and long neck, was slightly out of proportion from the rest of her body. Still, her soft, round eyes and quick wit gave her all the charm that the wife of a carpet merchant needed to help her husband, while keeping her sanity. She wondered what Balid would do if he knew she was a member of the Black Robes. *He would have a conniption, no doubt, and then he would convince every member of the organization to buy a carpet.* She repressed a smile and continued:

"I suppose you would like to give a piece of your mind to the priestess, hmm...?' Your Honor, Arfaad is the butcher of Alep?' Hmm...?"

"Are you insinuating that this Arfaad is a real hero?" he asked, hurt. "Maybe you are unhappy with a carpet merchant, or maybe you do not like my carpets. Yes, yes, my dearest, let the truth come forth. We have been married for twenty-seven years, and in all these years, you have not told me, not even once, that you liked my carpets. These carpets have been sold in royal palaces in seven kingdoms and in faraway lands. They are the best you will find from the golden shores of Mitani to the majestic cliffs of Lurca."

"You have never been to either place," pointed out Foosh, while setting the table. Balid had not yet noticed that the lamps inside their richly furnished tent were burning brighter. Comfortable cushions now surrounded the low table. "Besides," she continued with a broad smile, "the children are growing, the horses are fed, and we have food for tonight."

"Ah, my beautiful Foosh, your words are like honey and your smile like nuggets of gold from on high."

"May you be preserved from harmful harm," came a voice from behind.

Balid turned around and opened his expansive arms. "Master Kwadil, we were getting worried." He lifted the dwarf up and hugged him as though he had just found his long-lost child.

"Put him down," protested Foosh. "He cannot breathe."

Kwadil laughed. "Your strength has not left you, my friend. It is my pleasing pleasure and pleasure most pleasing to stand in your presence."

"The feeling is all mine," exclaimed Balid, rubbing his hands. He enjoyed Kwadil's friendship, but enjoyed Kwadil's purse even more. "I am delighted by your presence amongst us, friend. You brighten our light and make the stars of heaven shine forth in the midst of our tent."

"Balid, you mistake my dwarfitude for your clientele," replied Kwadil with a smile. "The lasting last time you sung sweetly and sweetly sung this song to my ears, my purse became lightly lighter and my canopy was graced with two carpets so magnificently magnificent that they were magnificent beyond magnifying compare."

"Ah, the royal Beluuch and the lush Bokhara. How long has it been since that fateful day?" asked Balid, with a misty voice.

"Thirteen years ago, right after the eventful events and events so eventful in Alep," replied Kwadil.

"Time flows like memories on the shores of the past... But tell me, how long did these carpets of mine last you?"

"I do not know. I sold them for twice their price to a princely prince of the Marada."

"See?" Balid gazed at his wife with a triumphant expression.

"Are you going to keep our guest standing by the door all night, or will you offer him a seat?" asked Foosh, with a wry smile. Balid motioned Kwadil toward the comfortable cushions, then he slipped his feet into his sturdy, leather mules and stepped outside to inspect the plaza. Despite his keen eyes, he saw no one and went back inside.

"The curfew is effective," he said, fixing his gaze on Master Kwadil.

"Hurry please, the food will grow cold," Foosh reminded them.

Balid removed his shoes and they washed their hands in bowls of fresh, rose-scented water and moved to the table where they relaxed on comfortable cushions. Kwadil examined the food, paying special attention to the olives: Some were black and some were green. Some were laid on a bed of mint leaves, while others sat on the edge of a plate surrounding a white sauce. Kwadil picked up one marinated, green olive with a mint leaf and caught sight of his friend staring at him. He placed them in his mouth and shook under a silent chuckle.

One green olive means Kwadil requires extraction of one young boy, understood Foosh. *The mint leaf implies that the extraction is urgent.*

"You are wondrously wondering and wondering in the most

wondrous of ways," explained the dwarf to his friend.

"What's so wondrous about my wondering?" asked Balid.

"How I made it here despite the curfew, yes? I gave the deadly servants of the high priestess a bribing bribery and a bribery most bribing," explained Kwadil, who lied as any good dwarf would when fortune or friends were threatened.

The high priestess wants someone dead, interpreted Foosh.

"And they accepted?" questioned Balid.

The High Riders were reputed for refusing all forms of bribery. The reality was a different matter.

"It is the feasting Feast of Light," retorted Kwadil, "and during the feasting feast, these soldierly soldiers act like boys who do not mind a bit of dangerous danger."

I see, the high priestess wants a boy dead, continued Foosh.

Seeing his friend thoroughly confused, Kwadil added in a conspiratorial tone, "You see, it was importantly important to see you today and no later than tomorrow."

Foosh glanced at Balid. His blissful expression reassured her. *Good. He is not aware of the hidden message—the high priestess wants the boy dead. He must leave tomorrow.* The message was now complete.

"By the highest heavens," began Balid, "Master Kwadil, you make absolutely no—"

"This food is excellently excellent as usually usual and in no other ways," interrupted the dwarf. "My dear Foosh, remind me to ask you for your recipe. This zaja is so good that I would travel hundreds of miles on a raging sea for her. If I did not know better—and I do—I would say, my dear Foosh, that you are a dwarf daughter of dwarfs."

"That's a dish of *zghazti*," corrected Balid. "We haven't had any *zaja* since our last trip to Tanniin," he added, rubbing his large belly.

Balid is right, thought Foosh. *Is Kwadil serious?* She saw him eye her without blinking. *He is serious. I see: most likely, he wants us to take the boy to Tanniin, and as usual, he must have a compelling reason.*

"Now, now, my friend," continued Kwadil, "these are extraordinarily extraordinary times we are lively living in. Yes, yes, indeed, extraordinary in the most extraordinarily of ways. Let us now feast on these wonders placed before us, for tomorrow is another day, and who knows what the sun might bring with him. Is it not true that the stone that was moved tonight may reveal a gem by the morrow?"

Stone, gem... He wants this boy trained and formed... Of course. Commander Tanios is in Tanniin, but why? wondered Foosh.

Balid, for his part, felt a familiar irritation creeping up on him. Dwarfs were known for their peculiar manner of speech. Every object had a gender: The sun was a "him" and the moon a "her". A pebble was a "him" and a boulder a "her". There was no discernable pattern, but a dwarf would be quickly offended if you used the wrong gender, particularly when speaking of stones and gems. Balid carefully avoided the entire subject, confining himself to carpets. To make matters worse, dwarfs were known to mingle two or more unrelated issues in the same sentence. Talking to a dwarf was an exercise in diplomacy.

"Life is full of wonders," continued the unflappable dwarf, "and she who is patiently patient and wisely wise, in due time, will reap good things from the fruits of her labor."

He will explain later, sighed Foosh. *How predictable.*

Balid, who was trying his hardest to make sense of his friend's words, perked up when he heard Kwadil say "she." A carpet was feminine in dwarfish (but a collection of carpets, masculine) and this was all he needed to steer the conversation toward more pleasant and remunerating shores: Pointing at his most expensive carpet, which happened to be hanging behind his wife, he intoned, "She is most welcomingly welcoming and welcoming most welcomingly, and so softly soft yet durably durable that she will be a wonderfully wonderful addictive addition to your luxuriously luxurious tent. More zaja?"

It was Kwadil's turn to be thoroughly confused. He leaned over and whispered loudly in the carpet merchant's ear: "Balid, this is zghazti, not zaja. More importantly, are you trying to sell me your wife?"

"My wife? What... No, not my wife," grumbled an exasperated Balid, "the carpet hanging *behind* my wife."

Poor Balid, thought Foosh, amused.

"So why didn't you say so?" asked Kwadil while scooping another large bite of zghazti. He added quickly, "You and I are about to engage in a mutually beneficial exchange, my dear Balid." Balid perked up. "One you and I will remember as a beautiful dawn on the seashore."

Foosh did the mental translation: *Balid will deliver a few carpets to his camp, and he will bring the boy back. I better prepare the special container.*

Balid's carpets were expensive and warranted the extra protection of sturdy, wooden containers to protect them. One of these containers—the handiwork of master dwarfs—had a cavity concealed by a dropped ceiling large enough for a man to hide in it. The intricate etchings inside the trunk created the perfect illusion, causing the hung ceiling to remain undetectable. Two copper pipes hidden by the carvings brought fresh air inside that space. Foosh had used this trunk on several occasions in the past to smuggle fugitives of Baal and help them join the Black Robes.

"Master Kwadil, you speak again riddles and mysteries. You did not come here under curfew to buy two carpets, did you?" Balid inquired.

"Ah, my dearest Foosh, you are the queen of spices."

Help me, I don't know how to answer your husband. translated Foosh silently. *Ha! This will teach Kwadil to underestimate Balid.*

"Your zghazti is delicious. It must be the goat cheese you use."

Is he telling me, to my face, that my husband is a goat? Involuntarily, Foosh frowned.

"He is so creamy," added Kwadil quickly. "I should like to know what you feed your goats."

Ah, he found a way out. I was going to let him stew in his own porridge a little longer.

"You should know, my dear friend and friend most dear," said Kwadil to Balid in reply...

Uh-oh, thought Balid, *I just offended a dwarf. May the heavens have mercy on us.*

"...that we dwarfs are not without our own resourceful resources and resources most resourceful. Andaxil may have not yet yielded all her secrets but not all our secretive secrets and secrets most secretive were locked up within her walls. We—"

"More zaja, dear Kwadil?" offered Foosh.

The dwarf's countenance brightened instantly. By saying "zaja," Foosh signaled that she understood and agreed to help him.

"Zghazti," corrected Balid wiping his forehead. "What is wrong with you two calling a zghazti dish 'zaja'? Back to the carpets; Master Kwadil, why did you come now and not wait until tomorrow morning when the curfew is lifted?"

"My estimable esteemed client and most esteemed estimable client will be leaving at the break of dawn tomorrow morning and not a moment later."

"Oh, where to? I was not aware anyone could leave Byblos so early."

"The *Noonoh*, a graceful, tri-mast ship, is leaving for Tanniin tomorrow morning. My richly rich buyer wants to attend the Games of the Mines."

Balid rubbed his chin dreamily. "The Games of the Mines, ah, yes, exciting. So many carpets to sell."

"I have never seen the Games," added Foosh innocently.

"Ah, yes, my dear Foosh, the Games are a wonder to see..." He lowered his gaze and shuddered. "So expensive this trip, don't you know?" With puppy eyes, he looked at Master Kwadil, "So very expensive."

"My customer is willing to cover the cost of travel if you throw in a third carpet," said the dwarf.

"Done," replied Balid. "Foosh, I shall take you to Tanniin, and you shall see the world, the Games, the mines. What an adventure. I had better go tell Parma to get busy," he said, rising. "We have much preparation to make."

"Then I had better leave."

"Before you taste the sweets? Out of the question. Besides, I'll need ten minutes at most."

"Fine. I shall wait for you."

"Foosh," said Balid, whispering, "serve the sweets."

"I am right here, Balid," said Kwadil. "I can hear you."

Balid smiled then slipped out of the tent.

"Who is he?" asked Foosh.

"The less you know, the better," replied Kwadil.

"I see. You want him out of harm's way. What shall I tell Commander Tanios?"

"Tell Tanios I am sending a slave to be trained under him. If, in the span of nine years, I do not send for him, the boy's fate will be in his hands. He may set him free if he so wishes."

"Why nine years?"

"Because, dear Foosh, the Tanniinites have learned that when an orphan slave is set free too early and they are left to their own devices, they leave their masters in haste and fall into the wrong hands. For the benefit of the slaves and the peace in the kingdom, a royal edict forbids an orphan slave from being set free before the age of twenty-one."

"I see," said Foosh. "How do we retrieve the boy?"

"I will come to you tomorrow morning, as soon as the curfew breaks, and the boy will be in my carriage. You will help Jendhi conceal him in that special trunk. Keep the boy sedated until you are far away from the coast. He must not, under any circumstances, mention the name of his sister, or else your lives and ours will be forfeited. Understood?"

Foosh nodded. "All of this for a slave?" she added quizzically.

"Tanios must not suspect anything. To anyone on that boat and in Tanniin, the boy must look like an orphan slave who is still in shock at the loss of his family. No more, no less."

"It is done," said Balid, walking back into the tent.

"Zaja makes you healthy. It prevents tooth decay," said Kwadil, beaming. "Have some more."

Balid did not bother correcting the dwarf. Instead, he obliged, wondering if he was still the host or if he had become the guest under his own tent. He knew his friend was a born leader, feeling at ease in a tent as much as in a palace. He, on the other hand, was content to play a more passive role.

"Time for some sweets," said Foosh, smiling. She served them and bowed. "Master Kwadil, I must retire early. There is much to be done tomorrow."

"May you be preserved from harm," replied the dwarf, bowing, and his words rung ominously in her ears. She smiled and left the tent.

Kwadil clapped like a child who had just been handed a wonderful gift. "Ah, my dear Balid, your wife's namoorah is without compare. I love her," he added looking at Balid.

"Master Kwadil," started Balid cautiously, "you are not suggesting what I think you have just suggestively suggested."

"Bravo, my dear friend," exclaimed the dwarf. "After twenty years of friendship, you are beginning to understand her."

"Who? My wife?"

"No, our language. Your sentence was perfectly dwarfish."

"Thank you," replied Balid beaming. Encouraged, he went on the offensive. "Have some more namoorah," he said grinning. "She has prepared her for you."

"Who?"

"My wife."

"Your wife prepared herself—"

"No, the namoorah."

"Ah, her. Very well, now, keep up your good work, and she will reward you greatly."

"Who, my wife?"

"No, the trip, of course. I suppose all has been said, yes? Good. Please give my highest regards to your delightful wife and do let her know how highly appreciative I am of her wonderful cuisine."

"Thank you, my friend, and do not worry. She will be very successful."

"Your wife?"

"No, the trip."

"What a peculiar manner of speech," said Kwadil, as he vanished into the night.

"I will never get it," muttered Balid. "I have known him for over twenty years, and I still do not get it. Dwarfish grammar doesn't make sense."

>✦✦✦<

Early the next morning, Foosh and Balid went aboard the Noonoh. The seventeen trunks filled with their choicest carpets went through customs and were loaded into the cargo bay of the tri-mast.

So it was, on Tébêt 2, 1141, that Balid, the carpet merchant, and his wife, Foosh, spirited Ahiram out of Fineekia to sell him as a slave in Tanniin.

"I sure hope we make it in time for the Games of the Mines," said Balid. "We've got to sell those carpets now."

"Don't you worry, Balid," said Foosh. "We will."

PART TWO

৹৵৹

Five Days to Freedom

5. Farewell, My Prince

"The Games of the Mines were a great invention of the Kingdom of Tanniin, preserving their national pride and identity. Year after year, the Games reenacted El-Windiir's victory, and year after year, the team from Baal won, reminding the Tanniinites that Baal was their master and they, his servants. To this end, Baal sent the finest juniors of the High Riders to win the Games."
–Teachings of Oreg, High Priest of Baal

"To the Games!"

Thunderous applause closed the inaugural speech of King Jamiir III of Tanniin on the eve of the Games of the Mines. The King smiled obsequiously, opened his arms, and gave a curt bow imbued with feigned humility. He raised his cup, surveying the guests fortunate enough to be admitted into the Royal Hall. The remaining 2,637 guests were confined to the Royal Garden, the lower hall on the first floor, and the middle hall on the second. The total number being exactly 2,929, to honor the span of years since El-Windiir, the kingdom's founder, fought the Lord of the Pit in the Wars of Meyroon.

"And now, dear friends, let us make merry. Let there be dancing and rejoicing on the eve of the great Games of the Mines."

Elliptical in shape, the Royal Hall was oriented east to west to honor Tanniin from the rising sun to its setting. The massive, vaulted ceiling held a masterpiece of dwarfish craftsmanship: a sun-shaped, alabaster-plated keystone—five feet in diameter—studded with two thousand diamonds. With its twelve gold sunrays sprawled over the white vault, the keystone shimmered like an inner sun. The high ceiling rested on twenty-four columns surrounding a gleaming dance floor large enough for seven hundred guests. Their bases of beaten bronze and hemmed, silver-fluted shafts rose to the capitals, where the ruby-eyed faces of kings long past cast an introspective gaze upon the guests below.

Twenty silver chains held a bronze lattice over the dance floor. Resembling the inverted frame of a ship's hull, it was the largest candelabrum ever conceived, holding eight hundred and sixty candles lighting the room as if in bright daylight.

Two additional columns of wider girth stood: one in the western corner behind the King's throne, and the other in the eastern corner. Marble-covered, each held a gold statue of Tanniin with his legs curled around the shaft and his neck lunging over the candelabrum with open jaws beneath ruby-red eyes gleaming in the light, while his wings fanned over the crowd in a protective gesture. Unlike Baal and Yem, Tanniin frowned upon revelries, and these two statues were a constant reminder to all of the god's wrath upon wanton behavior.

In the space between the columns and the back wall, the musicians sat busily tuning their instruments. Behind them, guests who chose not to dance were mingling. An arched wooden double door led to the marble balcony outside. The door was flanked by eight lancet stone arches with strip moldings of rosewood and oak. Across the dance floor, an identical double door opened to a wide corridor from which one could glimpse the glittering dark walls of the Lone Tower.

Between every pair of windows stood a table laden with dishes to satisfy every whim and fancy.

King Jamiir extended his white-gloved hand to Queen Ramel and the large hall fell silent. The rulers of Tanniin formed a striking couple. He was of fair complexion, skinny and freckled, with a receding hairline over a hawkish nose and a thin curled-up moustache. She was olive skinned with shoulder-length, straight, black hair parted midway and studded with pearls. A high forehead and deer-like, black eyes over a pair of thin lips that rarely smiled, gave her the conceited air of a perennially young goddess gracing the land of mortals by her presence.

He wore a white, satin shirt hanging loosely over linen tights with rubies stitched along their outer seam. She wore a purple, sheath dress of alternating ruby-studded, velvet and silk strands. A large freeze adorned the King's neck, while the draped neck of the Queen's dress, inlaid with white pearls, was fronted by one large diamond. His crown was of dark iron in imitation of meyroon, the rare and precious metal of legends—so elusive, that even the King did not possess it. His shoulder signets were two pairs of gold wings. A thin silver chain held the felt sheath of his inoffensive sword. This matched a pair of fur-lined bootees which mimicked El-Windiir's shoes of bronze. She wore a triple-band, gold crown inlaid with four emerald tears and long silk purple gloves with matching leather boots.

Delicately, Queen Ramel placed her hand on the King's and walked with him to the dance floor. Her dress shimmered as if she were a creature of light. They stood apart facing each other and waited for their guests to join them. Elders from the neighboring, western kingdoms of Togofalk and Oronoque, in their white saris patched with pastel tones, were the first to come forward. They were closely followed by the dark-skinned guests from Quibanxe, Edfu, and Kemet—each wearing a dozen thick serpentine chains of gold over their bright red and green saris. In contrast, the northerners from the kingdoms of Thermodon, Var-Kun, Bar Tannic, and even from the northernmost reaches of Val Halon favored tunics of interwoven fur and wool, studded with beads of black onyx. Their long, blond tresses were threaded with thin strands of silver, and the soles of their leather boots rang joyfully on the immaculate silver floor.

Those that hailed from the eastern kingdoms of Mycene, Teshub, Mitani, and Uratu came in their traditional caftans and boubous, with earthy tones of warm summer and glorious fall. The men of the faraway Kingdom of Atlant, nearly nine thousand miles away, wore brown, leather vests, pants, and white linen shirts over pointy, black boots. The women wore long, sheath dresses in cream-colored leather with matching jewelry and sandals. Last to join the dance were two couples moving in graceful layers of silk, swaying silently with the fluidity of water as if they had emerged from a primordial springtime of youth. They hailed from Ophir, the most powerful and wealthiest kingdom outside Baal's dominion, which lay at the southern edge of the land.

The orchestra of twenty lyres, six cymbals, ten flutes, and four sitars started playing. King Jamiir bowed gracefully and the Queen smiled as they opened the *Naddah,* a dance known in most royal houses.

And they all danced. *An Adorant's smile,* thought Bahiya observing the Queen. She was referring to the feared order of women serving Baal with their voices. No man could resist their songs or gaze into their eyes too long without becoming their willing slave. The Temple used the Adorant mostly to cement the loyalty of the High Riders and the army, but these feared servants had other uses as well, darker powers which Bahiya preferred not to think about.

She stood close to the throne in the western corner wearing a beige, satin dress that covered her from head to toe. Her hair was held in a simple high ponytail, and a strand of pearls was the only piece of jewelry she wore. Despite her austere countenance, she looked cheerful and festive next to the man behind her. Six-feet-three inches tall, broad shouldered and muscular, Commander Tanios stood, hands behind his back, surveying the dance floor as if it were a battleground. His steely-blue eyes beneath thick eyebrows were cast in a face chiseled from flint, which wavy, black hair held in a ponytail could not soften. He wore the Silent's uniform: a crewneck sweater over a pair of pants, both covered with a seemingly random pattern of different shades of green, brown, and black patches. The pant cuffs fit tightly around the ankles over a pair of soft leather, black boots. The strange pattern helped the Silent move unseen, even in daylight. Silk strands, judiciously mixed with the linen, added a confusing shine and gave the garment a semblance of fragility.

Commander Tanios would have dressed in more appropriate clothing for the occasion, but the King had sent for him two weeks ago and asked him to personally watch over Bahiya as commander of the Silent Corps.

"The high priestess of the Temple of Baalbeck?" the commander asked, taken aback. "Why should she cross twenty-five hundred miles to attend the Games? Are there no priests of Baal in Mycene? Are they all on vacation, or better yet, dead?"

The King sighed, tapping his index finger impatiently on his throne. "I need you to find out for me why the Temple is sending the powerful Bahiya to the Games."

"Could it be the slave's participation?" asked the commander.

The King shook his head. "I highly doubt it. The Temple dispatches slaves routinely, my dear Tanios. Frankly, that is why I consented to this silly idea of yours. I appoint you as her personal bodyguard from the moment she sets foot on the kingdom's soil, to the moment she is on the ship and headed back to the Fineekian shores."

Grim-faced and tight-lipped, the commander now stood next to the high priestess of Baalbeck while the music played. Bahiya's glance lingered for a moment over Hiyam's slender frame. *How she has grown,* she thought as her daughter moved gracefully on the dance floor with her partner, Prince Olothe. *Now, he is something else altogether,* she thought with contained disgust.

Olothe's long, silky hair flowed gently as he fawned over Hiyam, his black sari glittering with diamond fragments. His black beard, black eyes, and black hair contrasted violently with his bleached skin creating an eerie impression of the walking dead. Hiyam wore a bertha-collared, white shirt with three-quarter length, puff sleeves over a light-blue, gored skirt, and a pair of gilded leather thongs. Her hair cascaded in dark, wide locks, and she wore a tiara with a single diamond.

She looks lovely, thought Bahiya misty-eyed, and she shuddered when she tried to imagine her daughter's betrothal to Prince Olothe. It was a marriage of convenience, to give Hiyam access to the wealth she would need to complete her formation in Babylon. Olothe was rich, greedy, and conveniently ambitious. Like fools who thought they could tame a high priestess' daughter and use her to gain access to a power they craved, he would end up as her daughter's driveling servant. On the night of the wedding, when he would come running to her chamber, an Adorant would be waiting to turn him into the willing instrument that Hiyam would need for her ascendancy in the order of the Temple.

"I wish for you to go to Tanniin," Sharr, the high priest of Babylon, had told Bahiya. "I am counting on your expertise to handle three delicate matters. First, the good King Jamiir has not delivered Tanniin into our hands. You will assist him in completing this task. Second, our informants have told us that representatives from the Kingdom of Ophir will be in Tanniin. My niece, Ramel, does not believe the King instigated this. Find out what these representatives want, and why. Lastly, the good King has allowed a slave, who is also a Silent, to take part in the Games of the Mines. I am certain the irony does not escape you. Dispose of the slave discreetly and stop these Games. Do this, and your entrance into the Inner Circle is assured."

Bahiya shivered. The Inner Circle was Baal's circle of power. Priests and priestesses belonging to the circle saw what no one else could see and wielded a power most men and women craved. This would be the culmination of her career, the peak she had longed for.

From the corner of her eye, Bahiya glimpsed a moving shadow. Turning away from the dance floor, she saw a Silent approaching. He could not have been more than six feet tall, but his stride was powerful, his stance assured, as if he was cresting a dark storm, dragging it wherever he went. He surveyed the hall, claiming the world for himself, and leaning against a column, he crossed his arms in an act of self-assured defiance. The thick locks of his auburn, curly hair fell untidily around his face, and his hazel eyes, which seemed gentle at first, burned with a fire she had never seen before. A wave of fear washed over her— sudden, unnatural.

As guardians of the King, every Silent was on duty this night. *This Silent would not be standing here unless he is the slave taking part in the Games*, thought Bahiya.

Before reaching the shores of Tanniin, she had told Prince Olothe she would give him her daughter's hand if he could take care of the slave quickly and discreetly. The prince nearly laughed at her, and only a modicum of self-control saved his life. Obsequiously, he then assured her that he would get rid of the slave, and she had felt she could focus on the two most pressing matters: the King and the Ophirian representatives. However, now that she saw the slave, doubt lodged itself in her mind like a worm. Bahiya knew this doubt all too well. The familiar angst turned her palms sweaty and constricted her breathing. This acute and unreasoned fear had always been for her the harbinger of failure. She glanced at Olothe and immediately regretted having done so, for she knew the commander was observing her and would pick up on her glance. She bit her lower lip and regretted that too, as she instinctively knew he noticed this as well. Bahiya chided herself for having revealed so much to the commander, for he must have guessed by now that Olothe would dispose of the slave. The high priestess slowed her breathing and regained her composure. The slave turned sideways, looking behind him, and she winced. A lone eagle's feather was embroidered on his right shoulder: the Solitary's insignia, the highest rank a Silent could achieve.

Olothe will fail, Bahiya thought with absolute certainty. The prince was a brute, using his cruelty as a substitute for skills, but he was no match for the drive of a Solitary. Few could face a Solitary and prevail, especially when they had trained under Tanios.

The dance ended to the guests' applause. The King bowed once more, and his shadow slithered beneath him as he walked toward the Queen.

Like a trembling snake, thought Ahiram, leaning against a column next to the northern door. He came late and had missed the King's address. *No one will notice anyway, for no one notices a slave.* He crossed his arms, a sad smile on his face. *Tébêt 4, 1197, the Festival of Light. They must be preparing to celebrate in Baher-Ghafé,* he thought. It was also his birthday, a fact he chose to ignore for fear of stirring deeply buried emotions. Looking for a distraction, he surveyed the audience, trying to locate Bahiya, the high priestess of the Temple of Baal. He saw her standing by Commander Tanios. Both were looking at the King.

Six years had come and gone since Master Kwadil had brought him to this strange land. Six years as a slave in the Kingdom of Tanniin. Six years of intense training as a Silent. Six years ago it was his twelfth birthday. Today, it was his birthday again. He was standing amid strangers, far away from the tender light of his sister Hoda and the reassuring voices of his mother and father. All he had wanted was to catch a shark, but instead, he ended up in the jaws of another shark: the dwarf Kwadil, who brought him to this faraway land and sold him as a slave to Commander Tanios. Though his status was that of a slave, Commander Tanios treated him as his own son and taught him everything he knew. Tonight, Ahiram stood at the threshold of freedom. The Games of the Mines were his chance to be set free.

Once more, the music filled the hall as the King and his guests stepped onto the dance floor. Ramel the Queen smiled her dazzling smile, and Ahiram averted his eyes.

"Baal needs to keep his grip on Tanniin," Commander Tanios had explained. "Our kingdom is the key to the north. If it slips away from the iron grip of Baal, the entire north will follow suit. Our beloved King, who, by the way, is not of the direct lineage of El-Windiir, was asked to marry Ramel, the niece of the high priest of Babylon. Stay away from the Queen; do not let her notice you."

Ahiram wondered why Tanios disliked the Temple so much. After all, Baal brought peace and prosperity to the whole land. Baal symbolized order and discipline, two virtues Tanios possessed to an eminent degree. His commander's mistrust of the Temple did not make much sense to him. Granted, the Kingdom of Tanniin was dedicated to the dragon Tanniin who, the legend says, was exiled to the Realm of the Void by Baal. As a whole, the Tanniinites resented Baal's grip. King Jamiir, who considered himself a skilled diplomat, was content with the prevailing peace, which was tenuous at best. Nearly everyone else considered him to be a weak monarch, and some went as far as to think that he was an outright traitor.

"Be very careful when you speak to the high priestess," Tanios had told him. "She is cunning and her knowledge of the kingdom is outstanding. She is very familiar with our legends, songs, and even our prophecies. In fact, it was she who introduced Ramel to Jamiir and arranged for their betrothal. She is also an accomplished athlete, but most of all, her magical power is great. The less contact you have with her the better."

Nearby laughter broke Ahiram's reflection. He glanced sideways at a group of young men and women to his left. He looked at the young woman with long, dark hair, who was standing among them, and he recognized her easily. She was Hiyam, the daughter of Bahiya, the high priestess of Baal. Hiyam was as slender and as beautiful as her mother.

Some thought she surpassed her mother's beauty. For Ahiram, Hiyam meant trouble of a different kind—her team of players from Baal was his most dangerous opponent in the Games of the Mines. Suddenly, Hiyam looked at him, and Ahiram immediately lowered his gaze, for it was not proper for a slave to look at a guest in the eyes. The laughter died. He heard a whisper followed by a hushed "ah." The group moved away. Ahiram smiled.

Hiyam and her team were favored to win these Games. It was an outstanding team that had the blessing of the King. Jamiir did not pay much attention to Ahiram's participation. Had the King thought Ahiram stood a chance to win the Games, he would have forbidden his participation. As far as the King was concerned, Hiyam had to win. It meant peace with Baal.

➤✿✿✿➤

"Ahiram, the Games are a moment of passing glory for the winner, an honorable commendation for each athlete, and four thrilling days in the vastness of the mines. For you, the Games are a different matter: if you win, you will be set free, but if you lose, you will remain a slave for as long as you live."

"Commander Tanios..." Seeing his master raise his hand, Ahiram stopped.

This exchange had taken place two months ago in a training hall of the Silent.

"You are eighteen now. By ancient, royal edict, I am not at liberty to free you before you are twenty-one. Can't you wait another three years? You are a Solitary: a rank reached only by Corintus before you, a rank your peers would only dream to reach. Setting you free would honor the kingdom, Ahiram."

"Is it not possible for the King to make one exception to the rule? I am a Solitary, not an ordinary slave. Can he not free me now?"

Tanios shook his head. "The King may have agreed with me, but Queen Ramel's opinion prevailed. No exceptions."

"Why?"

"Her Majesty must have her reasons," replied the commander. "Still, it *is* three years living with your friends, enjoying the honor of a Silent. Why bet your life and all you hold dear on these treacherous Games?"

"Commander Tanios, my father used to say that when hunting a shark, we should either kill it or let it go. To cage a shark is sheer cruelty, and I cannot live like a shark in a cage anymore."

The commander was not convinced. He drew closer to his pupil and started pacing.

"Ahiram, the odds are stacked against you. Since you are a slave, you cannot be part of a team. You must race alone. Furthermore, you will begin your race half an hour after everyone else. You must win all four Games and any contestant can kill you during the race if they so choose, and no one, not even I, can prevent them."

"Yes, Commander Tanios, I am aware of all the rules of the Games."

"And you wish to participate, even though no slave before you has come out alive from these Games?" Tanios was pacing.

"Except El-Windiir."

"He does not count." Tanios' pace quickened.

"Why, Master? After all, the odds were stacked against him. He faced the Lords of the Deep and kept them from entering the mines for four days until the Malikuun came and—"

"I know the story. There will be no Malikuun to rescue you."

"And no Lords of the Deep to attack me."

"Will you stop arguing with me? Assuming you are able to win all four Games and survive the attacks of the teams, you must know the Temple of Baal will most surely send assassins after you. A slave who wins his freedom through the Games might cause an uprising and break the tenuous hold the Temple has on the kingdom." He walked back and faced Ahiram. "Giving you permission to enter the Games is sending you to your death, Ahiram. I cannot do it."

Ahiram winced as if the commander had slapped him. His jaw tightened and his eyes clouded. "Commander," he said in an altered voice, "I will be dead either way. My temper... it is as if there is a raging fire within me, a power bent on destruction. Despite my training, I can barely control it now. Noraldeen... I cannot bear the thought of what I can do to her, to Jedarc... to everyone. I am like a caged shark about to tear everything to pieces. The Games, Baal and their assassins, all of it: I would rather face the entire army of the Temple than harm Noraldeen or Jedarc."

The commander's expression softened immediately. "You have great friends, Ahiram, but you should remember, they are Silent as well. They can defend themselves."

Before Tanios had finished his sentence, Ahiram's fists stood a hair away from the commander's forehead. Tanios felt as if the world had come to a standstill. He was an accomplished athlete, a fearsome warrior whom few would dare face one-on-one. The commander was fast, *very* fast, and he knew instinctively that Ahiram's speed was other-worldly. The boy was an amazing fighter, but now with this ability to move almost instantaneously, there was no telling what he was capable of.

"When did you learn to do this?" He asked quietly, "When did you find out you could move this quickly?"

"I cannot do it all the time," replied Ahiram. He averted the commander's eyes, "only when my temper flares... and it has been flaring a lot lately and for no obvious reasons." His shoulders slumped, and he felt suddenly very tired. "I cannot go on like this for much longer. I would rather die in the mines than hurt Noraldeen or Jedarc. You said they are my friends, and you are right, but so is Banimelek. Noraldeen and Jedarc are very different. There is a purity, an innocence, a joy in them that is reassuring, that is... hopeful. I need it, the world needs it. Even if I were at the other end of the world, the thought that there are people like Noraldeen and Jedarc would comfort me. I don't know how to say it differently, but they are like a shining light that keeps me tethered to the day. I want to see my parents and my sister before I die. I want to stand honorably before my father and tell him I have upheld his name. I want to hold Hoda in my arms one more time. With my temper burning like lava, three years is a long time." Ahiram raised his head and looked at his commander with a silent supplication in his eyes. Tanios had seen this gaze before. This was the last wish of a man condemned to death.

Ahiram lowered his eyes, assuming once more the posture of a slave. A long moment went by without either man speaking. The Commander sighed. *So be it then.*

"Fine," he had whispered, "you have my permission to enter the Games of the Mines."

Ahiram bowed his head. "Thank you, Commander Tanios. The Silent prevail." He looked up and saw his master's back. He saluted him and left the room.

>❂❂❂<

"So, this is your protégé, my dear Tanios."

Ahiram was brought back abruptly to the Royal Hall. Bahiya and Tanios were facing him. He looked at them and lowered his gaze.

"Yes, this is the fool who dares oppose your daughter."

Bahiya laughed. Ahiram glanced quickly at both of them. She was radiant, while Tanios was somber.

"Do not worry, dearest. I will tell my daughter to spare his life. He will not be lost to you."

Ahiram's temper flashed. He bit his lip and held his fists tightly behind his back. He closed his eyes and saw the high priestess as a raven about to pluck out his eyes. He opened them and snapped at her.

"I do not need anyone's pity—the Games are mine."

"Shut your mouth, slave," said Tanios with fury. He moved forward to slap Ahiram on the mouth, but Bahiya held him back gently.

"Not tonight, dearest. This is the night when even slaves can speak their minds. Besides, his spirit pleases me—that is of course, if he learns to control his temper. For otherwise, he will surely die in the mines." The pair moved away, leaving Ahiram alone.

Ahiram bit his tongue. Commander Tanios had warned him—on countless occasions—about his temper, "Your temper is your worst enemy. Control it, or it will get the best of you."

If this were a different night, his temper would have spelled his doom. Disrespecting the high priestess of the Temple of Baal was punishable by death. Ahiram was smart enough to realize that Tanios wanted to slap him to protect him from the priestess. He sighed, went around the dance floor passing behind the King's throne and stood in front of the display of food. He piled as much food as he could onto a tray, walked toward the door, but stopped when he heard a goblet tumble onto the floor.

"Slave, pick it up."

Ahiram turned around to look. Prince Olothe stood before him. A goblet lay at his feet, its contents spilled. Ahiram sighed. Ever since his arrival, the prince had not stopped remonstrating his participation in the Games.

"I said, pick it up." A hand gripped Ahiram's neck and almost choked him. "Are you deaf, slave? I said, pick it up."

Ahiram struggled to keep his tray from falling. He said in a faint voice, "Let me put my tray down." The hand gripping his neck relaxed enough for him to turn around and put the tray on the table. Oddly, his temper remained subdued, almost indifferent to the prince, as if he did not matter, or maybe because Ahiram was able to handle the prince without the aid of his mysterious temper. Presently, the Silent was tempted to break the prince's arm. It would be so simple: grab and snap. A clean break of the arm would make him writhe in pain. Breaking the elbow would immobilize him, and may never fully mend. Then, to finish it by shattering the ankle would cause the greatest pain, and more than likely, maim the prince for life. Right now, maiming the prince was very tempting. Yet, he did none of it. He lifted his eyes and in the reflection of a silver bowl of strawberry wine, saw the commander staring at him. Quietly, he knelt down to pick up the goblet, when Olothe suddenly thrust him forward, nearly slamming Ahiram's head against the floor.

"We would not want to waste such good wine, slave. Lick it."

In the posture he was in, Ahiram knew that the prince was vulnerable to two types of back kicks. One would paralyze him, the other would kill him. Ahiram was still too young and impetuous to notice that he was being provoked into action and that Olothe was setting him up. A fraction of a second before he struck the prince, the commander spoke.

"That is enough, Prince Olothe, let him go." The hand tightened around his neck and pushed him further down. Ahiram was struggling to keep his head above the wine.

"Commander Tanios, he dropped the goblet and splashed me with it. Surely, you do not object to him being properly punished."

"With all due honor to your rank, Prince Olothe, you are overstepping your boundaries. No one is allowed to punish a Silent— even though he is a slave—unless he is willing to stand trial before the Silent's tribunal."

"Come now, Commander, I did not mean to ruffle your Silent's feathers. You do not need to bring in court and judgment. This is the free night, and we are entitled to a little amusement. You can take this slave of yours back now."

Prince Olothe released Ahiram.

"But if I may, your slave must be reminded of his status."

Ahiram tensed his muscles instinctively at the slight change of tone in the prince's voice. When the blow came, it did not take him completely by surprise. He rolled with it, ending up under the table. Luckily, the prince was at an odd angle, and his kick was not as strong as it could have been. Instead of hitting Ahiram directly in the stomach, his blow grazed the arm Ahiram had placed on the floor in order to stand. The prince's laughter rang loudly in his ears.

"Surely now, my dear Tanios, your men do not mind me teaching your slave good manners, hmm...? After all, it is Baal who taught your lot civility. Without the Temple, your so-called kingdom would be nothing more than a land of ragged savages, hmm...? Well, now, my dear Hiyam, I am sure Commander Tanios will see to it that this slave will not disgrace the evening by his presence. Shall we?"

Ahiram, who was still under the table, saw the group of guests that had formed around the prince quickly disperse. He rubbed his neck. *This prince has a grip of steel; I shall remember this the next time we meet.* Someone came and knelt by the table. He looked up. It was Tanios.

"Are you all right?"

"Yes."

"Pick up your tray and go eat outside and do not come back in. They do not want you here; most athletes are insulted that you are participating in the Games. Prince Olothe wanted to disqualify you. Your self-control saved you tonight. Now remember, the point of the Games for you is to gain your freedom, not to kill anyone. You are a Silent, and a Silent does not take revenge. A Silent wins. Now, go before they come back."

Ahiram got out from under the table. His tray was still intact, and the chicken was still warm. He hated cold chicken, which is what he usually had, if any. He went outside and followed the bend to the northeastern corner, where he found a quiet and dimly lit spot to sit and eat in peace. The crescent moon shone brightly in the summer night, and the breeze that blew from the valley was warmer than usual.

"Eating alone, I see."

Noraldeen's slender silhouette caught him attempting to shove a massive piece of chicken into his mouth. She was staring at him with her usual elusive smile, between a gentle irony and something else he could not pinpoint. Her long, blond hair was held back in a ponytail, and like him, she wore the Silent's uniform.

"What are you doing here?" he said gruffly.

She shrugged her shoulders and looked away. Ahiram continued eating his chicken, trying to ignore her. She looked at him, exasperated.

"What are you trying to do? Kill yourself?"

"I am not."

"Do you think you stand a chance of winning these Games? All the Silent know about Prince Olothe. We all know what he had tried to do, and if it were not for Commander Tanios, this petty prince would have been dead by now." Her voice quivered with contained anger. "Who does he think he is?"

"A prince," said Ahiram, who was on his third chicken leg.

"Do you think he will spare you in the mines?"

"No."

"And you think you can win the Games?"

"Yes." Ahiram concentrated on his chicken. Her questioning annoyed him. He knew what she was getting at.

"I knew you would say that," she sighed.

He put his chicken down. "Nora, do you think I would have entered the Games if I did not think I could win? 'The Silent weighs his options and acts prudently.' *Book of Siril*, Chapter 7, verse 8."

She sighed once more. "Ahiram, these Games are rigged, don't you know? No one from Tanniin is supposed to win them... only the Temple's team."

Ahiram's anger flashed as hot iron. "Since when do we let the scheming of those in power stop us from doing what is right? Besides, I know these mines better than anyone else. I will win these Games."

" 'How many Silent were caught unaware in the silky web of pride?' Chapter 11, verse 3, of the Book of Lamentation."

" 'O Silent, take courage for the darkness will most assuredly be broken by your hope.' *Book of Siril*, Chapter 2, verse 12."

There was a moment of silence during which the only sound that was heard was Ahiram chewing his chicken.

"Is the chicken good?" asked Noraldeen with sadness in her voice.

Ahiram looked at her once more. He put his food down and started laughing, he got up, stretched, and walked to the parapet. He looked into the valley plunged in darkness. Now and then a wolf or an owl would cry as though bemoaning Ahiram's imminent fate. She joined him.

"Noraldeen, you are one of my best friends, you know that. Yet, you also know that between you and me, there is an insurmountable chasm. I am a slave and you are a free woman. You are also the daughter of Lord Orgond, the most respected and most beloved man of the kingdom. If it were not for your rank, you would be flogged for talking to a slave after hours."

"Do you have to bring up the subject of slavery every time we get together?"

"No more than a man in prison would talk of freedom."

She moved closer to him, her hand almost touching his. "But there are other ways..."

He looked at her straight in the eyes. "Of regaining my freedom? Really? How?"

"Well," she started hesitantly, "I could ransom you."

"No, you cannot, and you know it," answered Ahiram with a smile, "You can pay only for the freedom of a slave born into your household. The rule is very clear."

"Well, then, I could take you as my slave and treat you like a prince."

Ahiram contained himself. As a slave, he had had the opportunity to do this often. Then, remembering his brooding temper, his features softened. *I wish my hatred of slavery was my only problem. Oh Noraldeen, if you only knew...* He smiled. "Noraldeen, even if I could live the rest of my life as a slave—and you know I can't since I was taken away from my parents—I want to go back and tell them I am alive. I have an idea," he said excitedly. "What if, after I win the Games, and I am set free by the King, you, Jedarc, Banimelek, and I travel back to Baher-Ghafé? You would be able to see the emerald sea and the white mountains, and meet Hoda. You two would get along so well—in fact, come to think of it, you are so much alike. Jedarc would have all the chicken in the world to chase after and Banimelek plenty of tall trees to stand under and brood properly. Wouldn't that be great?"

Noraldeen was dumfounded. In the six years she had known Ahiram, he had never spoken so many words in such a short period. Seeing him animated and smiling with dreamy eyes was wonderful, and she would have loved to share his excitement and hope.

"My childhood was spent on the sea," he continued. "I grew up with free men, Nora; noble men who gave their word and lived by it. The life of a slave chokes me. I can't live like this."

Noraldeen looked at Ahiram as he gazed at the valley below. She could clearly see the three small, dark circles at the base of his neck. He had once told her that these were birthmarks. When she had asked him for an explanation, he had said that his mother craved melons while pregnant with him, but it was the middle of winter, and none were available. As a result of her unfulfilled craving, he ended up with three small melons on his neck. He had made her laugh so hard with his melon story. And on that beautiful day when Tanios had taken all the Silent apprentices for a military exercise in the mountains, Noraldeen had told Ahiram that the melons made him absolutely unique. Back then, he had looked away silently.

Noraldeen smiled. Just now, Ahiram had looked away.

Noraldeen was beautiful and sharp, perhaps the most beautiful woman he had ever met. Everyone in the Silent Corps knew she was destined for a princely love. Already, many contenders had knocked at her father's door, only to be told that it was too soon. Ahiram cared deeply for her, more than he was willing to admit, but something tugged at him, pulling him away.

Ever since he had joined the Silent, his goal had been to regain his freedom and return home. This single-minded focus, coupled with an almost compulsive drive to perfection and an exceptionally athletic constitution, allowed him to move up quickly in the ranks of the Silent, until he became a Solitary—one who is sent alone on the most dangerous missions.

Noraldeen knew how powerful his thirst for freedom was. She was aware of the deep wound he carried and wished she could take his pain from him. Her love for Ahiram had grown imperceptibly over the past six years. Their shared life gave her ample opportunities to discover his strength *and* his broken heart. As their relationship matured and her love blossomed, she intuitively realized that her inner strength exceeded his. His physical prowess was astounding, equal to his temper in intensity; and his temper was the scream of rage hiding his fear and pain. He was a Silent, screaming "never again"; she was a Silent, singing "I love you more," and she hoped her singing would allay his fears and heal his heart. *Once your heart is healed, my love*, she thought, *you will shine like the stars.*

A veil of sadness fell over her eyes. The life they had shared was passing away. Soon, he would be gone. The yearning for his parents that compelled him to regain his freedom called him home; and this desire was his driving force, his strength, and the sole purpose of his life—a life she so ardently desired to share.

"You know we could help you in the mines."

"Don't even think about it. I do not want you in harm's way, no matter what," he said, alarmed.

"Are you afraid for me?" she asked, looking at him with that sincere smile that melted his heart. "Look at me, Ahiram... you are afraid for me, are you not?"

"Yes, I am," he replied tearing himself from her gaze. He turned his back to the valley and looked up. "I care for you more than I care for life itself," he said softly. "You know that."

"But you do not care enough to be in love with me," she replied, frowning. "Why is that? Sometimes I feel you treat me like your sister."

Ahiram lowered his gaze.

She looked at him, sorrow mingled with joy. "Your sister? You love me like your sister?" She slapped him on the chest. "I cannot believe this. I love you and you think of me as a sister?"

He raised his eyes and looked at her. "When you are a slave and an orphan in a foreign land, the love of a sister is the warmth of a hearth, the sun in the sky, the tender presence that cares about you, Nora. Do not belittle my love for you; it is all I have."

Instantly, her eyes filled with tears.

"Oh no, don't do that now. You will cry, and I will lose my appetite; and this is the one night when I get to eat warm, delicious food."

She wiped her tears and laughed. He caught her by the shoulders and held her against him.

"Nora, I am telling you, I will win these Games. Don't worry."

She gazed at him lovingly as tears streamed down her cheeks. He felt guilty, not really knowing why, but whenever Noraldeen cried, he felt as though his heart was being torn apart. He wiped her tears.

"Don't cry, Nora, please don't."

"I have come to say good-bye."

"You are leaving?" Suddenly, loneliness fell on him like a thick blanket. A feeling of foreboding rose in his soul. "Why? Why do you have to go?"

"My father is calling me back. He has a suitor for me..."

Ahiram looked at her. "A prince, I suppose?"

"Yes, the son of a very powerful king. Apparently," she added in hushed voice, "an alliance is being forged against the Temple."

"What did you say to your father?"

She looked at him and smiled, "My father will not marry me off against my consent."

"But what if this prince can provide you with a good life?" asked Ahiram, "It..."

"I don't want a pampered life in some palace far away, Ahiram, and you know that." She replied softly with sorrow in her eyes. "The prince is enchanting, and he will make a good husband, but I already told my father I will not marry him."

"So why do you have to leave then?"

She sighed. "No need to provoke the king whom my father is trying to forge an alliance with. I must think it over, I was told. So I will go to my father for two weeks and come back."

Ahiram laughed. "And in two weeks I will be free."

"And you will marry me."

He looked at her, startled. Before he knew it, she held him and kissed him affectionately.

Suddenly, a powerful light lit up the sky, turning the night into dazzling day. It startled them both, and forgetting everything, they watched in awe, unable to believe what they were seeing.

Drapes of weaving light from the highest heavens to the bottom of the valley danced before them, filling the forest with resplendent colors. The guests streamed from the open doors and stood enchanted.

The sheets of light swayed gently in the valley, as though moved by a breeze. Then they parted, forming four large pillars of light, which shone so brightly that everyone covered their eyes. One by one, the pillars faded, leaving behind the quiet twinkle of a starry night. After a moment, the guests burst in applause and congratulated the King.

"Your Majesty," exclaimed someone, "what a magical spectacle; this honors us much."

The guests thought this was a welcoming gesture on the King's part. They were used to the court of Babylon, where acts of magic were performed on special occasions. Yet, Babylon, in all its might, had never produced a show remotely close to what they had seen tonight.

Bahiya was one of the few not to congratulate the King. She knew this was beyond human prowess. This was of a different nature. *Something is stirring*, she thought, leaving the balcony.

Ahiram took Noraldeen by one hand, his plate with the other, and slipped quickly out of the crowd to a quieter place.

"This is incredible," whispered Noraldeen.

"It is," replied Ahiram, gazing at the sky with eyes full of hope. "Somehow, I believe it is a good omen. Light in the midst of darkness is usually impossible, and a slave freeing himself is usually impossible. See? The two go well together."

"And a slave marrying a princess is usually impossible. See? The three go well together."

Ahiram imagined Noraldeen in the great hall of the Amsheet, the northern fortress where her father, Lord Orgond, ruled. Suddenly, he felt lonely. She had been a ray of warmth during these six years of intensive training. She was always there when he needed her and had never asked anything in return. He feared losing her the way he had lost his family.

"Noraldeen, listen. Before you leave, I want you to promise me, promise me that no matter what, you will not forget me. Promise me on your father's name that your door will always be open to me."

Gazing lovingly at him, she promised.

"And I promise," said Ahiram, "when I am free, I will be at your side whenever you need me."

Ahiram placed his right hand on Noraldeen's left shoulder and she placed her right hand on his left shoulder.

They had sealed their oath. Noraldeen then swiftly kissed him again. "Farewell, my Prince."

She then vanished into the night. Ahiram stood there for a moment rubbing his lips. He scratched his head and sat back on a nearby bench. He forced his emotions to quiet down. He refused to think about her; he needed his focus for tomorrow. A vague sense of regret formed on the surface of his consciousness before disappearing. "Regret? Regret for what? You saw an incredible light. You have at least one faithful friend, so what are you regretting?" Ahiram was now muttering. The answer solidified immediately in his mind: "The chicken, it's cold."

6. GAME OF BRONZE

> *"The Games were initially conceived to honor El-Windiir's remarkable victory over the Lords of the Deep. The team with the greatest endurance, physical stamina, perfect self-control, determination, and focus would win."*
> **–Principles and Rules for the Games of the Mines, The Great Judge Bayrul III**

> *"The Games? A paradox, I say. A rigged cry of freedom, a deadly doorway to freedom, an illusion of reality, a concrete illusion. A marvelous remembrance of El-Windiir's fate, the Games would kill any participating slave. After all, if the King sets all the slaves free, who would cook the chicken and clean the parsley?"*
> **–Soliloquy of Zuzu the Hip, Jester of the Royal Court of Tanniin**

Ahiram opened his eyes just as the sun's rays splashed over the rough, wooden floor in his small room. Two narrow rectangles of light lit the usual spot, the only one the sun could briefly reach as it lurched sideways between the high guard tower opposite the slaves' wing and the branches of a nearby oak. His gaze strayed to the tiny particles floating aimlessly in the shaft of light. Other slaves he shared this wing with believed the strange, shiny specks were remnants of the souls of the dead. Makombians, the gentle slaves from the Kingdom of Makombé, who worked the kitchen, feared to touch a shaft of light, preferring to wait until the light moved away before entering the premises.

Ahiram rolled onto his back, cupped his head with his hands, and absentmindedly watched the shiny particles go through their chaotic dance. He felt the familiar sadness linger around him for a while before dissipating right when the sunrays moved away from his window; the same sadness he had felt ever since Master Kwadil brought him to Tanniin. But today, the veil of sorrow was heavier.

I woke up crying last night, but over what?

A thick curtain lay over his childhood memories in Baher-Ghafé, preventing him from recalling the tragic events that led to his exile in Tanniin. A knot of sorrow mixed with apprehension filled his heart.

Noraldeen must be gone by now.

Her leaving left a gaping hole in his heart, but her absence was not the main source of his sadness. He could no longer remember his father's and mother's voices. He relied now mainly on forged imagination; he could still see them, as in a faded dream. Only his sister Hoda stood clear and bright in his memories, as if he had seen her the night before.

I was certain I had seen Hoda yesterday. What is wrong with me?

Firmly, he drove these thoughts deep within—below the Silent's iron-fisted discipline, deeper than the layers of generosity, magnanimity, and courage his family had instilled in him, and deeper still than the raging magma of his anger. There, in the depths of his soul, the sense of despair and abandonment lurked and festered, feeding the anger and fury above. Still, these were not the dominant forces in Ahiram's life. His enduring love for the sea, his hunger for freedom, and the care he had for the weak and downtrodden were powerful drivers. Ahiram knew the dark rage within, a rage he carried with him from Baher-Ghafé; fueled and strengthened by six years of slavery. This darkness frightened him, which is why Noraldeen had become his anchor. She had become the light of day, the faithful guide that brought him back to sanity. He knew he was broken, and he loved to see her whole, radiant and full of life.

Ahiram knew he would never be like Noraldeen or Jedarc, another Silent and great friend of his; but he simply rejoiced that they both existed and felt privileged to be their friend. Observing them, he came to believe that a wrong could be righted, that injustice would end, and that one day, he too, would rejoice the way they did.

Cut it out, Ahiram, he thought. *Enough with the sentimentalities. Let's go win this game.*

Still tired, he rose effortlessly to a sitting position and after a rigorous round of stretching, he rolled off his sleeping mat and performed one hundred and sixty slow knuckle push-ups. With one fluid movement, he raised his body to a vertical, upside down position and stood on his knuckles. He stretched his legs to a 'V' and raised his right arm, now supported by his left knuckles alone. Slowly, he lowered his raised hand, and now stood only on his right hand's fingertips, then alternated between left and right. Next, he balanced on the palms of his hands, arched his back and moved his feet over his head. Ever so slowly, he lowered them until they rested on the ground. Bending arms and knees, he sprang up, flipped one hundred and eighty degrees, and landed silently on all fours.

Continuing his regimen, he got up and stood in front of a wooden, vertical pole holding a dozen short rods pointing in different directions. He took a thick, linen band hanging from a rope on a nearby hook, and blindfolded himself. Standing in front of the striking pole, he completed the one hundred and one daily, precision strike exercises required of every Silent. The pole shook under the heavy rain of blows. Fists, elbows, shoulders, knees, and feet all struck the wood with frightening power and accuracy in a flawless dance, beautiful, yet deadly.

Next, he turned his back to the wooden contraption and performed another set of side-kicks, back-kicks, and elbow strikes. Although shorter, this sequence was just as deadly.

Ahiram yawned.

I wish they would have started these Games at ten o'clock instead of seven, he thought, for he was not an early riser. He took off the blindfold and jumped rope, building speed as he went until the rope became a blur.

"Six hundred," he said, as he slowed to a full stop, then hung the rope back in its place. Standing with his feet side-by-side, he bent down and pressed his palms fully on the floor. Slowly, he slid, moving his legs further apart and landed in a split. He leaned his body forward until his nose brushed the ground, then leaned back until his hair was a few inches above the ground. He straightened his position and got up, having completed his morning routine in a little over an hour.

He had not broken a sweat.

Quickly, he changed into his uniform and buckled the famous Silent's belt around his waist over the thick, linen undershirt and beneath his crewneck sweater.

The belt held an assortment of fifty specialized darts. Quickly, he inspected its contents, counting five loop darts—used to loop ropes around a target when climbing or when needing to immobilize someone. *Ten arrow darts, five thin stunt darts with needle heads,* he counted, *and another five with suction heads.* The former injected their contents, mostly soporifics, into their targets, while the latter delivered a slow acting poison through the skin. *Let me see now, do I have the escape darts? Yes, all ten of them.*

These darts carried explosives or corrosives in their large heads. The Silent used them to blow up obstacles or dissolve iron. *The smoke darts,* he muttered. *I wish I had a few more of these. They'll certainly come in handy against the team of Baal.* These darts exploded loudly in a billow of thick, dark smoke that induced coughing and itching. He checked that the five vanishing darts were strapped tightly in place. When thrown against a solid object, these darts would instantly burn, leaving only a discreet streak invisible to all but the trained eyes of a Silent.

'*These darts burn only in the horizontal position,*' Commander Tanios had explained on several occasions. '*Before you put your belt on, make sure they are stowed and tightly strapped in the vertical position. If you try to throw them like the other darts, you will end up with a severe burn. Hold them by their tip,*' he explained, '*and throw them the way you would throw a knife so they begin to burn once the tip has slammed into the wood.*'

Besides these, Ahiram counted one dozen smoke pellets whose effects were identical to the smoke darts but were easier to use when he needed to create a smoke screen around him. He pulled at the two foldable crossbows and checked that they were in good working condition. A marvel of dwarfish engineering, they could hit a target one hundred and fifty feet away. Lastly, he slid his curved dagger into one of the belt's sheaths.

Heaving a deep sigh, he opened his bedroom's door that creaked, just as it did six years ago when Commander Tanios brought him to this room for the first time. Ahiram glanced at the gray walls with the small window up high, next to a ceiling of dark beams. *Soon,* he thought, *soon this will no longer be my room. Soon I shall be free.*

He donned his lightweight, white coat, closed the door, and quickly crossed the long, narrow passage where nineteen of the sixty-nine slaves' bedrooms were located. Most slaves slept four to a room, attending to their tasks long before dawn. They did all the menial jobs in the kitchen, garden, and castle. He was one of the few who slept until sunrise. He reached the gate to the slaves' quarters, crossed the guards' hallway, and went down a narrow set of stone stairs, zigzagging as he did through a maze of crates filled with fruit and vegetables. The head cook had managed to flout the repeated demands of the Royal Guard's headmaster to keep the stairs free from any obstacles. The cook contended that fresh produce was preferable over tidy stairs, and since no one confiscated the crates, Ahiram concluded that the head cook was more powerful than the headmaster of the Royal Guard.

The thought of Prince Olothe tumbling down the stairs and landing in a crate of rotten tomatoes flashed luridly in his mind, but he stayed it. Commander Tanios taught his Silent that "Fantasy weakens the mind and dissolves the will," (*Book of Siril,* chapter 9, verse 12). He told them to avoid it like the plague.

The delicious taste of chicken lingered in his mouth. "Cold chicken," he muttered as he entered the servant's kitchen. It was already buzzing like a busy beehive, so no one took notice of him, save Habael, the royal gardener who had just come back from the garden.

"Lad, come and eat," he said, gesturing for him to sit at a large table.

"I cannot, Master Habael, I must be at the mines."

The old man, who walked with poise, came to him and gently took him by the arm. His tanned and smooth face housed two eyes of light, as Ahiram called them, because of their peaceful gaze. Habael was the one who kept Ahiram going, even during the worst moments of his training.

"Come on, lad, there is warm bread, the way you like it, with eggs, roasted ham, goat cheese, grapes, and figs. Come and eat before you go."

These were Ahiram's favorites.

"All right, Master Habael, all right."

Ahiram sat down and ate with great appetite. As his teeth sank into a thick piece of bread, he realized how hungry he was.

"You know, lad, the other night I had a dream. I was crossing a suspended bridge and looked down into the water when, lo and behold, I saw a bird, a big, beautiful, crystal bluebird. But when I drew closer, I noticed the bird was dead and decaying."

Ahiram looked at the old man, waiting for the rest. He wondered once more how Habael managed to have such thick, white hair and eyes as blue as the bluest sky. The gardener was six feet two inches tall, but at times, he could appear even taller in his oversized, light gray sweater and pants. He had wrapped a dark-blue, wool scarf around his neck. His sturdy, leather sandals were a source of mystery, for the Silent had never seen them dirty despite Habael's long hours in the garden.

Habael seemed lost in his thoughts. Ahiram realized that what the old man told him must have been a disguised warning. He glanced at the servants, but no one was eavesdropping. Still, the Temple had spies everywhere. He wanted to ask questions, but refrained from disturbing the old man. If Habael had more to say, he would have said it. The food was delicious, and there was nothing he enjoyed more than eating a good breakfast in silence. Habael stirred and smiled.

"Well now, you are done eating, I see. Too fast. You always eat too fast. Take this," he said handing him a leather pouch. "In case you are injured, rub some of this ointment on the wound. It will sting, but you will feel better."

"Thank you, Master Habael," replied Ahiram as he inserted the small pouch into one of his belt pockets.

"Off you go now. I shall expect a full report when you come back."

Ahiram stood up and bowed before the old man, who took his head in his hands and kissed him. Master Habael then lifted Ahiram's face, looked into his eyes and said, "Never cease to hope." He smiled, then let him go. Ahiram was doubly grateful to the old man, first for the wonderful breakfast, but more importantly for the warning he had just given him under the guise of a senseless story: Beware of what looks good at first sight. Inspect, but do not touch.

He stepped outside to the servants' garden. The court smelled of sheep and chicken. At the far end, steam billowed from the blacksmith's shop while a rhythmic thud shook the mason's shop. The shepherds' keep was empty—the shepherds preferring to stay up in the surrounding hills this time of year. The two soldiers manning the narrow gate—the only other way out of the castle besides the royal gate—nodded and let him pass. Ahiram buttoned his long, white coat while walking briskly along a dirt path. He walked across the narrow bridge over the Adulaan

River and quickly crossed Royal Road which, as a slave, he could not use. Instead, he walked—hidden in the canyon—on the dirt path running parallel to the road. The Mines of Bronze, Silver, and Gold were half a mile away, south of Taniir-The-Strong, in a maze of mountains and hills known as the Doral Highlands. The mines had been in use for centuries, until the constant excavation depleted them. Mining then moved farther south a century ago to Dabâr, the southern end of the Karian Chain, near the fortified city of Beit-Windiir.

In Doral, El-Windiir, Tannin's founder, slaved for the Lords of the Deep. On Nissan 1, 2756, of the Age of the Second Covenant—when the Wars of Meyroon broke out—the Lords of the Deep opened Hawâl, the Heart of the Pit, or the "Pit of the Abyss," as the Babylonians called it. They unleashed bestial hordes in three waves, each more powerful than the last. No forces on earth could stop their advance until the Malikuun stooped down from their high reaches in heaven and waged a relentless war against the Lords of the Deep. El-Windiir rebelled against his masters and cut their supplies of meyroon for four days, depriving them from their most powerful weapon. His action tipped the balance in favor of the Lords of Light, who defeated the Lords of the Deep and locked them in the Pit of the Abyss. As a reward, the Malikuun gave the Land of Tanniin to El-Windiir before departing to their heavenly abode.

Not long after, the servants of Baal rose against El-Windiir. He forged weapons: a sword and wings of the most pure meyroon, a fiery mask of pure gold in the image of the great dragon Tanniin, and a belt of silver, which he endowed with navigational power. Finally, he took shoes made of silk and dipped them in clarified bronze, a formula the great magician Inshetaar invented that yielded a light metal stronger than iron. El-Windiir called this pair of shoes *Giril Sarisil* (Swift Ones). He then raised a great army and laid siege to Sokhor Dur, Baal's fortress, and destroyed it during the famous Battle of Shanganar. In their desperation, the guardians of the Temple committed a terrible sin. They invoked the power of the Pit, and devised a terrible weapon that they used during the Battle of Monsabe in order to defeat El-Windiir and exile him to a remote island. So it was, on Chesbân 21, 3098, of the Age of the Second Covenant, El-Windiir left Tanniin. After his death, his grandson, El-Windiir II, brought his body back for burial, but no one ever found his weapons.

Yet, Tanniin knew peace during the last period of the Age of the Second Covenant. The kingdom managed to weather the Age of Chaos, then the Age of the Temple began and Baal started expanding his dominion. Initially, Tanniin repelled the forces of the Temple, but Baal was relentless, and eventually the kingdom fell. El-Windiir's story became a folkloric play, *The Song of El-Windiir*, which in time, gave birth to the Games of the Mines.

There were four Games, one per day, each aptly called by its matching metal in honor of the artifacts of El-Windiir: bronze, silver, gold, and meyroon. All four Games took place in their corresponding mines, with each team required to find all of El-Windiir's replicated weapons. The first team to leave the mine of bronze with shoes of bronze, would win the first round, the Game of Bronze. The first team out of the mine of silver with the shoes *and* belt of silver would win the Game of Silver. The third day, the team that reached the mine of gold's exit first with a mask of gold, along with the belt and shoes, would win the Game of Gold. However, qualified teams still in the race were eligible to win the final Game, provided they could produce the proper artifacts at the end of each round. Finally, the first team to leave the Mine of Meyroon with the wings and the three other artifacts would win the Games of the Mines.

Four judges oversaw the Games, but the disqualifications began with the Game of Silver on the second day. They disqualified teams that did not possess all the required artifacts. Teams could steal from other teams, leading to stunning reversals of fortune during the final game. Victory remained elusive until the end.

There was one exception: a slave could have no teammates. To win the Games, he had to come out first, all four times, and prevent the others from stealing his artifacts—an impossible feat which Ahiram set out to do.

The Game of Bronze was a warm-up to prepare the teams for the three remaining Games. The number of metal artifacts matched the number of teams. As a slave, Ahiram was not entitled to a pair of shoes, so he would have to find and steal one. The rules also provided the teams with a half-hour head start ahead of him. Since the pairs of shoes were typically easy to spot, his chance at winning this first game was slim.

Most players want me out as soon as possible, but I have plans of my own. Ahiram smiled to himself and began whistling "O Flag of My Heart", a popular song allegedly sung by Layaleen, the widow of El-Windiir, when his body was brought back to Tanniin, wrapped in a torn Tanniinite flag. Supposedly, Queen Layaleen prophesied that "liberation from Baal will come when a slave rings the bell, and raises the flag of Tanniin". Ahiram had no clue why he was whistling this song. Perhaps the song's vibrant theme of freedom called to him.

He reached the wide circular plaza, where the Game of Bronze would start momentarily. Shaped like a bowl two hundred feet in diameter, it could easily hold a crowd eight thousand strong. The flat face of the Doral Hills flanked its southern end where the entrance to the mines lay. The slaves had erected stands on the northern side over a grassy area that ran half a mile back to the edge of the woods surrounding Taniir-The-Strong. The King had not yet arrived. The stands were filling rapidly. Hungry men and women lined up to buy a bowl of hot *praniti*, a local specialty with beans, bacon, chicken wings, spicy lamb or other sweet chunks of meat, and topped with seasoned bread crumbs. The man and woman staffing the praniti stand liked to cook it with a generous portion of paprika and curcuma. Children waited patiently for the sellers of roasted chestnuts to open their stands. Still others haggled with jewelers and clothing and carpet merchants. There was even an itinerant butcher who set up shop behind the stands. He was a tall, burly man with a beard to make even the hairiest dwarf jealous. He sharpened his knives while a long line of local farmers stood in a row, ready to sell him their geese, pigs, ducks, lambs, and calves. Visitors from nearby villages were indignant that the butcher conducted his dirty trade during this noble occasion. Their indignation quickly faded when he pointed to the animals outside his shop, then pointed at the delicious praniti bowls they were holding.

To the east of the plaza, a gently sloped canyon led to the narrow neck of the Sandoraal. This luxuriant valley started at the foothills of Taniir-The-Strong and ran southward in an ever-widening span, until it reached from sea to sea a few hundred miles south. The western side of the plaza led to a ravine, which abruptly fell several hundred feet into the Renlow River, snaking its way up north through mud swamps that were still freezing cold despite the heat of the summer. A narrow, rocky road linked the plaza to the western reaches of the Doral. Sandwiched between the cliff walls and the ravine, it followed a wide right bend, then disappeared from view. It reappeared across the ravine, rising rapidly to a flat plateau a mile and a half away.

Twelve posts stood, six on either side of the large doorway leading into the mine. All but one post carried colorful oriflammes bearing the teams' insignias. The flags flapped joyfully in the morning breeze. Ahiram knew that the last post, the one without a flag, was his, and he started walking in its direction.

The other teams were already present, chatting in small groups. The smallest team hailed from the Kingdom of Oronoque and consisted of three members recognizable by their long, black hair worn like a turban. Hiyam's team was the largest, with ten participants. Prince Olothe was also there with his team of seven. Everyone knew that the prince cared nothing for the Games. He was courting Hiyam, and it was anyone's guess whether her beauty or her status was foremost on his mind.

Hiyam was smiling at Prince Olothe, yet her gaze caught Ahiram entering the plaza, and she gave a start. Prince Olothe caught sight of the Silent, tightened his fists and strode toward him. Ahiram stopped. This time he was ready. The prince stopped a few feet away and clapped, commanding attention.

"Fellow athletes, I adjure you to refuse to take part in these Games as long as this slave's presence sullies this noble competition. O men and women of noble birth, faithful subjects of the great Temple of Baal, let us ask the judges to order him off these premises."

A trumpet sounded, imperious and impatient. Two trumpeters walked gracefully side-by-side. They wore dark green, knee-high velvet tunics over light gray tights and green and gray striped boots. The royal dragon was stitched in gold on their shoulders and on their hennin, which partially covered their blond hair. Next came the standard-bearer, dressed in like fashion, but with a white, silk tricorne instead of the conical hennin. The large, white standard showcased four stylized eyes looking in the four directions—a symbol of the far-reaching wisdom of the four judges presiding over the Games.

A fourth man, of shorter stature and wider girth, walked behind the standard-bearer. He wore a long, flowing golden and open tunic over a white, silk shirt and a pair of white, linen trousers, with a red, silk scarf around his neck. A black bicorne—with a pair of wings engraved on both sides—sat awkwardly on his nearly bald head. It matched the odd looking pair of black and gold gaiters he wore as the head judge.

"Master Garu," said the prince addressing him, "I command you to remove this slave from the premises at once."

"Prince Olothe," replied Master Garu, speaking like a tired grandfather, "may I remind you, these are the Games of El-Windiir? The prevailing rules allow any able man or woman to compete."

"Well, then change the rules. The presence of this slave disgraces the Games and disgraces us."

"May I recommend that you submit your wise and worthy thoughts to the members of the jury? I am certain they will consider them with utmost care before next year's Games. Presently, the rules stand and are not subject to change. Slaves are permitted to participate. If you would do me the honor of rejoining your team, we are about to begin." Having said this, Master Garu turned around and joined the other judges.

Olothe turned toward Ahiram. The prince was so close that Ahiram could almost feel Olothe's breath on his face.

"You get to go in," he whispered, "but don't count on getting out alive." He punched Ahiram in the stomach before returning to his team.

Ahiram fell on the ground, gasping for air. The crowd roared with laughter and applauded the prince, who bowed with a gloat. No one guessed that Ahiram concealed strength and feigned weakness, for a Silent is not so easily taken down. He pretended to stand up with difficulty and wobbled to his post. He unfolded the banner he had specially sewn for this day, tied it to the rope, and hoisted it up. It boasted a shark beneath a boat. The crowd booed him, but he ignored them.

He did not lift the banner for them, but for his father, his mother, and for Hoda. Mostly for Hoda.

The trumpets sounded three times, and the crowd sprang to attention. The King and the Queen made their entrance into the plaza and sat in the royal enclave. The King wore a yellow, satin shirt over a pair of red, leather trousers, a brown, sleeveless surcoat extending to mid-calf with a thick band of fur running along the edges, and matching hat. Queen Ramel stood next to him, clasping the edge of her long, fur coat that was firmly wound around her. High Priestess Bahiya of the Temple of Baalbeck, stood to the left of King Jamiir, dressed in the traditional gray, priestly justacorps with its twelve gold thunderbolt buttons. The coat was fitted to the waist and flared below. Knee-length, it revealed a long, flowing, linen robe reserved for the priesthood. The emerald eyes of the large, crystal skull pendant she wore blazed in the sun—a clear symbol of her power and authority.

Of all the kings that had reigned in Tanniin, King Jamiir III was the most despised by his people. Even though the priests of Baal effectively ruled Tanniin, they did not dare build a temple. Under Jamiir's reign, this changed. The Queen was the main instigator and at her behest, builders from the nearby Kingdom of Mycene erected the first temple to Baal in Taniir-The Strong, but what the people begrudged their King for was marrying a Babylonian woman.

Yet, the reality of governance was altogether different. Jamiir saw himself as a defender of the kingdom. To resist the Temple meant deposition and exile. Baal would end El-Windiir's dynasty and install a governor. By comparison, a temple in honor of Baal was a benign act. Besides, it was unavoidable. Better to preserve the dynasty in the hope that one day, one of his descendants would lead his people into freedom from Baal.

The skeptics—who were far more numerous than the King had imagined—retorted that since the King had never set foot in the temple of Tanniin, he preferred Baal. Moreover, he was childless, and as such, had no dynasty to speak of.

Rising to his feet, the King turned to the high priestess and bowed. "Dear Bahiya, my dear friends and dignitaries of noble kingdoms: Master Garu, head judge, Masters Ibromaliöm, Hylâz, and Ramany, judges of the Games, and my dear people; united, we commemorate my illustrious ancestor, El-Windiir, who, at the dawn of time, withstood the might of the Lords of the Deep and won the Day of Light that brightens our hearts. We have with us the finest of the friendly kingdoms that live under the banner of Baal. These young men and women have come to take this test of endurance, courage, and strength. They entered the Games to win the coveted sword of El-Windiir."

That last name drew warm applause from the audience.

"The most honorable and worthy of all acclaims, high priestess of the famed Temple of Baal in the city of Baalbeck, Lady Bahiya, gifted us with this year's prize, which bears witness to her lavish generosity." Two arbitrators carried the decorative weapon on a red, silk cushion and showed it to the crowd. "As you can see, it is made of pure gold with twelve rubies adorning the handle, symbolizing Tannin's twelve virtues."

The public applauded politely and the applause was sustained—an expression of the admiration and fear surrounding the priestess like an aura. She bowed with a natural grace and bestowed her enchanting smile on the crowd.

"And now, my dear people, let us salute the athletes who are prepared to take part in these Games."

The trumpets and drums attracted the attention of the audience. Each team stood beneath its banner. Everyone focused on the competitors. Master Garu stood to introduce the teams.

"First, I should like to present the favored team hailing from the famed city of Baalbeck, the famed team of the Temple of Baal. It is led by none other than High Priestess Bahiya's daughter, Lady Hiyam."

Dressed in red and black—the colors of Baal—the Junior High Riders received a standing ovation. Baal's line-up was an all-time favorite year after year, for they always managed to overcome—with great ease— every obstacle they faced during the Games.

"Next, we have the team of the Kingdom of Lurca, who finished second last year. This year, the team's leader is new to the Games, and we salute him warmly: Prince Olothe."

Prince Olothe and his team of seven saluted. They wore crimson and light blue vestments to honor Astarte, the goddess of love.

Master Garu introduced the remaining teams in succession: the team from the Kingdom of Oronoque, two teams from the farthest land of Lickmerick, two teams from the Isles of Quibanxe, one team from the southern Kingdom of Mitani-Nahariim, two teams from the neighboring Kingdom of Togofalk, and one team from Babylon in the Land of Aram, a new participant this year.

Master Garu stood before Ahiram. An awkward silence fell over the crowd. The Silent lifted his head, listening to his banner flapping joyously in the air.

Master Garu continued, "And in the great tradition of our venerable Games, we have this year, a daring, new participant. This young man wishes to stand where El-Windiir once stood and repeat his victory, so to speak. One who wants to win, not only the Games, but his freedom: the slave, Ahiram. Let us therefore salute his courage—"

Someone shouted, "His stupidity," and the crowd guffawed. Master Garu waited until the cackle subsided before continuing, "...and wish him the best of luck." An awkward silence followed, and the two teams from Quibanxe applauded. Ahiram looked at them, startled. Their applause died quickly when the crowd began to boo Ahiram once more.

The King and the high priestess sat down and the Queen, holding a white handkerchief, stood up. Eleven arbitrators ran to the posts and lowered the banners. The drums started beating, first slowly, then faster and faster, until at last, the Queen dropped the handkerchief. The twelve trumpets blared to the cheer of the crowd. The teams rushed into the mine, except for Ahiram, who had to wait half an hour.

Since the Games took place inside the mines and out of sight of the spectators, jesters, actors, acrobats, musicians, and singers would soon invade the plaza to entertain the crowd. Arbitrators, strategically posted in the mines, kept the spectators abreast of the players' progress. As each team neared the exit, the arbitrators would raise that team's banner.

Ahiram surveyed the crowd, trying to recognize any friendly face. The sun was in his eyes, and he recognized no one. He stared at the dark, gaping hole leading into the mine and shuddered. Now that the goal was so close, he felt afraid. This half hour seemed the longest of his life.

Prince Olothe and his team entered the mines last. This, Olothe did on purpose. He let the other teams take the lead, while he and his men lingered behind. When he was sure that only his men could hear him, he gave three of them a simple and stern order:

"Get rid of this slave, understand? Do what you must."

With the rest of his team, he took off running. The men left behind decided to wait for Ahiram around the first bend, in a hidden alcove where the daylight, seeping from shafts high above, could not reach. The Silent would have to be as thin as a shadow to avoid their blades.

Ahiram looked at the hourglass on the judges' table; the half hour had elapsed a moment ago. Hylâz, one of the four judges, took notice and at last, gave the signal. His fear and anguish instantly forgotten, Ahiram leaped into action. However, instead of going into the mine through the main entrance, he continued along the western path. Someone shouted, "Lo, the slave is running away!" Promptly, the crowd stood up. Many ran after him, nearly trampling the performing mimes who scrambled to higher ground. Ahiram glanced back and saw the crowd surging like an angry wave. He winced and sped up, following the bend in the road. He sprinted toward a boulder and leaped, grabbing a rope lodged there. He climbed quickly. By the time the crowd reached the boulder, he was already halfway up. One man tried to pull on the rope, but luckily, the trumpets sounded. The crowd quieted and made way for the judges. Ahiram was now two hundred feet high, near the top of the rock face, and the judges caught only a glimpse of him.

"Climbing up, I see. Rather original," said Hylâz. He adjusted thin spectacles over his prominent nose and squinted in the light, trying to see Ahiram. The Silent had fully disappeared from view. Hylâz inspected his velvet, light-brown coat, struggling to cover his wide girth with it, and was relieved that it had not been sullied in the excitement.

"Is this action against the regulations?" asked Ramany, a second judge. He scratched his bald head, shaped like an elongated egg gleaming under the sun, and tensed his neck muscles, as if he was having difficulty swallowing. His deep-blue, velvet coat floated around his tall, thin frame, like a ghost hovering over a pole.

"I do not believe so," replied Master Garu, standing nearby in his white, velvet coat. "We must check the exact wording of the rules. If memory serves me right, the regulations stipulate that the judges shall declare as a winner the first team to come out of the mines with a validated pair of bronze shoes. Nowhere does it say that the participants have to enter the mines, let alone enter through the main doorway."

"Hmm... this is awkward, we must amend the rules," mumbled Ibromaliöm, the fourth judge. He was tall, perhaps not as tall as Ramany, but with a stronger build. Unlike the three other judges, Ibromaliöm's pepper-black beard seemed perennially unkempt, hardly able to cover cheeks so hollow they looked emaciated. A pair of thick, dark eyebrows loomed like two vultures over tiny, black eyes. The judge's bony frame gave him the appearance of a scarecrow, and whenever he flashed a smile, his white, sharp teeth startled those standing nearby. He looked like a predator about to devour his prey.

"Most certainly," replied Garu, "but amendments will do us no good in the present circumstances; they can apply only to next year's Games. Meanwhile, we had better return to the plaza and let these poor mimes resume their show. Let us see what this action portends. My friends, something tells me these Games shall be keeping us very busy."

With these words, Garu started walking back. He walked impatiently, and the three other judges had difficulty keeping up with him. When they arrived in the open space, he immediately reported the events diligently to the King and Queen. The crowd lingered, inspecting the rope that hung lifeless against the mountainside. Some touched it, others yanked it. One by one, they went back to the plaza, wondering what the slave hoped to achieve by climbing that rope.

Ahiram peered inside the dark, gaping hole. The long rope, neatly wrapped on a short ledge, was still there. Tied sturdily to an iron ring by one end, it was ready to be lowered. He closed his eyes and listened for the slightest movement below, but heard nothing. He removed his white coat, appearing in the shimmering green and gray uniform of the Silent. When Olothe drew attention to Ahiram earlier, every player saw him in white. "Your best disguise is the strong impression your enemy has of you," Commander Tanios had said. "Strong... and dead wrong."

He dropped the rope down the hole and waited for it to unfurl quietly before starting his descent. It swayed in the cold draft circulating in the upper parts of the mine. He suspended his descent for a moment to allow his eyes time to adjust to the dimmed light, and then resumed. He lowered himself soundlessly. No one was around when he reached the sandy ground. He stayed motionless for a moment, surveying the surroundings until he was certain that no one had spotted him. Quickly, he hid the rope by rolling it up and wedging it between two rocks, then he began walking toward the exit. He moved rapidly from cave to cave, the sand muffling his footsteps.

Whether these caves were related to the mines—where El-Windiir slaved under the bane of the Lords of the Pit—was a favorite topic of debate for the judges of the Games. What was certain is that over time, treasure hunters—questing for the tomb where the weapons of the founder allegedly resided—expanded the subterranean complex, turning it into a huge labyrinth of hallways and rooms which included the circuit that Ahiram was presently following. Some even say an entire community of Undergrounders hid in large caves below, waiting for the day of liberation. Others whispered of hidden temples and dark magic in secret chambers deep within the belly of the mountain. Ahiram did not care much for these folktales. Instead, he spent two years crisscrossing the upper levels of the mines where the Games took place until he knew his way around them like the back of his hand.

The idea of participating in the Games was not his. It was old Habael who planted this seed and helped him to organize his plan of action: study, train, and win. The old man was a mystery. Some say Habael entered Magdala, the forbidden forest, and came back changed. Although he was a gardener, he seemed at times to wield more power than the King himself. In fact, the King, on more than one occasion, had asked Habael to interpret a few of his disturbing dreams. The King wanted to make Habael a personal adviser, but the old man stubbornly refused, stating that his place was in the garden. Ahiram would have been surprised had he known that Habael refused the advisory position in order to stay close to the one he affectionately called "the lad". Ahiram would have been very surprised, indeed, if he had known what Habael thought of him.

The caves where the Games took place were huge. It would have taken anyone several days to cross them from one end to the other, assuming that the traveler knew his way. Often, arbitrators rescued a team that had wandered too deep into the mines. When not mediating, they earned their keep by leading pilgrims into the safest section of the caves, where the ground was clean and the walls safely smoothed. They made most of their earnings during the busiest two weeks of the year; the end of the month of Ayyâr, which signaled the close of the harvest. At that time, thousands of pilgrims came for the festival of El-Windiir and thronged the mines.

Traditionally, the head arbitrator hid the bronze shoes two-thirds of the way into the Hall of Rippling Pillars. The players in the Game of Bronze raced to the hall, frantically searched for the shoes, and made a mad dash to the exit. The last stretch wound its way through a real maze of honeycombed caves, where teams were bound to get lost. Frequently, laggard teams would catch up, steal the shoes, and reach the exit before their victims could manage to stop them.

As far as the arbitrators were concerned, the Game had been too easy if the players' clothes were clean when they reached the exit.

Nearing the Hall of Meetings, Ahiram heard an arbitrator speak clearly, as if he were standing next to him. He stopped, leaned against the nearby wall, and listened. In this peculiar cave, one could hear a whisper as clearly as a shout. Allegedly, El-Windiir met with his men here before the last onslaught of the Lords of the Pit.

"How many teams so far?"

"Only one."

"Bahiya's?"

"Yes. Her team is fast, traveling like it had a map of the place. You should have seen them zipping by here and taking the right turn without hesitation. I tell you, they know what they are doing."

"I suppose..."

"What do you mean, 'I suppose'? You suppose what?"

"Oh, come on. Are you so naïve? Don't you know the lead arbitrator has rigged the Game?"

"Rigged?" exclaimed the first arbitrator.

"Not so loud. Do you want us hanged?" cut in the second, in a hushed voice. "Of course. It is political. They want the team of Baal to win. Imagine if a local team won these Games over Baal." The tone was now conspiratorial. "Some might just take this victory to be *the* signal..."

"Signal? For what?"

"I was having a couple of ales with Arif a few nights back—"

"Oh, where did you go?"

"Well, you were on your night shift, so that's why we didn't tell you. We went to the Flying Tankard—"

"The Flying Tankard? Are you out of your mind? That tavern is for cutthroats. We're not supposed to go there."

"Arif has connections, and besides, that's where you'll find the best ale. Anyway, while there, I heard that liberation will soon be at hand. The underground movement is ready to free us from Baal. All they need is a signal to rouse the people. The Baalites have increased their patrols.

They do not feel as comfortable in our streets as they used to. Even the King wants Baal to win."

"The King?" The first arbitrator was shocked.

"Of course. Where have you been these last few years?"

"Well, you know me, when I am not arbitrating or serving as a guide, I am up there with the shepherds."

"Oh yes, I forgot, you are one of *them*."

"What do you mean? Oh, never mind, tell me about the King."

"Without the Baalites, I tell you, he would be as much of a King as a dead fish. Baal maintains him in power and he knows it. In fact, he sacrifices also to... you know... the foreign god."

"He does?"

"Yes, why do you think he is childless?"

"No. That would be taking it too far."

Ahiram sighed. The arbitrators were known for their gullibility. They were ready to believe anything and everything. That the King had sympathy toward Baal was obvious, but that he sacrificed his newborn children to Baal was simply not true. The Silent were guardians of the castle; they knew more than people thought they did. Arbitrators liked to mistake goats for children.

"Tell me then," continued the first arbitrator, "Why did the King give the team of Baal a map revealing where the shoes are hidden in the Hall of Rippling Pillars?"

Ahiram froze. If the team of Baal knew where every pair was, they may have picked up all the bronze shoes. He would already have lost. Before the second arbitrator had a chance to speak, Ahiram leaped and stood between them.

"Is this true?" he asked, as if he had been part the conversation

The startled men jumped from fright, seeing Ahiram appear out of nowhere.

"Is what true?" asked the second arbitrator in a shaky voice.

"What you said about the map and the location of the shoes?"

The chubby man opened his eyes wide. "I don't know what you are talking about."

Ahiram pinned him against the wall while keeping an eye on the first. "Is this true?" He relaxed his hold and continued quietly, almost on a friendly note: "If you do not want Baal to win, you had better help me, if I win, then the team from Baalbeck will lose."

"I don't know, I don't know," repeated the man, glancing quickly behind the Silent's back.

In one swift movement, Ahiram lifted the man, pivoted sideways and threw him on top of the three attackers who were creeping up behind him. "Prince Olothe," said Ahiram, anger flaring in his eyes, "I should have guessed."

The prince was moving slowly, quiet as a cat, sword in hand, when the arbitrator crashed into him and his men. By the time the prince managed to get the screaming arbitrator off of him, Ahiram had disappeared.

7. BAAL IN THE LEAD

"O my soul, fear the poison of envy, for it will burn your heart and tear you apart. Envy is, and will always be, your worst enemy."
–Book of Lamentation, chapter 9, verse 7

"Fools, idiots, incompetents!" Olothe exclaimed, as he brushed the sand off his clothes. He looked at his team. "Wait until I get my hands on those three monkeys I stationed by the entrance. I enjoined them to kill him, and look, the slave is ahead of us. Well, what are you waiting for? After him."

His men looked at him and then looked at all the pathways that sprang out of the Hall of Meetings.

"Which way?" asked one of them hesitantly. "He could be anywhere."

"He went this way," said the second arbitrator, pointing out one of the pathways.

Immediately, the three men bolted down the path. The prince picked up his sword and looked at the two arbitrators. "Say a word about what happened here and your ears are gone." He whipped the air with his sword a hair's breadth away from their ears. "Understood?"

"Yes, Your Highness, yes," stammered the second arbitrator. The first was trying to control the clattering of his teeth.

"Very well, then. You said this way?"

"Yes, Your Highness, this way."

"I hope for your sakes that you are not lying."

>❁❁❁<

Presently, Ahiram was in the Hall of Rippling Pillars, a large triangular space where a stack of smooth, round slabs stood in all three corners. A shaft of light flooded the area around each stack, and the combined reflection of the three sources on the glittering ceiling lit the hall with a soft-amber light. The stacks were sixteen feet high, and of unknown origin and purpose. The Silent was crouching on top of the northeastern pile. Having finished surveying the room, he stood up. The shoes of bronze were nowhere to be found.

Most likely, the team of Baal grabbed all of them, thought Ahiram. *Right before they leave the mine, they'll keep one pair and drop the rest.*

Carrying more than one pair while in the mine was licit, but leaving the mine with *more* than one meant instant disqualification.

I have to reach them before they get out, thought Ahiram. He was about to jump when Olothe and his men entered the room. One of them inspected the ground.

"So?" asked Olothe, exasperated. "Where is he?"

Ahiram was lying on the flat rock. *What madness possesses this man?* he wondered. *Why is he so hell-bent on stopping me? I am beginning to think his mission is to kill me, but why? What does he have to gain?*

"Not too far, Your Highness," replied his teammate.

Ahiram preferred not to confront the prince, but Olothe, it seemed, did not leave him any choice.

This one knows how to read tracks. Better get rid of him first, thought the Silent.

Olothe's acolyte was still inspecting the ground, while the prince and the two others were watching him. He drew closer to the pile of rocks, where Ahiram was perched. After hesitating for a second, he lifted his head to inspect the rock. At that moment, Ahiram jumped and landed a few feet away from him. The Silent's opponent reacted swiftly, faster than Ahiram had anticipated, so his kick landed on the shoulder rather than the head. Nonetheless, it was strong enough. The prince's teammate fell, moaning with pain.

The two others charged Ahiram, with the one on his right being slightly faster than the one on his left. He waited for the first attacker to come within reach and pivoted quickly, grabbing his opponent by his shirt and propelling him against the rock. The man slammed hard on the surface and crumpled to the ground. Ahiram reversed his pivot, shifting his body so that his back was purposely turned to the prince. He treated the second man like the first, with good results.

Olothe took advantage of the situation and charged Ahiram with his sword over his head. This is what Ahiram was hoping for. He bent backward, letting the blade whiz over him harmlessly. Then, as the prince's arm moved away from Ahiram, exposing Olothe's side and back, he kicked the prince in the side, throwing him onto the floor. He followed through with three powerful blows that caused Olothe to reel in pain. Ahiram kicked the sword away, and as the prince tried to lift himself up, Ahiram kicked him in the face. The prince fell flat on his back, unconscious. Ahiram heard a rustle behind him and crouched down. The first attacker slung a jagged rock at him, which ripped into his shoulder, sending a shock of pain deep into his joint. He turned around, ignoring the pain, and delivered a powerful blow that knocked his opponent down. Ahiram took off running, but the pain in his sliced shoulder was acute and he knew it would hinder him from reaching

Hiyam and her team before the exit. Reluctantly, he stopped in a secluded alcove to dress the wound—the gash was deep. He opened the pouch that Master Habael had given him, and gently applied the pungent, dark red paste. His shoulder burned, but he knew the medicine would have its effect soon. He secured the pouch back in his belt and resumed his sprint.

Outside the mines, fervor had reached its peak. Baal's team members were in the lead with the slave on their heels. They were fast approaching the exit. The sun had gone past midday and the artists, despite their excellent performances, drew distracted applause from the audience. The crowd was worried; many had bet on Baal. A few fools chose the slave with odds of fifty-to-one. Habael was smiling. Some paced nervously, while others sat by the entrance, which doubled as the exit, for the trajectory in the mine was a loop starting and ending at the same entryway.

Ahiram stopped to catch his breath. He had to admit that the team of Baal was fast. Unnaturally so. He looked up and saw the shortcut. It bypassed the honeycomb labyrinth by moving in a near-straight line, rejoining the main passage one hundred yards from the exit. Its entrance was a narrow hole hidden from view, forty feet above ground, and to reach it, Ahiram had to climb along a flat wall with grooves so tiny that he could grip them with only the tips of his fingers. Few could climb this wall, which is why the arbitrators were unaware of the passage's existence. Ahiram reached the top and went through the hole gritting his teeth as the rough edge scratched his shoulder. He stood on a narrow ledge and jumped over a five-foot gap into a corridor wide enough for only one man. Ignoring the throbbing pain, he bounded forward. Catching up with the team of Baal was what mattered now.

There was a sizable crowd waiting eagerly by the exit, kept back by a row of arbitrators keeping the excessively curious from entering the mine. Suddenly, the crowd became agitated, as an arbitrator, still panting, burst out of the mines. He had news. The arbitrators guarding the exit commanded the crowd to move back. Slowly, a comfortable space opened up. The crowd looked at the arbitrator, who stood bent down, hands on his knees, waiting for his breathing to calm down. He stood up, tried to speak, but could not. He waited a little longer. Finally, he stood erect and spoke in a loud voice:

"The team of Baal is in the lead. They are twenty minutes away from the exit and..." He took another deep breath. The crowd tensed, "The team of Quibanxe is in second position, an hour behind."

The crowd relaxed, cheered, and recovered its festive mood. Men and women boasted to whoever would listen that all along they knew that Hiyam and her team would win the Games. Some shook their heads at their own credulity that led them to imagine that the slave could have been a serious threat to the well trained Junior High Riders. Master Habael, who was listening to a fat and sweaty woman ranting through a similar monologue, did not smile. He was starting to worry. *Could the lad have failed this simple test?*

Inside the mines, Hiyam and her team relaxed their pace. Early on, they had taken the lead and no one challenged them. This first Game would be an easy win for them. They felt a cool draft flowing toward them, an indication that they were nearing the exit. Shortly after, one of them pointed to a small source of light ahead. It was indeed, the exit. They all cheered. Their strongest man had all eleven pairs of miniature, bronze shoes strung around his neck, and they surrounded him on all sides, forming a strong barrier against any would-be attacker. They went under a natural bridge, talking excitedly about the prospect of winning the Games, when three small, white clouds billowed from the ground at their feet. They were caught in a fit of sneezing and coughing. A dark shape leaped from the bridge, lithe as a snake, and a dagger whizzed by, slicing the laces of the bronze shoes. Ahiram snatched one pair and threw the rest at his opponents. Before they understood what had happened, he thrust his way through them and ran toward the exit. He heard Hiyam yell an order, but only two men were able to run after him, being less affected by the coughing powder. Ahiram ran faster. He had to outrun them, which was no easy feat given that these men were among the fastest runners in the land, and his lacerated shoulder was throbbing. He thought about Hoda and felt a surge of renewed energy. He ran like he had never run before and dashed out of the mines with the two men on his heels. All three of them stopped amid the crowd, who cheered at first, and then fell dead quiet. The two men of the team of Baal moved toward Ahiram, but the trumpets sounded. "Make way, make way for the judges!" The tension eased a little. The four judges reached the circle and looked at Ahiram.

"Well, young man, do you have a pair of bronze shoes?" asked Master Garu, eyeing him the way a frog would a fly.

Ahiram handed the pair to the judge. Each of the four judges inspected the seal on the shoes and nodded his approval.

"Indeed, this pair is genuine," decided Garu. "Well then, young man, you have won the first Game. Arbitrators, sound the trumpet and declare that..." The judge hesitated for a second, "what is your name, young man?"

"Ahiram, sir."

"Ahiram has won the first Game. Now, I suppose, I should report all of this back to Her Majesty the Queen, who is greatly interested in the Games. Meanwhile, gentlemen, you should take time to deliberate, for this incident creates a unique set of circumstances requiring utmost attention to the subtleties in the rules of the Games. I will rejoin you as soon as I can. Come now, gentlemen, this young man has us occupied tonight."

The judges left. The crowd looked at Ahiram with hatred. Suddenly, a scream came from the exit. Hiyam emerged and walked resolutely toward Ahiram. Her eyes were red.

"You swine! Filthy slave! Who do you think you are? Do you not know who I am?"

Ahiram felt like saying, "a loser", but he bit his tongue. He looked down. She slapped him so hard his ear rang. He glared up at her, and seeing the dark fury in his eyes, she stepped back. "I will get you." she shouted as she left the plaza with the rest of her team.

The crowd stood around him, sullen and silent. Still, it did not feel as hostile as it did this morning. Perhaps, the fact that he took the slap tacitly brought about a subtle change in the crowd's attitude toward him. Resolutely, he forged a path through the crowd by staring at those in his way, and one by one, they moved aside. The last man he faced was smiling. Ahiram relaxed and smiled back.

"I knew my boy would come through," said Master Habael, embracing him. "Come, let's walk back together. I knew you would do it, lad. I am very proud of you, just as your father would have been."

"Do you think so?"

"Sure. You bested the best, and tonight you sit at the King's table."

Ahiram froze.

"At the King's table? Impossible—I am a slave."

"And the winner of the first Game." Habael laughed. "You have created a headache for the judges. Should they seat you at the royal table or not? Should they raise your banner or not?"

"My banner?"

"Well, yes. Since you are a slave, your banner must be below every other banner, but since you are the winner, it must be above all others. What to do, what to do? They must be anguishing over it."

"I am sorry for them, I—"

"Do not even think about it. Do you think they are upset? They are delighted. Those four judges would love nothing more than to debate the rules. At last they can argue, and for good reason. They love it. I only hope we will get to eat at a reasonable hour tonight."

Ahiram laughed, Habael patted him on the shoulder, which turned his laughter into a moan of pain. Habael looked at Ahiram's shoulder, his expert hand going over the wound. "A minor laceration, I will take care of it when we get to the kitchen. You have to look presentable tonight." Ahiram followed, thinking that if this was a minor laceration, what would it take for Habael to call it a serious one? "You have had good training with the Silent Corps, but you should learn to stomach pain a little better," said Habael, as though he was reading his mind. "Before the end of the Games, you will be injured far more than you will care to remember. Let us hope that they will be only minor injuries like this one. Now hurry. Otherwise, I will not be able to take care of your shoulder properly."

> ❁❁❁ ⟨

"Yes, yes, I know he is a slave," cut Garu. "You said it over and over again, so there is no need to repeat it. The fact remains that he has won the first Game. The stipulations are clear: he must be seated at the royal table."

Hylâz, Ramany, and Ibromaliöm had been debating for a couple of hours now, with no end in sight. Garu was briefing the Queen.

"Wait, I think I have it," said Hylâz. "As a slave, he is allowed to stand by the table to serve, so let us decree that he will stand at the table, while everyone else sits. He shall eat standing."

"But if he is standing in their midst, and they are all sitting," asked Ramany pensively, "does it not give him, how shall we say, a semblance of authority?"

"Well then," continued Hylâz, "let them all stand, and Ahiram may be seated."

"The King, the Queen, and their retinue standing around a table while a slave sits in their midst? You must be out of your mind." snapped Ibromaliöm angrily.

"Fine, let them all stand a couple of feet away from the table. Alternatively, they can sit *on* the table and put their food on their chairs, or let him sit while chewing one bite and stand while chewing another. Perhaps he could sit on half of a chair? Better yet, he could sit on the rung of a ladder, or a rope, or he can..."

"Hylâz, will you please stop this nonsense?" pleaded Ibromaliöm. "This is not a game; the King will have us hanged before we suggest something so outlandish that not even his jester would dare say it."

Garu joined them at this point, and they briefed him about their dilemma. He seemed distracted and indifferent, which surprised them.

"Gentlemen, gentlemen," said Ramany, "let us collect ourselves and observe the facts. These facts are incontrovertible. On the one hand, a slave may not sit at the kingly table. On the other, the winner must sit at the royal table. To do the first is inconceivable, and to not do the second, impossible. Yet, here we are, and I must proclaim my ignorance. I say, let the King decide."

They all looked at each other. It was late, the supper had been delayed to allow them to reach a conclusion, and they were getting hungry. They shouted unanimously: "Let His Majesty decide." As they moved toward the door, Ibromaliöm said, "What about the banner?" The three others looked at him. His tall, skinny figure, with the large protruding nose, brought to mind images of a scarecrow.

"The banner? What about it?" asked Garu, exasperated.

"Well..."

"Oh, you are correct, my dear friend, the banner." He sighed. "What to do with the banner?"

Ibromaliöm continued with his raspy voice. "I have given the matter some thought, and I have formulated a rather unusual but workable solution. Whereas, we cannot split the slave in two, we can duplicate his banner so that one will float above the others to indicate a winner, while the second will indicate a slave by hanging below."

Garu smiled approvingly.

"I say, this is a rather happy compromise given the circumstances. Are we all agreed?" Hylâz and Ramany nodded. "Very well then, let us announce our resolution to His Majesty." Garu sighed deeply, and Hylâz wondered if Garu was sick. Hylâz was interrupted in his train of thought by Ramany's booming voice.

"What about the second banner?"

"What about it?" replied Garu, who was getting exasperated by these interruptions.

"Well, where are we going to get a second banner like his? It is rather unique, would you not agree?"

"We will have someone make one like it tonight. I am most positively convinced that we will find able hands within these walls to create a banner like the slave's, regardless of its complexity. Would you not say so, my friend?"

"I wanted us to consider the matter thoroughly, that is all."

"And it has been," said Garu. "In my opinion, we have moved rather serendipitously from serious cogitation to confabulation. This could have been amusing under different circumstances. However, the King is waiting." With this, he opened the door and left.

The King was not happy. He and his guests had to wait two hours for the judges to supply a solution, and instead, they handed him a problem. Yet, there he was in the midst of this great company, having to decide one way or the other. If he asked Ahiram to eat somewhere else, his detractors would say he was siding with Baal. A band of fanatics out there might riot. If the King allowed the slave to share a meal at the royal table, Baal might take umbrage and depose him. He glanced at Bahiya, and in a flash, found a brilliant way out of this quandary.

"My friends and most honored guests. I thank the gods for the wisdom and enlightenment of our highly esteemed judges. It is with men like these that this kingdom shines forth throughout the world. They have asked me to rule in this important matter. In the spirit of Tannin's hospitality, I should like to bestow a special and privileged honor upon our beloved High Priestess Bahiya. I should like to hear her advice in this matter, for she is reputed for her prudent and forthright judgment."

The King looked at Bahiya and saluted her with a slight bow. The high priestess smiled and bowed before the King. *The old bore, he is nothing but trouble*, she thought. She had to decide now. She looked at Ahiram, who was leaning against a colonnade, seemingly disinterested by all this, and smiled a mischievous smile.

"Your Majesty," she bowed before the King, and again before the Queen, "The Temple of Baal has bestowed peace and security upon the whole world. Baal is known throughout the land for his generosity to those who show strength of body and mind. In the spirit of this great god, I would suggest to the great and wise King Jamiir III to let the young man be seated by my side." Bahiya ignored the horrified gasps and continued. "If it is dishonorable for him to be present at the kingly table, let a second table be set by His Majesty's, where the slave and I shall be seated there together. It shall not be said of the sun god Baal that he is lacking in generosity, even toward the lowliest of slaves."

Tanios, who was standing behind Ahiram and enjoying the diplomatic joust, smiled. *She has not changed one bit*, thought the commander of the Silent Corps. *She has always known how to turn every situation to her advantage, even if it tears out someone's heart.*

Ahiram was rather worried, for he had no desire whatsoever to be seated with the high priestess. He would have been perfectly happy to eat on the balcony by himself.

The King eyed the priestess with a surly smile. "Let a plate be added to the royal table, and let the slave be seated next to the high priestess."

Queen Ramel hid her rage behind a benign smile: although the King did not fulfill Bahiya's every wish, he nonetheless acquiesced to her demand by allowing the slave to sit in their presence. She was repulsed by her husband's servile attitude toward Bahiya, for he seemed intent on satisfying all her whims. Had it been up to her, she would have sent the slave to the kitchen to eat with the servants. Unbeknownst to her, Prince Olothe shared her rage. He wanted to tear the slave apart, but kept a calm countenance and a well-disposed facade. Hiyam looked placidly at the dragon etchings on her plate. Her mother's request confused her. *What are you up to, Mother?* she wondered. Still, the King had spoken. They took their places at the royal table. Tanios gave Ahiram a gentle, but firm push. All eyes were on him, and for once, he was glad he could keep his eyes down. He got to his chair and waited until all the guests were seated before taking his place. Ahiram sat on the edge of his seat and kept his eyes focused on his plate, waiting to be served. Most conversations were hushed. Bahiya was amused by the stiff reaction of the nobility.

"What are we eating tonight?" asked Master Habael jovially. He was seated at the table of the Silent, along with the commander. Both were greatly enjoying the situation.

"I believe it is shark tonight," replied Tanios in the same tone. "I love shark steak, Master Habael. What about you?"

"Me? Oh, I would not want to go a day without it."

Suddenly, someone screamed, as if in sheer agony. Plates and cutlery crashed to the floor and goblets tumbled. Tanios sprung to his feet and ran to the royal table. Ahiram was up, standing behind his seat while Bahiya lay on the floor, unconscious.

"You swine!" screamed Prince Olothe. "I am going to kill you!"

"Prince Olothe, contain yourself," snapped the Queen. "The slave is innocent. The high priestess simply looked at him, screamed, then fell."

Prince Olothe muzzled his mouth with great pain. He was not about to create a diplomatic incident by contradicting the Queen.

"Mother is back to herself," said Hiyam, helping Bahiya to stand.

The high priestess rubbed her forehead, and sighed deeply. "May His

Majesty the King live forever," she said with a quivering voice. "I should ask His Majesty permission to take leave for the night. It has been a rather long day, and the worries of the temple construction are exhausting. I am fatigued, but will be fine tomorrow, I assure His Majesty. May we all forget this incident."

She bowed before the King and walked out of the room, followed by Tanios' gaze. *This is abnormal*, he thought. *She is up to something.*

Ahiram was still standing with eyes cast down, when he heard the familiar footsteps of Master Habael.

"May the King live and prosper." said the old man.

"My dear Habael, what is your wish?" asked the King.

Habael bowed deeply. "Perhaps the King would consider the advice of the King's servant. By sitting with the royal assembly, Ahiram has fulfilled the requirements for the winner. If the King were to order him outside, he would satisfy the requirements for a slave."

The King looked at Habael, impressed and relieved. "Indeed so, my dear Habael. Slave, go eat outside."

Ahiram bowed before the King, picked up his plate and made his way to the terrace without incident. He was grateful for Habael and relieved to be on his own. The tension had been diffused. The King and his guests were relieved to see Ahiram leave, and he was even happier to be out of sight. *For once*, he thought, *I will eat a warm dish in peace.*

8. GAME OF SILVER

"An etching on the Bridge of Silver depicts a man holding a libre over his head before an altar of Tanniin. As I prepared for the long journey home, I saw in a vision, an altar of the flying god. On this altar, a libre lurks, waiting for a man of greed to find it, and fall prey to the madness within."

> —*Introduction to the Book of Knowledge,* **Ussamiah the Togofalkian, 123rd Guardian of the Empty Seat of the Librarian**

"An ancient malice lurks deep within the Pit, thirsting for man's soul. The Temple's mission is to keep the Dark Abyss locked. If we neglect this imperative, we doom our children to the darkness of the Pit."

> —**Teachings of Oreg, High Priest of Baal**

His dinner finished, Ahiram climbed up the crenated wall of the prison's tower to the castle rooftop, where he lay on his back, gazing at the star-studded, heavenly cupola. Wafts of laughter reached him from the castle below like a fading memory. He lay there, still as a stone, letting the vastness of the heavens wash away his sadness. Even though he refused to admit it, the past six years had become an integral part of his life. He had forged strong and enduring friendships with Noraldeen and with two other Silent—Jedarc and Banimelek—who had become his best friends. Commander Tanios had sent the men on a mission two months ago, and Ahiram did not know when they would return. He feared having to leave without saying good-bye and hated the thought of losing them. Yet, his duty and his great affection for his family called him back. He knew he had to go, no matter the cost.

> *To battle I leave, my love, in sorrow unsurpassed*
> *Our flag flies atop twelve hundred vessels' masts;*
> *Proud ships set sail for seas of promised spoil,*
> *Yet war is a flowing river of blood, sweat and toil.*

> *My battle-filled travels will forever remain*
> *The shortest road back to you; through blood, toil, and pain.*
> *My beloved, my sweet hope, do please understand,*
> *For you I go to war, for freedom, for our land.*

> *Alas, my heart cannot contain the beauty of your eyes,*
> *Where light shines and shimmers in the splendor of the skies.*
> *I am but a silent man before the raging sea,*
> *I leave to fight for you, for to stay is to flee.*

> *If only I could hide you in the silence of my heart,*
> *Safe from this raging madness that tears us apart.*
> *Alone, I take my leave in sorrow unsurpassed,*
> *So do remain my love, my shining love, my first and my last.*

Ahiram got up, stretched, and hid his muddled feelings behind a contrived yawn. Commander Tanios had them memorize poetry, "...because it jogs your brain and will keep you from turning into a frozen turnip when in royal courts," he had told them. "A Silent fights with words then with darts. You cannot be a Silent if you have the vocabulary of a slug negotiating with the chicken about to swallow it. Learn poetry."

This poem belonged to the *Dirge of Layaleen*, El-Windiir's wife, and allegedly, the great founder declaimed it extemporaneously before he left for the war against Baal. It came to Ahiram, unbidden. He sighed and wished all these feelings would go away.

He firmly repressed his sadness and Noraldeen's haunting smile by performing six batteries of strenuous exercises, as he jumped from one part of the vast rooftop to another, until he reached the slaves' wing. He knew that the Silent on night duty had seen him and was grateful that they had turned a blind eye to his nocturnal regimen. He washed and fell asleep. Midway through the first watch, two Silent woke him up.

"Banimelek, Jedarc, you're back." he exclaimed. "Praise El. I was just thinking how sad it would be to leave without saying good-bye. I thought you were still on your mission." Realizing what time it was, he eyed his friends. "What are you doing in the slaves' wing in the middle of the night? Isn't it a little early for breakfast?"

"We will talk later, Ahiram. Commander Tanios wants you in the Silent's wing," replied Banimelek in his customary taciturn style.

"What's going on?" asked Ahiram, rising from bed.

"The commander will explain," replied Jedarc. Ahiram had never seen him so serious before. "We must hurry."

Ahiram dressed quickly and followed his friends. *Is it about last evening's incident? What is the high priestess up to?* he thought, *Did she find something else to accuse me of? The commander would never ask me to leave the slaves' wing unless the King's life, or mine, were in danger.*

The slaves' quarters were located on the second level of the castle. This peculiar feature of Taniir-The-Strong was the result of a tragic accident. Originally, the slaves lived on the first level and the servants on the second. King Dilandiir IV swapped the two wings after a diplomatic incident that nearly started a war. He had hosted a series of talks with representatives of the Empyreans, the dwarfs, and the Temple, to reach a long-lasting peace agreement. Midnight tolled, waking the head of the dwarfish delegation. His throat was parched from much ale and salted chicken cooked in garlic sauce, so he yanked the service rope and waited for a slave to show up. No one did. He yanked it again with equal results. Impatient, he sent his personal adviser to fetch the water. The dwarf lost his way, took a wrong turn, and entered the Empyrean quarters, where he was mistaken for an assassin. There, blood and water mingled on the marble floor. The King barely managed to avert a war. A subsequent investigation found several broken ropes that failed to reach the slaves' wing. The King restructured the first and second levels, moving the slaves to the second floor, closer to the guests, and the servants to the first floor, closer to the kitchen.

Ahiram, Banimelek, and Jedarc left the slaves' wing, crossed the main hallway, and walked into the Silent's training wing. A moment later, they reached their sleeping quarters. They led him to a room adjoining the main door.

"This will be your room," said Jedarc.

"It's a bit smaller, but it's all yours," added Banimelek.

"No one has the honor of a private room, save his Grand Lordship Beardless I," added Jedarc.

"Beardless the First?" asked Ahiram, puzzled.

Banimelek pointed with his thumb at Jedarc. "Prince Jedarc over here insists I grow a beard."

Ahiram chuckled and pointed at Jedarc, "The day this prince braids his hair," he said, then pointing at Banimelek, he added, "that caveman will grow a beard."

Banimelek slapped his forehead. "Ahiram," he said reproachfully, "do you think he needs any *more* ideas?"

"Hmm?" replied Jedarc. "Braided hair. Yes, I could walk around with a harp singing 'I am a lonesome bard, lonely atop my donkey—'"

"Don't sing." shouted Ahiram and Banimelek, in unison. They looked at Jedarc, their hands pleading their eyes wide open, as in fear.

"You look like you have seen a ghost," said Jedarc, glancing behind him. "What's wrong?"

"It is late," said Banimelek, "and we need some rest."

"Good idea," added Ahiram quickly. "I need silence, peace, and quiet. Lots of it, especially silence... and quiet."

"Hey, is there something wrong with my singing?" asked Jedarc.

"Not at all. Your singing is... unique..." said Banimelek.

"As the ultimate weapon to decimate an invading army," continued Ahiram. "Even the High Riders will die of fright hearing you sing, 'I am a bard, atop my lonely donkey that is still with me because he is deaf'."

"Fine," grumbled Jedarc, "I'll keep my singing for noble folks with refined taste."

"Great," chorused his friends.

"Oh, I nearly forgot, Ahiram," said Jedarc, "the commander wants you to leave before the first bell," he added in his customary, gentle smile. "He does not want you, I mean, us to—"

"To break protocol. Yes, I know," completed Ahiram. The law forbade a slave from breaking bread with free men. "Don't worry, Jedarc," he said smiling. "I much prefer the servants' kitchen."

"We will see you back here after the Game," said Banimelek. "You are not to return to your room."

"Why?" asked Ahiram. "What happened?"

Banimelek shook his head. "The commander's order."

>✦✦✦<

"No, Your Majesty," replied the commander. "We cannot acquiesce to the prince's demands. His accusations are groundless."

The prince, Commander Tanios, and Lady Bahiya stood before the

King's throne in the Hall of Judgment, located behind the Great Hall where they had dined a few hours ago. It was a long, marble room with twelve obsidian columns jutting out of its southern wall. Each column boasted a bronze statue of Tanniin bearing down with gleaming red eyes to strike terror in the hearts of the guilty.

"Groundless?" The prince winced, feeling acute pain in his shoulder and neck. His face, where Ahiram's kick had left its mark, was swollen and red. "A poisonous dart of yours killed one of my men, and you tell me that my accusations are groundless? Your slave is guilty of murder."

"Your Highness," replied the commander calmly. "Will you swear under oath that you saw, with your own eyes, Ahiram kill your teammate?"

The prince felt uneasy. "Commander Tanios," he said with a low, threatening voice, "are you telling me you put as much faith in the word of a slave as you do the word of a prince?"

"No, but yours against mine."

"My dear friends," intervened the King, "let us consider this case calmly, shall we?" He looked at the prince and the high priestess before continuing. "Olothe, you have convoked this noble assembly in the middle of the night after your ghastly discovery. I understand your feelings, and I share them. However, my dear Olothe, accusing a Silent of murder, even if he is a slave, is a grave offense against the Corps."

The King raised his hand to stave off a reply from the prince before continuing, "As you know, the Silent are the elite guard of Taniir-The-Strong Castle, trained to protect the royal family. Each Silent swears an oath never to commit murder. As bizarre as this may seem, even a slave swears this oath and his word is binding. This should tell you, my dear prince, how serious this oath is. Many candidates, fearing this oath's curse, balk at the last moment and forgo their entry into this prestigious group." The King looked down briefly and smiled, "I was one of them." He looked Olothe squarely in the eyes while rising from his throne. "My dear prince, the family of a Silent who commits murder is outcast, even by lepers. They are driven to the desert to die and the curse prevents anyone—even a stranger—from burying them."

"But Your Majesty, this slave is an orphan."

"Ah yes, yes," said the King smiling, "we forgot this small detail. Commander Tanios?"

"The Silent unanimously voted for Ahiram to become a Solitary," explained the commander. "The Solitary's peers, those enrolled with him, bind themselves to him as family. If Ahiram, or any other Solitary, commit murder, he curses all his peers, every single one of them."

"The exalted Temple of Baal is aware of this rule and does not believe that the Silent Corps is dangerous. It grants the Corps, even in these troubled times, the privilege of guarding the castle; they do not commit murder. You see, my dear prince, the sensible course of action is to stay our accusations until someone produces supporting evidence."

All who were present considered very carefully the implications of the King's words.

"If not a Silent, then who?" asked the prince. "Who is the killer?"

"This, we shall find out, my dear prince," said the King. "I assure you, the commander is far more eager to uncover the truth than any one of us. Now, if you do not mind, it is time to retire for the night." With this, the King descended from his throne.

All present bowed and waited for him to leave. Prince Olothe looked at Commander Tanios for a moment, wanting to say something, but instead, dashed out of the room.

Bahiya eyed Tanios quizzically. "A Solitary. My dear Tanios, I see you have pampered this slave of yours."

"Do you believe the prince?"

"The King has spoken. What else is there to say?"

"Spare me your sarcasm, Priestess, I have a murderer to catch." Without waiting for a reply, Tanios left the Hall of Judgment. Bahiya remained alone. Her composure changed. She looked weary and tired. She stood in the room for a moment, and whispered in a sad voice, "Tanios," before leaving.

Directly below the Hall of Judgment, a short distance away from the Silent's wing, Ramany stood in the common area shared by the judges. While lying in bed, a thought mushroomed in his mind and would not leave him. He tried to ignore it, but it gnawed at him, keeping him up. One thought led to another, and the mushroom mushroomed. He tossed and turned for a couple of hours before admitting defeat. He got up, coughed a dry cough, filled his large mug with fresh water, and sat comfortably in a chair to think the matter over. Soon, his throat was parched again, something that happened only at night. He felt queasy and flustered, wondering if he had angered a god who plagued him with a nightly parched throat, and if so, which god could it be?

He leaned forward to grab his mug and knocked it over instead. It tumbled loudly onto the marble floor, splashing water on his sandals, but oddly, did not break. Relieved, he picked it up.

"This must be a good omen," he grumbled softly.

Ibromaliöm, who the judge Hylâz had nicknamed "the Scarecrow," opened the main door to their quarters and walked in. Ibromaliöm was still wearing his ceremonial toga, even though the Game of Bronze had ended several hours ago. *How odd*, thought Ramany, *but then again, Ibromaliöm is rather odd.*

"Up, I see," said Ibromaliöm jovially. "Something the matter?"

He smiled and Ramany shivered. The tall judge's white teeth flashed like two rows of fangs, and his black eyes were watching Ramany, the way a spider eyes a fly caught in its web.

"This slave... he is becoming a real headache, you know," he grumbled looking away.

"Why?"

Hylâz walked in from his bedroom and plopped himself onto a chair opposite Ramany. He struggled for a while, trying to pull his tunic from behind his back, stretching it over his expansive belly.

"Hylâz," protested Ramany waving his hand, "Could you please comb what little hair you have left? You look like a peacock."

"Look who's talking," grumbled Hylâz, combing his hair with his hand. "Your hair is pressed down on one side like moss, and standing up on the other like a prickly cactus."

"Gentlemen," sighed Ibromaliöm, "could we please focus on the matter that keeps our good friend Ramany awake."

"Yes Ramany, what is keeping you up?" added Hylâz.

"I see you are still awake," said Garu, walking in from the main door. Hylâz and Ramany were surprised to see him up this late. They knew the lead judge was an early riser, unaccustomed to late nights.

Involuntarily, Ramany glanced at Ibromaliöm, who stood leaning against the wall, arms crossed and eyes closed. He glanced at Garu and felt uncomfortable for no apparent reason.

"You came just in time, Master Garu," said Hylâz. "Our good friend, Ramany, was about to tell us what we must consider."

"Indeed," added Ramany. "Who is first tomorrow?"

"Well," explained Garu patiently, "the rule is clear: the winner of the previous Game goes first."

"And who won the first Game?" asked Ramany.

"The slave—"

"Who, according to said rules, should go last," continued Ramany.

Garu shook his head. "Judge Bayrul did not make up these rules with winning slaves in mind."

"Precisely," said Ramany.

"In your opinions, my dear colleagues," said Ibromaliöm, "what is more significant? A winner, or a slave? Clearly, a winner must go first. A slave would go last, but a slave that won the Game of Bronze symbolizes most closely our illustrious El-Windiir. We should consider this resemblance very, very carefully."

Placing his hands behind his back, he started pacing. "The rules apply for a winner who is not a slave, and for a slave who is not a winner. Combining them yields either a winning slave, or a slave who is a winner. You can elevate the slave, or demean the winner. Tanniin holds these Games to honor El-Windiir, so it seems fitting that we should raise the slave, rather than degrade the winner. I rest my case."

The remaining three men were speechless. Garu stood up and said, "Just what I was thinking. My dear Ibromaliöm, I congratulate you on your well-thought-out argument, and I charge you in repeating all of this to the King tomorrow morning. Good night." Ibromaliöm bowed and retired. The two remaining judges looked at each other.

"He is a smart one," said Ramany.

"Smarter than you think," answered Hylâz. "I have known him since he was four years old. If he puts his mind to it, he can convince a king to sell his kingdom for a cow on the verge of dying. Anyway, have a good night, Ramany; tomorrow will be a long day, a very long day indeed."

Ramany spent most of the night reflecting on Ibromaliöm's words. The argument was brilliant, but Ibromaliöm bent the rules, which forbade the judges from playing favorites, even in an exceptional case such as this one.

Seeing Ibromaliöm bend the rules so subtly makes me wonder what this man is capable of, he thought. Ramany shivered and decided he had best go back to bed.

Ahiram woke up with a strange feeling. This new room was larger than his cell. The floor was covered with shiny, laminated oak slabs and the walls were paneled with rosewood. A large mural of two Silent sparring with training staffs covered the wall opposite his bed. The two young women stood in a golden field against a backdrop of snow-covered mountains. An iron-beaten statue of the god Tanniin—all six wings extended—was embedded in the marble ceiling above. Its ruby-red eyes gazed at him in the darkness.

How odd, thought Ahiram. *No window.*

He got up and performed his morning regimen, then left the room. Commander Tanios' door was closed. *He may be still sleeping, or maybe he left*, thought the Silent. Regardless, he would not dare disturb his master. Quickly, he walked out the main door into the eastern hall, and went down the staircase located inside the Garden Tower. He reached the first floor just in time for the changing of the guards. Taniir-The-Strong could host a garrison of three hundred and twenty soldiers with their captains and commanders, but King Jamiir had cut the number of soldiers by half. Ahiram knew the barracks closest to the Garden Tower were empty and the servants now used the northeastern dining area for storage. Ordinarily, nothing disturbed the peace of the first floor, aside from the familiar noises from the kitchen. Standing in the shadow of the spiral staircase inside the tower, Ahiram could tell that something was different. Guards stood along the wide corridor of the Lone Tower. A mute tension suffused the air, as if an invisible hand was changing air into lead. *Something evil took place here, I am certain of it.* He could not pinpoint the source of his certitude, but it overwhelmed him, as if he had witnessed the evil himself. Suddenly, he felt relieved that Noraldeen was gone. *At least I don't have to worry about her.*

Just then, Master Habael and Commander Tanios came out of the royal kitchen. The commander was talking and the old man was listening intently. They went past the Lone Tower and disappeared behind the soldiers' quarters. *So, the commander was up before dawn*, he thought. *This must be serious.*

He strolled into the corridor with poise, just as the guards would expect. The granary's door was wide open, and he saw a group of soldiers conducting searches inside. Two Silent barred anyone from entering the royal kitchen, but the servants' kitchen was open. Leifa, the head female servant, hollered, motioning Ahiram to sit at the table.

"Master Habael asked me to look out for you and to make certain you ate your breakfast before you leave." She set an omelet before him with two thick slices of bread, goat milk, and six dried figs.

"Thank you, Frey Leifa," replied Ahiram.

Leifa grinned and ruffled his hair. "Always polite, this one," she said to no one in particular. "He called me 'Lady Leifa' the first time we met. Look at him, a Solitary with eyes to melt an Empyrean heart, and he calls me 'lady.' May El give me long life to meet her."

"Meet who, Frey Leifa?" asked Ahiram.

"The Empyrean, silly, the beautiful Empyrean whose heart will melt when she sees you."

Ahiram shrugged his shoulders. "Do you know what happened during the night?" he asked, gulping down his food.

A twinge of sadness cast a shadow over her bright eyes. "Soldiers found one of the guests dead in the storage room," she said softly.

"Dead? Who did it?" Ahiram's mind was racing. No doubt the prince must have accused him. This would explain why Commander Tanios wanted him in the Silent's quarters.

"No one knows yet, my boy," she said, wiping the table. "Don't you worry about it now. You have a Game to win today." Leaning forward she whispered mischievously, "We're all counting on you." She straightened her posture and continued with a normal voice. "Leave the rest to your commander. He will find out who's behind this. He always does."

Ahiram smiled and said nothing. He finished eating in silence, thanked Leifa once more and slipped quietly out of the kitchen.

When he reached the circular plaza in front of the Mine of Silver, the crowd had already filled the stands and were showing signs of impatience. The participating teams were already in place.

Many considered the Game of Silver, also known as the "Game of Bridges", to be the first *real* Game. To win, the contenders had to cross several dangerous bridges. Its entrance was high up the mountain face, across the ravine, reachable only by the Bridge of Evergreen, a suspended bridge which stood six hundred feet over the Renlow River. It measured four hundred yards long and linked the two sides of the path that Ahiram had taken the day before, shaving two miles off the length of the rocky road. Unwary travelers who chose this crossing invariably ended up stuck midway trying to survive the bridge's wide and deadly swings caused by the capricious northwestern wind.

Those who were rescued suffered severe bouts of dizziness, even days after, and those who were not rescued were carried away by the river into the swamps.

The first salvo of trumpet blasts filled the plaza. The crowd cheered and applauded expectantly. King Jamiir's carriage had just arrived, followed by the royal retinue. The teams stood at attention by their posts. Ahiram was surprised to see a second flag above his own, attached to his post. No one had bothered to tell him about the decision the judges had reached the night before. The second trumpet call echoed in the valley. An arbitrator ran to him.

"As the *current* champion, your first flag must be the highest, and your second, the lowest to match your... state."

"You mean because I am a slave?"

"Exactly."

"Fine."

The arbitrator ran back. Ahiram began lifting the flag. In the surrounding silence, he could almost feel the crowd's gaze upon him. The blinding sunrays occluded the standard as he continued pulling on the rope until it locked in place. Next, he lifted his own banner, careful to keep it beneath the others.

"To the honor of Father's name," he whispered, and turned around. The crowd's roar startled him. Men and women were clapping and chanting, ostensibly looking at him. *Me? Have they gone mad? Or did old Habael bribe them?* Ahiram bowed and the crowd thundered. Then, amid the great brouhaha, a chime rang and a bell tolled. The crowd quieted immediately. A ruddy, young boy on the fourth bench stood holding the bell. Solemnly, the crowd stood up and many waved white handkerchiefs as they began singing. Surprisingly, their voices were mellifluous.

O flag of my heart
You are bleeding.
The love of my soul,
His life receding.
O flag of my heart,
Why are you fleeting?
The love of my youth
Has left me pleading,
For you and the day
Of dancing on high,
Embracing the rain,
The blue of the sky.
The blue of his eyes,
The crest of the moon,
The silk of the light
On the rim of Aramuun.
O flag of my heart,
O flee my demise.
My love that once soared,
My love is no more.
Death passes
By me at last.

The land is past,
Yet as I go today;
Where my beloved has gone;
Arise, O my flag,
O hope from the dawn.
Arise!
On the rays of the sun,
On the crest of the moon,
On the rim of Aramuun.
And fly in their hearts,
O fly on their lips
Across all the land,
All over their ships.
Keep them company, until the happy day
When you will be restored
Above all the land.
By their voices, by their hands,
Until the day when you, forevermore,
Will fly in the wind, by the toll of the bell,
And fly El-Windiir, by the toll of the bell.

Ahiram looked up at the flag incredulously. It bore three pairs of wings in the rising sun.

"Astounding. The flag of Tanniin and the bell, just as Layaleen foretold," he whispered. The sight of it, flapping in the wind gave him goose bumps as he remembered the prophesy of El-Windiir's wife: "Liberation from Baal will come when a slave rings the bell and raises the flag of Tanniin".

This incident frustrated Jamiir and annoyed him. These Games were turning out to be a real headache. Clearly, the crowd now sided with Ahiram. *A slave flying El-Windiir's flag—how poetic*, he thought. He stepped out of his carriage, signaling the start of the procession. *I better do something before they dethrone me,* he thought, smiling. The crowd's roar drowned the third trumpet blast.

Events are beginning to get out of hand, thought Tanios, walking behind the King. *The crowd has a champion now. I wonder if the Baalites will impose the curfew tonight.* He followed the King and gave Bahiya his biggest grin. She looked away.

"The priestess is annoyed—how charming." He laughed, knowing she could hear him.

The Silent formed two ranks flanking the King. The crowd hushed. The lead arbitrator motioned for Ahiram to go first. Confused, he complied. *What is going on here?* he thought. *As a slave, I am supposed to go last.* Since no one protested, he assented.

Ibromaliöm, who had followed the entire scene from the rightmost side of the amphitheater, slipped away unnoticed.

The procession snaked its way through the eager crowd toward the Bridge of Evergreen. Many hands tried to touch or grab Ahiram, but the Silent company in charge of the King's safety kept everyone at bay. They reached the bridge without incident. There, the Silent had to make use of their full authority to clear a circle wide enough for the King and the athletes to stand within. Presently, Ahiram faced the swinging bridge. The path around him overflowed with people, with some standing precariously on boulders overlooking the ravine. Ahiram could see the entrance to the Mine of Silver perched sixty feet above the bridge's landing area. To reach it, he would have to cross the bridge in less than a minute, jump, grab one of the ropes hanging from a pole near the entrance, and climb to the cave. A minute after Ahiram would set foot on the bridge, Hiyam and her team would come after him. If they stepped onto the bridge before he managed to leave it, they could try to throw him over, and he did not doubt their proficiency. He could heard them snickering behind him. *Dirty murderers,* he thought.

If I reach the Hall of Echoes before them, I will be fine, he thought. *They won't dare use magic in front of the crowd.* The hall was a large cavern where, traditionally, the belts were hidden. It could comfortably accommodate five thousand spectators who were privileged to watch the teams contend for the concealed artifacts.

Ahiram braced himself and focused solely on the bridge. He waited for the signal: three short trumpet blasts that rattled the crowd's nerves and echoed down into the valley. Immediately, he leaped onto the bridge, running. "Do not look down, do not even try to see where you are placing your feet: run, run as if you are sailing on water. You must be as nimble as a lynx, fast as the wind, and the bridge will carry you like a powerful river. Slow down for an instant and all will be lost." He could clearly hear the voice of Master Habael. He smiled and kept running. The cheer of the crowd reached him and reverberated down the valley. He was nearing the end when the bridge shook violently. He gripped the right hand rail, a thick, rough rope, and looked back. Hiyam's team was fast approaching. They swung the bridge on a wide arc and jumped forward whenever it passed through its upright position. Ahiram did the same. Finally reaching the other side, he ran as fast as he could and began his climb. Hiyam's team stopped swinging the bridge and came after him.

Incredible, thought the Silent, *I cannot believe anyone could run that fast on this bridge.* He doubled his efforts. Suddenly, his rope started swinging wildly, and he grazed his head against a rock. Looking down, he saw two of Hiyam's teammates holding the end of his rope and began swinging it. Hiyam and the rest started their ascent on another rope. Ahiram's situation was becoming precarious. He had stopped climbing now and was desperately clinging to the rope. The two men swinging the rope changed tactics. Holding the rope, they moved back, pulling him with them, then ran forward to slam him against the wall. This new maneuver brought Ahiram closer to Hiyam's rope. In one quick jump, he switched ropes. The sudden loss of weight propelled the two riders holding his rope forward. They slammed against the wall and collapsed. *Now let them swing this rope*, he thought, while climbing quickly. He reached the cave with Hiyam on his tail. *I need to slow them down*, he thought. He took a small vial from his belt and broke it on the rope, then he ran up the winding path into the mine.

The constricted path wound through the mountain like a coiled, slippery serpent. It led to the Bridge of Light; a cylindrical slab spanning a narrow but deep chasm. Natural light streaming through deep shafts bounced off the bridge and the surrounding stalactites in a blinding prism, turning the bridge into a shimmering halo of bright colors. A contender abruptly crossing into the intense light could be momentarily blinded and would fail to notice how slippery the bridge was. To cross it, one had to crawl, and quickly, to avoid being burned by its icy-cold surface.

The low ceiling forced Ahiram to crouch, and the light was so dim now that he relied on his hands to avoid bumping against the ceiling. Suddenly, he heard a scream and a commotion behind him. *Good. The itching powder is at work.* Presumably, some of Hiyam's teammates had touched the portion of the rope affected by the contents of his vial.

That should slow them a bit, he thought. Encouraged, he pushed forward. By now, he was crawling, and his progress was painfully slow. The tunnel constricted further, stalling his movements. He felt like an insect trapped in a spider's web. Ahiram knew he could not defend himself should his pursuers attack him now. Vulnerability turned into anger, and anger spurred him onward. *Faster*, he thought. *I must move faster.* He crawled like never before, ignoring the agonizing burn in his knees and hands. After a short time, he felt the ceiling rise, and finally he could stand, hunched over until, at last, he could stand unhindered.

He trekked around a bend and was dazzled, almost blinded by the ambient light that surged from thousands of glittering stars. Even though he had seen this bridge before, the beauty of the dancing light made him forget the Games for a moment. But he jolted back into action when he heard the muffled sounds of footsteps behind him. He stepped onto the bridge, wanting to cross on foot, but one slippery step convinced him that it was not possible. He got down and again, began crawling, cringing as the icy-cold stone pricked him like a thousand cruel thorns. He reached the other side, and managed to stand up just as Hiyam entered the room.

How did she make it up here so quickly? he wondered. *Later,* he thought. *Now the real challenge begins.*

He eyed the steep descent ahead of him and took a deep breath. He had to get down this path—a frozen, interior river—and reach the bottom unscathed. Many contenders would plummet to the frozen lake below with broken bones or worse.

Ahiram put on a pair of leather shoes with small spikes to help control his decent. He slid down, gaining speed as he went, when he heard a stifled noise behind him. He looked back and stared wide-eyed at Hiyam running down the path as if she were running on dirt. She overtook him, threw a lasso around his neck and yanked. He nearly choked as he fell onto the ice. He loosened the knot around his neck as he tumbled down the ice—the High Riders gliding gracefully around him. He focused on avoiding obstacles and softening the blows he was receiving as Hiyam swung him from wall to wall. The descent lasted forever. Finally, they made it to the bottom of the river and Hiyam swung him against the wall, then dropped the rope.

They have ordinary shoes, thought Ahiram. *How did they manage to slide so easily?* Warily, he stood rubbing his sides and back.

"You are wondering how we are so fast, are you not, slave?" said Hiyam, who seemed to read his mind. "I may as well tell you, since you will be dead soon: magic."

"Magic? But the use of magic is strictly forbidden."

Hiyam and her team laughed at him. "For a slave, maybe, but not for the daughter of the high priestess of the Temple of Baal."

He looked at her. "Ah, so you win by cheating."

She blushed, and her eyes became hard as steel. "Get rid of him." she ordered, "Now."

Ahiram had found a weakness and was determined to exploit it to the full. "A cheater and a coward, I see," he said nonchalantly. "Like mother, like daughter." he added, snickering. He pretended to rub his back muscles while his hands were searching for just the right dart.

Everyone froze. Hiyam looked at him with murderous eyes.

"I was going to let my men kill you quickly," she said, edging a bit closer, "but now..." She turned sideways to give an order, when she heard a loud popping sound and felt something prick in her neck. Instinctively, her hand went to her neck and discovered a dart lodged above her collar. Fear seized her and confusion set in as she looked at Ahiram, wide-eyed. She felt the tip of the dart. *Rubber*, she thought contemptuously. *Another of this slave's stupid tricks.*

She was about to pull on it when she saw Ahiram raise both hands. "I would not do that if I were you," he blurted out. She stood motionless, her hand on the dart. "It is poisonous. Remove it the wrong way and the poison will seep into your skin, and you will die a rather painful death. The poison in this dart will paralyze your muscles. Your lungs will collapse, and you will drown—slowly."

"You are lying," she said breathless.

"How are you going to find out?" he replied, grinning. Her hand tensed on the dart.

"Do not do it, Hiyam," interjected one of her men. "The Silent are known for being cruel and ruthless, and they are masters of these infernal tricks."

"What do you suggest?"

"Let us keep moving. We will find someone else to remove it."

"Ah, but you see," said Ahiram, pacing, his hands behind his back. "This dart is motion sensitive. One wrong move and you release the poison. I suggest that the daughter of the high priestess stay calm while the rest of you murderers send a message to Commander Tanios. With any luck, he might send a Silent to safely remove this dart. Also..." he added with a wry smile, "I have not yet fully tested this dart, so I wouldn't wait too long if you wish to save her." He looked at Hiyam with disdain, "But I am not certain there is anything worth saving here." Ahiram spat on the ground. Hiyam's men surrounded him. "Delay me and she will surely die. Let me go and she will live."

"How do we know you are not lying?" asked one of her men.

Ahiram gave a curt bow. "You will have to trust the word of a slave."

9. FURY UNLEASHED

"Emotions are powerful steeds. The Silent shall neither stifle them nor allow them to run wild but will discipline them in conformity with right reason."
—**Book of Siril, chapter 8, verse 8**

"The Silent must forego the instant gratification of his senses in favor of what is just and good, for the fruit of justice is peace and contentment, while the fruit of selfish desires is wrath and grievous regrets."
—**The Book of Lamentation, chapter 2, verse 4**

Ahiram left the River of Ice and was happy to feel firm ground beneath his feet. The shortest path to the exit was over thirty miles long. The first twenty-five miles weaved their way through a maze of tunnels, caves, archways, and paths until they reached the Laughing Staircase—a spiraling staircase of one thousand steps with no safety rail, cut into the outer edge of a steep cliff. Ahiram would have to climb down as quickly as possible without falling to his death. Then, after a short distance, he would reach the Room of Echoes where the belts were usually hidden and from there, it would be a straight, five-mile uphill sprint to the exit.

The Silent took off running at a measured pace which was faster than what most of his opponents would be able to sustain. Still, he needed to conserve his strength, so he resisted the impulse to accelerate. Besides, the path kept on twisting, turning, and spawning side-paths in dizzying numbers. The slightest wrong turn and more miles would have to be traversed to reach the end. He knew the years of reconnoitering in the mines were paying off. *Next is Jedarc's tall chicken cave. Take second turn to the right... now it's the cave that has a rock that resembles Banimelek's future beard. Take fourth turn to the left.* And so went Ahiram's thoughts as he navigated the massive maze like a ship crossing the mist. Caves succeeded each other in an unrelenting blurred monotony of silent stone walls, torches burning brightly or sputtering their last fiery breath, dust that swallowed every sound and distant whizzing of bats in the belly of the mountain. Time had no meaning, space became a starry, subterranean night where the distant torches twinkled like the heavenly flames of night and life, a confusing path amid inconvenient and sometimes deadly choices. After a few hours, Ahiram thought he knew the meaning of eternity, and then toward the sixth hour of his run, he began to doubt he would ever leave the mines, as though the madness of the Pit had consumed the mountain and all that is in it to punish him for his past deeds, his bursts of anger, his betrayal of his sister Hoda.

Ahiram stopped in his tracks, and raising a fist to the high, dark ceiling, he began to scream, "I did not betray her. She did. She did not come for me. She left me alone. I waited for her like she asked. She promised. She promised."

The anger and sense of betrayal he had bottled up all these years flowed freely, now that his angry outbursts were more frequent and more powerful. His temper was like hot lava ready to consume the world around him. His anger burned fiercely, ready to destroy anyone it found on its path. Thankfully, he was alone in the depths of mines too haughty to be concerned with the plight of man. Eventually, he calmed himself and noticed then that he had been crying. *These mines,* he thought, *they would drive anyone insane. Better get out as soon as possible.*

His injured shoulder was bothering him again. When Hiyam dragged him down the frozen river, his arm had sustained repeated blows. Despite the discomfort, he picked up his pace and kept to the true path. His mood worsened for he could feel now his anger closer to the surface, the raging darkness was ready to pounce if given the chance and woe to whom would stand in his way.

Two more hours went by during which Ahiram saw no one. His initial sense of loneliness had become oppressive. His initial desire to be set free had started eroding as if another voice, a different voice, was whispering words of comfort and repose.

"Who cares if you are free or not? What is the purpose behind all of it? You have a princess who's pleading with you, she wants nothing else than to pamper you and treat you like a king. You could live better than most, so what are you fighting for?"

"Freedom is not a thing to take or receive. Freedom is who I am," replied Ahiram out loud.

"Freedom is an illusion. Men choose comfort over freedom every time they can. Take your sister, for example. She ran and never looked back."

Ahiram's temper flared and curled on itself. He knew he was being played, and he was determined not to let the voice win him over. He came out of a cave and crossed a bridge over a vast, deep chasm. *I am like this bridge, hanging over a darkness about to swallow me.* He laughed a nervous laugh. *What am I talking about? I must be losing my mind.*

"No, you're not," answered the voice, this time sounding a little closer, right beneath his feet in the soundless, gaping hole below. "At least not yet, but I will make certain that you will be when we meet next."

Ahiram stopped midway. "Who are you?" he yelled. "Show yourself."

"Not yet," snickered the voice. Ahiram's hair stood on end. The voice was terrifying now. "But soon."

The Silent's anger flared and clashed with the incoming terror and stayed it. Fear without, rage within. Ahiram felt dizzy and breathless.

"Who are you? What is your name?" he insisted.

"Soon, you will know me as your master. I am the Urkuun of the Ninth Order." Ahiram felt a shadow creep up on him, heard a popping sound and then, suddenly, he knew he was alone.

He grabbed the railing—which was freezing—and rested a bit.

Urkuun of the Ninth Order, thought Ahiram, *What's an Urkuun? Why would such a creature living in the depths of the mines bother with a slave wanting his freedom? He sighed. There's more to these Games than meets the eye. Well, no sense in worrying about it now. I'll ask Master Habael later.*

A strange wind rose from the deep and howled mournfully in the massive cave. Ahiram ignored it and resumed his run. He ran up a sandy path and after a wide bend, reached a narrow promontory overlooking the largest cave in all the mines. Two hundred feet below, a wide plateau was split midway by a steep canyon one thousand feet wide and five hundred feet deep. The roar of rushing water from below the canyon echoed like the laughter of a madman, as if the rocks were caught in an eternal shout of rage. Two thousand torches lit by the arbitrators failed to dispel the thick darkness. Ahiram could barely make out the Bridge of the Last Meeting over the river, which he would have to cross before reaching the Room of Echoes. Few had ever seen this bridge, for this cave was seldom open to tourists.

Nimbly, Ahiram grabbed the rope prepared by the arbitrators and slid down to the plateau. He crossed the length of the mesa with ease and stopped before a triple stone arch flanked by two statues of laughing dwarfs. One dwarf leaned on a pick, while the other pointed with his left hand to a bag he carried in his right. The original contents of the bag had been lost long ago, and spiders nested in its hollow for as long as anyone could remember. Some arbitrators believed that two miners had incurred the anger of Sureï the Sorcerer who had turned them into these two statues.

Ahiram walked through the archway and reached the entrance to the

Laughing Staircase. Silently, he began the long descent.

"The only way to move up or down this staircase," Master Habael had advised him, "is with eyes closed. Trust your feet and your hands, and open your eyes every ten steps. If you do not, you will either get too dizzy to continue and lose precious time, or fall to your death."

The dwarfs had carved a spiraling stairwell down to the canyon. Midway through, they had hit an impenetrable layer, and being the practical dwarfs that they were, continued the staircase in the softer, outer face of the cliff. One hundred steps spiraled in the open air, and although a handrail protected the original miners, it fell into disrepair when the dwarfs abandoned the mines—and no one had bothered to replace it. A few corroded metallic stumps remained, compounding the danger. Unwary participants of the Games, who were already dizzy when they reached that point, fell to their deaths, and this portion of the Laughing Stairs became known as "The Steps of Sudden Death."

Either Master Habael will save my life or I am going crazy, Ahiram thought as he ran down the stairs at breakneck speed. *I have gone down these stairs twice now, but never that quickly. I suppose I will find out sooner than later if the old man was right.*

"Are you sure you saw the flag of Tanniin?"

"Yes, master. I saw it with my own eyes. I may be getting old, but my eyesight, the gods be praised, is as clear today as it ever was. It was the flag of Tanniin floating on high."

"And, so, you believe the prophecy is about to be fulfilled?"

"If there was ever a time when I believed the prophecy would come true, it is today."

The dimly lit table in the Tavern of the Last Meeting hosted a peculiar group of men. At one end there was Abiil, a servant of the castle.

Facing him sat Soloron and his two lieutenants. Abiil hated the Temple of Baal. A year ago, a company of High Riders accidentally killed his brother, and he never forgave the Temple. Over the year, his hatred became acute, and he joined the Undergrounders—those who oppose the presence of Baal in Tanniin. Soloron was the head of the Undergrounders. They considered the King and his court as apostate and wanted to bring back the true Kingdom of Tanniin by ousting the Baalites from the land.

The Undergrounders initially began with a dozen men of dubious valor—ill-trained and poorly equipped. They stole from merchants traveling from Taniir-The-Strong to the southern ports of Mitriil or Tyra-Min. Things changed when Soloron assumed power. A former officer of the High Riders who fled the Temple for personal reasons, Soloron immediately relocated the Undergrounders' headquarters from the exposed mines to remote caves abandoned by the "desert people"— tribes so reclusive that the Temple left them alone. Under his iron grip, the scattered band of revolutionaries became a small army, well trained and well equipped. How Soloron financed his operations, none of his men knew nor dared to ask.

"And what do you suggest we do, Abiil?"

"Well, master, if the slave wins the Games, there will be a celebration the likes of which has not been seen in Taniir-The-Strong. Mount a surprise attack during the ceremony, kill that apostate of a king, and hail the slave as El-Windiir reborn. The people will side with you and overwhelm the soldiers. You won't have to fight, you wait and see."

"The Temple will not approve," objected Soloron.

"Baal will want to avoid a military confrontation. If we could find common terms, then everyone wins and you are the hero. If we go to war and the Temple wins, you give them the slave and negotiate terms of surrender. On the other hand, if the Baalites loose the war, well, it would not surprise me if the slave dies young due to ill health or accidents."

Abiil smiled. Soloron and his men laughed buoyantly. Soloron leaned over the table to get closer to Abiil.

"And how do we get inside the royal castle without being noticed?"

"I found a secret way in."

Soloron's eyes narrowed to a slit, but his voice remained level. "How did you manage to do that?"

"By accident," replied Abiil, unfazed. "One of the judges was on the second floor of the castle, and instead of using the main stairs in the hall to go down to the first floor, he used the staircase inside the Lone Tower. It is steep, narrow, and slippery. Only slaves use it nowadays. I followed him just in time to see him disappear through a hidden door."

Abiil could tell that his boss was not buying it. "Yes, that's what I am saying. I got there right when a portion of the wall closed behind the judge. I swear to Tanniin, I am telling the truth. This secret door is very well hidden. It took me a long time, but I found a hinge inside a tiny hole next to the ground. You press it hard and the door pivots."

"So where do you end up in the mines?"

Seeing his boss listening intently, Abiil leaned over the table, scanned the tavern and continued in a whisper. "Into the Mine of Meyroon. Once the Games are over, I can take you there and show you."

Abiil straightened up, glanced sideways at the tavern's entrance, leaned over and whispered, "It'll be easier than you think, master. You and your men can take the stairs, I'll have men disguised as guards waiting for you. They will guide you to the Royal Hall. You depose the King and set the slave on the throne. Everyone will follow you. You'll be the hero instead of that pampered slave."

"Very well, my friend, but what if the troops of Baal prepare a little surprise of their own?"

"Do not worry, master," continued Abiil, "I have spies among them: young, ambitious men who are easily blinded by a glimmer of gold. They keep me informed of Baal's plans. I know when the Baalites come and when they go, when they sit and when they stand. I will alert you in case of danger."

A moment went by when each of the men sipped their ale. The raucous ambience shielded them from eavesdroppers. Besides, the High Riders seldom ventured into this part of town. As an added security measure, Soloron had his men posted outside, ready to warn him in case of trouble. Abiil finished his beer and stood up.

"I had better go back before they notice my absence. The royal castle is full of men of Baal. It makes me sick to my stomach."

"Very good, Abiil. You shall keep quiet, hmm?"

"Do not worry, master, I will be as quiet as a snake in the snow." Abiil covered his head with his hood and left.

"This Abab-liil—" started Soloron's brother. Frajil was also his assistant, a giant of a man whose stature alone was enough to open a passage for Soloron in the most crowded streets.

"Abiil," corrected Soloron.

"...he sharpens the ax and hardens the wood."

"You mean he is double-tongued?"

"Yeah, that too. I no like his head."

"Do not worry, Frajil, after we make it to the top, his head will be so low that it will take a shovel to pick it up."

The three men erupted in laughter and the massive frame of Frajil rocked the table so hard that the earthen goblet containing his beer crashed onto the floor. Frajil pointed his finger toward the smashed goblet and said, "The King."

>◉◉◉<

Down at last, thought Ahiram, as he made it safely off the deadly staircase. He panted from exertion and took a moment to catch his breath. The young man could not hear anything over the din of rushing water and could not tell if Hiyam's men were trailing him. Seen from down below, the cave looked twice as large. In the eerie emptiness, he sensed an invisible presence following his every move. *Is it the Urkuun following me or am I imagining things? It must be these caves. No wonder some of the miners went crazy down here,* he thought, shrugging his shoulders.

He ran along a rocky path and reached the Bridge of the Last Meeting where allegedly, El-Windiir had met Layaleen for the last time before going to his demise. Some say that if one were to stand on this bridge, and remain still for a while, one could hear the echo of their voices trapped between the walls of the mine. Ahiram sprinted across the bridge. He had no time for such fairytales.

At the end of the bridge, he glanced back out of habit, just in time to see a rock crashing down from the spiraling stairs. In the dim light, he could barely glimpse a man dangling from the staircase several hundred feet above. He heard Prince Olothe scream, "Idiot, be careful."

"Be careful... careful... careful..." replied the echo.

So the priestess' daughter sent her dogs after me, he thought. *How very nice of her.*

The stairs on this side of the mines were large, square slabs sloping gently up along a winding path. Ahiram ran up a dozen steps, looked back and was shocked to see Olothe and his men at the bottom of the cave. *How did they do it?* he thought. *This is incredible. I am fast and well trained, yet it took me a lot longer to get down here.* Ahiram nearly panicked. He threw himself behind a large boulder and watched them. Instead of running to the bridge, they leaped and crossed nearly twenty feet in a single jump. *That's impossible—it is almost magical.* Suddenly, it dawned on him: *These men are using magic. They are cheating. I bet the priestess is behind this.* Raging anger bubbled up, but he stayed it. *No use running away from them, but I can use their weapon against them.* Looking up he saw a burning torch across from the large boulder. He crossed the path and inspected the two iron rings holding the torch, yanking them forcefully. They did not budge.

He produced a thin rope from his belt, tied it to the top ring and looped it around the second ring. He let it dangle to the ground and went back behind the boulder.

Olothe and his men will naturally look at the light, and with a little luck, they will miss the rope. Minutes later, he heard Olothe.

"Faster now, do not lose him. I want him dead before he reaches the Hall of Echoes."

Ahiram's temper flared like raging magma. Seeing the extended shadows of the three men profiled on the opposite wall, he gripped the rope tightly. By now, he was able to hear the bounce of the three men close by. He waited a little longer, then yanked the rope with both hands. Suddenly, the last torch before the rocks where Ahiram was hiding projected the shadow of the foremost runner, who ran into the rope and yelled as he fell back. Knocking his head on the slab, he lay unconscious. The second attacker was in mid-air when this happened. He managed to avoid his companion, landing next to him, but the mysterious power that he relied on to move so quickly, propelled him forty feet in the air with a frightening force. He screamed, lost control, smashed against the boulder, then fell to the ground where he lay in an awkward position, blood coursing from his mouth and nose.

Olothe, who came last, managed to stop in time.

"Slave," he shouted, "I know you are hiding behind this boulder. Come out from your lair, so I can squash you like the rat that you are." Ahiram remained still. He was waiting for his foe to make the first move. Olothe unsheathed his sword. "Come out, you coward," he said, as he moved up the stairs slowly. "Come out, you sniveling dog, son of a dog, coward, son of a coward, slave, son of a slave."

This, the prince should not have said. Startled, he watched Ahiram attack with a speed and a fury he had never seen before. He lifted his sword in a futile act of defense. But how could a sword defend against a raging flood, a howling wind, or an all-consuming fire? A fist of stone exploded in his chest, sending waves of unbearable pain through his body. Prince Olothe was a trained military man, but nothing had prepared him for the speed and accuracy with which Ahiram pummeled him. The Silent attacked the prince without any restraint. He hit to hurt and punish, using all that he had learned to break, dislocate, and destroy bones, joints, and ligaments. In the span of a few minutes, Olothe lay on the ground writhing with pain, shaking violently. Ahiram placed his hand on his opponent's throat and squeezed. He whispered in the prince's ear, "You will not be able to make use of your arms or your legs for the rest of your miserable life. A slave will live a better life. If you ever call my father a slave again, wherever you may be, even in the depths of the earth, I will find you and inflict even greater pain upon you than now, then I will leave you to the dogs. Do you understand me? To the dogs."

The prince, now unable to speak, moaned. Ahiram's voice had resonated within his heart like the commanding voice of a god. The words the Silent spoke were indelibly etched in his mind. Ahiram, unaware of the effect his voice had on his opponent, loosened his grip on the man's neck and spat on the prince's face before leaving. He ran for a short while, stopped, and unable to control himself anymore, burst into tears. He did not know why he was crying. Regret overwhelmed him. He knew the damage he inflicted upon Prince Olothe was irreparable and nothing would ever heal him. The prince would now be a cripple, simply because he, a trained Silent, had lost his temper. He could not even remember how he moved so fast. He could almost hear the commander speaking, "Control your anger or it will destroy you." Now it was too late. A man was paralyzed, broken and useless, and it was his doing. He could not help but feel sorry for Olothe.

Ahiram forced himself to calm down and resumed the ascent. "I have a Game to win, and I will win it," he muttered, gritting his teeth. He reached the top without any further incidents. Once there, he saw the Bridge of Silver crossing the Chasm of the Deep, forty feet wide and sixty feet long, with magnificent carvings on its high railings. Glittering softly, the polished bridge was out of place in the belly of the mountain, like a princess amid lepers and paupers. No one knew what this masterpiece—rivaling Taniir-The-Strong's drawbridge in beauty—was doing so deep within the mines. As he crossed, Ahiram immediately noticed the twelve framed panels covering the handrails, six on each side.

The Silent was simultaneously attracted and repulsed by them. Forgetting the race, he crossed the bridge with deliberate slowness, staring at each panel as he walked passed it. They seemed to tell a story, tragic and sad, that started at the feet of a high tower of monstrous proportions, while on the opposite hill, two men stood observing it. On the tower's peak, a dark figure sat on a spiked throne, gazing at the two men who held their arms straight, palms open in a gesture of warning. The tower then crumbled and the taller of the two men was no more. In his stead, Ahiram saw a beautiful woman with a haunted look in her eyes, standing by the second man, who was bearded now.

Ahiram saw the bearded man standing atop the ruined tower with the woman in his arms. A close-up portrait showed him screaming with rage. The tower was now gone, replaced by a pool of dark water. Another panel showed the bearded man as he stood gazing at the pool, while a second shadowy figure watched him. From the pool, a book emerged— something Ahiram had never seen before and could not recognize. The man leaned over the book as the shadowy figure now stood behind him, holding three orbs.

The last panel on his left showed the bearded man dressed as a priest of Baal, but the panel to his right was black. Ahiram glanced at it and leaped back. He had the distinct impression that the panel was about to pull him in. *These mines are getting to me,* he thought, rubbing his hair. *I must be seeing things.*

As he stepped off the bridge, he was startled by a distinct popping sound. He looked back and saw, or imagined, the black panel throbbing like an exposed, dark heart. He ran from the bridge as fast as he could.

After a short while, he entered the brightly lit Room of Echoes in search of a belt of silver. The waiting crowd gave him a standing ovation. He blinked in the light and saluted. The cave was large and spacious and served as an ideal spot for the crowd to watch the contenders in action. The trumpets sounded and the crowd hushed. Just then, the team from Quibanxe reached the cave, and the three tall men fanned out in search of the artifacts. Ahiram concentrated on the ceiling, for it was the most natural and most difficult hiding place. At the extreme southeastern corner, he saw something glitter. He looked closer, and there it was: a belt of silver, hidden behind a stalactite. One of the men of Quibanxe called the two others, pointing at another spot on the ceiling.

They found a belt too, thought Ahiram. *This is going to be close.* He knew they could form a human ladder and reach the ceiling. He was alone and had to rely on other means. He pulled a rope from his belt, clipped it to a dart, and hurled the dart up. The looping dart swung around a stalactite, reeling the rope up. Ahiram pulled on it, and the noose tightened and held. Using his arms, he climbed up so quickly that the crowd gasped. Without stopping, he looped the rope around his feet and swung back and forth, gathering momentum until he managed to reach the belt of silver. He clipped it onto a hook on his left leg and was about to grab the rope with both hands, when it came loose. The crowd screamed.

Ahiram dropped the rope and slammed feet first into a neighboring stalactite. The crowd shrieked. Knees bent, he pushed away, extending his body to reach another stalactite which he held on to with both arms. He heard scattered applause. Cautiously, he began to slide down, but the structure broke, and he fell, barely evading the fractured rock. Instinctively, the spectators ducked, howling and cheering. Shifting his body, he managed to grab the peak of a stalagmite with his left hand. He swung his legs, and his body slammed into the rock. Despite the shock and momentary dizziness, Ahiram held on. All eyes were on him. In one fluid movement, he slid down the freezing surface, then pushing away, performed a perfect flip and landed on his feet. The crowd gave him a standing ovation in a deafening roar. Ignoring the cheers and applause, he saw the men of Quibanxe about to leave the hall with the leader holding a belt above his head, so sure they were of their win. Ahiram pulled out his folded crossbow, opened it, cranked it, slid an arrow dart into the shaft, aimed, and fired. The belt flew from the hands of the surprised leader and slammed against the wall behind the howling crowd. Ahiram sprinted, hoping the Quibanxian would try to pry the belt from the arrow dart instead of running after him, for they were amazing runners. He ran the last five miles as fast as he could, not daring to look back, and reached the exit barely two steps ahead of the fastest man on the team of Quibanxe.

Outside the mines, the crowd, twice as numerous as the day before, exploded in cheers, ululations, and applause. The judges came forward and asked him for the shoes of bronze and belt of silver. Ahiram handed them both. They inspected them and declared him the winner of the second Game. Four men carried him on their shoulders in jubilation through the cheering crowds toward the King's castle. Ahiram would have preferred to walk alone on the slave's dirt path, but this was not possible.

Once inside the main gate, he went through the garden of the officers to reach the garden of the servants and climb up to the second floor. Having forgotten that Commander Tanios wanted him in the Silent's quarters, he headed straight back to his room.

He opened the door and saw someone lying in his bed. He raised his fist, about to strike, when the young man turned and stretched.

"Your mat is far more comfortable than mine. Can I buy it from you?"

"Jedarc," said Ahiram with tired smile, "What are you doing here?"

"Wrong question," replied his friend standing up. "What are *you* doing here?"

"Me?" replied Ahiram confused. "This is my room."

"Really?"

Jedarc slapped Ahiram on his shoulder and winced. "I win," shouted his friend, while rubbing his hand. "Do you eat stones for breakfast?" he asked. "I win."

"Jedarc, what are you talking about?"

"I made a bet with Banimelek. I told him that by the end of the day you would have forgotten Commander Tanios' order, and he said that you wouldn't. You didn't remember, so I won the bet."

"That's true, I wasn't supposed to be here. Alright, Jedarc, you win. What is the object of the bet?"

"A song," replied Jedarc, grinning.

"A song? What song?" asked Ahiram, feeling sorry for Banimelek.

"A wedding song. If I lost I would have to sing a song at Banimelek's wedding, but thanks to you, he will have to sing a song at *my* wedding."

"What song?"

Instantly, Ahiram regretted asking, for Jedarc took his question as a cue to begin singing:

Across the vast, empty plain,
In the summer, under the rain,
Through snowy mountain roads,
I sing ballades, love songs, and odes.

I am a lonesome bard
Atop his lonely donkey.
Your joy is my reward
With a dish of meat and barley.

"Stop singing!" yelled Ahiram.

"What?" said Jedarc, puzzled. "You don't like my singing?"

Before Ahiram could answer, his door was flung open by a band of frenzied slaves who thought someone had died, and a band of wailing women had been hired for the funeral.

"Well," said Jedarc, offended after Ahiram had managed to reassure everyone, "your friends cannot appreciate refined singing."

"That's it," said Ahiram, "you got it. Now that I am *fully* awake, let's be on our way before my *friends*—as you call them—change their minds and come back for the kill."

"I am a lonesome bard, atop his lonely donkey," whispered Jedarc. Ahiram elbowed him.

"You are cruel," groaned Jedarc.

"I can be when needed," replied Ahiram sharply. They walked the rest of the way in silence. As he was about to enter his room, their way to the Silent's quarters, "but tell me, what's the point of that bet? Neither of you are going to get married any time soon."

"We shall see about that," replied Jedarc as he spun and bowed. "That, we shall see."

Ahiram shook his head. "What's for dinner?" he asked.

"The usual," said Jedarc eyeing him closely. "Cold chicken, bread, salad, water, and apples."

"I hate cold chicken," muttered Ahiram.

He went to his assigned room and closed the door without another word. Exhausted, he threw himself on his bed and fell into a deep sleep. He dreamed that he stood before the ruins of a tower. Suddenly, an earthquake shook the ground and volcanoes erupted on all sides, threatening to engulf him. A large hole opened before him. Inside, he saw a shark, a bull, a dragon, a jaguar, and a host of unknown creatures dancing amid flames that were growing brighter by the minute. He wept, but he did not know why. He looked up and saw a lady of ravishing beauty. She smiled at him, and he felt at peace.

Tanios woke him abruptly.

"Get up. The evening ceremony is about to start."

Ahiram looked around him in a daze. It was dark. He must have been asleep for a while. "Ceremony?"

"Yes, you won, remember? Hiyam came in third, and one of the team of Quibanxe, second. Olothe has left the Games. Apparently, he sustained a rather serious injury as he was coming down the stairs. Good riddance."

"Commander," interrupted Ahiram as he was getting dressed.

"What?"

"The prince. He did not fall. That is I, I..."

"You what?" asked Tanios. "You what?" His voice was hard.

"I lost my temper. I beat him badly."

"How badly?"

"He will not walk again, and he will not be able to use his arms."

"You left him paralyzed?" Tanios was scandalized. "One of his men is dead, and you are the prime suspect. I had to plead with the King to keep you out of jail, and you lose your temper and beat Prince Olothe to a pulp? You left him paralyzed? What will it take before you curb that temper of yours? Don't you know what this means? He will be treated worse than a slave. He is now unclean, and will be shunned by his family."

"I am sorry, Commander Tanios, so sorry..."

There was a moment of silence. Tanios sighed. "You are in deep trouble. The Temple of Baal will not tolerate the slightest insurrection. You have become a symbol of freedom for Tannin. Expect the next Game to be a lot harder and far more dangerous than this one." He sighed and rubbed his eyes. "Did he insult you again?"

"No," whispered Ahiram.

"Did he insult your father?"

"He said I was a slave, son of a slave, a dog, son of a dog."

The commander winced. He could only begin to imagine the fury Ahiram had unleashed on the unsuspecting prince. Guilt surfaced once more, and he wondered if he had failed this pupil. Six years of harsh training would have tamed a tiger, but not Ahiram's temper. *What went wrong?* he wondered.

"Olothe should not have treated you contemptuously. With his arrogance and stupidity, he was looking for trouble, but it does not excuse your behavior. Your actions were reprehensible. You were reckless, and consequently, you will be demoted from the rank of Solitary. Now come, His Majesty the King is waiting."

Commander Tanios left the room and closed the door behind him. Ahiram shook his head and looked at his hands as if he were seeing them for the first time. *Are these the hands of a murderer? Is this what I have become? I could have killed Prince Olothe today. When I became a Silent, I took an oath not to kill unless my life is in grave danger. But at the first occasion, at the first test...*

He flopped back on the bed and gazed at the ceiling. Remorse and grief filled his heart. *I was prepared to lose everything in order to gain my freedom, including my rank as a Silent; but was I prepared to take a life to be set free? What will Hoda do when I tell her what I have done? What will she do?*

Slowly, he rose from his bed, put on his clothes, left his room and walked down a deserted corridor; as his footsteps echoed softly on the marble floor,

Ahiram felt alone like never before. Before, alone meant being bereft of his sister and parents; over the years, it came to mean being separated from his friends. But now, being alone, meant being ashamed to be in their presence.

"I will always be alone," he whispered.

He heard a popping sound and a voice whispered back: "You are not alone; I am with you."

10. A Restless Night

"Throughout my years of service to the Empress, I have met many remarkable men—some I have admired, some I have loathed. None have won my respect as much as Commander Tanios, for he gave us a measure of courage and integrity that is truly exceptional."

–Diplomatic Notes of Uziguzi, First Adviser to Her Majesty Aylul Meïr Pen, Empress of the Empyreans

"To prevent anyone from reopening the Pit of the Abyss, the Temple will curse anything that reeks of magic. Some priests have been accused of larceny, embezzlement, or profiteering. Others have been guilty of racketeering, threatening to curse the innocent unless hefty payments were made. The Temple is aware of all this and never fails to punish the guilty. Yet, this evil is nothing next to the opening of the Pit."

–Teachings of Oreg, High Priest of Baal

"You told him what?"

Bahiya was beside herself. Her daughter took two steps back, her hand lifted before her face in a sign of protection. She had seldom seen her mother so angry. The high priestess' features were drawn, and her eyes betrayed extreme fatigue.

"How could you be so irresponsible?" she snapped. "Don't you understand what that means?"

"I thought he would not make it out of the mines alive."

"You *thought?*" yelled Bahiya. "I didn't bring you here to *think.* I gave you direct orders and expected you to follow them. It is a miracle that you survived. If the commander did not remove that poisonous dart, you would be dead by now, do you understand?"

"I thought he was bluffing," said Hiyam. She bit her lower lip, wishing she had not spoken.

"Bluffing?" said Bahiya, grabbing her daughter's wrist and twisting it sideways. Hiyam winced under the pain. For a woman with a slender frame, her mother was unusually strong.

"You threaten to kill a Solitary who can handily take on the best of the High Riders, and you expect him to use a cheap trick? Haven't you learned *anything* about them? Will I have to flog that worthless tutor of yours to teach him not to waste the Temple's funds?"

"But Mother—"

Bahiya pushed her daughter against the wall. "I do not want you to think. I want you to execute my orders as I give them to you, when I give them to you, and how I give them to you. Do you understand? I had specifically ordered you not to lay claim to his life, and you have disobeyed me. Fail me one more time and your chances of becoming a priestess, much less a high priestess, will vanish."

Hiyam lowered her head. "Yes Mother." Bahiya let go of her and moved back.

"What would you do if the slave were to tell Commander Tanios that I used magic, Mother?" Hiyam questioned.

"Nothing. Nothing at all. The commander knows that I would accuse the slave of lying, exile him to a remote island, then wait for these fools to forget about the entire affair, and sentence him to death."

"But if he wins, he would be speaking as a free man."

"Are you trying to infuriate me?" snapped her mother. "That worthless Olothe failed like the miserable worm that he is, and now *you*? And to think I wanted him to marry you. Good riddance."

"Well, it is not that easy. This slave is—"

"What? Are you telling me that he can withstand a well-trained team of Baal that enjoys the full support of the god of gods? Is this what you are trying to say?"

"Not exactly, but there is something strange about him that I cannot explain. I feel as if someone is watching over him."

"What do you mean?"

"I mean that I think he is..." Hiyam shrugged her shoulders with exasperation and blurted out, "I mean I think he is protected."

"Protected? Protected by whom? Explain yourself."

"I cannot explain it. It is nothing tangible... for instance, when he threw his dart. It was a perfect throw."

"He is a Silent. What did you expect?"

"Well, I know, but—"

"But what?"

"Mother, calm down. Do you think this is easy? Don't you know that I am more distressed about this whole matter than you? I am losing this Game, Olothe is gone, a slave is besting me, and you..."

The priestess sighed and stopped pacing. She sat on a chair and looked at her daughter who was still standing against the wall.

"Tanios may be right after all."

"What do you mean?" asked Hiyam.

"I may be pushing you too much, asking too much from you."

Hiyam went to her mother, knelt before her, and held her mother's hands to her cheeks.

"But I want to be like you, to do what you did, all the wonderful things in Alep. I really want to, Mother."

"I know, I know... so what were you trying to say?"

"Well, you see, I was sure that he was going to die because before I started talking to him, I invoked the protection of the orbs."

Her mother straightened her position in her chair. "You did what?"

"I did not want to take any chances, and I knew I had received protection because of the usual burning sensation. That is why I acted so... carelessly. I figured a mere slave would not know how to penetrate the protective shield, so when his dart hit me, it was like a dream."

Her mother fell quiet for a while, and Hiyam did not dare interrupt her meditation. Her mother looked at her disbelievingly. "You mean to say that you invoked the protection of the orbs, and you obtained it?"

"Yes, Mother."

"And his dart went through the magical shield?"

"Yes, Mother."

"Which is impossible unless..."

"Unless a greater power than the shield is at work here."

Another moment of silence went by during which Bahiya mulled over the problem. "I know for a fact that the Silent Corps does not dabble in magic. Of this, I am certain. Only a master with the prescience of the Inner Circle would know how to penetrate the shield of the orbs; and this slave is certainly not a master... Was there anyone else in the cave?"

"I cannot be certain, but I did not sense anything unusual."

Bahiya's apartment was located near the Royal Hall on the third floor of the castle. A large wooden door opened directly from her room onto the balcony that circled the entire story. Opening the door, she motioned to her daughter who followed her. She crossed the wide veranda and leaned over the marble rail, peering into the night. Hiyam stood next to her and was startled by an owl screeching loudly, as if something, or someone, had disturbed the bird. Hiyam looked up, admiring the glittering stars in the beautiful, summer sky. The stillness was total; the young woman was no longer comfortable in this land. She longed to go back to Baalbeck and bathe in the sun.

"This is a lot more serious than I thought," said the priestess softly. "The flag of Tanniin has risen and the shield of the orbs has been pierced. A lowly slave evades a deadly trap. There may be a mightier hand behind all of this. I need to consult with Babylon. Go back to your room and await my instructions." Bahiya's order brooked no argument.

"Good night, Mother."

Bahiya did not answer. Hiyam walked out on the balcony, toward the Royal Hall, intending to go down the royal staircase to her room directly beneath her mother's. As she crossed the Hall of Judgment, Master Ibromaliöm stepped onto the balcony and nearly ran into her.

"Master Ibromaliöm, you startled me."

"My apologies, dear lady, I was taking a stroll on the balcony and somehow ended up here." He laughed uncomfortably. "I hope I did not scare you too much?"

"No, I am fine. I wish you a good night."

"And likewise, my dear lady."

He stood on the balcony watching her, and she could not help but wonder what he was doing in the Hall of Judgment. *Was he eavesdropping on us?* she wondered. *I know my mother's shield of protection is incredibly powerful. That's why she does not need guards at her door. Therefore, he could not have heard us, but still, I should let Mother know.*

She walked into the Great Hall, deserted at this hour, and was about to take the stairway back up to her mother when she saw one of her men climb the stairs four by four.

"You're here, Baal be praised! We were looking for you everywhere," the Junior High Rider exclaimed.

"Who is looking for me and why?"

"Come, you must see this."

She followed him down the main corridor and saw a group of soldiers standing next to the Lone Tower with more men streaming in the hallway. She heard the distinctive voice of Queen Ramel.

"This is inadmissible!" the Queen was screaming. "This is intolerable!"

"What happened?" asked Hiyam.

Her companion signaled for her to move faster. A sense of dread fell upon her. *Something bad has happened,* she thought.

"I demand you clean my dance floor at once," shouted the Queen.

"I am sorry, Your Majesty, but we cannot. We must wait for the commander. He is on his way."

Her teammate moved aside to let her walk in first, then followed her. The soldiers parted to let them pass. Hiyam walked into the Queen's Ballroom and froze. She even forgot to bow to Queen Ramel. On the ground, near the door, one of her men lay in a pool of blood, his hands clutching a dart planted deep in his chest.

"It is poisonous," whispered her companion while bowing before the Queen. "He was murdered much like Prince Olothe's teammate."

"Young man, if you have something to say, say it. Do not *ever* whisper in my presence."

"My apologies, Your Majesty," answered Hiyam. "My teammate thinks the Silent are killing us."

"How do you know the murderer is a member of the Silent Corps?" asked the Queen haughtily.

The Junior High Rider felt uncomfortable. "Well, the poison, the dart. Is it not obvious? They must be..."

"Just because someone is killed with a High Rider's sword does not mean that the criminal is one of us, does it?" interrupted Hiyam.

"Are you defending them, Mistress Hiyam?" snapped the young man.

"No, but your mistress would do well not to repeat the errors of Prince Olothe," replied the Queen. Hiyam sensed the veiled threat but did not reply. "We shall wait for the good commander to come here and clean up this mess."

"With your permission, Your Majesty, I would like all of my

companions to be accounted for," requested Hiyam.

The Queen nodded distractedly.

"Go," ordered Hiyam, "and get everyone here, but first alert my mother," the young soldier nodded.

Hiyam leaned against the velvet covered wall and closed her eyes.

>❋❋❋<

"So, my dear Bahiya, if I understand you correctly, the flag of Tanniin has risen once more and a slave has won the first two Games."

"Yes, master, this is correct."

"Fascinating. And so far you have not intervened?"

"I was counting on Olothe to dispatch the slave. If you would like me to intervene, I am—"

Master Sharr lifted his hand up into the orb of communication as a motion of silence.

"That will not be necessary. You have acted wisely. As I see it now, we have two issues of concern. Let me start with the lesser of the two, the slave. While we most certainly could have put this young man's remarkable talents to good use, he must not live beyond the fourth day, I am afraid. In crushing him, we put an end to the people's dream of freedom. This champion's supporters will see their hopes dashed and will go back to their cattle and their crops."

"What about the King?" asked Bahiya.

"Why don't you tell me about the leader of the Undergrounders? His name is Soloron, is it not?"

"Nothing escapes you, master," said Bahiya, bowing. "He has the wherewithal to depose the King, but he will be a mediocre leader; capable soldier, wasted talent."

"Use him to get rid of King Jamiir. I never thought Jamiir was fit for ruling Tanniin, but Kalibaal thought otherwise, and he will one day succeed me as Babylon's high priest. So, I consider Jamiir's rule a convenient experiment to teach Kalibaal a lesson. I hope you will consider my entreaty and become his mate; Kalibaal will need a steady hand to rule the Kingdom of Baal and you would be a perfect match."

Bahiya nodded appreciatively.

"Once the Games are over, do not go back to Baalbeck. Tomorrow, you will use the orbs to influence Jamiir. Have him order Commander Tanios to protect you, no matter the cost. Leave Soloron to me; once his little charade is finished, I will send Kalibaal—who will convince him to abdicate in favor of Lord Orgond. Do what you must to get the commander to take you to Lord Orgond, and remain there until he is crowned King. Then, you will lend him all the necessary help to broker a truce between the Temple and the Empyreans. Although Sureï cursed most locations where a Letter of Power is hidden, he never managed to do so inside their kingdom; so you must find the Letter hidden there and curse it. The Letters of Power must never be used to open the Pit. The sole reason the Temple exists is to protect the world from the Lords of Chaos. No matter the cost, no matter the sacrifices we make, the Pit must never be opened. Is that understood?"

"Yes, master," replied Bahiya, straining under the pressure of the orbs. Keeping four orbs stable required tremendous energy and concentration, and this exchange had lasted far longer than she had expected.

"One last thing, daughter. I ask you to spare Jamiir's life for the sake of my niece. I want them both back in Babylon."

"I will see to it that they are both well protected."

Sharr nodded. "Now, on to the last most and troublesome matter. We must do what is necessary to identify the one who managed to pierce through your daughter's shield. I trust your daughter is proficient in these invocations?"

"Yes, master, I taught her myself."

"Then, there is no reason to think that she may not have performed the invocation correctly. You, my dear Bahiya, will see to it that whoever has these powers may not be able to put them to use during the fourth Game. You must not fail."

"Yes, master."

"Very good then. We will meet again after the third Game. Rest assured, my dear Bahiya, that Babylon is following your movements very closely, and whatever assistance you require shall be provided immediately."

"Thank you, master."

Sharr's image faded slowly, and the milky vapor hovering between the four motionless orbs was absorbed by them. Carefully, Bahiya lowered the hovering orbs from smallest to largest back into their designated compartments, inside a silver box. Shaking with exertion, she managed to prevent the orbs from rotating in the slightest during their descent. Heaving a deep sigh, she staggered to the nearby sink and washed her face. Manipulating the orbs took a greater toll on her now, and she wondered if she was getting too old for this magic, or if a power hiding within the castle had set itself against her.

Wearily, she lay down on her bed and mentally reviewed what Sharr had told her. The offer of assistance concerned her. *This does not bode well,* she thought. *He does not fully trust me. Still, none of it will matter in two days.*

Bahiya heard a discrete knock at the door. She got up, closed the silver box, and placed it inside a wardrobe. She stepped back, waved her left hand, and the wardrobe's panels closed soundlessly.

"Come in, Menla," she said firmly.

An older woman, with long, curly, white hair held in a simple ponytail, stepped in. "My apologies for disturbing you at this hour, Mistress, but Commander Tanios requests an audience with Your Ladyship."

Bahiya knew what was coming. "Please, convey my regrets to the commander. I would be delighted to receive him in the morrow. I am afraid I would not be much of a guest at this hour of the night."

Before the servant could reply, Tanios stood at the door. He dismissed the servant and eyed Bahiya angrily.

"Well, my dear Tanios, what can I do for you?"

"I am here on behalf of His Majesty the King. You are hereby notified that any further infractions of the rules by your daughter will mean her immediate disqualification."

She had expected recriminations or complaints, but this was downright crazy. "Are you out of your mind? Do you know how Baal will react if the Temple's team is disqualified?"

"And how will Baal react if news of its team relying on magic to win were to reach the crowd?" retorted the commander with a faint smile.

"How dare you?"

"Precisely what *I* wanted to know: how dare *you*?"

Bahiya looked away.

"This is not the time, nor the hour to open old wounds," continued Tanios, "but I am warning you, Priestess..."

"My *name* is Bahiya."

"That is the name of someone I knew, a long time ago. You are a priestess of Baal, and that is who I am warning. If you do not want to deal with major civil unrest, get your daughter to play by the rules."

"Why did you give this slave permission to take part in these Games?" snapped Bahiya. "If you had refused him the right to participate, none of this would have happened."

"I know that a slave earning his freedom means nothing to you..."

"That is not what I said."

"But that is what you mean; gold, power, and ambition, no matter the cost—isn't it, Priestess? To you, anything or anyone who stands between you and gold is an annoyance, someone to be rid of. Well, this slave is exceptionally gifted in all respects. He could remain a slave, become the leader of the Silent Corps, and lead a well-respected life here at the castle. In fact, as a slave, he could wield more power than most free citizens could ever dream of. Yet, he put his life on the line because he wants to return to his father, his mother, and his sister. They mean more to him than any amount of gold. I respect that."

"But he may die in these Games and never see them again."

"Don't you think I tried to stop him from taking part in these crazy Games? Do you not think I..." Tanios sighed deeply and continued in an even tone. "I can no longer control him," he said, turning his back to the high priestess. "His temper is a raging sea. It frightens even me."

Bahiya felt dizzy. She took a couple steps back and held herself against the drapes that covered the wall. "Don't tell me that the famous Commander Tanios is incapable of taming a slave—"

"Yes, that is precisely what I am saying, Priestess. If this was a natural anger, I could have taught him how to control it..." He turned around to face her. "Do I need to remind you that I have had my share of loss and betrayal?" He gripped a nearby chair and closed his eyes. "No," he said in a measured tone. "This is something entirely different."

"So what are you saying?"

"I am saying we are running out of time. By the laws of the kingdom, I must wait until he is twenty-one to set him free. I am afraid that soon his temper will get the best of him; like it did when he disrespected you the night before the Games. What if his temper flares against the Queen or the King? The first five years went well, but now I can see him slipping away. If he lashes out against the King, the law will demand his head. I did not allow him to enter the Games so he may win his freedom; I did it to give him a chance to stay alive."

They stood facing each other silently. Tanios sighed and was about to leave when Bahiya held his arm and squeezed.

"Babylon is issuing orders as we speak. If you value the life of your slave, do not, under any circumstance, mention which village he is from.

If you do, he will certainly die."

Tanios stared at her in shock. A high priestess would not voluntarily disclose valuable information to one such as himself unless she wanted something else in return. Disturbed, he pulled away gently, nodded, and left the room.

Slowly, Bahiya slid down against the wall and sat on the floor.

"Tanios, if you only knew," she said, crying softly.

>◈◈◈<

Kalibaal was a priest of Baal of the Inner Circle, which comprised the select few who could walk alone behind the deepest curtain of the Temple and into the terrifying spell world without losing their sanity. Ponderously, he walked barefoot on the cold, dark stones of the inner temple—a reminder of the nothingness of man when standing in the inner sanctum of Baal. He ignored the searing pain caused by the icy-cold stones, pushed out a dark curtain, and entered a small alcove where High Priest Sharr stood facing a blank wall. Sharr briefed him on his latest conversation with Bahiya and then casually added, "Tell me, Kalibaal, what do you make of the lights that appeared on the eve of the first Game? What do you think these lights mean?"

Kalibaal winced. Inwardly, he chided himself on his carelessness. *How did I not notice it before?* He looked his master in the eye and answered softly: "There is no mistaking; the Seer yet lives."

"The Seer yet lives," nodded Sharr. "Our last attempt has failed. He managed to escape."

Kalibaal waited for the rest. He knew that Sharr's knowledge and experience of the spell world far exceeded his.

"Eighteen years ago," said Sharr, "a mysterious messenger uttered a prophecy in the northern realm of the dwarfs foretelling the coming of the Seer of Destruction. Six people were present and heard it. Some years later, one of them, a woman, fell severely ill and in her delirious state, spoke of the prophecy. Her nurse, a devotee of the Temple, related the news to the local priest, a faithful child of Baal, who unfortunately, dismissed the story as the ravings of a sick mind. By the time we heard of it, the woman was gone and all our efforts to locate her have failed."

"Is this the Pit of Fire prophecy?" asked Kalibaal.

"Yes indeed, this is the infamous Pit of Fire prophecy. We tell everyone it is apocryphal, but we cannot ignore it."

"So then, how was it possible that we could not find this woman?"

"She must have had powerful allies. Be it as it may, the prophecy spoke of a great sign in the heavens four days before the Seer would be set free. Isn't it peculiar that these strange lights were seen the eve of the Games of the Mines?"

"Surely, the prophecy could not mean freedom from slavery?"

"Good point, my dear Kalibaal. If this were a local prophecy exclusive to Tanniin, freedom from slavery would be justified, poetic even. But this is a prophecy pertaining to the Seer of Power. Its meaning is far reaching and clear: in two days hence, the Seer will be set free from the bonds of ignorance and will discover his first Letter of Power."

"What are your orders, master?"

"I fear the Seer is slipping away from us. Release the Béghôm."

"The Béghôm, master? I do not understand. This creature was made to fight the Marada."

"Any creature of the spell world will help us ferret out the Seer. The Béghôm is the least of the creatures we can release. Release him."

"He will wreak havoc—"

Sharr waved his hand dismissively. "Victims are always required to keep the Pit shut. Release him."

"Yes, sir."

"Has the Urkuun reached the Empyrean Kingdom yet?"

"Yes, sir. The being of power you unleashed from the spell world is there now, and he has begun rallying many to his cause."

Sharr glanced at Kalibaal briefly. "My son, you must not fear these creatures. They are yours to command."

"They are creatures of the Pit, master," replied Kalibaal. "The Temple's knowledge is deep, I know. Still, much is hidden from us."

Sharr shrugged his shoulders dismissively. "The Urkuun will do as instructed. He cannot break the curses that shackle him."

"Your wisdom is far-reaching, master," said Kalibaal, bowing.

"Command him to move to Tanniin. The Fortress of Hardin sits atop an ancient lair of the Urkuuns. Let him take his abode there."

"But sir," replied the man, alarmed, "surely the danger is not as..."

"It is the Seer of the Letters we are dealing with here," replied the high priest dryly. "If, as I suspect, he is alive in Tanniin, we must stop him. If he finds but one of the twenty-two Letters of Power—only one, you hear—he will set in motion a series of events that will spell the doom of the Temple and unleash forces on the world, the likes of which we have never seen before. It must not be. In this matter, as in all matters pertaining to the Letters of Power, the Temple must not fear the loss of life—even innocent life—for the alternative is unthinkable. If the Urkuun destroys an innocent boy, then we will mourn our loss, and the world will be safe from all danger. If the Urkuun slays the Seer of Power, then all the lives we have taken will be vindicated."

"Are we certain there is a Letter of Power in Tanniin?"

"Every indication we have suggests Sureï went to Tanniin for that express reason. My suspicion is that the Letter is hidden somewhere deep within the mines. The slave Bahiya spoke of may be thinking he is trying to win his freedom, but I think he is unwittingly attracted to the Letter of Power lurking beneath the mountain. Certainly, there is no reason to doubt the sincerity of his motives, but they matter very little. The Letters will call the Seer to them just as the flowers call the bees."

"In this case," replied Kalibaal, ruefully, "the curse Sureï imposed on every location where a Letter of Power is hidden will take care of the Seer. Has he not directed his curse specifically against the Seer, and are not these curses terrifying? Surely, the Seer cannot escape them."

"Unfortunately, Sureï was unable to curse *every* location. We know of at least one place that he was unable to curse. Why? No one knows exactly. We cannot take this risk. This is why I want the Urkuun in Tanniin. The Seer must be destroyed."

There were no more objections Kalibaal could raise. As a priest of the Inner Circle, it was his duty to question the decisions of the high priest, but he could see Sharr's far-ranging wisdom. He bowed and left with a heavy heart, for the Urkuun was a monster created for the subjugation of mankind. Kalibaal could not help but wonder if the Temple, with all its might and knowledge of the spell world, would be able to subjugate the monster after it had managed to destroy the Seer. The biting cold of the dull stones reminded him how important humility was. *We do not know everything,* he thought. *In fact, we know so very little.*

><center>✦✦✦</center>≺

Tanios rose up. He had finished his inspection of the body and was holding the dart in his hand. The Hall of Dancing was cordoned off and no one was allowed in or out. Hiyam and her team stood nearby.

"O my soul, seek not a coward's solace even if he be a trusted friend for he will strike you at an hour you do not expect."

"What do you mean, Commander Tanios," asked Hiyam, drawing near him.

"Book of Lamentation, chapter 7, verse 5," replied the commander, a puzzled look on his face.

"Do you see this dart?" he asked, pointing at the weapon used to kill the man. "It is three-pronged and each of its prongs is slightly curved inward which makes it harder to pull it free from its target."

"It takes barbarians to create weapons such as these," interjected one of Hiyam's men.

"Shut your mouth." Hiyam's order suffered no reply.

Tanios ignored the outburst. He seemed deep in thought.

"You were saying, Commander?"

"I am saying this dart is old. Very old. In fact, it is so old that none of the Silent under my command have been trained to use them. When thrown, these darts would wobble and seldom hit their mark. We dropped them from our arsenal ten years ago." Tanios threw the dart straight at the wall. It wobbled and fell clumsily to the ground.

"Why attack someone with such a coarse weapon when you have far more effective means to do the job? Why not use a needle dart that can deliver a quick poison without leaving a trace? Why risk missing your target by throwing a wobbly dart, unless..." He got up and inspected the room once more, as though he was seeing it for the first time. "Lady Hiyam, look around and tell me, what do you see?"

Hiyam inspected the hall. A series of comfortable chairs surrounded an elliptical dance floor.

"I don't see anything unusual," said Hiyam pensively. "Aside from these chairs, there is nothing else here."

"Precisely, my dear Hiyam, precisely. Nothing else. I take it everything is as it was since the incident?"

The man who found the body nodded. "We did not touch anything."

"An undisturbed hall and a wobbly poisonous dart. What is the implication? Your man let the killer get very close to him without a fight." He leaned over and examined the body once more. "No signs of injury, no bruises, no signs of struggle." He stood up. "Your man was not afraid of his opponent, who stabbed him with this poisoned dart at close range. Can you imagine Ahiram entering this room, trying to convince one of your men to come close to him? I do not think so. Whosoever committed this crime knew the victim very well and was able to draw close to him in confidence. Then, the murderer used this dart, trying to confuse us into thinking Ahiram did it. Clever, but only by half."

"But who would do such a thing?" asked Hiyam, anguished. She glanced at her men. "This makes no sense."

"A very good question, my dear Hiyam, and I assure you, I will find out who is killing these men. In the meantime, I would suggest that you and your teammates do not open the door to anyone and be on your guard. I will send servants to help with the preparation for the proper burial of this unfortunate young man."

"As if you cared," interjected one of Hiyam's men. She rushed to him and was about to slap him when Tanios gently stopped her. He looked at the young man who had spoken.

"Your brother?"

"My cousin."

"I am sorry, and I will find the killer. But if I may say, do not use the dead as an excuse to hate the living, especially those who are innocent of this crime."

Tanios opened the door and left. Hiyam watched the young man step out of the Hall of Dancing into the dark hallway. She saw him walk out to the balcony and knew he was crying.

>✦✦✦<

"It is the shark, I tell you."

"Yes, yes, of course. Yesterday it was the oysters. The day before... what was it again? Oh yes, the lamb, and tonight, the shark."

"Well, it is not my fault if I snore."

"Of course not. It is not your fault that you snore. Your snoring is what's faulty that's all; it wakes me up."

"Well, you should sleep in a different room."

"As if this would change anything. Your snoring is so loud; I would be surprised if the King upstairs, or anyone else in the entire castle is able to sleep."

Ramany and Hylâz were sitting in the common room, looking at each other dejectedly. Ramany, the fat, short judge, had a gruff look on his face and his hair looked like a bunch of broken straws shaken by a violent wind. Hylâz's face was wrinkled from lack of sleep and his frown furrowed his forehead, splitting it in two. Whatever hair he had had, he seemed to have lost tonight.

He passed his hand over his scalp. Ramany followed his gesture attentively.

"What are you doing?"

"I am combing my hair."

"Your hair? But you barely have any."

"If you did not snore, I wouldn't be losing my hair."

"My snoring causes your baldness?" asked Ramany. "This is incredible."

"Your snoring would cause crows to go bald," scoffed Hylâz. "In fact, do you see any crows around here? No, there you go."

"Crows? But it's the middle of the night. You are impossible."

Ramany started laughing. Hylâz joined him.

"So, why did you wake me up?" he asked, remembering now what was bothering him.

"Well, it is only justice, is it not?"

"So, if you cannot sleep, I should not sleep either?"

"I was getting bored sitting here by myself listening to you filling the night with your poetic expressions."

"You could have woken up Garu. He is the lead judge after all."

"I tried, but neither Garu nor Ibromaliöm are in their rooms."

"Ibromaliöm is a night owl, so this is not surprising, but Garu? Usually, he is more disciplined than the Silent."

"Well, Garu, Ibromaliöm, and the King wanted to join the Silent

Corps when they were young. They enrolled in the Silent's training program the same year, but the oath scared them enough that they dropped out the day before the oath ceremony."

"Garu? A Silent?"

"Yes, I know. Most of us underestimate this man. Behind his quiet, seemingly bored face, is hidden one of the sharpest minds I have ever known. I tell you, sometimes he scares me."

"Ibromaliöm scares me."

"Me too, but not in the same way as Garu. Ibromaliöm is not as subtle as Garu is. You can tell that he is trying to impress you. Garu hides it. He does not want to attract any attention to himself."

"And what is it that scares you about me, old friend?"

Ramany and Hylâz almost fell out of their chairs. Garu was standing before them, as if he materialized from nowhere.

"Garu, this is most unsettling, and if I may add, lacking in taste and gentlemanly manners."

"My apology, dear Hylâz, but I could not resist. You are afraid of me? I must say, I am grieved. I thought we were friends."

"I do not think it prudent to annoy our good friend, Ramany, with this rather private matter, do you not agree?"

"You have been annoying him, as you say, for quite some time now with this private matter, so why not pursue it a little further?"

"I am not annoyed," said Ramany quickly.

"And why are you up, Master Ramany?" asked Garu.

"It is the shark—"

"Ah yes, indeed. I found it too heavy for my taste."

"See?" exclaimed Ramany, looking triumphantly at Hylâz.

"It must be the garlic," said Garu, smiling.

"Yes, the garlic, that's it."

"Well, my dear Hylâz, I am sorry if I have put you on the spot, but the events of this night are rather unnerving, if I may say so."

"Events? What events?" asked Ramany.

"One of Hiyam's men was found dead."

"Dead?" exclaimed Ramany and Hylâz.

"As dead as can be. He was murdered."

"Murdered?" exclaimed the two men in unison once more.

"Have you ever considered singing together?" asked Garu, smiling.

"Garu," snapped Hylâz, "this is not the time for your sarcasm."

"You are right. I am sorry, dear friend," said Garu, sighing. "Something is wrong and I am on edge."

"But how did you find out?" asked Ramany.

"Tanios woke me up. He wanted to question me about my whereabouts. Apparently, I am one of the prime suspects."

"You mean to say that Tanios thinks you may have committed the crimes?" Hylâz's voice was shrill with fear and excitement.

"He did not say it in so many words, but he told me that he will send some members of the Silent Corps to protect me."

"Well, is it not a prudent decision?" asked Ramany.

"It would be if Tanios allowed the Silent to be at my disposal. Instead, he said that the Silent would protect me. The difference is subtle, but very real: it means he does not trust me, and this, in turn, implies he considers me a suspect." Garu stood up and went to the door. He put his finger on his lips, asking both men to be still. He opened the door quickly and looked out. "Nobody. These Silent are truly amazing."

Ramany and Hylâz joined Garu and looked into the corridor. There was no one to be seen. They went back to their seats, and Garu closed the door.

"Are you sure someone is guarding these doors?"

"Well, you have only to ask Tanios. I am sure he will be paying you a visit very soon. He told me he wanted to speak with Ibromaliöm first. In any event, I am going to bed. Tomorrow will be a long day, so I suggest you do the same. Good night, my friends."

Garu left. Ramany and Hylâz sat around the table waiting for Tanios to appear at their door. After waiting for a long time, they grew tired and went to bed. Hylâz waited anxiously for Ramany's powerful snore, but it never came. Ramany's fear of being murdered kept him awake all night. But he would be quick to lay the guilt of insomnia on the shark steak they had eaten—served with a creamy garlic sauce, salad, and a fresh loaf of bread. His stomach grumbled and he fidgeted in bed wondering what would keep him awake longer: his fright or his bloated stomach.

>❁❁❁<

"No, my dear Tanios, there is no one besides the four of us."

"What are we to conclude, Your Majesty?"

"That Master Ibromaliöm, Master Garu, you and I, are prime suspects in this matter."

"But this is absurd."

The King walked toward the window. Dawn had begun coloring the clear skies with a deep golden hue.

"It is going to be another fine summer day in the kingdom, my dear Commander," said the King. Looking at Ibromaliöm, he added, "The facts are undeniable: whosoever used this dart knew how to use it at close range and was known to the victim. All of us– you to a lesser extent–fit these two conditions rather well, would you not agree?"

"Yes, Your Majesty."

"Commander Tanios, you and I have had our differences. We may not agree on the presence of Baal, the building of the temple, nor the honor I accord to the priestess. Nevertheless, my father—the gods be praised— made an excellent choice when he placed you at the head of the Silent Corps. I have never questioned this; some have suggested that I demote you but I have always refused. I feel secure knowing you are the head of the Silent Corps. You know that the Temple of Baal would be very glad to see the Corps dismantled. I do not want this to happen. The murderer must be found and stopped before it is too late."

"What do you suggest, Your Majesty?"

"Why would anyone want to murder these young men? There is no relationship between them; they belong to different teams and different families. What is the motive for their murders?"

"I do not know, Your Majesty. Granted, both teams have tried to get rid of Ahiram, but this does not explain why these two young men— and no other members of their teams—have been killed."

"True, indeed. So what do they have in common?"

"They are both men and they have been murdered in the same way."

"By a poisoned dart," said the King. "Hmm… I think it is time we had a conversation with the old man, Habael. Where do you suppose we should find him in a few hours hence?"

"In the quarters of the Silent, Your Majesty."

"Ah yes, Master Habael does take good care of your protégé, does he not? Very well, I will pay that remarkable Silent a visit. No need to bring Master Habael here. Also, we need privacy while talking about such matters and your quarters are as good as any, my dear Tanios."

Tanios bowed and left the Royal Hall smiling to himself. *The King said remarkable 'Silent' rather than 'slave.' Ahiram is starting to make a name for himself.*

>❋❋❋<

"There, there," said Habael, as he removed the last elixir pad he had placed on Ahiram's shoulder the night before. "See what a good night's rest did? You are nearly healed. Are you ready for the next Game?"

Ahiram examined his shoulder and smiled. "What would I do without you?" he asked, looking at the old man.

"What would *we* do without Habael?" interjected Jedarc, who was sitting by Ahiram.

"We would have to put up with the moaning of Ahiram all night long, that's what we would be doing." said Banimelek.

Ahiram, Banimelek, and Jedarc erupted in laughter.

"You beat the team of Baal," said Banimelek approvingly.

"They were at a disadvantage," said Jedarc. "Twelve against Ahiram, come on." They all laughed again.

"Are you trying to defend them, Jedarc?" asked Banimelek, teasing.

"Me? No, not at all, never, you know me, Banimelek. Me, defend the High Riders? Outlandish, preposterous, ridiculous, absurd. Perish the thought. The mere fact that I find Hiyam... *very* pretty should not be construed in form or manner to mean, imply or intimate that Jedarc of the Silent Corps is defending the High Riders."

"Look at him," chuckled Banimelek, "Jedarc is in love."

"I am *not*," replied Jedarc. "All I said was that she is—"

"Very pretty," completed Banimelek. Their laughter died down when they saw Ahiram's expression.

"What?" asked Jedarc. "You don't find her pretty?"

"She's a snake, Jedarc, a snake who wants me dead. Beware the women of the Temple, they will chew you live and spit you out like an olive's kernel. You would be nothing but dead weight to her."

"I hear you," said Jedarc, sighing. "But are you certain she's doing this out of her own free will or..."

"I don't know and I don't care," snapped his friend. "It doesn't matter. As long as she belongs to the Temple, you will never know, so drop your sentimental dirge and wake up: your beloved wants me dead."

"She is *not* my..." Jedarc sighed and became suddenly serious. "You've got nothing to worry about, Ahiram. You can trust me."

"That's not the point," cut in Ahiram quickly. "I trust both of you with my life. It is *you* that I'm worried about. The creatures of the Temple are not real. Never trust them, ever."

"You are right, Ahiram. I am being a sentimental idiot."

"Not a complete idiot," replied Banimelek. "If, by some miracle she leaves the Temple, courting her will be like a wide open field, now that Ahiram has given Olothe the beating of his life."

Ahiram's mood darkened instantly. Jedarc looked at Banimelek as though saying, "What is wrong with you?" Banimelek shrugged his shoulders and looked at Habael. Having missed nothing of this quiet exchange, he looked at Ahiram with great tenderness and put his hand on his shoulder.

"Does it still hurt?"

"No," said Ahiram, almost imperceptibly.

"Well, then this is good. You heal fast." After a moment of silence, he continued, "Now, my boy, I will say this to you: never grieve beyond hope, and do not let sorrow overwhelm you. Instead, let your sorrow be your daily bread to remind you of what you have done. The prince is also to blame; he acted rashly."

"But he could not have known what I am capable of when my temper rages." Ahiram stammered. "I cannot blame him for that."

"He knew, my boy. I told him."

"You did?"

"Yes, the morning of the Game of Silver, I had asked to have an audience with him, and I explained to him the danger he was placing himself in by attacking you. I told him about the love and admiration you have for your family and how it was most important for him to treat you with respect."

"What did he do?"

"I kept this from you, but given the circumstances, I believe I should tell you... He had one of his men slap me on the mouth."

This was an insult of the worst kind in the Kingdom of Tanniin, for it was a punishment reserved for rebellious slaves. By slapping Master Habael, the prince intimated that the old man was like a slave to him and therefore anyone who valued and respected the gardener was foolhardy.

Unwittingly, with this single gesture, the prince insulted the royal house of Tanniin.

"He did what?"

Ahiram, Banimelek, and Jedarc were on their feet.

"He did what?" repeated Ahiram. His indignation was beyond measure. Habael motioned for them to sit down and waited for the young men to recover some semblance of self-control before continuing.

"That he slapped me and threw me out is something I permitted him to do for reasons which are all my own. My lad," he said, addressing Ahiram, "I have made this unfortunate event known to you because I want you to understand that you do not know everything. The prince was vindictive, arrogant and reveled in his own cruelty. He was determined to kill you, and you defended yourself—which was the right thing to do—but you gave free reign to your selfish desires, abused your strength, and maimed a man for life. As you can plainly see, I do not excuse nor justify your violence against the prince. I grieved when I learned of your actions, but if you have any respect and affection for this old man, then do not wallow in self-judgment in the hope that someone might console you; instead, atone for the evil you have committed, and find a noble way to make reparation to the prince if you can, and if not, to others in his stead."

"How?" asked Ahiram. "How do I do that? Just tell me."

"Your eagerness is commendable," replied Habael, "but do not assume that it is as easy as training for combat." Habael looked at Jedarc and smiled. "Consider this, Ahiram: a Silent attracted to a Junior High Rider is a good omen, my lad; it is a hopeful sign."

Ahiram stiffened and his jaw tightened instantly.

"She wanted to kill me."

"Would you say that her desire to kill you was greater than your eagerness to hurt and kill the prince?" asked Habael softly.

Jedarc and Banimelek held their breath, fully expecting Ahiram to fly out of the room in a bout of anger. Instead, their friend simply lowered his head.

"No," answered Ahiram, "I don't think so."

"So then," continued Habael, "if you, who has committed a worse action, cannot forgive Hiyam, how would you be able to accept what you have done and find ways to avoid doing it again? Ponder this well, Ahiram, for your future and so much more than your future hangs in the balance."

Six quick trumpet blasts announced the coming of the King, who entered, flanked by six guards and Commander Tanios. The Silent assumed their military positions and Habael bowed.

"At ease," said the King, who inspected the Silent. He stopped by Ahiram. "Congratulations once more on your second victory. Your victories are an honor to the entire body of the Silent." Ahiram bowed before the King, who then looked at Habael. "My dear Habael, may we have a word with you?"

"Certainly, Your Majesty."

The commander invited them to his private apartments and closed the door behind him.

"This must be serious," said Banimelek, "for the King to be up in the middle of the night."

"You didn't hear?" asked Jedarc, and, before his friends could ask him, he added, "One of Hiyam's men has been found dead in the Queen's Ballroom. He was killed with a poisonous dart."

The two young men glanced at each other and then looked at the closed door, wondering what the three men could be discussing inside the commander's quarters.

$$\succ \circledast \circledast \circledast \prec$$

"My dear Habael," started the King, "do you recall the poem about the rising of Tanniin?"

Habael thought it was an odd hour for such a request, but did not show any sign of surprise.

"I believe so, Your Majesty."

"Very well. Now, my dear Tanios, I want you to pay close attention to the words of this poem. The Queen told me once that this poem is very ancient, perhaps predating the Age of the Temple. I believe you will find these few verses of special interest to you in light of the latest unfortunate events."

"As you wish, Your Majesty."

"Habael, please start."

Habael began:

> *"Tanniin-the-Strong was on high,*
> *Above Baal and his Temple,*
> *Strength to rule the sea and sky,*
> *Power before which all tremble.*
> *In the darkness of his lair,*
> *Baal plotted death and despair;*
> *Seeds of sorrow,*
> *By night and morrow,*
> *Using stealth and machination;*
> *He made of stolen meyroon,*
> *Three spears of desolation.*
> *And in the shadow of the moon,*
> *Threw his spears, wounding the flying liege*
> *Who fell, and fell, and fell unto earth beneath;*
> *Where he moans his fate, a broken sheath,*
> *And the toil of his sons under siege.*
> *Silently, he awaits the day of his strength,*
> *When freedom shall be his at length.*
> *To be free, he must heal his woes,*
> *By dealing Baal four blows,*

Four sons, four lives,
By stealth and silver knives.
Blood sprinkled on the corners of the seal
Will break the curse and end his ordeal.
It will reveal the sword hidden within,
When the hour shall toll for the surge of Tanniin.

The deep voice of Habael fell silent. The King looked at Tanios, who stood, eyes closed, unmoving.

"Much to ponder, do you not think so, my dear Tanios?"

"Yes indeed, Your Majesty," replied the commander slowly. "This has proved very helpful. Thank you."

"What are your plans, Commander Tanios?"

"Tighten the security around the castle and the teams of participants, then get a few hours of rest. I will want to follow a few leads from the poem Master Habael recited. Hopefully, tomorrow will be uneventful. After all, there is still a Game to be won."

"Very well, my dear Commander. Remember, I am counting on you to find the murderer quickly."

Tanios bowed before the King, who opened the door and turned around with a sigh.

"My dear Habael, I envy you."

"Your Majesty, peace awaits you in Magdala's heart."

The King pondered the enigmatic words of the old man. Habael had often spoken to the King about the forest and the beauty within.

"Someday, Habael, someday."

Outside the castle, across from the balcony on the royal floor, an owl suddenly took flight. It hooted as if it were trying to warn them that, hidden beneath the shadows, a murderer was stalking the castle.

11. GAME OF GOLD

"The Game of Gold is a rite of passage. Death by water, rebirth by fire, and then the long, painful ascension through the Pit of Thunder. Above all, beware the masks of gold hiding in the midst of the many faces of Tanniin. Of all the Games, the Game of Gold is my favorite."
–Principles and Rules for the Games of the Mines, The Great Judge Bayrul III

"The Game of Gold. O My! O My! The excitement, the adventure, the heroes, the winners, the dead left behind, bobbing up and down on the surface of the still cold water; round and round they go, and no one remembers."
–Soliloquy of Zuzu the Hip, Jester of the Royal Court of Tanniin

"The dwarfs, having carved the mines, knew them better than anyone else. Yet, the mines remained shrouded in mystery, as though the mountain housed ancient beings of great power deep within its bosom."
–Philology of the Dwarfs, Anonymous

"Jedarc, what are you doing in the servants' kitchen?" asked Ahiram.

"What does it look like?" replied Jedarc, spreading fresh goat cheese on a slice of warm bread. "Having a scrumptious breakfast, reserved only for slaves."

"But this is where *I* have breakfast," objected Ahiram. "You're supposed to get your fancy food upstairs, not down here."

"Fancy food, fancy food…" grumbled Jedarc. "Do you hear that, Banimelek? They treat him like a prince down here and serve him the freshest ingredients, while *we* get the stale porridge and the wilted apples."

"Sit down, Ahiram," said Banimelek, smiling. "You should eat, or you'll be late again."

"Late?" said Ahiram, sitting. "I'm never late." He took the ladle and served himself a generous portion of cooked oats and mixed in raisins, dried apricots, a spoonful of crumbled walnuts, and two swirls of honey.

"See?" said Jedarc, pointing his spoon at Ahiram. "What did I tell you? Raisins and apricots! When was the last time *we* had raisins and apricots?"

"You wouldn't eat apricots anyway," said Banimelek. "It thickens your beard."

"Really?" asked Jedarc, eyeing the apricots suspiciously. Seeing a glint in Banimelek's eyes and the beginning of a smile, he frowned and slapped his tall friend's shoulder. "Look who's talking. If this were true, you'd be able to hide a cow in your beard, if you let it grow."

"So, what are you doing here?" asked Ahiram again as he cut three thick slices of bread. He covered the first slice with goat cheese, the second with a piece of ham, and the third with a thick, gooey, light-brown sauce, and a swirl of honey.

"What is that?" asked Jedarc suspiciously.

"Marinated goat's brain with aged yogurt," replied Ahiram, "Why do you ask?"

Jedarc's jaw dropped as he gazed at his friend, mingling pity with horror.

"I thought this was the marinated goat's tongue," offered Banimelek.

"They ran out," explained Ahiram, who gazed innocently at Jedarc. "My favorite is the dish over there," he said, pointing to a bowl with a dark, thick sauce. "That's marinated goat's eyes with turmeric and mint, but we get it only on feast days."

"Too bad," sighed Banimelek.

Jedarc shook his head in disbelief. Unable to contain themselves any longer, the two broke into laughter. They laughed so hard that tears welled up in their eyes.

"All right, all right," grumbled Jedarc, shrugging his shoulders. "You got me, but I am glad you did. I thought I had stepped into a nightmare." He shuddered, shaking his shoulders like a man getting rid of a slimy substance. "So, what are you eating?"

Ahiram took a piece of bread, spread the gooey sauce on it and added honey. "Go ahead, try it," he said, handing it over to Jedarc.

Jedarc looked at him suspiciously at first. Then he relaxed and grinned. "What am I doing? This is Ahiram after all," he muttered to himself. "If you're telling me to try it, then it must be good." He shoved the piece of bread in his mouth and chewed energetically. "Hey, that's not bad at all. It's nutty and sweet."

"Crushed almonds," said Banimelek, "with honey."

"They serve him crushed almonds, too?" moaned Jedarc. "What do I have to do to become a slave? *Please* tell me."

"So, what are you doing here?" asked Ahiram for the third time.

"Someone murdered two men, and you are still the prime suspect. We are in charge of your protection, so we will escort you to the plaza."

"But, Banimelek, if anyone wants to attack me, they'll do it inside the mines."

"Assuming that the attackers know there way around the caves," retorted Jedarc. "The priestess has stationed soldiers along Royal Road from the castle to the mine."

"These guys are slower than a slug," grumbled Ahiram, biting off a massive piece of bread. "They can't catch me."

"They don't have to," replied Banimelek. "they only need to slow you down. If they can do this, it'll be all over for you."

Ahiram conceded the point. He finished his breakfast in silence and a short moment later, the three friends reached the plaza in front of the Mine of Bronze.

The crowd was twice as large as yesterday's. *At least seven thousand people*, he thought. *I wonder how big it will be for the Game of Meyroon tomorrow.*

"Are you ready for this?" asked Banimelek, standing behind him.

"As ready as I can be," said Ahiram, smiling.

Banimelek nodded. "We will keep an eye on you inside the caves," he said before slipping away with Jedarc, just as the trumpet blasts signaled the start of the Game. Immediately, the procession formed, headed by the King and his retinue, followed by the four judges, and the athletes. Two rows of Silent kept the people at bay. The sun peeked over the mountaintops in the bright blue sky, and the crowd cheered three times. Ahiram stood behind the King. Hiyam's team was in second position, followed by the team from Quibanxe, the team from Marduc, and the team from Togofalk. Ahiram glanced at Bahiya's daughter. She stood forlorn, as if she had lost all interest in the Games, and for once did not laugh or jeer at him.

With the third trumpet blast, the procession lurched forward, moving along the western path leading to the Bridge of Evergreen. Just as they passed it, someone in the crowd started chanting Hiyam's name. Soon, others joined the lone voice and the chorus grew loud. Someone else picked up Ahiram's name and many joined him. The singing grew louder as each camp tried to drown out the other, until a strident shriek rose over the din. The crowd parted, forming a circle around a man lying on the ground with a bloodied face. The mass became agitated. Another man leaped into the circle, crouched next to the wounded man, and started screaming, pointing an accusatory finger at Hiyam. He stood up, raising a closed fist to the heavens. The crowd surged toward Hiyam. Immediately, several Silent moved forward and faced the angry mob, which threatened to lynch the Junior High Riders. An arbitrator managed to alert the King, who had not noticed the commotion. King Jamiir lifted his hand, and the trumpets sounded authoritatively above the crowd's fury. Everyone calmed down.

"My dear people," said the King in a loud and clear voice, "I share your excitement and I am pleased to see many of you have decided to support the team of Baal, while others chose a different champion. I am proud of you and would like to encourage you to keep this highly competitive spirit. Today's Game is harsh and fraught with dangers. The teams will need every ounce of courage and strength to make it through the Mine of Gold. Therefore, can we count on your warm but dignified participation?"

A rumble went through the crowd, then quieted. *Like a scolded child,* thought the King with satisfaction. He smiled and added with a loud voice, "In the name of the participating teams, I thank you." The trumpets sounded once more and the procession moved forward.

A few hundred yards past the bridge, a set of stairs carved into the slope led to a flat promontory overlooking Lake Renlow. Known as the "Lake of Hiding", its quiet surface hid a submerged grotto. Eighty feet inside this cave lay a narrow, vertical siphon, easy to miss in the ambient darkness. However, if a diver were to enter it and swim upward for a distance of twenty-five feet, he would break through the waters inside a vast, upper chamber. Allegedly, El-Windiir had hid there for ten days and fooled his masters into believing he had run away from the mines.

Reaching this cave was the first challenge for the contenders. Since an icy, subterranean river flowed into the lake, the water's temperature was bitterly cold. Players in former Games had died of hypothermia, and the arbitrators had retrieved their bloated bodies from the River Renlow.

In the past, the players would begin their swim from the shore, but diving from the edge of the promontory, fifty feet above the lake, had turned the Game into a show the crowd enjoyed. From that height, the divers would hit the water at a speed of thirty eight miles per hour, swiftly submerging to a depth of thirty feet. Any miscalculation could prove deadly.

Presently, the King and entourage sat on a raised platform. Since this side of the hill sloped gently downward, the contenders had to jump twelve to fifteen feet out, to avoid slamming against the lake's rocky bottom. To gather speed, they ran the forty-foot stretch from the back of the promontory to its edge.

The trumpets blasted, and Ahiram moved to the starting point, waiting for the King's signal.

>❂❂❂≺

King Jamiir glanced at Bahiya sitting by his side. She looked worn out and tense. Knowing that he was not the only one who had spent a sleepless night gave him a grim satisfaction. He glanced at her once more. Her sunken features were visible, despite the expensive kohl she artfully used to accentuate her almond-shaped eyes. Ostensibly, she was looking at Ahiram. *I would not want to be in his shoes*, thought the King, *I wonder what she has planned for him. Nothing good, I suppose.* He imagined the slave dead and managed to curtail a grin of deep satisfaction. He resented the slave and blamed him for the recent murderous events even though he knew that Ahiram was innocent. As far as Jamiir was concerned, preserving his crown justified the Silent's death. Should the priestess decide that he must die, then so be it. The King looked at Hiyam standing among her men and sighed. A second member of her team had disappeared in the early hours of the morning, and incredible as it seemed, no one had noticed anything until the team assembled for the third Game. *I hope I will not have to deal with a third victim when I return to the castle*, he thought, shuddering. Tanios was already on the case, but the damage had been done. The crimes of the past few days had heightened the tension between Taniir-the-Strong and Babylon. This was the last thing the King wanted.

"Will her Majesty the Queen grace us with her presence?"

Bahiya's crisp voice startled him, but he managed to keep his countenance. "Unfortunately, not. Her Majesty is not feeling well. The news of the two killings, especially the ghastly discovery in the Queen's Ballroom, distressed her much, and being delicate by nature, the Queen fell ill during the night. Her Majesty prefers to rest and avoid any further commotion. Nevertheless, she should be with us tonight."

Bahiya nodded out of customary politeness.

The final trumpet blast called everyone to attention. By now, the rumor that the slave would fulfill Layaleen's prophecy had spread south to Beit-Windiir and northeast as far as Tan-Aneer. The constant stream of the newly arrived swelled the ranks of the already dense crowd, ringing the bend of the western road all around the lake.

The King stood up, holding a white handkerchief. Judging from its fluttering, Ahiram determined that the wind blew from the east. *It'll be at my back if I veer slightly westward*, he thought, relieved. The King dropped the white cloth and the Silent leaped forward to the cheers of the crowd. His feet pounded the dry ground as he gained momentum, keeping his gaze focused on the edge of the cliff across the lake, as if he wanted to fly. Looking down would orient his jump along a descending arc and he would not reach the deep waters of the lake. Fixing his gaze on a flock of geese passing by, he quickly pumped his arms and legs and leaped—gliding for a second—then flipped and dove headlong into the icy lake below.

The water slapped him like a giant fist, and the cold whip nearly sent him into shock. He let the momentum of his dive carry him as far down as possible, and then transitioned to a vigorous swim that led him straight ahead to the mouth of the underwater grotto. His lungs began to burn and he felt his head ready to explode. Looking up, he saw the circular hole leading to the upper level and kicked his legs hard until he slid effortlessly through the two-foot-wide hole. A few seconds later, he finally broke through the water, gasping. But the hot, smoky air nearly choked him. Coughing and sneezing, he looked around and saw that the rim of the small lake was on fire. Fumes billowed up and his eyes stung. The pool was getting hotter, and he wondered if he was going to drown in boiling water.

Soon, the members of the four other teams were treading water with him. Ahiram started to feel dizzy. The flames surrounding them were rising. The air was steadily growing hotter and heavier. Fumes rose from the fire and Hiyam felt as if her lungs were about to explode.

Ahiram looked at the ceiling and saw stalactites. They were huddled in a narrow space, but the leftmost pillar was slightly distant from the rest and it looked sturdy enough to hold a man's weight.

This would require others to cooperate. He winced at the idea, but their situation was precarious and precluded diplomatic negotiations.

"I need someone to hold me while I throw a dart," he yelled. Sharp streaks of pain ran through his lungs.

Immediately, the Quibanxian athletes drew near and offered to help. Ahiram saw Hiyam glaring at him. "I give you the word of a Silent that I will not leave anyone behind," he said. This mollified her, but neither she nor her teammates offered to help. *She is too proud*, he thought. Two men from Quibanxe treaded water side-by-side, and Ahiram climbed onto their shoulders.

He reached for his belt and took his crossbow, a looping dart, and one of the compressible, thin ropes that he carried with him. Thankfully, his belt was waterproof, for his crossbow's critical midsection was susceptible to long immersions in water. He cranked the crossbow, clipped the rope to the dart, and locked the dart in place. He aimed and was about to shoot, when Hiyam interrupted him.

"Are you crazy?" she shouted, "You can't possibly hope to tie this rope up there. You do not have enough leeway. The stalactites are too close to one another."

"Do you have a better idea?" answered Ahiram sharply.

"Can you kill each other later?" cut in one the Quibanxian supporting Ahiram. "We're drowning here!"

He focused, trying to compensate for the constant movement beneath his feet and pulled the trigger. The dart ripped through the air, the rope in tow. Ahiram lost his balance and fell backward into the water, but managed to keep his crossbow from also falling in. Ahiram saw his rope drop lazily next to him. He picked up the dart, climbed back up onto the men's shoulders and tried again; and again he missed but managed not to fall. He repeated his attempt another five times and was ready to give up, when on the seventh attempt, he heard a slight popping sound as the dart coiled around the stalactite forming a tight knot.

Everyone cheered, including Hiyam. Ahiram was stunned. He could have sworn the dart's trajectory had changed, as if an invisible hand was guiding it. *Is this another of Hiyam's tricks?* he wondered. *Probably not. I must be imagining things.*

"You can't climb on such a thin rope," objected Hiyam. "It will cut through your hands."

He gave her a cocky smile, the kind that said, "You are not a Silent." Before she could snap back, he unlocked the two hinges holding his crossbow together, folded it, and stowed it safely away in its pocket. Then he pulled out two steel handles, each with a hollow, thin compartment. He released a small latch, and the handle opened along its length. He inserted the rope inside the hollow compartment, snapped closed the handle, and locked the hinge back in place. Hiyam, who drew close, noticed a clamp protruding from each handle. Ahiram verified that the two handles slid freely along the rope. Then, grasping them firmly, he rose over the water with a few quick movements.

"Grip the handles," he instructed them. "Grip them hard, and they will clamp in place. Release and slide to move up," he explained. "Do one hand at a time. It's a bit awkward but works well. Once up there, release the handles and they will roll back down freely."

"Then what?" snapped Hiyam, resentful. "What will we do up there?"

Ahiram contained his mounting irritation and forced himself to respond calmly. "I will figure out something once I am up there." And without another word, he quickly climbed.

He reached the top without much difficulty and looked around him. The fire was at least fifteen feet wide; yet to survive, they would have to cross it. He looked farther into the large cave and saw another cluster of stalactites beyond the zone of fire. He clipped the two handles to his belt to free his hands, took an arrow dart, clipped the second rope, loaded it in his crossbow and aimed. He knew he had one, maybe two chances, because each failure would land the rope in the middle of the fire. The rope might resist the fire once but not twice. He pulled the trigger. The arrow slammed into a stalactite, shattering it. Fragments of rock fell to the ground in a cloud of dust. Quickly, he yanked the rope back, hoping to save it from the fire. Instead, he managed to land the dart and the top section of the rope in the flames. He yanked at the rope again, and it fell into the water. Ahiram reeled it up, reloaded his crossbow and focused, ignoring the tightening in his muscles and the strain on his injured shoulder. He fired. The rope zipped through his fingers, and this time, the dart sank into a second stalactite; it did not explode. He pulled on the rope and tied it to the stalactite he was hanging from, creating a bridge over the fire.

"I am crossing," he yelled. "When you see the rope yanked twice, start climbing. The fire is at least fifteen feet across. Tear pieces of cloth to protect your hands," he added. He unclipped the end of his long sleeves and unrolled the thick, leather band that protected his wrists, forming makeshift gloves which he used to grasp the rope. He then swung his legs and crossed them around the rope; it bent and swayed under his weight, but did not break.

Good, thought Ahiram. *I don't want to roast like a chicken.*

With one hand, he unclipped the handles from his belt and watched them slide down, then proceeded quickly forward. He could feel the heat on his back and his neck, but it was tolerable. Fortunately, the heels of his sturdy boots shielded his ankles and after a short while, he managed to reach the other end safely. He wondered how he would reach the ground, twenty feet below, without breaking his neck. Still holding the rope with his feet and hands, he arched his neck and looked around. He spotted a small platform protruding from the left side of the cave, five feet ahead and ten below. He hung by his arms, swayed his body to gain momentum and jumped. His clothes brushed against the wall and he landed on the platform, but lost his balance at the last moment and fell back. The reflexes he honed during years of training took over and he flipped, somersaulted and managed to land on his two feet.

The ground was hot, but bearable. He looked around him, wondering what lay ahead in the dark passage leading away from the cave. As he approached, a powerful, hot draft engulfed him, followed by a distant rumbling. Standing still, he waited. When nothing else happened he left the cave walking cautiously but rapidly to get ahead of the others. He knew Hiyam and her team would move swiftly. The commander assured him there would be no magical gimmicks, but could he trust the Baalites to refrain from magic in these dark caves?

He walked briskly inside a narrow corridor shaped like an elongated egg—clearly the handiwork of men when the mines were turned into a tourist site. The light from a series of small oil lamps, set twenty feet apart, seemed to mock him. It cast long shadows that swallowed the ceiling and hid the ground three feet away from him.

Odd, thought Ahiram. *Last time I came this way, the light was brighter. I wonder what the arbitrators are up to now?*

The arbitrators were probably roaming around silently, watching the participants. Suddenly, he realized the air and the ground were hotter. He felt the wall to his right. It was also hot. *It can't be the fire around the pool,* he thought. *I'm too far for that. Where's the source of heat then?*

He heard a gurgling sound rise from the ground. A geyser shot up several feet behind him. Steaming water hit the ceiling like a fist, splashing the passage with burning hot droplets. Ahiram jerked back. He knew the water was near the boiling point and would scald him severely.

He turned back wanting to warn the others, but could see no one. He forged ahead cautiously, watching for any bubbling sound. A few feet ahead, a second, more powerful geyser erupted. Ahiram waited for the path to clear before resuming his trek. He managed to get to the end of the track unharmed, even though several geysers jetted from the ground. He had avoided them thanks to their predictable gurgling.

He walked into a large cavern with a dome-shaped ceiling. A lake, at least one thousand feet wide, filled it. The walls of the caverns twinkled brightly, even though no source of light burned in the cave. The dwarfs, who used these burning stones in their mining operations, had gifted this batch to the Game. The water was bright blue, as a thousand shining stones floated on the surface inside glass cups. He stood on the sandy beach listening to the soft ripple of waves licking his boots, engrossed in the dazzling light show. The silent lake was linked by a siphon to the hidden lake outside and to the 121-foot-tall Falls of Wonderment located deep within the caves of meyroon. Reluctantly, Ahiram broke free from the enchantment and focused on the Game.

He went to the five small boats moored at shore by thick ropes and picked the smallest of them. Before pushing away, he tangled the ropes of the four remaining boats to slow down the other teams.

Rowing alone was a serious disadvantage, and he feared the incomparable rowers of the Quibanxian teams most.

After pushing the boat away from shore, he rowed vigorously and his shoulder started hurting again. It was not healing properly and Habael had been worried. "After the Games, you better rest for a week or two to let it heal, or else it may hamper you for the rest of your life." Ahiram had smiled.

My dear Habael, he thought as he pulled on the oars, *if I win these Games, I intend to rest for more than two weeks in the house of my father.* That thought gave him courage, and he rowed with more vigor. Halfway across the lake, he saw the team of Bahiya enter the cave, followed closely by the teams of Quibanxe. He noticed that the team of Baal was carrying a man. *Probably burned,* Ahiram thought. He could not restrain the feeling of satisfaction. A burned man meant one less pair of arms for rowing. He wanted to reprimand himself for thinking this way, but he simply could not. To avoid losing, he had to get to shore well before the other teams, so he rowed with renewed energy. Just as the boat skidded onto soft sand, he jumped out and glanced at the other teams. As expected, the Quibanxians had crossed over three-quarters of the lake, leaving him with a slim margin. Hiyam's team was right behind, and in the distance, the two other teams were moving in, rowing with vigor.

Ahiram ran to the wall and free-climbed the straight façade to reach a platform sixty feet high. From there, he had to jump and catch a rope dangling in midair through a shaft piercing the dome.

This shaft, known as the Pit of Thunder, started three thousand feet above in the Mine of Gold and ran downward in a straight line, ending as a large, gaping hole in the roof over the lake. The masks were hidden in the Hall of Statues, and the shaft was the quickest way there. The steep staircase led to fifty-six intermediate levels; therefore none of the contenders—not even Hiyam's team running up these stairs—could beat a fast climber up the shaft.

The rope was three thousand sixty feet long and hung from an iron pole high above. It dangled in the air sixty feet over the lake and fifteen feet from the platform that Ahiram wanted to reach. Contestants who failed to grab it fell into the lake, which was thankfully deep. The climb proved arduous, for the wall was humid and caused him to lose his grip a few times. As he reached the platform, he heard the muffled sound of boats sliding onto the sand. Ignoring his competitors, he leaned against the wall, forcing himself to rest and catch his breath. He could almost hear Commander Tanios' teaching: "No Silent shall begin an arduous climb without a proper squat leg wrap. During the climb, the Silent shall remain recollected and anchored to the rope, which he shall keep motionless as if he was a shadow gliding on a wall. Remember this technique, it may save your life."

I have one chance at this, he thought. *I cannot miss. Once I grab that rope, I'll have to climb at a steady pace to stay ahead of them.*

The rules required a slower contender to step aside onto one of the resting slabs jutting from the circular wall, but impatient and faster climbers never waited for a sluggish competitor to reach the wedge of stone and would simply climb over him. Sometimes, the unfortunate player fell, taking others with him.

Ahiram focused with the intensity that was second nature to a Silent. He ran hard and jumped, grabbing the rope with both hands. It swayed under his weight. Pain exploded from his wounded shoulder. A moan slipped through his tight lips, and he released his left arm to ease the throbbing a little. Once the rope settled, he managed to grip it with both arms and legs. He quickly rubbed his shoulder with some of the pungent ointment Habael had given him, dulling the pain to a bearable level. He looked down and saw the quiet surface of the lake calling to him, urging him to let go, to allow himself to fall into the cold embrace of the water and be carried away. He looked up and could barely see the top of the Pit. Resolutely, Ahiram started the arduous climb.

Initially, the dwarfs had used the Pit to move provender down, and precious metal up. They had found a small crack through which water seeped, and they dug into the rock with the determination of termites until it became this gigantic pit, wide enough for a vertical cableway used to hoist miners and goods up and down with relative ease. After the miners left, the cableway fell into desuetude and was altogether removed when the Games were introduced.

To the athletes in the Game, it was a singular challenge requiring strength, stamina, and a focused mind. They had to manage their speed and the time they took to rest on the slabs located every three hundred feet. Once out of the Pit, they had to sprint to the Hall of Statues to locate a mask of gold. Therefore, they could not afford to reach the top exhausted. Ahiram knew that many athletes were climbing the rope below him. He wondered if the rope could hold all the contenders without breaking.

Feverishly, he went on, forcing himself to rest as needed. He was one hundred and fifty feet high in the Pit, and twelve climbers had come after him already. *This is it*, he thought. *By now, every athlete still in the Games must be climbing.* He looked up and saw a bright, white spot far away, and felt like a snail inching his way on a dandelion's stem. Why he thought of a dandelion, he did not know, but the image popped in his head when suddenly he saw the face of a young boy before him—a face he had seen before, six years ago. The young boy looked concerned.

"He found you. To defeat him, you will need El-Windiir's sword."

Ahiram was slowly becoming incensed by these impromptu visions of people he had never met, who blurted mysterious sayings about swords needed to defeat a creature whom he had never seen—without bothering to introduce themselves, or explaining how they knew him in the first place—or why they thought he was connected to all of this. He wished he could sit with the young boy around a warm plate of chicken. He even felt like asking the mysterious, young man if he liked chicken, but then the image of Jedarc popped in his head. *Now, that's too much, even for me.* Ahiram breathed deeply and shook his head, trying to regain a semblance of control.

"Who are you? Who found me? What is all this about?"

"No time for questions now," replied the young boy. "Find the sword, you *must* find the sword."

The boy's image disappeared. Just then, he heard a strong rumbling from the lake beneath. Ahiram froze. He did not recall the arbitrators saying anything about a rumbling. *Better move,* he thought. He gripped the rope and climbed as quickly as prudence allowed. The next few minutes were soundless—except for the quick shuffle of his hands and feet on the rough rope—and just when he began to wonder if he had imagined it, the rumbling was back, and it was now louder. Ahiram felt a knot in his stomach. He was no longer climbing to win; he was climbing for his life. He reached the first slab and took a forced rest to ease the pain in his shoulder when a thunderous explosion filled the pit. *The Pit of Thunder,* he thought as he started climbing again.

Then it happened. He heard the screams of the players down below, which were silenced abruptly right when a powerful surge of water reached him. For a split second he lost his grip on the rope as the water slammed him against the wall. *A geyser?* He thought, stunned. *I did not know there were geysers in the lake.* The mass of liquid passed him by, continued its ascension for a little longer, slowed down and stopped. It then fell on him with a powerful rush. He gripped the rope and gritted his teeth and waited for the water to recede. Once in the clear, he resumed his ascent, hoping that all the players had survived the ordeal.

The rope was soaked now, making his grip precarious. He inched his way up, knowing that if there were still others below, they were doing the same. The rumbling started again. This infuriated him and boosted his strength. He moved up the rope, determined to get out of the next geyser's reach, but he heard the thunderclap, and screams from below told him the water was coming. He gripped the rope tighter and the water hit him like a furious bull. This geyser was more powerful, toying with him like a child toys with a doll. It flung him against the wall, and he lost all sense of direction. The returning water pounded his shoulders, renewing his pain.

After a short moment of rest, he resumed his climb, his grip slipping now and then. Halfway to the next ledge, he heard a third rumbling.

Hold it. The water is cold. A geyser needs heat, he thought, *This is not natural.* Then it struck him. *Magic. This must be magical. Does the high priestess want me dead so badly that she is willing to risk her daughter's life? Then again, this boy—whoever he is—told me "He found you." If he meant the priestess, he would have said she. But if it is not the priestess, then who is after me and why?*

The geyser shot up, exploding like a booming thunder. The rushing water swallowed the screams of pain from below. Frantic, Ahiram climbed the rope, bracing for the incoming jet, but it only managed to lick the heels of his boots. Encouraged, he moved quickly up the rope, which was now dry, and reached the next ledge, where he rested.

I have two thousand four hundred feet to go, he thought, looking up and wondering what insanity pushed the dwarfs to dig this bottomless hole. *One has to be driven mad by gold to be willing to dig so deep,* he thought. He resumed his climb just when the thunderclap resonated through the Pit. He glanced down and saw the water rushing toward him faster than an arrow. He stopped climbing, brought up his knees, and when the geyser reached him, he let it carry him, loosely holding the rope, then gripping it fiercely when the turbulent waters threatened to slam him into the walls.

At last, the water receded. Ahiram again tightened his grip on the rope and was amazed to see how far he had traveled. *I must be two-thirds of the way up.* He climbed another hundred feet to the next ledge.

Feeling confident, he let out a shout: "Let Baal bring forth this geyser again. I will show them the strength of the Silent."

"It is I, not Baal, who is moving the waters. Know this, slave: if it were not for me, you would be dead by now."

The Urkuun. Ahiram nearly lost his grip. The raspy voice had sounded near and far in his ear, strong and weak, the way a voice form the past would sound in his memory.

"What do you want from me?" He stammered.

"My quarrel is not with you at this moment, but with the assassins the Temple has dispatched to kill you."

"*You* are helping me?"

The laughter, or whatever that screechy, high-pitched sound was, hit him like a fist. He felt weak.

"You are far more valuable alive than dead. I will teach you all that you need to learn and you will serve me in this age and the age to come."

Abruptly, the imperious voice—and the threatening presence— vanished. Ahiram sighed. *I am not looking forward to meeting this being,* he thought, *But first, I need to get out of here.*

A scream of rage chilled the air. Ahiram fought to control his fear. A deafening explosion filled the Pit, and judging from the strength of the tremors shaking the walls, he knew this was the strongest geyser yet. Driven by instinct, he began to climb, fearing once more for his life. *This is far more powerful than anything I've seen,* he thought. *It's as if the lake is rushing up the Pit.*

He looked down and saw the water moving with a fury he could not have imagined. *It's too strong,* he thought. *I won't be able to ride this wave,* but he continued his frantic climb.

Two blinding bolts of light appeared out of thin air and hit the incoming water before it reached him. The bolts slithered down the raging mass, breaking its momentum. The surge slowed down and crested ten feet below, having lost its strength and deadly purpose. A gargling moan bubbled through its surface as it receded.

What was that? he thought, breathless. *Where did this come from? What does it mean?*

Not waiting to find out, he resumed his climb. After what seemed like an eternity, he finally reached the top. He crawled out, moved away from the Pit, and lay breathless on his back. He waited for his breathing to return to normal and for the waves of pain to recede before sitting up and opening his kit. Fortunately, the contents of his belt were still dry. He took a vial containing two murky liquids, one yellow and the other brown. Ahiram shook the vial vigorously before quickly opening it and gulping down its contents.

"And this is *assin*," Master Habael had told him. "It is a Togofalkian mixture of *usmask* and *timrand*: two potent herbs that grow deep in the forest. Use it to regain strength."

Ahiram felt as if fire surged through his aching muscles. He followed Habael's advice and fought the urge to throw up, then in order to help the medicine course through his weary body, he got up and paced until the pain receded.

"Start walking slowly after the pain recedes, and soon you will feel much better," Habael had advised him, "because by walking, you help the medicine move quickly through your body."

Ahiram heard the rumble one more time and turned back to look. Should he stop and help those who were still below? But how could he? He could not hope to pull all the climbers out of the Pit.

The arbitrators, he thought. *They must be in the Hall of Statues. I must warn them.*

Hiyam clutched the wet rope and braced herself for the next geyser. She had already lost one of her men in the rush of water, and the two below her were moaning in pain. She was exhausted and involuntarily did what she always did when faced with extreme danger: she receded into her mind, to a place of safety. As unlikely as it may seem, the gurgling sound of the receding geyser reminded her of the water font which graced the inner courtyard of the temple where she played when she was little. The fount would bubble and water ebbed gracefully, like a crown of pearls in the blue sky. She remembered vividly the day when she fell into the fountain and nearly drowned. Her mother had pulled her out and scolded her. The salty taste of her tears—now running down her cheeks—brought her back to the present.

Irritated with her momentary weakness, she pushed the memory away, wiped her tears, and regained her focus. The rumble started again, and she was barely able to contain her tears. She was frightened; none of her magical incantations were working. She felt powerless, as if someone was toying with her and she was incapable of stopping it. At that moment, Hiyam finally understood what it meant to be a slave. *If I survive this*, she thought fiercely, *I will never own a slave for as long as I live.* Gingerly, she began to climb, relying on the strength of her arms and legs to move her upward.

The water pummeled her back with mighty blows. She whirled uncontrollably round and round and bounced into the walls of the Pit, nearly suffocating under the flow. She closed her eyes, and using the magical lore she had learned from the Temple, she tried one more time to reach her mother, but without success. She opened her eyes and looked around her. Her last two men were still holding on. Suddenly, the image of her mother crystallized in her mind. "Hold on, I am intervening." Her mother gave her a reassuring smile and Hiyam burst into tears, surprised and confused by the love shining in Bahiya's eyes.

The rumbling started again. Hiyam opened her mouth to scream, but could not. Down below, a dark storm tore the lake. Lightning pounded the cave and thunder boomed repeatedly. The water churned so fast that it became a blur until suddenly, it disappeared from view and she saw the ragged bottom of the lake far below. Then, a terrifying tornado assaulted the Pit, tearing her and her companions from the rope, slamming them against the walls—nearly breaking her back—and lifting her at breakneck speed. She lost all sense of direction and thought she was about to die when she saw two lightning bolts zap through the water, breaking the tornado's power. Suddenly, Hiyam found herself underwater in a quiet pool. Swimming briskly, she broke through the surface and frantically reached for the rope. Slowly, the water receded below her. Up ahead, the Quibanxians were gingerly climbing, but she dared not look down for fear of seeing no one. Instead, she resumed climbing, pulling herself up the rope, holding back tears.

At last, Hiyam reached the top and with the help of the Quibanxian, she crawled on all fours and lay shivering from exhaustion. Waves of nausea washed over her and she retched. As the last member of the Togofalkian team came out of the Pit, they heard another strong rumble. Fear brought them to their feet and they backed away, half-expecting a sudden gush of water to surge from the Pit and pummel the roof; but instead, the ground shook violently. "An earthquake," yelled someone. A chunk of earth fell from the ceiling and crashed mere inches from Hiyam, who fell down. As she rolled over, she felt as if the power lurking below had lashed vengefully at them one last time.

>✿✿✿<

Ahiram had been staring at the statue of a dragon when the earthquake struck. He was in the chamber of Tanniin, otherwise known as the Hall of Masks. This chamber was a circular cave hewn into the rock and contained three circles of thirty-three gold statues each. The outer circle honored Tanniin, who, according to ancient lore, belonged to the outer ring and possessed only three pairs of wings. The middle circle honored his ancestor, Lamatanniin, who lived during the Wars of Riharon and served the Masters of the Dark. Lamatanniin belonged to the second ring and had five pairs of wings. The innermost circle honored Lamatanniin's ancestor, the greatest of all dragons, Tanniin Ashod, known as "Daron Ashod" among the dwarfs, and as "Black Dragon" by the Empyreans. With nine pairs of wings, the mighty Tanniin Ashod was without compare in all the kingdoms–except for Baal. Tanniin rebelled against the Masters of the Dark and helped El-Windiir resist them. The people of the kingdom revered him as the god of light.

Originally, there were 101 statues in this hall that, according to popular belief, had been protected by powerful spells. Anyone who attempted to steal them would be plagued by terrible curses, die a horrible death, and suffer the eternal pains of hell. So strong was this belief, that even if these statues were exposed in the lowliest parts of town, no one would dare touch them. But in the center of the innermost circle, two pedestals were missing their statues. In the common lore of Tanniin, Sureï, the great sorcerer, fell in love with the two innermost statues, and waving his hands, broke the curse and took them with him to Babylon where he hid them. Thus, the empty pedestals became a stubborn reminder of Baal's oppression. Despite the Temple's repeated attempts to clear Sureï's name, this belief perdured, for the people reasoned, who, but Sureï, had the wherewithal to break powerful spells such as these?

The statues were of pure, white gold with rose gold masks on their faces. This made them the perfect hiding place for the golden masks that the participants had to retrieve. The arbitrators would layer the fake masks on a statue's face, and the teams would have to find and remove them; all this, without falling under the curse by inadvertently touching the statues.

Standing in the innermost circle, Ahiram was scrutinizing the face of one of the statues, carefully examining the double rim along the edge of its mask. *That's the only statue with a double rim,* he thought. *This is it. The top rim is the edge of the arbitrators' mask, and the bottom one is the edge of the original mask, the one that's cursed.*

He climbed onto the pedestal and was about to touch the mask when the earthquake occurred. Ahiram lost his balance and fell back, barely managing to shift his weight to avoid hurting his shoulder. All around him, the statues shook as though suddenly endowed with inner life. Whichever way he looked, statues were moving. It was as though Tanniin was coming back to life. The statue with the double gold rim he was looking at had moved past the pedestal's edge, when suddenly, the earthquake stopped as abruptly as it had begun.

Slowly, Ahiram moved back, then got up, surveyed the damage, and was amazed that all ninety-nine statues were still standing. A glimmering object on the ground attracted his gaze. He drew closer and smiled: it was a golden mask that undoubtedly had fallen from the statue during the earthquake. Ahiram scrutinized it carefully, looking for the judge's stamp, a circle containing four small squares. He breathed a sigh of relief—seeing it on the lower, left corner—and picked it up quickly. He looked at the statue of Tanniin watching him from its pedestal above and saw an identical mask over its eyes.

How clever of the arbitrators to hide the two masks on the same statue, he thought. He suddenly froze: had he touched the other statue, he would have fallen under the curse. He shuddered at the thought and was glad the earthquake had happened. Ahiram slid the mask inside his leather bag, adding it to the shoes of bronze and the wings of silver, then took off running. The exit was thirty miles away.

Hiyam and her team must have recovered, and they are coming after me, he thought. *There is no time to waste.*

12. Two Drops of Blood

"Priests of Baal who read these, my words, consider that Alissaar's curses never harmed innocent passersby. Reflect on their stability and longevity through the centuries, and you will realize the debt of gratitude we owe Alissaar. His curses are the pillars sustaining civilization. His curses are our high wall against the madness of the Pit.

"Alone, this founding father of our order continues to protect us long after he is gone. He is the arch-model of the High Priest."
—Teachings of Oreg, High Priest of Baal

"Baal banished Tanniin to the outer realm by thrice pouring blood upon him, once for each pair of wings. Only blood poured out twice, and twice again, can bring him back."
—Book of Siril, 22nd Apocryphal Act, verses 4-5

Commander Tanios watched Ahiram dive into the cold water of the Lake of Hiding before heading back to Taniir-The-Strong. Tanios breathed deeply as he walked, trying to ease the knot of apprehension gripping him. He chaffed angrily at "the boy's stubbornness." But when his anger failed to hide his fears, he tried to distance himself from the Games. He reasoned that he had advised Ahiram against participating in the Games.

What else could I do? he thought. He reminded himself that Ahiram was at the peak of his abilities. *He should survive...* he repeated several times until his anxiety subsided. As he walked toward the castle, he glanced absentmindedly at the snow-covered peaks of the eastern Tangorian Chain, glittering in the haze of the morning heat. They reminded him of the icy-cold lake where he had seen Ahiram plunge. His fear returned stronger than before, and the lack of a solid lead to apprehend the murderer killing the athletes made matters worse. Royal Road was empty. He glanced at the tall oak trees lining it. The King, at the insistence of the commander, had decreed that destroying one of these trees was a criminal offense, punishable by flogging. During one of Ahiram's proverbial bouts of anger, he had broken several branches from the trees and smashed them in the middle of the road, making a spectacle of himself. The decree had helped the young man find other, more discrete ways to vent his frustration and anger.

Tanios walked through the main gate and paid no attention to the guard's salute. He was relieved when a servant told him that Master Habael was waiting for him in the third training area of the Silent Corps.

"Master Habael? Why meet here when Training Area 1 is open?" he asked as soon as he entered the room.

Area 1, was the Silent's largest training hall, designed for martial arts, hand-to-hand combat, acrobatics, stealth tactics, and endurance. Area 2, was reserved for dart training, and Area 3, the smallest training hall, was filled with dangling cordage, wooden, hollow circles, and pulleys used for all sorts of acrobatics, staff combat, and dart shooting.

"I chose Area 3, because it is windowless, Commander Tanios," replied the old man, a glint in his eyes. "There is a map I wish to show you," he added, turning his gaze to a sheet of parchment laying on a table next to a simmering teapot.

"I don't recall seeing this table here before," said the commander suspiciously, "and since there is no stove here, how did you get this pot to simmer?"

"I assure you, Commander, this table is perfectly innocent; I brought it from storage," chuckled Habael, pointing with his chin to a door, "and this teapot was specially designed by the dwarfs for me. It has a double hull with a metallic coil encased between them. When heated, it keeps the tea simmering for much longer than an ordinary teapot. Now, judging by your question about the teapot and the tea, I would say you are worried, are you not?"

"Hot," said Tanios, "boiling hot." He set down his cup on the table. "I will breathe better once the Game of Gold has ended and Ahiram comes out alive."

"Would you like me to pour cold water into your tea?" asked Master Habael. "I can have a jar of fresh water brought here."

Tanios glared at the old man as if he had asked him to eat stale fish.

Habael laughed. "Now, now, Commander Tanios, you do not have to growl at me so; even the King likes a little cold water in his hot tea."

"I am not of kingly stock, my dear Habael; I enjoy my tea piping hot. Why do you not leave my tea alone and tell me what you have found, old friend?"

"I have gone over the poem," said Habael, drawing closer to the table, "and I think it may hold a clue to these murders."

Tanios was gently blowing on his tea, and his head jerked up when he heard his friend's reply. "This is surprising. Please, Master Habael, do explain."

"Glad to oblige," said Habael, smiling. "Please listen to this excerpt from the poem:

> *Yet, he silently awaits the day of his strength,*
> *When freedom shall be his at length.*
> *He must, to heal his woes,*
> *Deal Baal four blows,*
> *Four sons, four lives.*

By stealth and silver knives
Sprinkle the four corners of the seal,
Break the curse, end his ordeal,
Reveal what was hidden within
At the mighty surging of Tanniin."

The commander winced, berating his impatience, for the hot tea had burned his tongue. "Too hot," he growled. "Blasted teapot."

"What was that?" asked Master Habael innocently.

"What do you make of it, Master Habael?" replied Tanios hastily. "I mean, this bit of the poem. What do you make of it? You know I do not deal well with metaphors. For instance, how can a seal have corners? King Jamiir's seal produces a round, red smudge of wax. It has no corners. But supposing it did, what would it mean?"

"Perhaps," suggested Habael, "the word 'seal' does not refer, in this case, to the signet that produced it. Instead, it may point to the extent of the power behind it." Seeing a confused expression on the commander's face, Habael raised his hand in a gesture of patience and explained further.

"For instance, if the King's deputy wishes to shut down a tavern, he seals the door with a bit of wax and the King's signet, yes?" The commander nodded. "The King's deputy does not need to apply a second seal on the back door of the tavern; once the citizens of Taniir-The-Strong realize that the front door has been sealed, they know not to walk through the back door. Thus, the power of the seal covers the entire structure."

"If I follow this line of reasoning," the commander argued, "four drops of blood translate to four corners. You are telling me that the locations of the murders mark the corners of a room. Is that it?"

Master Habael nodded. "It is a bit farfetched," mused the commander, "but who am I to judge poetry? All right, I can work with this. Tell me, Master Habael, what is in that chamber? How would dropping blood on the corners free Tanniin from Baal? You do not believe this will cause the forces of Baal to withdraw suddenly from the empire, now, do you?"

"Your skepticism is well-founded, Commander, if in fact, this was a political move."

"Whatever it is, Master Habael, eventually, it will involve sweat, blood, and the clatter of weapons."

"I may be able to offer an answer, Commander, but first, let us look at the map, shall we?" invited Habael.

Tanios eyed his friend and smiled ruefully. "Sometimes, I wonder who the real king in this place is," he said, as he drew closer to the table. Carefully, he placed down his cup of tea, then grasped the edge of the table with his hands and leaned forward, his powerful frame overshadowing the map.

"So, there are four drops of blood and four corners," he muttered. "I had assumed that the precise location of the murders to be irrelevant, but if the murderer killed these men of Baal simply because they happened to be in the right location, well, this changes everything."

"Exactly," replied the old man. "Exactly."

"Thus far, we have two 'drops,' if we may call the victims so. One drop occurred in the storage room on the first floor, and the second, in the Queen's Ballroom on the third floor. Since these 'drops' are happening on different levels of the castle, then the height of the drops relative to the corners of the room should not matter, is that not so?"

"I would think not," said Habael. "What matters is to perform these crimes as close as possible to the corners of the room."

The commander peered at the parchment and visualized the castle in his mind. "There is no room in the castle whose corners match these locations."

"Indeed, the room in question must be beneath the castle."

Tanios nodded approvingly. "So someone is committing these crimes to free Tanniin from Baal. Since the Temple has been tightening its noose around the kingdom, it would stand to reason that a desperate soul in Tanniin has decided to put faith into these old stories and murder two men in cold blood."

The men exchanged a silent gaze in which they both realized they were thinking the same thing: *could the King have killed these men?*

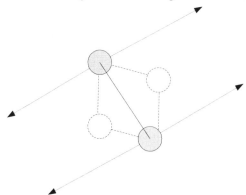

Tanios looked at the map once more, and penciled a shaded circle around the location of the two murders. He traced a line joining them. "If the two locations are two corners of a rectangle, then either they are adjacent, or diagonally opposed. In the first case, we do not know where the two other murders will take place, for we have no idea of the length of the other side of the rectangle." He drew two dotted arrows pointing in opposite directions.

"Still, we know that the two other murders will take place either left or right of the line joining these circles, and inside the band delimited by the four arrows. Master Habael, how big is this room of yours?"

"Difficult to say, Commander. If it is a secret chamber, then it would be relatively small. If, on the other hand, it is a secret temple, then it would be sizeable indeed."

The commander shrugged his shoulders and grunted in approval. "If these two circles are diagonally opposed, then our task becomes easier, for we would know where the two other murders would take place." As he said this, he drew two other hollow circles and joined the four together into a diamond. "They would take place at these two locations."

"Presuming, of course," added Master Habael, "that the corners of this room are at right angles."

"A safe assumption, Master Habael, since this is the case in every rectangular room of the royal castle."

Master Habael nodded. He peered at the map. "Is it to scale?"

"It is a good rendition of the castle," explained Commander Tanios, "enough to know where everything is in relationship to everything else, but I do not believe it was drawn to scale."

"Then how can we be sure that the corners of the squares are where they are supposed to be?"

"We cannot be sure, so I am not taking chances. The Silent will be keeping a tight surveillance on all three levels."

"Commander Tanios, why do you think El-Windiir III abandoned Taniir-On-High and built the castle of Taniir-the-Strong?"

"Huh?" asked the commander, confused. "How is that relevant?"

"Call it a hunch."

"As far as I know, he thought Taniir-On-High was under a curse, but I have never been able to find out the real reason."

"If the locations of these murders delineate a secret chamber, then the story of this castle, Taniir-The-Strong, might contain important clues, wouldn't you say?"

The commander gulped down his tea and served himself a second cup. "Excellent tea, Master Habael," said the commander after a few sips. "Clues you say? Hmm... that is a possibility. The King's knowledge on this subject would surprise you."

"Forgive me for being so bold, Commander, but I believe Her Majesty the Queen may know more about this than His Majesty."

"The Queen?"

"Yes. She has taken a great interest in the history of these legendary castles and has often questioned me about their history. I would not be surprised in the least if during one of her customary walks up the mountain, she even managed to reach Taniir-On-High."

"Indeed, my dear Habael, I would not be surprised either. Her Majesty likes trekking up the mountain; the women among my Silent are keenly aware of this. They have told Her Majesty that she should join the Silent Corps, for no one can climb this mountain like she." Tanios paused for a moment before continuing. "Do you think we should bother Her Majesty with this case?"

"I am certain that Her Majesty would like this mystery solved as soon as possible," replied Habael.

"Then we will go and see if we can have an audience."

They left the Silent's quarters and walked toward the Lone Tower.

"Let us first stop by the Silent's common area. I need to give a few instructions."

The two men crossed the Lone Tower and walked into the Silent's area through the door adjoining the commander's quarters. Banimelek stepped out of his room just as they walked in.

"Banimelek," said the commander, "please call the Silent. We have much to do and very little time."

"Certainly," replied the young man. He closed his door, which quietly reopened as soon as he let go of the handle.

"Still not fixed, I see," said the commander, who stood several feet away. Banimelek was startled; Tanios did not see him close the door. "I do not need to look, Banimelek," he growled. "I can tell from the sound of your footsteps that you stopped and turned around. Get this handle fixed today."

"Yes, sir," said the young man.

He knew the commander was a stickler for order. Using a whistle, he sent out three shrill calls. Immediately, the thirty-four Silent came into the common area and stood at attention, forming seven teams. The last one to make it was Jedarc, who was still buckling his belt.

The commander ordered two teams to patrol the second and third floors of the castle, when a new recruit interrupted.

"Sir," asked Sheheluth, "what are we looking for?"

The Silent stood rigid, wondering how their commander would handle the interruption. Silent were supposed to be just that—silent—unless afforded an occasion to speak. This was a grave breach of their code, but Sheheluth thought the gravity of the hour justified a few questions.

"It's a loose chicken," blurted Jedarc. "It escaped the kitchen, and it's threatening the safety of the castle. No telling what it can do, you know."

The Silent were stunned by Jedarc's glib remark. The commander's eyes bore into the young man, who smiled innocently. "Isn't it so, Commander?" he asked.

"Two murders have been committed," replied Tanios calmly. The Silent held their breath, waiting for the punishment that was sure to come. "We have reason to believe two more will take place in short order," he added. "I want to prevent these crimes. You will protect the team of Baal and apprehend anyone walking in the castle unescorted by our soldiers or by the Silent. Is that understood?"

As he said this, the Commander gazed intently at Sheheluth.

"Yes, sir," she replied quickly.

"Permission to speak, sir," said Roman, a tall, third-year Silent.

"Permission granted."

"Thank you, sir. Question, sir. Does this command extend to the judges, the guests of honor, and the priestess of Baal?"

"Yes, Roman. Very good question. To everyone without exception, and most especially, the priestess. Her murder would amount to a declaration of war. It would be the end of Tanniin as we know it."

"Yes, sir," said Roman. "Thank you, sir."

"Sheheluth?" The commander's voice was even and steady.

"Yes, sir?" The ebony-skinned young woman was lithe and slim, with wide brown eyes and a smile to light the night. She waited expectantly, hoping her natural charm and youth would excuse her behavior.

"After you finish your shift watching that corridor, you will go down to the kitchen and offer your services to Leifa. The cooks have begun their preparation for the end of Games celebration. Usually, forty or fifty chickens are plucked for this event. You will tell her I want you to pluck the whole pile by yourself, and you will not go back to your room until this chore is complete. Is that understood?"

Sheheluth's shoulders slumped. She lowered her gaze, swallowed hard, and whispered "Yes, sir."

"What was that?" asked the commander, his voice rising slightly.

The young woman stood to attention. "Yes, sir!" she replied.

The commander nodded. He did not have to glance at Jedarc to know the young man was already regretting his bit of humor.

Tanios directed three more groups to patrol the first level and added, "Jedarc, Banimelek, you've got your orders. The rest of the Silent will remain here on stand-by. Any questions?"

There were none. The commander gave a quick bow and all of the Silent responded with a deep bow. He walked out with Master Habael, who noticed that Banimelek's door was ajar. He closed it discreetly as they stepped outside the Silent's quarters and back into the main corridor of the castle's second level.

"You need not protect them, Master Habael. It is their duty to protect this castle."

"Indeed," replied Master Habael, "but I do wonder, commander, how will Sheheluth protect the royal castle by plucking thirty chickens. They can't be too dangerous now, can they?"

The commander glanced at his friend as they walked by the Lone Tower. "I am beginning to wonder if assigning Jedarc to your protection is a good idea. You are acquiring his sense of humor." The old man chuckled. "Sheheluth's hands, wrists and arms are still weak. In their present condition she can hardly parry with the staff or put enough power into a dart to hurt anyone fifty feet away. This will provide an excellent training for her."

"Plucking chickens, you mean?" asked Master Habael.

The commander did not answer. Instead, he walked briskly to the large window at the right of the Officer's Tower and leaned down to examine the marble floor. Master Habael joined him.

"What is it, Commander?" he asked.

The commander stood up muttering unintelligible words. "Look," he said indignantly, "look at the floor."

Habael peered at the floor and only noticed some dirt by the window. "You mean, the bit of dirt?"

"The *bit* of dirt? The *bit* of dirt? It is dirt on the marble floor, and it is a breach of protocol. I shall have a word with the head slaves, they are responsible to keep this floor impeccably clean with no *bit* of dirt *anywhere*. If they cannot keep their slaves in check, I shall have both of them flogged."

"It must be serious then," said Master Habael.

"If I cannot trust the slaves, servants, soldiers, and Silent to do what is required—whether small or great—how can I be certain of the King's safety?" asked Tanios pointedly. "Cleaning is not just about cleaning—it is about security. A slave who cleans this area regularly can tell immediately when something is out of place. I count on them to keep the Silent and myself informed of any change, however subtle, however insignificant. This smudge on the floor should not be here, and I was not alerted."

Master Habael eyed the commander and refrained from any comment. After all, he was not in charge of the King's security.

Tanios sighed. "Let us be on our way. I shall deal with this after we have spoken to the Queen." Their steps echoed in the vast hall while a shadow—barely visible—moved with unnatural speed toward the Lone Tower. Shortly after, Banimelek and Jedarc came walking with Zumbra, Alviad, and Sheheluth.

"Don't worry, Your Highness," said Sheheluth, addressing Jedarc, "I don't mind plucking chickens."

"Will you stop giving me the 'Highness' thing? You should call me Jedarc, and that's all."

"But I thought you were a real prince," interjected Zumbra, who like Sheheluth, was in his first year of training as a Silent.

"We call him such," growled Alviad, "because his pinkish sensitive hands have never plucked a chicken before."

Jedarc sighed. "Don't listen to Alviad," he told the two novices. "He is as strong as an ox, but slower than a petrified slug."

Alviad shrugged his shoulders. "Just because you can run with the wind does not mean I'm slow," he muttered.

"Cut it out you two," snapped Banimelek. "Jedarc, I cannot believe it. Haven't you learned your lesson yet? What will it take before you learn that you cannot deflect a well-deserved punishment?"

"That's true," said Alviad, grinning. "I had nearly forgotten the bunch of coriander in the second training room."

"Why? What happened?" asked Zumbra.

"Don't listen to them," Jedarc cut in. "They exaggerate everything."

"Really?" asked Banimelek mockingly. "Let me see... who was it now? Was it you, Alviad, or was it Parito?"

"No," Alviad corrected. "Silvanly. Parito was sick that day."

"That's right," confirmed Banimelek, "Silvanly was in his first year, like the two of you, and we were in our third. Silvanly had promised Master Habael a bunch of coriander from the garden. He's always been interested in all things botanical."

"Yes, so he had gone out," continued Alviad, "to the garden and stared at some plant—I don't recall now what it was. He was so engrossed by what he was seeing that he lost track of time, so when he heard the whistle calling for our morning meeting, he panicked and ran up to the second floor with the coriander bunch and nearly collided with the commander."

"So, he stood there," Banimelek added, "like a young man with a bouquet of flowers. He stood there," stuttered Banimelek, who was trying hard not to laugh, "like a frozen statue before the commander and then he said—"

" 'I surrender,' " guffawed Alviad, his massive frame shaking under the strain. " 'I surrender,' he said."

Jedarc, who had been sulking, joined in, "Yeah, that was funny."

"Then Jedarc walked in—" continued Alviad.

"Late as usual," slipped in Banimelek

"...he looked at the scene and said with a straight face, 'Commander Tanios, what a great idea. Chicken stuffed with coriander and cheese is delicious. When do we eat?' "

Sheheluth and Zumbra gasped.

"What happened next?" asked Zumbra.

"Well, Silvanly had to learn to pluck coriander one stem at a time, with a dart, and Jedarc was assigned to kitchen duty for three months."

"That was not funny," grumbled Jedarc, involuntarily rubbing his stomach. "Working in the kitchen when you're allowed to eat only dried meat, bread, and steamed vegetables is tough."

They had reached the bottom of the stairs.

"Don't fret, Sheheluth," said Banimelek gently, "every Silent gets kitchen duty at one point or another. We all get punished for these trifles. But the commander usually assigns punishments to help us grow strong. You'll see. You'll thank him for this assignment later." Having said that, Jedarc and Banimelek took leave from their companions.

"Sheheluth," Alviad explained, "you run with the first shift until the second afternoon gong, and I'll be your backup. Before supper, Zumbra will take over so you can go to the kitchen."

"But then you will have to be his backup," protested Sheheluth.

"Don't worry," said Alviad, raising his large hand. "I'm used to it. Then I'll cover the night shift, and you will be my backup."

"Why are we here?" asked Zumbra, "What are we looking for?"

"This is nothing you haven't done before," reassured Alviad, smiling. He pushed the heavy, curly locks from his face, but they stubbornly fell back in place, forming a thick curtain over his forehead partially hiding his eyes. "You stalk the corridor the way you've been trained to do: silently and invisibly. If you see or hear anything suspect, you alert your backup. Chances are nothing will happen, and it will be yet another boring day. Any questions?"

"Alviad," said Sheheluth timidly. "Banimelek said everyone has to do kitchen duties, so did Ahiram do kitchen duties?"

"Ahiram? Are you kidding? He practically lived in the kitchen. He's got a temper of a locked-up dragon and got punished more than the rest of us combined."

Hearing this, Sheheluth's spirits lifted, and she straightened her posture.

"Don't worry, Sheheluth," said Zumbra, "you'll do just fine."

"Zumbra, go get some rest while you can, and Sheheluth, I'll be practicing in the empty dining area over there. If you see or hear anything suspicious, come get me at once."

Moments later, a soldiers' patrol walked into the corridor and passed noisily by a stone pedestal holding a large, marble flower pot. The soldiers saw three slim dragons holding the pedestal and failed to realize there was one too many. Sheheluth smiled beneath her cloak. *It's true,* she thought, proudly, *We Silent can be undetectable if we choose to be.* Then she thought of the crimes of the past two days and shuddered. *We're not the only ones who can be invisible; the murderer may be in the castle, may even be in this corridor, unseen.*

13. DEEPENING MYSTERY

"Taniir-The-Strong lives in the shadow of Taniir-On-High, like a man living in the shadow of his mother-in-law. She may not speak much, nor complain, but he knows she's always watching him. Unless you know she's there and you know what she's up to, you'll misunderstand why the man acts and behaves the way he does. Study, study, I say! Castles have their mysteries, but in the end, it's all about a man and his mother-in-law."

—Soliloquy of Zuzu the Hip, Jester of the Royal Court of Tanniin

"Taniir-The-Strong is the visible part of a castle hewn out of the mountain's heart. Its visible walls are but a small fraction of its walls within. We dwarfs never distinguished between the castle and the mines—they are one and the same."

—Philology of the Dwarfs, Anonymous

 The Queen was in a good mood when she received Tanios and Master Habael. The commander noticed her flushed cheeks and wondered if she had come back from a strenuous walk. *They do enhance the beauty of her deep, black eyes,* thought the commander, *and I do wonder what could eyes such as these do to the hearts of men.* He shuddered inwardly, as though warned by a mysterious instinct to keep his distance

from her. She wore a long, golden dress hemmed with fine red silk thread. Her hair was tied in a tight braid and hung down her back. Ramel was without her crown.

Then again, thought Tanios, *Her Majesty is not known to obey the royal protocol of dress and deportment.*

"Commander Tanios, my dear Habael, what a pleasure to see both of you on this bright sunny morning."

"Your Majesty does us much honor," replied Tanios.

"And it is well deserved. What, may I ask, brings you to these forlorn quarters of the castle?"

"Surely, Her Majesty is aware of the two unfortunate events that have disgraced the walls of this august castle," answered Tanios. "It has occurred to Master Habael that these actions may be connected to an old prophecy concerning four drops of blood. Is Your Majesty acquainted with this prophecy?"

"I am," replied Queen Ramel, who, by now, had seated herself on a raised rosewood chair studded with silver pins and cushioned with purple damascened pillows. She bid her guests to stand before her. "Continue, Commander Tanios, please."

"If it is so, then the first two murders are located directly above two of the four corners of some secret chamber. Without further information, we cannot proceed. We do not know why this alleged room is important or where it lies. Master Habael thought perhaps the history of Taniir-the-Strong may shed some light on this sordid matter. I should like for him to explain to Her Majesty what he has in mind."

Habael bowed before the Queen and continued. "Ever since Your Majesty has graced these walls with your presence, we have all been delighted to see Your Majesty take to heart the affairs of the kingdom. It is common knowledge that Your Majesty has a keen interest in the history of Taniir-The-Strong and of Taniir-On-High, and your knowledge of this subject is unmatched in the entire kingdom. We thought that perhaps Your Majesty may be so kind as to share with us the reasons that led El-Windiir III to leave Taniir-On-High, and why he chose to build Taniir-The-Strong on this side of the mountain."

The Queen looked at the two men for a moment and smiled. She stood up and went toward a window that overlooked the beautiful interior garden of the castle. She remained motionless, collecting her thoughts, then turned to lean against the windowsill.

"As you know, gentlemen, I came to you from the fair land of Babylon, where the highest and deepest mysteries lie within the Supreme Temple of Marduc, or Baal, his more familiar name. Taniir-The-Strong, though magnificent in its design and architecture, seemed like a peasant's hole to my eyes when I first arrived here, and soon I felt the desire to widen my horizons, to seek and explore the surroundings. Rapidly, this proved enchanting and the majestic beauty of this mountain attracted me. Then one day, I found my way to the top where I spent countless hours exploring the ruins of Taniir-On-High. This you have knowledge of, my dear Tanios—through your faithful Silent—and I am grateful to you for not intervening, despite the fact that these ruins are forbidden ground."

"You are our Queen," answered Tanios with a smile. His answer did not conceal his disapproval of her behavior, and if she understood the underlying reproach, she did not show it.

"I explored the ruins and they fascinated me. The account I received from the shepherds and local peasants I met was fragmentary and disappointing. Yet, bit-by-bit, I pieced together what I believe is the history of Taniir-On-High. Masters Garu and Ibromaliöm proved to be invaluable aids. The breadth of their knowledge is truly astounding.

"As you already know, El-Windiir built Taniir-On-High after the victory of the Malikuun. The size of its ruins tells us it was a formidable fortress; the greatest perhaps, save for Bashan-Sulmaron in Marduc. Her builders must have studied under Babylonian masters, for the analogy between Taniir-On-High and Bashan-Sulmaron is striking. Anyway, it must have been impregnable. No assault could have penetrated her defenses."

"So why does it lie in ruin?" asked Tanios with a tone of voice that betrayed his emotions. Like many of his kinsmen, he considered the ruins of Taniir-On-High as a personal wound.

"Because it fell under a curse, a terrible curse," replied the Queen.

"From Baal?" asked Tanios prudently.

Queen Ramel looked at him and smiled. "No, my dear Tanios, I know your feelings, or rather your ill feelings, toward the great god Baal, and though I respect them, I do not share them. In this case, however, Baal had nothing to do with it, El-Windiir himself imposed the curse." She raised her hand to prevent any interruption on the part of Tanios. Habael, who was standing behind Tanios, smiled. None of what the Queen said so far succeeded in eliciting a reaction from him. It was as though he had heard it all before.

Queen Ramel continued. "The songs that the shepherds and peasants of the highlands sing contain fragments of the truth behind the legend. Listening to their songs, I was struck by the similarities between the lyrics. It occurred to me that what the shepherds sang was possibly a missing fragment of another song the peasants were singing. Both shepherds and peasants attribute their song to El-Windiir, even though these two groups do not speak much to each other. I asked Garu to piece it together for me, and I believe that he came up with a plausible version. It goes like this:

"How shall I describe you, O beauty of my eyes,
You, whose abode is far above the skies?
Could a broken man describe perfection,
Can I, whom you loved, speak well about love?

Thrice have I risen higher on high,
Thrice have I ridden the winds and the storm,

Thrice have I beheld the height of the world.
Once did I love and love brought me low.

Since, long have I pursued you, O lovely of my soul,
Long have you hounded me and have made me whole.
You brought me beyond the reach of mortals,
Through gates resplendent and mighty portals.

To you, I give what I may not have taken,
By my life I swore that none would open
What unspeakable splendor has closed,
And none shall close what my love has opened.

O wisdom, standing by the river,
O beauty, beyond compare,
O lovely of the light deliver
My spirit from despair.

Only one may utter what mortals may not
beware..."

The Queen stopped and looked at Tanios smiling. "It is a pity that we do not have the rest, is it not, Commander Tanios?"

"A pity indeed," replied the commander, breathing deeply to clear his mind. The deep, velvety voice of the Queen had entranced him, and for a short moment, he felt transported into another world.

Tanios managed to speak. "According to this poem, El-Windiir had sworn a door would be shut that no one could open, except one who would utter what mortals may not. Is this the curse?"

"I believe it is. Let me tell you more about Taniir-On-High. Until I climbed this mountain, I had little respect for El-Windiir and what he did when he fought against Baal. The Priests of Baal teach that he fought with the Malikuun, but later fell in disgrace and served the Pit. I was convinced that he was a tyrant, vain and surfeit, who would have brought back the chaos from which Baal had freed us," she said.

Ramel whirled around and looked through the window toward the mountain. Her voice altered and became almost a whisper. "When you go up the mountain, following the old trail that is still visible, you begin to understand why he wanted to fly. The view is breathtaking. I come from a plain, and I had never beheld the world from the height of a mountain before. Standing up there, your feet in the clouds, you feel the exhilaration that he must have felt, and I confess, I wished I had wings to fly like El-Windiir.

"But this desire of flying is not the only reason why I changed my opinion of the founder of your kingdom, my dear Commander. The sheer size of these ruins and the delicate carvings on the walls made me realize the beauty of this place. It must have been of colossal proportions, yet elegant and majestic. The castle must have sprung from the mountaintop like an eagle in flight: a masterpiece.

"I was astounded by what this man, once a slave, ignorant and unskilled, managed to accomplish. I could see the able hands of the dwarfs all over the ruins, but still, beauty comes from a vision, from something beyond. It comes from the heart and soul of an architect who knew how to build an impregnable castle wrapped in beauty and majesty never seen before. The castle should have stood the test of time. We should have been standing up there now. Yet, it is now desolate: a heap of ruins. Why? What misfortune befell it?"

The Queen fell silent and the men waited.

Tanios looked at King Jamir's wife as if he were seeing her for the first time. He was impressed by her perspicacity and analytical mind. *I have underestimated you, my Queen,* he thought, *I can see this now. I wonder, to what lengths, will you go to fulfill a dream?* His heart grew suddenly heavy

"According to tradition," the Queen continued, "a mighty beast rose from the bowels of the earth under El-Windiir XIII. The King fought it and that led him to insanity. His son, Namiir IV, continued the battle, became blind and died mad. With him, the lineage of El-Windiir ended. The brother-in-law of Namiir styled himself King Dilandiir I, abandoned Taniir-On-High and began building Taniir-The-Strong."

"Unlike Garu, Ibromaliöm does not doubt the existence of the beast, but he believes El-Windiir XIII did not become mad fighting the beast; he believes the king became mad because of the curse which brought the beast."

"I do not understand," said Tanios.

"You asked me what this curse was. Well, according to Ibromaliöm, El-Windiir established a curse against anyone who would open what he had shut. His unfortunate descendant, El-Windiir XIII, brought upon himself this curse by attempting to open what he should have left closed. The curse had a direct effect on him because he died insane and so did his son. With the death of Namiir, the entire lineage of El-Windiir ended. According to Ibromaliöm, the beast is the physical manifestation of this curse, preventing anyone entry inside the closed room."

"What might that be?" asked Tanios, intrigued.

"The power of Tanniin," replied Ramel. Seeing the frown that creased the commander's forehead, she explained further. "According to ancient Babylonian traditions, when Baal pacified the land at the close of the Wars of Meyroon, he asked Tanniin to refrain from deploying his wings, lest he destroy what Baal was building. Tanniin complied at first, but later he rebelled. What this rebellion was, we do not know. All we know is that Tanniin was banished to the void, formless and without power. Yet, somehow, Tanniin contacted El-Windiir. Garu believes that El-Windiir forged his sword with meyroon so that no mortal blade could ever break it. Apparently, meyroon is lighter than a feather, yet harder than tempered steel. It cannot be melted by fire, nor shattered by the coldest ice and cannot be cursed. Garu has extensively studied the lore of the dwarfs, and it seems to point to some connection between meyroon and Tanniin. It may be that the meyroon El-Windiir possessed linked him to Tanniin. The god instructed El-Windiir on the design of the shoes, the belt, the mask, and the three pairs of wings."

"Six wings?" interjected Tanios. "I thought there was only one pair."

"This is the popular belief. Garu noted that the verse with the triple 'thrice' refers to three pairs of wings, each with a specific function. The first pair gives El-Windiir the power to reach 'higher on high,' which is an ancient idiom for 'higher than anyone else.' The second pair gives him speed and the strength to move through wind and storms. The third is mysterious. 'To behold the height of the world' may mean increased vision, but it is not clear how this relates to the wings."

"So then, the shoes, the belt, the mask, and the wings are the power of Tanniin?" asked Master Tanios.

"Yes," replied the Queen. "These artifacts are the tools the god uses to communicate his powers."

"But if he was locked away," wondered the commander, "how could he do this with Baal knowing? The Temple would have reacted..."

"Swiftly and without pity," completed the Queen. Her voice was steady and did not betray the slightest emotion. "But even the gaze of the mighty Baal cannot reach the depths of these caves, so El-Windiir's work went undetected. Furthermore, Bahiya told me that every god has his own secret way to contact seers and mediums. The Temple suppresses them whenever possible. I know that you perceive the Temple as cruel and domineering, and you are right. The Temple is filled with ambitious men and women. It attracts them and wants them to join its ranks. Then, it bends their ambitions to its own purpose. There is one true constant across the ages: no magic shall be used lest the Pit is reopened. You see, dear Tanios, the Temple does not worship Baal because he is just or benevolent. We worship him because he is the most powerful."

"I do not understand," replied the commander.

"Perhaps you might find this analogy helpful: consider an inhumane tyrant who rules over the world until the Malikuun defeat and lock him away in a deep pit. Then the Malikuun, for reasons unknown, leave us to our own devices. Human tyrants spring up and vie for power. They battle each other for supremacy, spilling the blood of countless men, women, and children. The cruel irony is that this supremacy will elude them, since no one is the equal to the tyrant locked in the Pit. This, my dear Commander, is the perennial lot of man: either we let the Pit rule over us, or we choose our own tyrants. Tyranny is our lot. If no matter what we do, there will always be a tyrant over us, then better a benevolent tyrant with the means to pacify the land than a so-called liberator, who would either turn into a worse tyrant, or end up reopening the Pit. This is why filling the heads of men with the hope of a liberator is sheer cruelty, for there is no freedom from tyranny. The choice is between law and order; between the benevolence of a moderate tyrant, such as the Temple, or the chaos of a liberator."

"Your Majesty believes the thirst for freedom in the hearts of men to be evil, and their subjugation to the Temple a good?" asked Tanios.

"Does it matter what I believe?" asked the Queen with a bitterness that surprised the commander. "Baal fashioned man from the spittle of the primordial chaos and the dust of earth. In my veins courses a blood tainted by darkness, and no matter what I do, or do not do, I will always tend to chaos. This is the unbending law governing man's heart: we are broken twigs amusing the gods for a passing moment and tossed into the fire to be turned into dust, and no one can change this fact."

"There is El," replied Master Habael softly.

"Dear Master Habael," replied the Queen with a sorrowful pity in her voice, "I would ardently believe in this benevolent, gentle god of yours, but where is he? Where can I find him? The might of the Temple governs the earth, and all around us the strength of the gods resonates in the heart of man. No, my dear Habael, I would rather believe that man is alone, the Pit a fantasy, and the gods a mere illusion before I believe in a benevolent god who stands back and impassibly watches our pain and suffering. According to the story you told me once, the Lords of Light came to the aid of man in the great battle of Silbarâd. Man then broke the covenant, and El commanded the Lords of Light to withdraw their aid. Tell me, my dear Habael, if your child is hurting, living the life of a slave, and you do not aid him, are you not just another tyrant?"

"Even as we speak, El is working in the world, Your Majesty. How else do you suppose, that despite the tyranny of the gods, man still finds joy in the world and the strength to hope? Yet, a broken covenant must be restored, or how else will man come to know El and worship him properly? Unlike the tyrants you spoke of so eloquently, who seem bent on imposing their will on man, El sent forth a call and waits for a response. But I do not wish to bore Her Majesty with a matter she is already familiar with," said the old man, bowing gracefully.

The Queen laughed. "I would more readily believe in you, my dear Habael, than in any god, for I have yet to meet such goodness so beautifully integrated with humility. Even though I do not agree with you, I thank you for your honesty and courage in sharing with the dreaded Queen Ramel, your deepest belief. Enough of this, you did not come here to hear me wax poetic about the gods. You are trying to solve a mystery, so let's get back to the problem at hand. As I was saying earlier, according to Bahiya, these artifacts are the Power of Tanniin, and El-Windiir hid them somewhere beneath Taniir-On-High."

"The high priestess knows about these matters?"

"She is more informed about them than anyone else, including the King and myself," replied the Queen, carefully watching the commander. He met her gaze, and she gave him her warmest, most charming smile. He bowed gallantly. The Queen's gaze lingered on the commander for a moment before she resumed her explanations.

"Not so surprising, my dear Tanios, when you consider that Bahiya is in charge of keeping peace in this part of Baal's Empire. When she came to Babylon to present me to the King, she spent countless hours studying these prophecies with the great masters of the Inner Circle. This is what my uncle told me. At the time, I did not give it any thought, but I confess that her sustained interest in these matters surprises me."

"Indeed," added Tanios, "surprising indeed. So what happened after El-Windiir fashioned his weapons? Did the Temple punish him?"

"That is what the legends say, but the shepherds living in the remote areas of the mountain have told me of two ancient songs that seem to tell a different tale. These songs are difficult to translate, and if it were not for Ibromaliöm's knowledge of these languages and ancient customs, we would not have been able to decipher them. According to these songs, Baal did not defeat El-Windiir; it is El-Windiir who asked Baal for help."

"What?"

"I know that this must sound blasphemous to your ears Commander Tanios, but listen to this slave's lament It is El-Windiir who speaks:

In the steely darkness that devour
The heart of man and his soul,
In the darkness of mines so deep
A slave's life is cruel and cheap.

Then came the day when I stood free,
Rejoicing in the land from sea to sea,
I beheld the beauty of a rising world
When I flew in the skies, wings unfurled.

Wings of steel now hound me,
A voice, I feel, now binds me,
Hounding, taunting, tempting.

My face and the land are foreign to my sight,
I lay awake in the depth of the night,
My hand never departs from my blade,
Alone, awake, cold and afraid.

Who will come, who will deliver
This Slave from a cruel slavery?
Who will rise, who will sunder
The shackles of this tyranny?

"This fragment is older than the poem I previously recited. It seems that El-Windiir is lamenting his fate. When a human entreats the god without sufficient foreknowledge, he becomes a slave to the god, and thus, under his total control."

"El-Windiir became a slave of Tanniin?" asked the commander, who was struggling with the implications of the Queen's words.

"Yes. This is a common occurrence. In fact, it is one of the most severe punishments the Temple of Baal inflicts on criminals."

"So, when El-Windiir called on Baal, he was freed?"

"This is what Bahiya says, but I do not believe it. Baal would not have delivered El-Windiir; he would have crushed him. This is Baal's customary law for those who oppose him. Something else must have helped El-Windiir: an encounter with someone he calls 'The Lady of the White Tower,' who seems to be endowed with amazing powers. Both Garu and Ibromaliöm are lost in mere conjectures here. We do not know exactly what El-Windiir saw, but whatever it was must have been more powerful than Tannin to set him free. This encounter was the turning point in the life of your founder. I cannot explain it. In any case, it seems El-Windiir—having been freed from his chains—imposed the curse on the power of Tanniin, and according to the last verse, he has hidden the power with him, in his sarcophagus. The sarcophagus was closed, sealed, and the curse applied. Anyone who opens it, and is not the Seer, will be cursed. It seems that the beast was set as the guardian over this famed sarcophagus."

"Why did he not destroy them?"

"Garu speculates that he may not have had the strength to do it. Ibromaliöm believes that somehow El-Windiir kept the power of Tanniin—his weapons—in the foreknowledge that someone would come after him and use them appropriately. The verse 'Only one may utter what mortals may not' makes him believe so. Bahiya is ambivalent on this point. Taken out of context, 'one' in this verse could refer to Baal, who alone may utter what no mortal can. But the context does not permit such interpretation, for it would be strange for El-Windiir to keep the power of Tannin until Baal takes it. Bahiya has come to believe that this power was kept for another mortal. At any rate, the real reason is lost amidst various contradicting hypotheses."

"So, he keeps them in his tomb. Then what happens?"

"In his sarcophagus," corrected Ramel before going on. "He utters the curse. El-Windiir XIII attempts to open the sarcophagus and tries to seize the Tanniin's power. What we know of him is not reliable, but it seems he was a ruthless ruler. That he may have been tempted by the power is not impossible. The curse sets in. The beast is its exterior manifestation, and madness its interior manifestation."

"So, then, Namiir IV succeeds him. He follows in his father's footsteps, fights the beast, and loses his sight?" Tanios clarified.

"He *may* have fought against the beast," corrected Ramel. "The dwarfs have a song titled 'The Last Battle of Xur', which is about a dwarf commanding the forces of Namiir IV. In it, they mention the beast. But Garu and Ibromaliöm believe the reason why Namiir IV lost his sight was not linked to the beast. Losing one's sight is an interior manifestation of the curse. It may have been because Namiir IV got even closer to the power than his father, and since no mortal may see this, he lost his sight."

"This brings us to the end of El-Windiir's dynasty and the beginning of that of Dilandiir I, the brother-in-law of Namiir IV, doesn't it?" asked Master Habael.

"Exactly," replied the Queen. "Dilandiir I, who seemed to be in good standing with the dwarfs, commissioned them to build Taniir-the-Strong, which they did. He moved the sarcophagus and hid it somewhere in the depths of the mines, where no one has found it."

"Amazing. How did he get past the beast?" asked Tanios.

"Amazing indeed. Garu and Ibromaliöm have spent countless nights trying to understand how Dilandiir accomplished this feat. To take the sarcophagus away from the beast is almost impossible, unless of course, one has at his disposal forces so great as to restrain the beast."

"Dilandiir was a magician?" exclaimed Tanios.

"Close, my dear Tanios, very close. Garu believes that Dilandiir did not move the sarcophagus; Ibromaliöm believes he did, but neither could advance solid evidence in support of their respective positions. Tellingly, I found the answer in Babylon."

"Babylon?"

"Yes. How great are you, O Babylon. While on a pilgrimage there, I visited the Temple of Baal. The Master Treasurer is an old friend of my father's, so he gave me a tour of the most prized gifts made to Baal. In one of the oldest sections, I found a gift from King Dilandiir to Baal in thanksgiving for the wonders accomplished by Alissaar Ben-Nadam."

"The legendary magician?"

"The very one. Now, who could have kept the beast at bay while transporting and hiding the sarcophagus? Who would have the power to contain the beast? Alissaar Ben-Nadam was one of the greatest magicians of Baal that ever was. If anyone could have done it, he could.

"I extended my stay in Babylon and talked to my old masters and other learned men and women. My pursuit seemed to be in vain. No one knew about Alissaar's travel to Tanniin, nor his feat here. I was about to abandon my search, when during the carnival of Adonis, I saw a play, a rather interesting play. Four clumsy men were carrying a long box, and a monster followed them. They were trying to enter into a cave, but men kept thwarting their attempts because they wanted to see what was inside the box. Every time the box was opened, the clumsy men would hide their eyes; the curious would fall dead to the delight of the crowd. The four men would hastily close the box and start moving away from the monster. Several unsuccessful attempts and a half dozen dead men later, a magician showed up. He repelled the beast, ushered the four men into the cave, and closed it on them to the delight of the crowd. Here is the best of it all: the play is called 'Alissaar and the Dead Slave.'"

They all fell silent, trying to absorb what they had been told. Tanios could not help but admire the Queen for her perseverance and tenacity. She was able to piece together an old puzzle that had stumped many. Truly, this was no small feat.

"So, Dilandiir calls upon Alissaar Ben-Nadam to hide the sarcophagus, right?" asked Tanios.

"Yes, but there is more. According to Bahiya, Alissaar Ben-Nadam was a Methodical. His school believed, and continues to believe, that an act of magic is part of a whole, and unless the whole is complete, the act is lacking. We are not certain how Alissaar hid the sarcophagus, but from similar sealing..." Noticing Tanios' confused look, Ramel explained further, "I mean sealing with a curse, of course." Tanios nodded. The Queen continued, "We can safely assume Alissaar hid the sarcophagus and cast an additional curse against anyone who would attempt to open it. Bahiya is convinced that Alissaar's curse is directed against the one who could utter the word."

"How so?"

"Alissaar's curse would be triggered when the one who can utter the word is in close vicinity. Even if he is unaware of the sarcophagus and has no intent to open it, the curse would be immediately triggered. Her explanation is justified, since this was Alissaar's usual mode of operation."

"Is she saying that, if the one who could utter the word were to walk by or look at the sarcophagus, the curse would be triggered against him?"

"Yes, my dear Tanios. This is what High Priestess Bahiya has implied."

"But how could this be? How could the curse distinguish between one man and another?"

"I do not know much about magical lore, but according to Bahiya, if the one who can utter the word were to enter the mines, then inexorably, he would be attracted to the sarcophagus. This is due to the work of Tanniin. This motion would be somehow detected and the curse triggered. More, I do not know, for I have a real dislike for magic. This might explain why I did not become a priestess," she added with a smile.

"Where did the high priestess acquire such a detailed knowledge of the works of Alissaar?" wondered Tanios.

Queen Ramel smiled. "Do I need to remind the master of the Silent to which school Bahiya belongs?"

"She is a Methodical," whispered Tanios, "like Alissaar Ben-Nadam."

"Exactly," said Ramel. "One of the founding principles of the Methodicals, states that magic consists in the precise alignment of forces and counter-forces to achieve the desired effect. Naturally, these acts require fine-tuning and precision and must be performed methodically, according to strict guidelines. Hence, the name attached to their school. They are famed for their curses and their shields of power."

"So Alissaar cursed this location, and you think these murders are connected to the four drops of blood?" asked the commander.

"Whether they are or not will be for you to find out, my dear Commander. I am merely a student of history," said Queen Ramel with a disarming smile. "Now, let us follow once more the flow of events: after Taniir-The-Strong was built, a break occurs in the songs that came to us through oral tradition. Any song written after Taniir-The-Strong does not mention El-Windiir's sarcophagus or curse. He is now depicted as fallen, under the forces of Baal, a hero who stood until the end for the freedom of his kingdom. There is only one obscure reference among the dwarfs where they speak of the room where 'silence is imposed,' which could be a reference to a royal tomb. Garu speculates that after Alissaar constrained the movements of the beast, Dilandiir sealed and abandoned Taniir-On-High."

"So, what about the prophecy of the four drops of blood from Baal and all the rest?" asked Tanios, who always favored hard facts over legends and lore.

"Well, this is the part I am least comfortable with. In order to break Alissaar's curse, you may need four drops of blood, as the poem prescribes. Ibromaliöm believes this to be the case. He said this song comes from Tanniin through a medium. Tanniin may have found a way to break the curse. Four drops of blood from four men of Baal must be sprinkled on the corners of the chamber where the sarcophagus lies. I believe this is a fabrication. It is pure folklore."

"The assassin of the two young men from Baal seems to believe it."

"And I confess that I find this frightening. Anyone who believes in this story enough to kill must be mad. When I was in Babylon, stories of this type were rife. The Sacred Valley of Marduc-Wad became dangerous. Charlatans took advantage of people's ignorance and gullibility. They convinced many that fabulous treasures awaited them in locked caves. They would demand from these wretched souls four drops of blood to break the curse protecting the treasure. I will spare you the accounts of the atrocious crimes committed in Babylon then. Finally, the Temple intervened and put an end to this madness. I must admit that I was very surprised when I heard of these machinations in this poem."

"Does Your Majesty have any idea who might be mad?"

The Queen sustained Tanios' look for a moment before answering.

"Commander Tanios, I find the history of this kingdom to which my fate has been linked, amusing. It helps me cope with the boredom of everyday life. Ask me if you will, about the past and about this man who would stop at nothing to be set free. I can relate to him, but spare me questions about murders. The mere thought of it is enough to upset me. Now if you will excuse me, I would like to rest. I am not yet fully recovered."

The two men bowed before Queen Ramel and left immediately. They walked in silence for a while until they reached the balcony overlooking the inner garden. High in the sky, a falcon sent forth his piercing shriek.

"So, Master Habael, what have you to say about this conversation? You have been rather quiet through it all."

"Her Majesty is very learned, is she not?"

"More than I had imagined. She is very articulate and seems to know this subject inside and out. She repeatedly called Masters Garu and Ibromaliöm, 'Garu' and 'Ibromaliöm'. I did not know she was on such familiar terms with the two judges."

"She has met frequently with both of them to study these issues."

"I knew Garu and Ibromaliöm were called often before Her Majesty's presence," said the commander. "Master Habael, do you believe what she said about El-Windiir? I find her story hard to swallow."

"I do not," replied Habael softly. "I subscribe to everything she said with one exception."

"And that is?"

"All the poems have the shepherds and the highlanders as their common source, so why single out the poem about the drops of blood? Either all these poems contain an element of truth, or they do not."

"Let me see if I have the sequence of events right: first El-Windiir strikes a curse against anyone who attempts to open his tomb, except for the 'one who could.' Did I get this part right?"

"Yes."

"Then he hides the power in his sarcophagus that a later descendant attempts to open. The curse is unleashed. Dilandiir becomes king and calls on the Alissaar Ben-Nadam to stem the curse. Alissaar locks up the beast, takes the sarcophagus, and hides it somewhere in the mines. He is a Methodical, so he decides to complement the work of El-Windiir. He curses the place where the sarcophagus is hidden and curses the 'one who could' so that, if he should enter the mines, even accidentally, he would be cursed. Correct?"

"Yes."

"Finally, Tanniin uses a mysterious medium who recites a verse from a poem: 'To remove the curse, kill four men of Baal and sprinkle their blood on the four corners of the seal,' whatever this seal is."

"Indeed, Commander."

"Have I missed anything?"

"I do not think so."

They walked silently for a while pondering what they had just heard. "I do not know who should be more ashamed of themselves," said the commander angrily, "the gods for putting up with such wretched scheming, or us for putting up with such ruthless gods." He heaved a deep sigh. "So then, we have a madman—maybe a group of them—who believe they can open the sarcophagus and grab El-Windiir's power by sprinkling four drops of blood. Right?"

"Sounds convoluted, but yes, I think this makes sense."

"All right, but why now? If I wanted to commit these crimes, would I wait for a powerful priestess of Baal to be here to commit them? No, I would not. This is sheer madness."

"Unless..." said Master Habael.

"Unless?"

"Unless time is paramount."

"The crime would be politically motivated, but this does not fit the way politically motivated leaders act. They may try to overthrow the King, assassinate High Priestess Bahiya, launch sedition, raise the populace, and start a revolution. People who yearn to free their kingdom are pragmatists. They deal with tangible facts, not misty lore and fables from the distant past. I am having a hard time reconciling the two."

"A desperate madman, then?" asked Habael.

"As if the royal court was not already complicated," replied the commander, sighing.

"Commander Tanios, Commander Tanios..."

Tanios and Habael turned around and saw a servant running down the corridor. Tanios welcomed the distraction. It sounded like a problem, but one he was used to dealing with. The servant stood before them panting. They waited until he had sufficiently caught his breath.

"What is it now?" asked Tanios.

"Commander Tanios, the high priestess is looking all over for you. She has an urgent need to speak with you. Please, follow me."

"One moment. Master Habael, what are your plans?"

"With your permission, Commander Tanios, I am going to have a little chat with Master Garu and Master Ibromaliöm. Who knows what I might glean from these conversations."

"Very good idea, but please send a servant and have him fetch Jedarc. He shall be your escort. He is sharp as a sickle. I would trust him with my own life."

"Thank you, Commander," replied Habael, bowing. He knew full well that an escort was not necessary during the day, but after what they had just heard, Tanios no longer trusted either judge.

"Come, young man," said the commander to the servant, "lead the way. Let us see what is on the high priestess' mind."

14. The Lone Tower

"Magic, it may be said, was rife in the land before the Temple established its dominion. Sureï, and the men and women who came after him, labored mightily to rid the land of magic. Their success was partial, for magic still lurks in the shadows, hidden in abandoned temples and ruins, deep within caves or on high in star observatories on mountain tops. Our efforts must be relentless, whatever the cost, even if in the process, innocent lives are lost."
–Teachings of Oreg, High Priest of Baal.

"The Lone Tower was not abandoned when the star readers ceased their occupation. It was abandoned when Kyliir, the last star master, inadvertently summoned the ring of fire. The Pit of Darkness split the tower's floor and swallowed him—and all those with him—down into the realm of demons."
–Memoir of Alkiniöm the Traveler

Tanios stepped out onto the royal balcony and beheld Bahiya leaning over the stone railing. She wore a long, black velvet dress with three-quarter length sleeves and a draped neck. A red silk veil framed her face as it shimmered in the light  streaming from her open door. *She is not in her priestly garments,* he noted as he drew closer. She turned to greet him, and he was struck once more by her beauty. Images from the distant past flooded his mind, filling his heart with long-repressed feelings. He remembered with surprising clarity their last peaceful night together, when they took a long stroll on the sandy beach of Bragafâr beneath a star-studded cupola. They had remained on the beach all night, and in the morning, they had toured the mysterious Whale of Bragafâr, a lifelike statue of a blue whale. He had held Bahiya's hand tightly in his own as they joined a group of tourists inside the whale and listened, fascinated by their guide, a tall, lanky fellow with a nasal voice.

"This whale is Takkan, harbinger of Kanmar, the god of the deep. She was forged from the scales of Numerej, the great serpent of the sea by Wogal, the blind, three-headed blacksmith. She is a sign from the great god reminding the people of Bragafâr of their sacred duty to protect the whales that grace our shores every spring."

He had invited them to follow him inside the belly of the sculpture before resuming his rehearsed recitation: "Takkan is one hundred and ten feet long, twenty-two feet at its apex, and twenty feet wide." Tanios no longer remembered all the details, but he never forgot the incident involving a small fish. The guide had led them deep inside the whale and showed them a small fish made of gold, floating freely above their heads.

"This is Tulloon, Kanmar's messenger. She watches over us and makes our deeds known to the god," he had said reverently. "Kings would give half their kingdom for this fish, and many a foolish thief—foreigners mostly—have tried to steal it in vain. No one has ever managed to lay a finger on the fish of gold. Kanmar protects Tulloon and punishes the wicked. When we catch a thief—and we always do—we slit his arms, throw him into the sea, and let Yemarak—Kanmar's executioners—do the ghastly rest."

Tanios' recollection of these events was vivid still. Back then, he and Bahiya were hired hands, working for the Temple of Baal, which sent them on difficult missions to steal, destroy, or disrupt centers of magic. The pay was good, and the Temple overlooked whatever they managed to keep for themselves. Bahiya had been a priestess in training when they met, and Tanios, a hired mercenary. The high priest of Baalbeck had said the magical realm reacted strongly whenever they were together. Tanios never understood what that meant; back then, he did not care. Bahiya was beautiful, witty, and shared his love of travel. Nothing else had mattered.

Their mission was to steal Tulloon. Sharr, priest of Baalbeck, had promised four thousand gold shekels if they succeeded. Tanios did not require a translator during that famous tour to know the "Yemarak" the guide spoke of, meant sharks. Still, the lure of gold and the love of adventure prodded him forward. That night, after the tour, they had managed to evade the guards, sneaked inside the whale, and tried to steal the floating fish. However, despite Bahiya's incantations, Tanios never managed to lay a hand on the strange creature. A patrol caught sight of them and they barely escaped. He could still feel her tears flowing down his neck as they hid beneath the jetty of the main port, waiting for *Yem's Fin*—one of Baal's military vessels—to dock. They boarded the swift three-mast, and when at sea, she had begged him to come with her to Fineekia and settle down.

"Next year I will be a priestess. We can live comfortably in Baalbeck," she had told him. "Come with me."

He had laughed her request away. "I will never live in the shadow of Baal," he told her. "Better to die at sea than to live in the shadow of death."

She had not replied and grew progressively forlorn. Not long afterward, she left him after one of their memorable adventures. He learned later that she had joined the Temple of Baalbeck. He went to Tanniin and settled in Taniir-The-Strong. Zakiruun carried urgent messages from her, but he refused to hear them. As her power grew, so did her fame. He would often hear the King's guests whisper her name with a respect bordering on awe. As the years passed, he began to forget her face and voice. He had shut the door on his past, and she had chosen to stay behind it; nothing would force him to open it again.

Nothing did.

Until now.

A few weeks earlier, King Jamiir informed him of her arrival and requested that he be her escort and protector during her stay in the kingdom. The news struck him like a fist in the chest and troubled him deeply, more than he was willing to admit.

"Why is she coming?" he had asked. His tone was harsher than he would have liked.

The King raised an eyebrow. He nicknamed Tanios, *Erilin—Dragon's Wrath*—for he sensed in the commander a burning fire that reminded him of the famous bronze head of Tanniin at the shrine of Erilin. In a large cave, at the back of the imposing Temple of Mitriil, the head of the god, twenty-seven feet tall, emerged from a bed of beaten bronze, symbolizing the primordial pool of chaos. Beneath a pair of eyes glittering with contained fury, the open jaws exposed three rows of sharp teeth, representing the god's swift justice, unbending judgment, and the painful death he reserves for the guilty. There were 6,243 hand sculpted scales on the god's face, each inlaid with a turquoise stone representing the farseeing powers of Tanniin.

"You will meet her at the military port of Mitreel in one week, my dear Commander, and you shall be your courteous and affable self, *as usual.*"

Tanios had quickly regained his composure, but his heart remained troubled. When he laid eyes on her as she stepped onto the ship's footbridge, he knew he was still in love with her. The strength of his feelings surprised and distressed him. Still, the keenest observer would not have detected the turmoil in his heart hiding behind a slight frown and the tightening of his jaw.

"Good evening, Tanios,"

Her voice, hard as steel, brought him back to the present. *How you have changed*, he thought, bowing courteously. *Your face is as beautiful as ever, but within, you are as hard as a stone statue, for Baal is molding you after his own image.*

"You have asked to see me?" he said.

Bahiya looked away, then closed her eyes.

"Simer, another athlete from Hiyam's team, is gone."

"Again? When?"

"Earlier this evening at curfew." She glanced quickly at him and closed her eyes. A lock of hair lay lazily on his forehead, partially hiding his right eye, and she caught herself wanting to push it away like she used to do when they were together. She clutched her left fist and crossed her arms, resisting the irrepressible desire to wrap them around his waist. The strength of her feelings surprised her. *Even after all these years,* she thought, *how strange is the human heart.*

Tanios felt like asking her what was wrong, but held back. "You mean the team's curfew?"

"Yes. He did not answer the rally call this morning. Hiyam and her men went to his room, only to find it empty and in order. They cannot confirm that he spent the night there."

He looked at her, and she gazed at him. The moment their eyes met, they knew they were still in love with each other. Tanios wanted to take Bahiya in his arms. She wished she could lean against him and close her eyes. But the moment passed, and the two lovers faded away, leaving behind a high priestess of Baal and the Commander of the Silent Corps.

"Anything else?"

"No."

"Very well," he said. "I'll see what I can do."

He started walking, then stopped abruptly and turned around. "By the way, why do you ask me to help you, when you could just as well use those magic powers of yours to find him?"

"Assuming I had such powers, a magical act of this magnitude is a dangerous endeavor. It would be felt miles around. If I knew the identity or location of the murderer, I might be able to help. Without it, I would do more harm than good."

Tanios gave a curt nod and left. He went straight to the room of the young man. As he walked, he could not shake the feeling that Bahiya was hiding something from him.

Habael was perplexed.

As he stepped out of the royal kitchen into the wide hallway of the first floor, he saw Ibromaliöm enter the Lone Tower's staircase. *Why is he going up the Lone Tower?* he wondered. *There is nothing up there, save cobwebs and mice.*

Intrigued, he followed the judge up the stairs until he reached the third level. Servants and slaves shuttled between the Royal Hall and the staircase in the Garden Tower as they made ready for the end of Games celebration in honor of the winner. The judge was nowhere to be seen. Puzzled, Habael turned around to continue his climb and came face-to-face with Jedarc.

"Well, well, young man, what brings you to this part of the castle?"

"The commander asked me to escort you," the Silent replied.

"Oh, he wants to keep me out of trouble."

"Well," replied Jedarc with an embarrassed smile, "he's trying to keep us ... I mean, *me...* out of the mines."

"I see," said Habael in a chuckle, "Well then, why don't you come up the tower with me? One of the judges went up those stairs and I wondered why. So I followed him, but he is nowhere to be seen."

"After you, Master Habael," said Jedarc.

They reached the top and saw no one. A massive oak door with thirteen stars carved along its wide frame stood locked before them.

"Is this the Star Room?" asked Jedarc.

"Indeed it is," said Master Habael, inspecting the door. "I see you were paying attention during history classes."

"I like history," replied Jedarc. "Knowledge of history is depth of vision," he added.

"Spoken like a true prince," said Habael, peering through the keyhole. He could see the edge of a wooden table, but nothing more.

"What a strange handle," observed Jedarc. Ever curious, he reached out to grab it, but Master Habael—moving with surprising speed—gripped his hand and pulled it back.

"Do not touch it," he said gently. "Look at it, but do not touch."

Jedarc relaxed his hand and Master Habael removed his. The young man bent down to examine the handle. It was half an inch thick and nearly five inches long, made of beaten iron and covered with tiny scales.

Its undulating shape reminded Jedarc of a snake.

"A headless snake," he whispered. "Who, in his right mind, would make a door handle in the shape of a snake?"

"Presumably, the head is on the other side of the door," replied Habael.

Jedarc gave him a puzzled look and shook his head. "What's wrong with people?" he wondered out loud. He inspected the handle once more and realized that its end was split into two inwardly curved scorpion tails. "Look at these scorpion fangs," he exclaimed. "They're sharp. They can cut you if you're not careful."

"Scorpions do not have fangs," corrected Master Habael, "they have stingers."

"Fangs, stingers, two chickens on opposite sides of the same road," replied Jedarc. Seeing the confusion on the old man's face, he added, "I mean, it's the same thing, they're both dangerous. Anyway, this is crazy."

"I wish these *were* fangs," said Master Habael, "but they are not. These are horns of power. When their tips—fangs as you called them—point to the object the horns are attached to, the way these point to the handle, they draw power from anyone who touches them, sapping their life."

"Really?" he said. "Magic? Someone is practicing magic here?"

"I don't know," said Master Habael. "The commander will need to get involved."

"You're right, Master Habael. I remember now Master Garu's lessons on magic." He pointed at the handle. "If the tips are curled outward, pointing away from the object, they would sting anyone who would touch the object, injecting him with a curse. But when they stand straight up, they draw the life force out, and then inject their victim with a curse."

"Master Garu taught you well," said Habael, "Sadly, my dear Jedarc, from this day on, you must learn to control your impetuosity. If I did not stop you, who knows what this handle would have done to you."

"I would have missed out on a lot of chicken meals, that's for sure."

"The world as we know is passing," said the old man with an altered voice. "A new age is dawning. The heavens are hidden and darkness falls." Jedarc stared at Master Habael with a look of confusion and concern. Habael chuckled and tapped the Silent on the back. "You are right, Jedarc, do not mind this old gardener. Nevertheless, be on your guard," he said, glancing at the handle. "Familiar objects can be deceptive."

Jedarc backed away from the door. "I have always thought that magic is for the cowardly lot," he muttered. "Nothing good can come of it."

Master Habael smiled appreciatively.

"If this object is so dangerous, why is it still here?" asked Jedarc. "Why not get rid of it?"

"I presume if the Temple knew how to, the priests would have done so already."

"So, the Temple of Baal is on our side?" asked Jedarc.

"They are sincere," said Habael, "but they are sincerely wrong."

The old man's bold answer surprised Jedarc. It required real courage to call the Temple of Baal evil, and yet, the old man did so without affectation or anger. Jedarc knew that Habael had simply stated a fact.

"Do you see the ring of fire carved in the wood around the handle?" asked Master Habael.

Jedarc looked carefully at the door surface near the handle. He saw a carving, faint and barely discernible on the surface of the wood. He looked at it intently, vaguely aware that Master Habael was calling his name. The voice of the old man faded away, and Jedarc was now peering inside a ring of fire at least a mile in diameter. Deep beneath the ring, in utter darkness so cold that nothing moved, he saw many faces: a bull with gleaming eyes and horns of steel, a many-eyed spider, a dragon, a shark, and a face of mud, barely discernible. Beyond these, he sensed the presence of other creatures, but he could not see them. He heard coming from the ring of fire the alluring chant of a women's choir. The voices called his name, whispering, goading him to close his eyes and jump, to fall in and fall down. His eyes began to close, his mind began to drift, and he was about to give in, when in a flash, the wings of a powerful being jolted him, and Noraldeen's face came into focus.

"Jedarc, wake up," she shouted. Behind her voice, he heard another saying these same words, but with a power that could level mountains and reshape the surface of the earth—a voice of command that amplified Noraldeen's own voice. "Come back. Get out of there."

Jedarc jerked and would have tumbled down had Master Habael not caught him in time.

"What happened?" asked the Silent, cold and shivering. "What just happened?"

>❁❁❁<

"Noraldeen," shouted Lord Orgond, springing up from his seat. He rushed to his daughter's side, who sat on the floor amid the flowers and the shattered pieces of the vase she had been carrying. "What just happened?"

"I don't know, Father," replied the young woman, wiping her forehead. "I was looking at the daisies, thinking how pretty they were, when suddenly, they became this giant ring of fire over a deep abyss, and I saw Jedarc falling. So I called him, and I heard another voice calling also. The voice was powerful. And suddenly, I am back here with you."

Lord Orgond placed his hands on his daughter's shoulders, gazing intently at her. "Come, let me help you up. Let us step onto the balcony; the fresh air will do you some good."

They stepped onto the narrow, stony balcony, overlooking the northern plain. There, the Lord of Amsheet stood by his daughter. He was as tall as Commander Tanios but with a slender build and a jovial face. His blond hair softened his features, exuding charm mixed with the right type of warmth: concerned, but not overbearing. Lord Orgond was beloved by his people for his fair and firm rule.

He had been a widower ever since his wife died in childbirth. Even though many a noble lady would have considered a union with him a high honor and a fortunate state in life, he never remarried. Some said the chief reason was the heavy burden the governance of the northern realm had laid upon him. Others, mostly women, believed he was still in love with his wife, Lady Layal. The portrait that graced the main hall of the fortress revealed a tall woman of darker complexion. Her smile was gentle, but her eyes showed strength of character and a resolve that her daughter had inherited.

"Have you been dreaming lately?" he asked after a short while.

Noraldeen shrugged her shoulders. "I don't know. I wake up crying, but I don't know why. I think I dreamt of something, but I cannot remember what."

Lord Orgond refrained from prodding further, for he did not want to bring up once more the subject of the slave, the only topic that set him and his daughter at odds. It was a painful rift between them. Still, these dreams, and the vision she had just now, worried him.

"Very well, Daughter," he said after a while. "Why do you not go and get ready? We have company tonight."

Noraldeen's anger flared, but she managed to control it. She sweetly replied, "Yes, Father," and curtsied obsequiously, mimicking the surfeited amiability of the noblewomen who fawned over her father, waddling like chickens before a rooster. Lord Orgond clutched his fists to the railing and looked away.

Since he insists on bringing young men to meet me, I might as well enjoy myself, she thought with a grin that would not have reassured her suitors. She walked into her room, closed the door, and twirled several times before falling backward onto her bed. Then, she got back up, went to a nearby trunk, opened it, rummaged through its contents and pulled out a small figurine that had a striking resemblance to a certain Silent with curly hair. She sat it on the edge of her bed and stood facing it.

"Well now, Ahiram," she said, "tonight Lord Derek Mistlefoot, Stewart of the Royal House of Argamon, ruling over the Kingdom of Bar-Tannic, comes for a formal visit with his son, Lord Braird Mistlefoot. Bar-Tannic, where the goddess Astarte mourns the loss of her beloved Adonis, is a land of rain nine months a year. The people are stout, determined, and courageous. Well, how else can they be living under cloudy skies for months on end? Their manners can rival the Court of Ophir. I suppose, when your food is dreadful, you overcompensate with great manners, so perhaps, my love," she said addressing the doll, "you should spend some time in Bar-Tannic, to learn how to treat a princess as she ought to be treated."

Noraldeen knew that by being unfair, she was contravening the Code of the Silent, but her anger had gotten the better of her. "You see, Ahiram, Lord Braird Mistlefoot comes to us highly recommended," she said, imitating her father's voice. She jumped to her feet and tried to imitate the gait of a prince she had never seen. "Why do I have to suffer the presence of this pampered prince? 'He loves dandies and his father cultivates the best dandelions north of the Great Sea.' But what do I care for dandelions? You have never mentioned dandelions in any of our conversations. Don't you like dandelions, my love?"

Angrily, she snatched a dart and aimed it at the thick, velvety curtain, then at a bust of an ancestor, and finally, at a portrait of an obscure ancestor with a prominent nose.

"I did *not* ask to be a princess," she muttered as she targeted the nose.

"Wait," she said, looking at the dart as if she were seeing it for the first time. "It occurs to me that I might be able to put my training as a Silent to good use." Noraldeen smiled mischievously. "What do you think, Ahiram? Maybe a little live dart competition? We can use poisoned darts to spice things up a bit. Or, we could swing from rope to rope in a romantic sort of way—like Jedarc does when he is chasing a chicken—and end it with a kiss. He could swing blindfolded from the northern balcony of the fortress, believing that I am going to meet him midway by swinging from the southern balcony. Instead, I send a blindfolded pig. Let's see how much Lord Braird Mistlefoot would enjoy the close encounter," she added fiercely.

She sat on her bed, grabbed the doll gently and fell back on soft pillows. "I bet Jedarc would laugh hearing me talk about it," she whispered, "but Banimelek would wag his finger and nod disapprovingly, and you, my love, would simply look at me and smile."

Tears welled in her eyes. "Oh, Ahiram, where are you now? I miss you so much."

➤✦✦✦≺

"That was scary," exclaimed Jedarc. "Scary, strange, and well, really strange and scary, and I have no idea what that was all about."

"Neither do I," said Master Habael pensively. "Still, the fact that Noraldeen came to your rescue is a good thing, a very good thing indeed."

"Master Habael, I have no idea what you're talking about."

The old man chuckled. "Yes, yes, indeed. I apologize, my dear Jedarc. I should have never told you to look at the ring of fire. I did not expect it to flare so soon. Never mind that," he added quickly. "Still, we know now there is some high magic at play here, and I am beginning to wonder what Master Ibromaliöm is up to."

"Magic?" asked Jedarc, bewildered. "Did I just experience magic?"

"Deep magic," replied Master Habael. "This handle is under a powerful curse. Some say Baal cursed this door, others whisper of a deeper magic still. It is best not to touch this handle, my lad," said the old man, smiling.

"Better yet, it is best not to touch any part of the door," said Jedarc, shuddering. He took a step back and did not hide his distaste for all things magical. He heard some footsteps.

"Someone is coming," he whispered.

They looked down and saw Master Garu shuffling his feet, wearily climbing the stairs. As he reached the last bend, he caught sight of Habael and the Silent, and froze, his hand clutching the rail, and his chest heaving as he tried to catch his breath. His eyes went from Habael to the Silent and back. He resumed his climb, a broad smile on his face.

"Habael, what a surprise. What brings you to the top of the tower?"

"I could ask you the same question, Master Garu."

Garu laughed as he moved toward the door. "We use this room for our secret deliberations during the Games. It keeps the inquisitive minds of overly curious individuals away."

"I see," replied Master Habael. "Very wise, and I suppose you are coming up here to meet with Master Ibromaliöm?"

"Ibromaliöm?" asked Garu surprised. "He is here?"

"Yes. I saw him go up these stairs a little while ago."

"So, you think he is in the Star Room?"

"Where else could he be?" replied Habael.

"Very well then, allow me."

Garu inserted a bronze key into the keyhole, careful not to touch the handle. He turned the key and the door pivoted quietly, giving way to a wide room that would have been brightly lit had its four large windows not been shuttered with a clumsy assortment of wood planks—as if someone had hurriedly blocked the windows. A round table stood in the center of the room. Its surface was covered with a two inch thick layer of black wax. The floor under and around the table was also covered with black wax.

Ostensibly, someone burned hundreds of candles here, thought Jedarc, *but why?*

The wind whistled constantly, rattling against the shutters like a tormented spirit trying to get inside the room. Jedarc shivered inwardly; something in the room caused his hair to stand on end, but he did not know what it was.

"Well now, he is not here, is he?" said the head judge in a patronizing voice. "If you are looking for Master Ibromaliöm, you may try his room. I think he went there to rest. Now, if you do not mind, I should like to remain alone. There are some important issues regarding these Games that must be resolved before sunset." With this, Master Garu accompanied Habael and the Silent to the door and locked it after them.

They scrambled back down quietly until they reached the second floor and walked toward the judges' quarters.

"Now lad, what do you think of all this?" asked Habael.

"I don't think the judges were going up there to deliberate. Something in that room scares me. I don't know what. Besides, you said you saw Ibromaliöm go up, but he was not there, so I don't know what to think."

"Now, let us see if Master Ibromaliöm is in his room," said Master Habael.

They walked silently along the wide corridor. The judges' quarters were directly behind the middle hall. As they passed the first door into the Silent's quarters, Jedarc was surprised to see it ajar.

"You had better take a look, lad," said Master Habael. He remembered closing the door behind him after they left, and they both knew Commander Tanios' strict orders to keep all four doors leading to the Silent's quarters closed at all times.

Quiet as a cat, Jedarc opened the door. The smooth, dark wood of the common area gleamed in the light. All bedroom doors were closed except Banimelek's, which was ajar. The area was deserted, since all the Silent were on assignment. Jedarc wondered if he should inspect the rooms but found the idea ridiculous. After all, the Silent kept nothing of value here. He was about to leave, when he noticed a red blotch seeping from beneath Banimelek's door.

"Master Habael," he called, "come quickly!"

The old man came rushing in. "What is it, lad?"

Jedarc pointed to the dark patch. "It's blood."

"Whose room is this?" asked Habael.

"Banimelek's," replied Jedarc. "It's Banimelek's room."

Master Habael opened the door and walked in, followed by Jedarc. They gasped before the ghastly spectacle: the body of a young man lying in a pool of blood with a rope around his neck.

His clenched right fist lay in the blood, as though trying to retain the life that betrayed him. Habael respectfully closed his eyes.

Jedarc breathed a sigh of relief. "It's not Banimelek," he whispered.

"No, it's another member of Hiyam's team."

"How many deaths is it going to take?" wondered the Silent.

"Please call the commander," said Master Habael. "He had better come and see this."

Tanios gritted his teeth in frustration. He had lost the trail once more. First, a slave working in the kitchen admitted seeing, earlier, a young man matching the description of the athlete leaving the castle by the narrow gate. He cantered away on a horse, seemingly in a hurry. The tracks of the young man's horse led the commander to the Rock-of-the-Sentinel, a promontory where one could see the entire countryside. The rider had waited for a signal there. Inspecting the ground, the commander found a small, red velvet ribbon.

"This explains why this young man... what was his name again... ah yes, Simer. This would explain why he came here. Someone must have slipped this ribbon under his door; a signal that the woman he was courting agreed to see him. Someone told him to wait here for a second signal." A quick inspection of the grounds confirmed his suspicions: the horse's trail led to the valley below the castle.

"Someone must have signaled for him to come down there." He followed a winding path between two hills covered with silveria—a foot tall shrub that gave the impression of being an evergreen on account of the thick flanges on the stem and the dense cluster of sharp, tiny yellow flowers. The golden field was peppered with oleander, a grayish, spiny shrub with a brilliant pink flowers. The commander kept a wary eye on the path ahead, knowing these hills were a perfect hideout for snakes.

"Did anyone warn him about the snakes, I wonder? Then again, this is a junior of the High Riders we're talking about. He must have known what he was doing."

Down in the valley, there were more hoof prints. "Three horses now" muttered Tanios. "A secret meeting was held here between three people, not two. This changes everything. This is no longer the case of a romantic encounter; the man I am after is a spy."

A quick inspection of the ground confirmed that the meeting had occurred early this morning. He followed the trail which led him to the hidden river. There, it looked as if the tracks crossed the river, but when

Tanios examined the other bank, there was no trail to be found. Clearly, the riders went up or downstream in the shallow part of the river.

Tanios turned around and returned to Taniir-The-Strong Castle.

He spent the next hour discretely questioning the young maidens serving in the kitchen, but it was in vain. None of them had seen the young man that morning.

Either they are sincere, or they rival the Adorant in the vice of lying, he thought.

The Adorant were servants of Baal known for their entrancing singing that could subdue the will of the strongest man.

One of young women, however, did point out that early this morning, she had heard muffled sounds coming from Whisper Grove. The others giggled, but one look from the commander convinced them this was no laughing matter.

"When was that?" he asked sharply.

The young woman took a couple steps back. He added in a softer tone, "I do not mean to scare you, but I need to know when you heard the muffled voices, and what business brought you to the Officers' Garden?"

"I did not go to the Officers' Garden," came the quick reply. The young woman stood wide-eyed, hands clutched, frightened, and upset. "I was watering the herbs like Master Habael said. He told me to do it when the first rays of sun hit the ground in front of the wall over there. This is what I do every day. Those herbs are very, very important to Master Habael, and he wants them watered every day at precisely the same time. Once, I forgot to do this, and Master Habael was very, very sad, and some of the plants with beautiful smells died. Then, all of us we were very, very sad, because we liked those plants a lot. One of them, the little green one with a small beautiful blue... no, velvet... velvet flower, cured my mother from fever, and the other one, with big furry leaves, Master Habael used for my nephew when he was teething and—"

"So, was it at the first or second hour of the day?" interrupted Tanios. The maiden took a couple more steps back.

"The first... no, the second... I think... I don't know." She started crying and ran to an old woman who consoled her.

"Do not mind her, Commander Tanios. She is a good girl. I would say it must have been closer to the end of the first hour because this is when the sun hits the hedge separating our garden from that of the officer's. You know, Whisper Grove is on the other side of that hedge, close to the wall, so I am not surprised if she could hear what was going on over there."

Tanios thanked the older woman and went out to inspect the bed of herbs that the young servant had told him about. Why Master Habael chose this spot to grow these herbs was beyond him. The ground was still wet, and the young woman's trail was easily discernible.

The Officer's Tower had two doors, one leading to the Servants' Garden and the other to the Officers' Garden. A short moment later, the commander stood in Whisper Grove. He peered through the hedge, but it was too thick to see the bed of herbs on the other side.

Whisper Grove was a secluded area behind a cluster of thick, tall bushes, ideally suited for romantic encounters. A cursory look at the signs of struggle convinced him that the murderer had come to the fateful rendezvous. He knew from the erratic imprints of boots that the man had tried to free himself from a powerful grip. The fight had been brief. *The murderer must have taken his victim by surprise. Either the criminal is a strong warrior, well trained in close combat to overcome a junior of the High Riders, or...* He inspected the grounds closely. *No sign of blood,* he thought. *The murderer struck at close range, confirming my suspicion that the victims knew and trusted him.*

Tanios saw footsteps nearby. *High Rider's boots,* he thought. *Someone light on their feet,* he added as he followed the trail. It ended abruptly at the wall of the Officer's Tower.

Why here? wondered a baffled Tanios. He inspected the surrounding grounds. *No signs of footsteps by either door, which means the murderer did not drag the body into the castle. But why bring the body toward the castle? It seems the murderer is intent on dropping the bodies inside the castle. But why? This seems completely senseless.*

He looked up. *The Silent must never go against the facts, however strange they may seem,* he quoted absent-mindedly from the *Book of Siril.* *If the murderer has managed to transport the body, then I might be able to pick up his trail on the second or third floor,* he thought.

Still disbelieving what he was seeing, he went back to Whisper Grove and followed the footsteps again; and again, they led him to the same spot. *Decidedly, whoever is plotting these crimes knows what he is doing.* He looked at the red ribbon he had found and wondered whether the young man who had left the castle earlier this morning, and the one who came to Whisper Grove, were one and the same.

I highly doubt a woman would have managed to kill a skilled athlete like this Junior High Rider, carry his body on her shoulders and climb the wall, unseen. She must have had an accomplice who went to the grove in her stead. But what if there was no woman involved? he thought. *Then, I would be chasing a ghost.*

Reluctantly, he went back inside the castle and climbed to the second floor. As he reached the wide corridor, he froze and remembered the bit of dirt by the window. He wanted to kick himself for his negligence.

The murderer must have been nearby while I stood venting my frustrations, he thought. He was now furious and felt as though the murderer was taunting him. He went to the window and examined the dirt once more.

So the murderer managed to climb the wall with the body and sneak in unseen.

Tanios was shaken, for that meant the security apparatus he had put in place had been breached without anyone knowing about it. He got up and was about to follow the tracks when Jedarc called to him from the Lone Tower. The expression on the young man's face told Tanios that he did not have to look any further for his answers.

High Priestess Bahiya came back to her room in haste. While speaking to the King, she received a *Metarim* (a mental image) from her daughter calling for help. At that same moment, the first giant geyser hit the participants in the Game of Gold as they were climbing through the Pit of Thunder. The athletes were bracing themselves for the second hot geyser, and Hiyam had started calling on her mother for help. Bahiya locked her door, went to a large, mahogany chest, opened it, and took out a small, round mat and a small, silver box.

She unrolled the mat. Its dark surface had three golden concentric circles. The image of two ram horns filled the inside circle. She stood on the horns and opened the small, silver box carefully. It contained an oddly-shaped prism and five small spheres of differing sizes, each nestled in its own compartment. The high priestess stared at a small, golden orb for less than two seconds until it lifted silently in the air and began circling her. Bahiya kept her gaze locked on the small object as it passed in front of her until a throbbing yellow light shone inside it. After a short while, a hazy sheet of light rose from it, and the image of her daughter appeared on its surface. She was hanging from a rope while water shot up, pummeling her against the wall. Down below, she could glimpse a strange, black light. *nar hittim*, she thought, frightened, *The black energy of the spell world. Here? Impossible. How could this be?*

She looked at her daughter and spoke to her in silence. *Hold on, Hiyam, I am intervening.* She saw her daughter smile before the image faded away. The priestess focused on the floating orb, slowing it down until it stopped in front of her. She picked it up and dropped it carefully in its compartment, for the orb was now extremely hot.

Bahiya stared at the prism and sighed. *This is going to be far more dangerous than I expected. I cannot do this alone. I need help.*

Resolutely, she focused her attention on the left golden circle on the strange mat she stood on. Immediately, a green, dull light throbbed along its rim. She looked at the right circle and a blue, dim light throbbed along its rim. Bahiya waited until the blue and green lights began to appear and disappear in unison, then she gazed at the middle circle.

"Tamri," she whispered.

The circle vanished and after what seemed like an eternity, Tamri materialized before the priestess, standing on the left and right circles.

"High Priestess Bahiya," exclaimed the Adorant. "Forgive me for not being ready, but I was not expecting you."

Behind the young woman, Bahiya could see the golden outlines of the city of Babylon. "I am facing a nar hittim, Tamri. I need your help."

The young woman blanched. Even though she was an accomplished Adorant, able to carry the most potent magic with her voice, she recoiled at the thought of facing the black light of the Arayat.

"Bahiya, this is deadly."

"It's my daughter, Tamri. She is under attack."

Tamri's face hardened. "What do you wish me to do?"

"Stand eight absorbers" Bahiya said, "but do not link them to the Arayat," she added quickly.

Tamri breathed. Absorbers are special glassy orbs made to absorb hostile energy that would then normally be dumped into the Arayat. A trained magician could stand eight absorbers with a flick of the hand when they are not linked to the Arayat. But since these defensive artifacts were not made to distinguish between sources of magical energy, a magician who would link an absorber to the Arayat carelessly could cause the absorber to take the energy from the Arayat, fill it beyond capacity, shatter, and release an explosive force that would wreak immense havoc and possibly shatter reality by causing the Arayat to leak into the physical world. No member of the priesthood of Baal was allowed to link more than two absorbers to the Arayat at the same time.

"I am ready," said Tamri.

Bahiya heaved a deep sigh. "Good. I am raising the conjoiner."

Not waiting for an answer, the high priestess stared at the prism inside the silver box. It lifted up slowly and stopped a short distance from her eyes. She lightly touched it with her right index finger and it moved away along a straight line. It went through Tamri's image until it reached the window sill.

The sun struck its clear surface, and the strange object shot out a thin, blue ray that hit the priestess between the eyes. Instantly, the image of Tamri faded away and formed clear and true within Bahiya's mind. Conjoining meant having the image of the person you were joined to inside your head. Bahiya could clearly see the thin, blue ray touching Tamri's forehead.

"To neutralize the nar hittim, I need to find its source in the Arayat and strike it down. Whomever is doing this will surely try to wrest control of the concentrators from me and use them to kill me. You will know I am under attack when the conjoiner begins to heat your forehead. I want you to use your voice to channel that power to the absorbers."

Tamri's eyes brightened. "Very clever, Bahiya. The attacker will not sense the absorbers and will not know what to do. Still, how do we release the energy inside the absorbers into the Arayat?"

"Let's worry about that a bit later," replied Bahiya dismissively. "One thing at a time." Ignoring her friend's inquisitive gaze, she added, "Whomever is using the nar hittim is a master magician. Let's hope our little ploy will delay him long enough for me to neutralize his attack. Are you ready now?"

Tamri nodded. Bahiya gazed at the silver box until her sight clouded.

Two orbs and two concentrators rose and began circling her. Tamri gasped. She had never seen anyone do this before. Not even High Priest Sharr.

"Bahiya, how——?" asked Tamri, but Bahiya ordered her to be quiet. Tamri held her breath.

The four objects were zipping along within their appointed circles. Bahiya had chosen a paired configuration with each orb being fed by one concentrator exclusively. *Time to raise the hunter,* she thought. She gazed at the small sphere the size of a pebble, inside the silver box, and as she was about to raise it in the air, a wave of power, unlike anything she had experienced before, hit her with the strength of a hammer. She nearly lost control of the concentrators and the orbs, but her hardened will and the long hours of training prevailed. Hearing Tamri's voice ring in her mind, Bahiya knew the Adorant had begun singing to deflect the attack away from her. Tamri had opened a channel to the Arayat and like a vortex, it was sucking everything into its path back to the spell world. Bahiya said a quick prayer of thanksgiving for the hours she had spent training to resist the allures of an Adorant's voice. *If I can't keep free from Tamri's voice, we will both end-up trapped in the Arayat forever.* After a short while, the unbearable pressure lifted and she breathed a sigh of relief. *Much better,* she thought.

"Tamri, this attack was vicious. How are you holding up?"

"I am fine," replied the Adorant. Her voice was low and shaken, but still strong.

"We are almost there. Time to fill the orbs…" Tamri smiled. Bahiya glanced at the orbs and gritted her teeth. *Next time I am in Babylon, I will have a word with the Office of the Procurator of the Orbs. He promised me that this new generation of orbs could be charged twice as fast as the old ones, but here I am, waiting still.* Gradually, the concentrators' color shifted from dark green to dark red, and finally, to a pinkish white. Bahiya was relieved. They were empty. Inside the orbs, a yellow light was glowing.

Bahiya shook her head. The effort they had already exerted was great, yet they were not even halfway through. Their opponent attacked anew. She felt nauseated. Glancing at Tamri, she saw that the Adorant was shaking under the effort. *We don't have much time*, she thought. With a flick of her hand, Bahiya dropped the empty concentrators to her feet and lifted the hunter from the silver box.

The spell world was the battleground for all things magic. It was the bedrock upon which the empire of Baal stood. Through the spell world, the priests of the Temple ruled the real world. The black light, she knew, had its source in the spell world. She needed to open a *jasron* (a sort of bridge between reality and the spell world) to find the source of the black light and neutralize it there. She had to locate it and do it quickly. But the spell world was immensely vast, beyond anyone's ability to reckon.

The hunter was an orb used for such an occasion. It was made of a spongy, green substance that was grown in the spell world. She focused on the image of the nar hittim. The hunter flashed bright red. *Good, it knows what I am looking for,* thought the priestess. The small object sparkled for a short while, then abruptly disappeared. How hunters worked was anybody's guess. Still, they usually located their source very quickly, as if they did not travel at all in the spell world, but somehow managed to appear near their target. As long as the source was native to the spell world, it could not be hidden from the hunter. Bahiya focused her gaze on the first orb, slowing it down until it stood perfectly still before her. With a slight movement of her left index finger, she hooked the orb to the blue ray of light. Tamri jerked and her voice nearly faltered, but she quickly regained her composure. Bahiya swallowed hard. She knew Tamri did not understand why she was fusing the orb with the conjoiners; something she had discovered on her own and was not yet ready to tell her friend. Ignoring the Adorant, Bahiya hooked the second orb to the blue ray. Her iron-fisted will kept them apart, even though their contained energy pulled them together. Bahiya's exertion was so great that she nearly collapsed. Waves of pain swept through her body as tears streamed freely down her cheeks. She was having difficulty breathing. She knew that Tamri was not faring any better. *The eight absorbers must have sucked enough energy to blow up the entire western aisle of the Temple of Babylon*, thought Bahiya. Both women were now drenched with sweat.

"Hunter, show yourself." The small pebble materialized before her. An intense green spark flared on its surface and moved along an arc to the ground—this was the jasron. Slowly, the hunter slid on the arc of light, stopped midway through, and disappeared inside a black hole. *The source of the black light,* thought Bahiya.

"Tamri," she said breathlessly, "On my command, channel the energy in the absorbers back to me." Tamri jerked and nearly stopped singing. "Keep singing," urged Bahiya. "Do not worry. I know what I am doing."

Not waiting for her friend's response, Bahiya unleashed the orbs on the black hole. Two green bolts hit it simultaneously. "Now Tamri, now!"

Tamri's chant switched from a melodic drone to a high-pitched scream and the blue ray turned black. The energy in the absorbers was flowing back. With a supreme act of the will, Bahiya channeled it down the black hole.

"Hold on Tamri, hold on!" pleaded Bahiya, "Just a little longer!" The hunter flashed bright red once more and abruptly fell to the ground, where it glowed portentously. *It lost the target,* she thought breathlessly. *It was a successful hit.* Still, the energy in the absorbers kept flowing. She glanced at her friend and saw fear in her eyes, for once the flow from the absorbers began, it had to run its course.

Bahiya nearly panicked. *This energy will destroy this room and a good portion of the royal castle unless I channel it somewhere else.*

Seeing the concentrators lying on the carpet. She brought them back up and directed the energy from the absorbers into the concentrators. This was uncharted territory, for no one before, as far as she or Tamri knew, had done anything like it. They both knew the Kerta priests trapped their victims inside the Arayat and somehow filled the concentrators with that energy. No one had ever attempted to use a different source. Bahiya feared the concentrators would explode, but instead they kept ingesting the energy as if they had become two bottomless sinkholes. At long last, the flow ended. Bahiya saw Tamri falter, so she channeled some of her own reserve of energy to steady her.

"Thank you," said the Adorant. "How did you know to use the concentrators?"

"I didn't," replied Bahiya. "Intuition, I guess."

"Bahiya, you are stronger than the high priest of Babylon and the Soloist combined. You will end up succeeding both."

Bahiya smiled. "Thank you, Tamri, I am in your debt."

"Not at all. I owe you my life," replied the Adorant.

With a nod, they both severed the conjoiner's link. Carefully, Bahiya lowered the concentrators back inside the silver box. She repeated the same operation with the two orbs. She could feel the intense heat radiating from the silver box, but did not have the strength to study the concentrators. *This will have to wait,* she thought. She managed to bend down and pick up the hunter. It was chipped and cracked. *Amazing! My foe managed to attack the hunter.* Hunters were too fast for anyone to catch in the spell world, so whatever attacked this one was fast, very fast. Bahiya dropped the hunter inside the box, then managed to bring the prism back to its resting place. She stepped off the strange, small rug and staggered. Bahiya managed to reach the bathroom where she retched, then fell on the floor shaking. The effort had nearly killed her. She lay on the cold marble shivering, drenched in sweat, with a massive headache that blinded her.

By the gods, what sort of creature have we awakened in the caves?

"Whoever has committed this act is as vile as a scorpion and deserves no pity," muttered Tanios, standing up after examining the corpse. Habael had seldom seen him so angry. They looked at the body of the young man lying before them.

"What do you make of this, Master Habael?" asked the Commander.

"It would appear that the murderer has tried to confuse us. He would have us believe that this poor man had been strangled first then slashed with the same type of dart."

"I am not so sure. Blood does not flow like this from a wound after death," explained Tanios, "No, the rope must have served a different purpose."

"Perhaps," offered Jedarc, "the murderer tried strangulation first and when his attempt failed, he used the dart?" Seeing neither men respond he continued, "But why here?" asked Jedarc. "Why in Banimelek's room? Is someone trying to attack the Silent's reputation?"

"Possibly, young man," replied Habael evasively. "Now, Commander Tanios, is it a murderer, or murderers?"

Tanios surveyed the room looking for clues, but he could not see what may have led Habael to suggest that there was more than one murderer. Having found none, he asked his friend.

"It is too well organized to be carried out by one man alone. Someone had to give him the red ribbon and make him believe that a woman wanted to see him. Then, there is the secret meeting. It may be that these two meetings are related. Who knows how many individuals are involved in this operation?"

"But," interjected Jedarc, "If those involved in the secret meeting wanted him dead, why this complication? Why murder him in a castle garden? Why drag the body and dump it here?"

"What do you make of it?" asked Tanios. He knew he had to follow this line of reasoning to the end, for he did not want to share what he believed to be the real motive for the killing with anyone, save Master

Habael. A hidden room, a curse, human sacrifices, all of it made sense when listening to the Queen, but now, standing before the body of a dead man, the whole thing sounded foolish.

"Perhaps," replied Jedarc, "because whoever was at the initial secret meeting discovered later that the young man was about to betray them and wanted him dead. To cover their trail, they murdered him in the same way they had murdered the first two victims."

"So, this murder may have been politically motivated?" asked the commander.

"It may well be the case," continued Jedarc. "The victims may be involved in a conspiracy of sorts, and Baal found out and decided to take care of the matter swiftly and discreetly."

"And in the process, discredit the Silent Corps and get the soldiers from the nearby garrison of Baal to take over the castle," continued the commander grimly. "It makes sense."

"Perhaps it is as you have said, my dear Jedarc," said Master Habael, kneeling by the body. "Commander, look at the neck of this unfortunate young man. Perfectly clean, is it not? No bruises other than those occasioned by the rope." Habael stood up. "Now, if someone attacks a Junior High Riders, we would assume that he would defend himself. He would try to take that rope off his neck, but there are no signs of struggle."

The commander nodded. "Like the two other victims," he said thoughtfully. "If this is the young man who took a horse ride this morning to meet with two other riders, then perhaps the two events are unrelated. I had assumed the assassin lured him outside the castle, but I am beginning to think that he left this morning for a secret meeting, then upon his return met with the murderer who then killed him. This accords better with the evidence. Still, I fail to see why this requires more than one murderer."

The two men considered the facts in silence. His hands behind his back, Master Habael paced back and forth before the dead man lying face down. By now, the blood had started to dry up. Suddenly, he stopped pacing and went back toward the body.

"Can we turn him over?"

Tanios acquiesced, and with the help of Jedarc, turned the body over. Habael took a cloth from his pocket and rubbed it gently on the lips of the dead man. He looked at it and shook his head.

"What are you looking for?"

"Lipstick," answered Habael. "If a woman is involved in this crime, she may have distracted her victim with a kiss. If so, she would have done everything in her power to look attractive and would have worn lipstick. It would have left a stain on his lips, but my cloth is clean, so I do not believe the murderer is a woman."

Tanios did not answer. Habael looked at him and saw that he was looking at the dead man.

"What is it?"

"Look at his right hand."

"It's hair, is it not?"

"Help me open his hand," answered Tanios.

Carefully, the two men pried open the rigid fist. Tanios removed the strands of hair and stood. He held it close to the light.

"It's impossible to tell if it is that of a man or a woman."

"So, when the attacker threw his rope around this poor young man, his hand must have grasped the assassin's hair and pulled."

"He pulled," repeated Tanios pensively. "Jedarc, fetch me a small towel. Banimelek must keep a pile somewhere."

"It's by his bed," replied Jedarc. "There you go, Commander," said the young man as he held the towel open before his superior. Tanios laid the strands on it and picked as many as he could from the pool of blood.

"Master Habael, Jedarc, come look at this hair. Tell me what you see?"

"Red," said Jedarc. "The woman is a redhead."

"Good," said Master Habael, "we are making progress."

"Indeed," replied Tanios fiercely. "Indeed. Jedarc, fetch a team of Silent to remove the body. Until further notice, I want you to station two Silent in our quarters at all times."

"Yes, sir, but, sir, what about Master Ibromaliöm?" asked Jedarc.

"What about him?" said Tanios.

Jedarc relayed to him what had happened that morning.

"Once the body is removed and you have secured our quarters, go and wait for Master Ibromaliöm. Tell him not to leave his room until I have spoken with him."

>✿✿✿<

Abiil, the Undergrounders' collaborator, paced feverishly in his tiny cell, located in the servants' sleeping quarters. "My spy has been killed," he muttered. "My spy has been killed. Maybe someone is aware of what is going on and is on my trail. Maybe they figured out by now what I am up to. This is not good." The servant had always known the risk he was taking in working with the Undergrounders. He had managed to enlist Simer in return for money and other less seemly favors. Simer was ambitious, young, and gullible enough to believe Abiil when he told him that he was preparing a feast in honor of the high priestess. Thanks to the young man's help, Abiil knew that Baal was preparing to overtake the castle the night of the fourth Game. But now, someone had killed Simer. Anguish filled his heart, and he looked at the door expecting a High Riders' patrol to slam it open and drive half a dozen spears through him. "I had better inform the master," continued the servant in a hushed voice. "I should let the master know right away."

Cautiously, he opened the door, and seeing no one, pulled his cowl over his head and walked briskly until he reached the door leading to the outside court. He waited for the court to empty before darting toward the stairs leading to the kitchen's garden. Moments later, he was gone.

15. Bats and Boulders

"The caves beneath the earth number like the stars of heaven. They groan in their great solitude, yearning to join hands and form Xirik Andaxil, the one undivided mine—a realm greater than the greatest empire of men. Beware of the mysteries hidden within, whose beauty will burn your eyes as surely as a thousand suns."

—Philology of the Dwarfs, Anonymous

 Caves, arches, stairs, passages, and bridges followed one another in a seemingly endless succession, as if a giant mountain swallowed sun, moon, and stars, turning the world into an endless labyrinthine mine, empty and desolate. Boulders, stalactites, and stalagmites, became, in the dim light of distant torches, High Riders, giants, and monsters.

Alone, he ran. The thud of his feet was the only audible sound he heard, save for the faint echo of water dripping in dark corners, or the dim sound of rushing rivers like the clamor of armies in battle.

Swiftly, like a fleeting shadow, Ahiram moved from cavern to cavern, following the less trodden path to conceal his presence from arbitrators all too eager to help the team of Baal. Holding a torch to light his way, the Silent passed through giant halls that had never seen the light of day.

Like a beacon of hope in unrequited darkness, he ran over bridges long abandoned by their makers—following deserted pathways, where long ago dwarfs and men toiled side-by-side to pry the precious metal from the stony clutch of the mountain. The miners were gone, swept by the tides of time and the passing seasons. Nothing remained of their toil other than the meandering caves and a few rusted picks and shovels he glimpsed in the trembling light of his torch.

He stopped in secluded corners of massive halls, where he knew fresh water flowed from the walls into dark pools. He drank and chewed on the dry pieces of meat and cheese he had brought with him. He had tucked them inside an empty pocket of his waterproof dart belt before he dove into the lake. Despite the monstrous geyser in the Pit of Thunder, the contents of his belt were still dry. Once more, he felt gratitude toward the dwarfs who created this little marvel of ingenuity that they commonly called a dart belt.

Having finished his meal, he crossed the large cave and as he was about to enter a narrow corridor, he heard muffled voices from the other end of the cave.

He snuffed his torch and crouched inside the corridor just when a High Rider patrol entered the cave. Silently, he followed the corridor, until he reached a rectangular cave with a low ceiling. *I'm back on the main exit route,* he thought, seeing the torches stringing the wall. Glancing behind him, he saw no one, so he used a lit torch hanging from the wall to relight his own and continued running.

Time seemed to stand still as Ahiram progressed from hallway to hallway. Once more, he had drifted away from the main route to follow the less trodden path. Shafts of light shone intermittently in the distance, shattering the ambient darkness that hemmed his torch's halo. The lack of light made consecutive caves resemble one another, and he began to wonder if he was not running in circles.

He fought the urge to leave markings on the walls, firmly trusting his training and the days he spent scouting the mines.

I know I am getting closer to the exit, he asserted silently. *In a short while, I will rejoin the main path again. Up ahead, there's the Hangman's Hall, and then, a little further away, the Cave of Bats. Then, I'll go up the spiraling stairs to the Red Hall, and from there, I'll follow a wide curve to the Merry Dwarfs Bridge. Then there is just the one hour sprint to the Shipping Hallway which leads to the exit.*

Ahiram reasserted these thoughts several times during the next two hours until he finally reached the Hangman's Hall, so called because of a massive stalactite that had been carved into the shape of a man hanging from the ceiling. The statue was grotesque with bulging eyes and a tongue dangling from the man's mouth. The man grinned madly, as if enjoying the torture. *Miner's humor,* thought Ahiram, averting his eyes from the intolerable scene. Beneath the statue's feet, the anonymous artist had carved an overturned hat where an abandoned spider web fluttered gently.

The Silent was about to exit when he heard footsteps behind him. He took a quick look and saw a High Rider patrol coming fast after him. *These men are rested,* he thought, *and I am not. I won't be able to outrun them.* Quickly, he reached into his belt, grabbed two pellets, and without stopping, whirled around and threw them between his pursuers' feet. He dodged the two spears thrown at him, whirled back around, and sprinted off. He heard them cough and sneeze as he leaped out of the hall and into a narrow corridor, which he recognized from his past visits to the mines. He took a quick peek behind him and saw the soldiers' shapes profiled against the corridor's entrance; he sped forward until he reached the fork. Holding high his torch, he followed the left corridor, threw his torch as far as it could go, ran back and sprinted down the right passage. As expected, the soldiers went after the light.

Presently, the passage inclined gently downward, easing the strain. He sped along, remembering where this path led. *No one who took this path even once, would ever forget it*, he thought.

"In the name of Baal," said a strong voice behind him, "Stop."

A third patrol was on his heels. They were carrying three torches shining brightly in the corridor. *They don't know*, he thought, *and I have no time to warn them.* He sprinted forward in the dark as two spears whizzed past. The ground leveled beneath his feet, and he felt the warm draft from the wide opening ahead. He ran into a large cave, made an immediate left turn, felt the big boulder he was looking for, and crouched in the small space between the boulder and the wall.

Less than a minute later, the High Riders ran into the cave with their torches shining brightly. The cave was vast, with a ragged ceiling extending far above their heads. Ahiram overhead someone speak.

"What do you think you are doing?"

Ahiram peeked from behind the boulder, crossbow in hand. Hiyam and her team were right behind the patrol.

Despite the shortcut I took, she managed to catch up, he thought. *She is using magic again, no doubt.*

"We are looking for the slave," replied one of the men.

"Under whose orders?" snapped Hiyam. "I gave strict orders to the captain of the High Riders. I want him to be left alone."

What? thought Ahiram, confused. *She gave that order? What is she up to now?*

"My apologies, Lady Hiyam, your order has been superseded by a higher ranked officer."

"Who superseded my order?"

"Lady Hiyam, I am barred from disclosing his identity."

So Babylon trusts the priestess no more, thought Ahiram. *Looks like she couldn't kill me fast enough. Well, no matter, I need to get out of here.*

"Hiyam," said one of her men, "if the slave is here, let the High Riders slow him down."

"No," she nearly screamed. "Enough is enough. Let him compete. I will not have his blood on my hands."

"And you will not, my lady," said the officer. "His blood will be on me and my men."

Not if I can help it, thought Ahiram, as he released the trigger. The bulky dart's flight was flawless. Silently, it arced over their heads and exploded in a dazzling bouquet of colors. *Not bad, Jedarc*, he thought. *This silly fireworks dart you requested might just save me.*

Hiyam, her men, and the High Rider patrol jumped. The bright light blinded them momentarily.

"Another one of the slave's silly tricks," jeered one of the High Riders.

A deafening shriek answered him. Ahiram's dart had disturbed thousands of bats hanging from the ceiling. They descended on the men of Baal like a dark storm.

They don't call this cave the Cave of Bats for nothing, thought Ahiram as he ran along the edge of the cave dodging the occasional bat. He reached the exit and saw that it was partially blocked by a boulder.

The earthquake, he thought. He glanced back toward the men of Baal. They were flailing their torches at the bats, which only made them angrier. *The best thing to do when in the presence of bats is to stand still in the dark*, he thought, amused.

He managed to squeeze through the narrow opening and then noticed a cluster of small rocks at the base of a boulder. *That's why it did not block the way*, he thought. *But I can fix this.*

He took a few explosive pellets from his belt and wedged them between the rocks. He ran a short distance, loaded his crossbow with an escape dart, aimed and shot, then sprinted away.

A muffled explosion snuffed the neighboring torches, and smoke filled the passage. Ahiram grinned: the boulder had blocked the exit.

Let them use magic against this, he thought, grabbing one of the extinguished torches from the wall which he lit from the first burning torch he came across a few hundred yards away.

He ran nonstop for a good hour and reached the spiraling stairs, which he climbed two-by-two. They lead him to the Red Hall, a wide room cut into a brown rock. The torches the arbitrators had strung to two opposite walls cast a red-tinged light, the color of blood. In this vast space where thousands of miners had taken their meals on rows upon rows of stone tables and benches, many a man and dwarf had died, either from sickness or strife. As he ran across the hall, Ahiram's gaze trailed on the pots, mugs, plates, and cutlery the miners had left behind after their last meal. Rats had long ago licked the plates clean and a thick sheet of white dust blanketed everything. The Silent heaved a sigh of relief as he crossed the threshold of the exit. He felt uncomfortable in the presence of these ancient, yet familiar objects, as if the dust that covered them had swallowed up the living, and no one was left to tell the tale.

Ahiram followed a narrow, winding passage that veered abruptly on a ten-foot-wide path. He smothered his torch, turned left, and settled into a comfortable jog, for he had a ways to go before reaching the Shipping Hall. The path hugged a series of underground hills within a colossal space that the miners refused to call a cave. Instead, they called it *Tanniin Sirind* (Dragon's Hollow) for they thought that only the god himself could have dug such a lair beneath the earth. They refused to mine it, and holding it sacred, they stuck to the path. Arbitrators were convinced that the Undergrounders had hid in the Dragon's Hollow, but these claims remained unsubstantiated.

The hillside to his left rose at least fifteen hundred feet, while the incline to his right fell precipitously to a narrow canyon that was supposed to lie four thousand feet below. Since no one had dared to explore the hollow, no one knew what lay in that canyon. A howling wind blew into a deep shaft behind the hills, an abyss separating the hills from the Dragon's Hollow's edge. The wind moaned and roared with a suddenness that sent shivers down the Silent's spine. Involuntarily, he glanced up, half expecting to see a dragon gliding overhead. Even the dwarfs, who reveled in acrobatics, left this entire section of the mines alone, refusing to climb the hills, cross to the edge, or even climb to see how high the roof was. "The hallow hollow is significant significantly," they would say in their odd manner of speech, "and a significantly significant signification that must be left alone in its lonely loneliness." Thus, the hollow stood as a stern warning and reminder to men and dwarfs, to stay their curiosity and control their greed.

The path followed the hills for twelve miles, which Ahiram covered in a solitary run that lasted an hour and a half until he reached the massive Iron Gate that guarded the Merry Bridge. This bridge consisted of a single stone slab linking the path Ahiram was on to the Shipping Hall. Here, in happier times, miners celebrated weddings. The groom would hold his bride's hand while she walked blindfolded on the edge of the slab. For as the miners' saying went, "To marry a miner, a woman's trust and courage must be deeper than Dragon's Hollow's abyss."

The gate was sixty feet high and twenty feet wide and made of beaten copper. Its latticed panels bore a giant hammer, the preferred insignia of the dwarfs. Presently, a High Rider patrol guarded the locked gate.

"How long before the next patrol?" asked one of the soldiers The High Rider spoke softly, but his voice resonated in the cave.

"Quiet," barked his superior. "Keep your eyes on the path. The arbitrators told us the slave is near. There's a reward for his head. The quicker we nab him, the quicker we can get out of this blasted place."

Silence fell, and the men resumed their observation, when two puffs of smoke rose from the ground before their feet. The men, whose nerves were already jarred by the oppressive surroundings, panicked, thinking that a dragon was rising from the abyss beneath. They retreated to the gate, leaning their backs against its reassuring shape. Their leader, a stout man unafraid of the darkness, rallied them with a shout of command. "It's the slave," he said. "Keep your eyes on the path."

Ahiram grinned as he flew down the abyss hanging on to the rope that his dart had tied to the gate. After throwing the two smoke pellets, he had fired his dart above the men's heads, and it latched on the gate. Before the men had a chance to recover, he flung himself down the abyss and flew along a wide arc that took him past the gate and over the bridge. He waited until the last moment before letting go of the rope, landed softly on his feet, and ran swiftly away, while the High Riders were still staring at the path, waiting for him.

At last, he reached the Shipping Hall and stopped in his tracks: a rock avalanche had sealed the hallway off.

"Now what?" he said out loud, wiping the sweat off his forehead.

"Now, you come with us," said a powerful voice.

Before he could react, two figures leaped in front of him.

"Jedarc, Banimelek, what are you doing here?"

"Checking up on things," said Jedarc, grinning.

"What things?" asked Ahiram wearily. He knew he should have refrained from asking, but it was too late.

"Someone has to keep an eye on you," replied his friend. "You could be in trouble."

"I am in trouble," grumbled Ahiram.

"Not *that* kind of trouble," exclaimed Jedarc. "Left alone in the mines, who knows? You could be courting Hiyam." Ahiram elbowed his friend, but Jedarc, swift as the wind, moved away. "What?" protested Jedarc with a sly grin. "She is awfully pretty."

"Jedarc, do you really think this is the right time to talk about Ahiram courting a High Rider?" asked Banimelek.

"Or courting anyone, for that matter," replied Jedarc pensively, "other than a cooked chicken, that is. You should have seen him shoving half a chicken in his mouth while sitting next to the high priestess. I think this is why she fainted. Speaking of chicken, do you know why chickens do not like vegetarian cooks?"

"What do we do now?" cut in Ahiram, looking at Banimelek. "Hiyam and her men may not be far behind."

"We climb," replied Banimelek. "There's a shaft fifteen hundred feet that way," he pointed to Ahiram's left. "It's a straight climb for eight hundred feet, then it inclines gently."

"Let's go," replied Ahiram, heaving a sigh. "There's no time to lose."

"So do you know?" asked Jedarc, as they began their climb.

"Know what?" replied Ahiram.

"Well, why chickens hate vegetarian cooks."

"No, Jedarc, why?" replied Ahiram as he negotiated a difficult reach.

"Because he beats the eggs," said their friend with a chuckle.

"Someone else will get a beating if an arbitrator hears us," growled Banimelek. "We saw a patrol of High Riders enter the mines, and we knew they were up to no good. Cowls on everyone, let's keep moving." he added.

They finished the first climb in silence and took a few minutes to rest before continuing.

"Hey," said Jedarc, as they began their final ascent, "What did the chicken say to the pig when they fell in a big puddle of mud?"

None of them responded, and his answer was lost high up in the mines; if the joke was funny, neither of his friends laughed.

They reached the surface without incident. It was already night. Ahiram realized that he had spent the entire day underground. Suddenly, he noticed that he was famished and started laughing.

"What is so funny?" asked Banimelek, scanning for a signal.

"Jedarc's useless jokes made me realize one thing," he said after a while.

"And what have you been able to draw from the well of my wisdom?" asked Jedarc. "I think I should sit on a mountaintop and spout words of wisdom in the form of chicken jokes."

"Don't even think about it, Jedarc," said Ahiram with a grin. "I am too hungry to hear you talk about chicken."

"There is the signal," said Banimelek, pointing at a light across the valley beneath. "The way is clear," he said, even though he knew both of his friends could read these signals as well as he. Quickly, they went down the hill until they reached the main western path a few miles past the Bridge of Evergreen where Ahiram sprinted back to the plaza.

16. GAME OF MEYROON

"Much has been said about meyroon, the numinous metal of Tanniin, but little is known about its composition, properties, or origin. Sureï the Sorcerer once said, "The Priests of Silbarâd fused white gold and andaxilian iron and immersed them in Haialynn, the primordial pool of life filled with Mey-El-Roon, the Water of Blessing...

"...they sprinkled one hundred and forty-four herbs over the pool while chanting mystical prayers. Water became fire, earth turned into wind, and the metals transmuted into meyroon."
–Teachings of Oreg, High Priest of Baal

 Dawn. Tanios stood on the balcony, peering into the night. He looked up and shuddered as the stars of heaven were fading away. "Have the gods turned their faces away from the mines, I wonder?" he muttered. "Have they sealed Ahiram's fate?" He clutched the railing and closed his eyes. Thirty years of dealing with the Temple told him Ahiram could not survive the snares of Baal. He was frightened—frightened and angry. He had been fond of the lad from the day he laid eyes on him—standing stiff and scared behind Master Kwadil's emissaries.

"Master Kwadil entrusted me with the following message," Balid had told him. "Esteemed Commander, it is a most opportunistic opportunity and an opportunity most opportune for the commanding commander and the commander commanding the silent Silent to carefully care and care with utmost care for this young lad," had recited Balid, using the customary long-winded speech of the dwarfs.

"My husband is not a Zakiir, but he could have been one. His memory never fails him," had explained Foosh.

"Considerable considerations and considerations most considerable," had continued Balid, "derived with attentive attention should be given to his training.

"Alas, a necessary necessity and a necessity of the utmost necessary nature necessitates that no visible visibility be given to his standing status. For if he is noticeably noticed and noticed in the most noticeable fashion by undesired undesirables, then the unfortunately unfortunate consequent consequence is that his life would come to an abrupt end and an end of the most abrupt fashion. Furthermore, his originating origin and original origin must be kept secretively secretive and be a secret most secretive."

"Train him as a Silent, treat him as slave, and conceal his place of birth," had replied Tanios. "I understand."

Tanios had followed Kwadil's instruction to the letter, for he trusted the dwarf with his own life. He didn't ask questions, knowing Kwadil had relayed to him all he wanted to say.

Ahiram's presence in Taniir-The-Strong Castle went largely unnoticed outside the tightly knit circle of the Silent, Master Habael, and a few servants in the kitchen. He was a slave among many, and none was the wiser. Over the years, his affection for the lad grew until he treated him like his own son. By the end of the second year, none of the Silent, save Ahiram, thought of him as slave. The commander admitted to Master Habael that he had underestimated the impact of the separation from his family on the lad.

"I thought time would soothe his wound, and he would accept the separation. Instead, it has grown worse. Nothing can come between Ahiram and the love he has for his family. His sole purpose in life is to go back home as a free man."

"I would not ignore his temper," Habael had added. "It is certainly a constant cause of grief and distress."

"Correct, as usual. Still, I wish he could see life and purpose for him, *right here*, in Tanniin."

Master Habael had smiled enigmatically. "You are not the only one to suffer from his single-minded goal, my dear Tanios. This lad has caused a princess to shed many tears."

"You are right as usual, Master Habael," replied the commander sighing, "He will break her heart."

"Or she, his," replied Master Habael.

The commander shrugged his shoulders. "Even if I lived one hundred lives, I shall never understand what motivates women," grumbled the commander. "He is a slave desperately trying to set himself free, and she is thinking of romance."

"Perhaps so, my dear Tanios, but this young woman's heart is an ineffable treasure holding the surpassing mystery of love. I have high hopes for Noraldeen."

Commander Tanios shrugged his shoulders once more. "That may be so, Master Habael, but look at Ahiram. He is so driven that he does everything with a frightening intensity. When I train the Silent, I am constantly reminding them that they must give me everything they have, and then give me more. But with him, I have to hold him back. His standard of perfection is even higher than mine. I have often heard him tell his peers that a Silent must move like the waves of the sea, the breeze in the forest, and the raging, all-consuming fire of the plains. When they ask him who gave him these ideas, he replies matter-of-factly, 'My father, because that's what my father would say.' That's Ahiram for you."

"His father's shadow has grown tall amongst the Silent," replied Habael.

The commander nodded. "Do not forget his sister, Hoda. Every Silent would have loved to meet her," said the commander softly.

The sun crested the distant mountains, and its first rays turned the indigo of the night into a soft blue. Tanios looked up and saw the stars dim, and then disappear altogether. *How appropriate*, he thought. *Just like Ahiram's first day of training.*

>✿✿✿<

Tanios remembered that day vividly. Ahiram had been with them for six months, during which he sat on the sideline watching the students' daily training. The Silent had been engaged in a game of agility tag, which Tanios used to help them hone their skills. Two teams had stood facing each other across a fifty-by-fifty foot square, covered with a preponderance of white tiles and fewer black tiles. Before the start of the game, an arbitrator had assigned each player a number as he handed them a dart dipped in a red tincture.

When the commander had called a number, two opponents leaped inside the square and sprinted to the midline. Once they crossed it, they could tag their opponent if he had not yet crossed the midline or if he happened to be on a white tile. A player on a black tile could not throw his dart, but he could not be shot at either. Further, if a player managed to reach the end of the square, he received an extra dart; and if he crossed the square back to his starting point, his opponent was disqualified. Since a player could be tagged while jumping from one black tile to another, reaching the back line was far from easy. As the Silent's proficiency increased, Commander Tanios decreased the black tiles until none remained.

Tanios would spice up the game by calling several numbers at once.

A player who tagged someone other than his designated opponent was disqualified and his number transferred to his closest team player. A dozen simultaneous players taught the Silent to rely on one another, to move in tandem, and to watch their backs while reacting to every move their opponents made.

One student had been ill that day, so Noraldeen stood without an opponent. Tanios had ordered Ahiram to join the opposing team. The students–who had not taken this order seriously–erupted in laughter. The commander, aware of the incongruity of the situation, had not objected. After all, asking a young slave to face a Silent was akin to asking a farmer to engage a soldier. Noraldeen alone had not laughed.

"Do not make us wait, young man."

The commander's voice had stilled the room. The students had seen the slave get up and take his place in their midst.

"Commander," had interjected young Jedarc, unable to keep his mouth shut, "do you want us to play *nice*?"

"I want you to do your best, Jedarc, as always," had replied the commander without taking his eyes off the slave. "Now, Jedarc, listen carefully: *'Who shall bemoan the fate of the Silent who, trusting his eyes, fails to take the full measure of his adversary?'* What have I just quoted?"

"Chapter 3, verse 1 of the Book of Lamentation."

With these sobering words, the game had proceeded. Then the commander had called Noraldeen and Ahiram. Noraldeen, a fast runner, had reached the midline first, but then Ahiram leaped, and everyone froze. Noraldeen's throw had been accurate, but futile. Later, she had admitted that tagging Ahiram had been like tagging the wind or the rain. Ahiram had landed behind Noraldeen and gently tagged her with her own dart that he had caught in midair.

That day, his team had been doing badly. So much so, that when he had been called a second time, he faced six opponents, yet managed to tag all of them. Tanios had been astounded at the speed, precision, and power of Ahiram's throws. Round after round, Ahiram had tagged his opponents. Eventually, there had been only two opponents left in the court: Banimelek and Ahiram. Banimelek towered over Ahiram. His powerful build was coupled with fast reflexes.

Tanios wondered if Ahiram had found his match. He had given the signal. Ahiram had leaped forward, barely touched the ground and rebounded in the air. They thought he had been flying. Tanios watched attentively as Ahiram interweaved well-known movements with movements of his own, that were unlike anything they had seen before. Banimelek had attempted to avoid the fury by sidestepping Ahiram and outflanking him, but it had been useless. Ahiram sped past Banimelek, had jumped, and performed a perfect backward somersault, landing behind his opponent. Banimelek whirled around and had been promptly served a dart on his nose.

"You're it," Ahiram had said with a glint in his eye.

Banimelek had stood frozen. No one could believe what had just happened. Noraldeen applauded, and they had all joined in. He blushed and had looked down. Banimelek had slapped him on the shoulder: his sign of approval and respect. They had surrounded him and drowned him with questions. How did he do this move? Why throw the dart the way he did? Tanios had to call them back to order. He then asked Ahiram if he would like to join the Silent Corps. The young boy had nodded, and they had all welcomed him with cheers and applause.

The young Ahiram was incredibly fast and the accuracy of his blows was frightening. Whenever a Silent became his prey, he moved like a dart, tearing through the air with a purpose that could not be deflected. In all his fighting years, Tanios had never met his equal, save perhaps a long lost friend whose absence the commander felt keenly, now more than ever.

By his talents and abilities, Ahiram had won the admiration of his peers. By his humility, he had won their respect. He was straightforward, truthful, and soft-spoken. Ahiram was technically their superior, but he behaved as one of them. Sure, he blushed with pleasure when they had all applauded, but he had not shown off, a behavior that would have been characteristic of a boy his age. This commanding maturity had earned him the Silent's friendship and admiration.

Gradually, and without anyone's intervention, his commanding role had confirmed itself. It seemed natural that Ahiram would become a Silent. It seemed fitting that he would lead his class. They learned to go to Ahiram for advice, and he would humbly direct them. Whenever the question of slavery came up, they avoided it with pained embarrassment; an aberration of sorts, that defied the natural laws.

>◌◌◌<

Ahiram was Tanios' star pupil, the best he had ever seen, and tomorrow, by all accounts, he would be dead.

Tanios sighed once more. *If only I could take his place*, he thought. His affection for the lad was so deep he was willing to lay down his life for him. But this was not to be. Ahiram would enter the mines, perhaps for the last time, not to be seen again.

"Restless, Commander Tanios?" Habael stepped onto the balcony and stood by his friend.

"I am not the only one, I see."

"A man of my age needs little sleep," replied Habael, with a smile.

The two men stood there leaning quietly on the stone railing and peered into the night. They seemed to comfort each other without words, as men do sometimes when sharing a burden uncharacteristically heavy. That stubborn lad was taking part in the Games tomorrow, and there was nothing to stop him, except death.

"I have done everything I could to make sure he will be rested and strong for tomorrow. He is sleeping soundly."

"Thank you, Master Habael." These words alone brought comfort to Tanios' soul, yet he could barely restrain a sob. He cleared his throat before continuing. "Do you think he will make it tomorrow?"

Habael looked at Tanios. He then placed his arm on the tall man's shoulder. "I have never been as hopeful as I am tonight."

"Why?" vehemently replied Tanios. "Tell me, my friend, how could you be so bold in the face of such a bleak prospect? Surely, you are not ignorant of the threats to his life? The Temple has decided his fate and neither you nor I nor anyone else can stop them."

"I am all too aware of the Temple's intent, Commander." Habael looked up at a sky resplendent with stars. He pointed at one of them, "Amalein, Lantern of Hope. Did you ever wonder why these stars shine so vividly? Night after night, they stand at their appointed places shining brightly, as they ought. There is in this heavenly order, a harmony that gladdens the heart and gives peace to my old age. For beyond these stars, in the confines of the heavens, Amalseer, Undying Hope, shines. It sustains us, even in the face of the most gruesome death. I believe Ahiram will overtake his enemies and come out victorious."

"Forgive me if I do not share your hope, Master Habael. I am a man of action who has learned to measure risks and determine their outcome. My hope rests on measurable facts. I pay my tribute to the gods, but I do not ask from them what I cannot do myself."

"Any progress in the case at hand?" asked Master Habael, mostly to give his friend something else to focus on.

The commander grunted. "No woman in the castle is a redhead, so this is rather frustrating."

"You mean apart from the high priestess?"

"Indeed, and it would be absurd to think that she would be killing her own, just as it would be absurd to think that I would be willing to kill a Silent. So, yes, apart from her there are no other redheads in the castle."

"Could this woman be someone exterior to the castle?"

"Yes, but I cannot question every redhead in the city. This investigation needs all of my attention, and I confess, I am distracted right now."

"I understand," said Habael.

A rooster crowed in the distance. The moon was cresting. Its cold, silver rays splashed the valley beneath with a ghostly glow. A jaybird took its flight, and below in a garden of the King's castle, a dog barked. Tanios caught himself wishing he had been stuck in a prolonged nightmare that would soon melt away at the rising of the sun, taking with it the Games, Baal and these bloody murders. Yet he knew better. Indeed, he knew better.

> ❖❖❖ <

Soloron surveyed his men training for battle. The sun had not yet crested the high peaks and a freezing cold wind whipped the soldiers like an impatient taskmaster stirring his slaves into action.

Soloron had relocated the Undergrounders from the mines to this hard-to-access canyon, south of Taniir-The-Strong Castle. Away from prying eyes, he gave his soldiers a proper training, modeled after that of the High Riders but with slight, yet important, modifications.

Being a well-traveled man who had fought under different skies and rulers, he had synthesized what he learned into a unique fighting style that became the Undergrounders' hallmark.

In the sky, a large vulture was gliding in circles. *Probably some beast dying of thirst*, thought Soloron, and he imagined the King running away to die of thirst in the scorching heat of the desert. This thought brought a broad smile to his tanned face, where two dark eyes glittered like the deadly gems of Haradoon. His gaze turned back down toward his men. They were ready. His company now numbered in the thousands—a small army that would surprise the King and the Baalites. Suddenly, the imposing frame of Frajil materialized beside him. Soloron, at six feet ten inches was by no means short, but he was dwarfed by his younger brother's height; at nearly nine feet, he towered over everyone else. Frajil's shoulders were broader than two strong men standing side-by-side. Still, this giant was quiet like a tiger ready to pounce on its prey.

"Soloron, we ready for chicken." Seemingly, Frajil had finally understood the hidden meaning of this expression.

"Yes, my dear Frajil, tonight we roast the chicken."

"No, Soloron. Cook says chicken ready now. I hungry."

"You want to eat chicken for breakfast?"

"No," replied Frajil, offended. "I no eat chicken for breakfast. I eat chicken for strength."

He paused a moment, as though vaguely sensing that, perhaps, "breakfast" had a different meaning than what he had thought. "What is breakfast?" he asked cautiously.

Soloron sighed. "Never mind. Let the men rest and eat."

"And tonight chicken, too?"

"Yes, Frajil, chicken tonight, too. Now, here is what I want you to do for me. Listen carefully. This is a hard one. I want you to go to the kitchen right now and see if I'm there, and if I'm not, I want you to stay there until you find me. Do you understand?"

"Yes, Soloron. I go."

Frajil nodded energetically before taking off on his new mission. He always liked new and challenging missions, and finding Soloron in the kitchen seemed challenging enough. Soloron sighed, *Keeping him busy is getting more and more difficult.*

Once Soloron had tricked simple-minded Frajil one way, he could not repeat the trick a second time. Frajil had an incredible memory for these things and would only respond to new challenges, even if they were minute variations of old ones. *What this boy needs is some real action, and he will soon get it aplenty.* Below, the men were preparing for the seemingly impossible task of storming the castle, dethroning the King, and declaring Soloron the new King of Tanniin. *If the Baalites only knew of the little surprise we are preparing for them,* thought Soloron with a grin on his face.

Soloron walked back down to the training ground and stepped inside a large cabin where a dozen smiths were at work under the direction of Kerk, the dwarf. They had been working day and night to forge the swords, spears, and arrowheads his men would need. Soloron picked up a finished sword and checked the angle of the blade; he gripped the finely fashioned hilt and felt the weight and balance of the sword by cutting the air with it. He smiled. Kerk was a master at forging and honing swords known for their strength and flexibility.

"Is the artful art of the artistic artists," asked Kerk, pointing to the blacksmiths, "to the satisfying satisfaction of the commanding commander? I am of the opinionated opinion that she is a most suitably suitable and suitable most suitably for your enterprising enterprise."

Soloron expressed his agreement with a grin and a bow. He understood the general meaning of the dwarf's words and did not want to offend him by saying the wrong thing; and with the dwarfs, the wrong thing is usually the part of the sentence he would consider safe. "Master Kerk, you are the best blacksmith I have ever known," he said cautiously.

Kerk bowed. "Thank you, Commander," and returned to his work.

Soloron left the smiths and stood outside contemplating the desert "Tonight, the throne shall be mine."

>❂❂❂<

The three previous Games had started from the plaza south of Taniir-The-Strong, but the Game of Meyroon was launched north of the castle, from a square plaza overlooking a narrow and steep canyon. Ramany, expecting a much larger crowd for the fourth and last day, had tasked the slave master in charge of the seating arrangements to speed up the transportation of the benches from the first to the second plaza. The slaves had worked tirelessly through the night to dismantle, carry, and rebuild the benches along the perimeter of the plaza that faced the starting location of the Game. By the time the sun lit the tip of the Lone Tower and even before the last nail had been hammered, the benches were filled to capacity by an eager mass.

Under the watchful eyes of the crowd, the slaves had raised a smaller platform for the King, high priestess, judges, and the King's retinue, in the center of the plaza. Twenty feet away, they were putting the finishing touches on a one-hundred-and-fifty-foot wooden ramp which jutted over the edge of the canyon.

To reach the ingress to the Mine of Meyroon, each contender would run along the ramp, picking up speed as they went, and jump into the canyon to catch a rope dangling from an arch thirty feet away. The ramp was gently sloped to direct the athlete's sight away from the bottom of the canyon which lay some two thousand feet below. A contestant who missed the rope would tumble to his death.

Having caught the rope, they would swing to the other side where they would have to land on a four-foot-wide ledge without slamming into the opposite cliff. Then, they would have to use two more ropes to reach the entrance of the Mine at the opposite end of the Canyon.

The canyon was known as *Terim Tanniin*—Dragon's Flight—and anyone who walked along its rims would be struck by the serpentine shape $\curvearrowright$ of its walls. From the spectators' vantage point, the ledge was located close to the left end-point of the snake-like canyon $\curvearrowright$. Running along this ledge—and not falling into the canyon—the athlete would "take flight" by catching a second rope with which he would cross the first bend. Midway through, he would let go of the second rope, catch a third that would carry him through the second bend and to the right end-point of the canyon where the entrance to the Mine of Meyroon was located. Three ropes were chosen for this Game in honor of El-Windiir, who "flew thrice", as the locals would say.

Food merchants and sellers of souvenirs walked among the crowd shouting their wares. Some had even managed to create small, wooden figurines of Ahiram. But in the prevailing stillness, their shouts sounded out-of-place as if this was a funeral and they the unwelcome intruders.

The royal procession sat on the raised platform surrounded by the Silent. The athletes stood in a single line facing the King. Jamiir nodded, and eight trumpeters facing each other—four on either side of the royal platform—let out a vibrant shout that cut through the foreboding quietude, signaling the beginning of the Game of Meyroon. Incredibly, the crowd did not applaud, but remained still, and the stillness was so thick that one could distinctly hear the cry of a babe in his mother's arms high up in the benches. Ahiram lifted his eyes and saw her trying desperately to calm her child. An image flashed back from his memory: his mother sitting under the great tree, consoling him. He looked away, surveying the crowd for friendly faces. *Father, if I do not see you alive, may you receive my bones and know that your son fought bravely.*

Hiyam glanced at Ahiram, but seeing that he caught her glance, she looked away quickly and regretted it. She glanced at him again and saw that he was staring at her with his annoyingly defiant smile. She tried to sustain his look but could not. Her conscience pricked her. She wanted to believe her mother's arguments, to be convinced they were noble and good. "Better that a slave dies than Tanniin be crushed," Bahiya had told her. "The life of a slave is not worth an empire," she explained, matter-of-factly.

Still, Hiyam could not accept that Ahiram had to pay the price for their peace with his blood. *But he is a slave, a thing. He is not even a person.* She repeated these words to herself, trying to subdue her conscience, forcing it to accept the Temple's logic, but like a wild horse, it stubbornly refused. *If you were to kill a horse half as good as Ahiram, you would be severely punished,* she told herself. *You would treat a dog better than they are treating him, and he is the most amazing athlete you have ever seen. Admit it, Hiyam. He is the only one who bested you despite the odds and Baal's magic.*

At long last, the slaves had completed their tasks. The slave master walked the length of the ramp for a final inspection and when he nodded his approval, the trumpets sounded for the second time, and again, only silence answered. The King looked back wondering if the benches were empty or if the people had forgotten about the Games. But no, the benches overflowed with men, women and children staring at him. The King, who had never been close to his people, believed their soundless stance stemmed from a childish disappointment. *These people must have heard that the Games are about to be cancelled,* he thought, *Still, better the Temple cancels the Games than overtake the Kingdom.* Had he perceived the years of pent-up frustration, anger, and pain simmering beneath their muted silence, he might have been scared and perhaps would have taken the appropriate corrective actions, for Jamiir was not an ill-intentioned king, but rather a king who expected people to bring their problems to his attention instead of being attentive to the unspoken problems of his subjects. But beyond sorrow and suffering the hush of the crowd carried hope forward like a silent wave about to crash on the Kingdom and overtake it.

The King composed himself and glanced at Bahiya sitting beside him. She was cooling herself with her small, gold-trimmed, ivory fan, one of his many gifts for the high priestess. He wondered if the crowd was offended by the Queen's absence. Earlier, Ramel had met with Bahiya. "I do not like these Games," she had explained, "and I would greatly appreciate it if you could do me the honor of standing by the King's side today."

King Jamiir looked at Ahiram and breathed a sigh of relief, knowing it would end today. The slave would not come out of the mines alive. The people's dream would be buried with him, the crowd would disperse, and life under Baal's shadow would go on. He would have to reassure the Temple of Tannin's faithfulness, but with Bahiya at his side, it should be a relatively simple procedure.

Then we will all be able to sleep soundly, thought King Jamiir, forgetting the murders still haunting the castle.

The third trumpet blast sounded and did not fare any better than the first two. Only this time, tension filled the air, and the contestants bowed low before the King. There were three teams left in the race: Ahiram, Hiyam and her men, and one team from Quibanxe. The banners of Ahiram were lifted high and all present, except for the King, the high priestess, and the royal retinue, stood up to salute the flag. Then Garu stood, walked to the King and gave him a white silk handkerchief. Jamiir's hand rose, the athletes parted, and Ahiram stood facing the ramp, readying himself for the final race. Jamiir kept the handkerchief in his hand for a little while longer, enjoying his ability to hold everyone in suspense, and then let it go. It whirled, buoyed by a sudden waft that twirled it rapidly before dropping it abruptly on the crowd.

The trumpets sounded, imperious and commanding. Ahiram leaped forward. A roar of joy answered back. Suddenly, the fervor of the Games was back. The crowd was cheering their champion. Ahiram sped up along the ramp and without hesitation, jumped along an upward arc, and as if to defy the gods, the King, or the Temple, he swung around facing the crowd as he caught the rope single-handedly, and let it carry him backward to the other side.

The crowd rose like a mighty wave and chanted his name. He reached the end of his flight and landed softly on the ledge, bowed and waved. A thunderous clap answered him. He bowed once more, and then looked down.

The view was breathtaking. Deep below, the valley glimmered like a thousand jewels beneath the sun. Straight ahead, the canyon's vertical walls shone, and above him the limitless sky was calling.

"Oh, how I wish I could fly," he sang in a low voice. "To taste the free skies before I die, I would shine like snow in the cold winter air and fly, fly away with not a care... I would soar in the empty space away from the golden fields of summer and would know the heavenly grace hidden within the evanescent flower..." He remembered once more that he did not know the rest of the song and had often wanted to ask Jedarc for it. The song was attributed to El-Windiir, and it felt right to give him the credit, even if the Kingdom's founder had never sung it.

I would have wished to know which flower this was... he thought as he prepared to run. Oddly, the thought that this may be his last time to sing did not scare him. His folks fished sharks, and sometimes the fisherman became the quarry, taken to the depths of the sea by the fearsome beast. He knew he was going against a much more dangerous foe. A shark was not cruel—he was not a monster. *No*, he thought, *sharks are beautiful. Baal is a monster.*

An eagle's screech startled him. He looked up and saw the majestic bird soar lazily above him. A brisk, cold air blew through the canyon, and in that moment, standing alone on the cliff between heaven and earth, Ahiram felt an exhilaration that he had never experienced before. Suddenly, he understood the thrill El-Windiir had felt when, according to the legend, he flew for the first time from the stone slab where Ahiram was now standing.

The Silent backed into the corner where the two sides of the canyon met. It smelled of moss and jasmine. Ahead and above him, an arbitrator stood holding a line tied to the second rope Ahiram would use to cross the first bend of the canyon. The other end of the rope was tied to a pivoting platform set midway through the first arc and as soon as the Silent grabs the rope, a mechanism would be released that would slingshot the rope—and him with it—at dizzying speed into the air.

The Silent closed his eyes and concentrated. The rope swayed gently, eagerly awaiting his embrace. *Run like a lion sprinting toward its prey,* he thought. He waited until he felt relaxed and ready and then sprinted toward his target. He ignored the walls, the narrow ledge, and the canyon below. As he reached the end of the slab, he jumped straight ahead. The arbitrator let go of the strand just as Ahiram firmly grabbed the rope and began his flight into the curved canyon. As he disappeared from view, the crowd cheered and their cheers filled the valley with a mighty echo. Then, the mechanism holding the other end of the rope was released, and the Silent felt as though his arms were being ripped from his body. The canyon sides became a blur as he was pulled forward with his body in a position nearly parallel to the valley floor.

The walls of the canyon drew closer as he entered the first bend and in a split second, he saw a big boulder jutting from the opposite wall. With supreme effort, he managed to bring his knees up and the soles of his boots brushed against the rocks' surface. There was no time to think or to ponder the vagaries of the Games; all he could do was to hold on to the rope.

He reached the end of the first bend and anxiously scanned the space ahead for the third rope. He located it just as his rope, having reached the end of its range, slackened. Ahiram released it and zipped through the air toward his quarry, feet first. He performed a half-flip and grabbed the end of the rope so quickly, that the assigned arbitrator did not manage to release the line holding the rope in place before Ahiram had pulled away. The arbitrator was yanked forward and he fell in a scream. Luckily, he was tied to a safety line that saved his life. *Hah. Failed to let go in time. No warm chicken for him tonight,* thought Ahiram as he entered the second arc of the serpentine canyon, his feet brushing against the opposite wall.

This time, Ahiram brought his knees to his chest. He heard the twang of the second mechanism, and once more, he was hurled through the air at an incredible speed. Despite having his feet curled up, he barely managed to avoid crashing into several small trees growing on the opposite side of the wall. As he reached the end of the turn, he glimpsed a gaping hole in the narrow wall where the canyon dead-ended. *That's the cave. I'm going too fast. I need to slow down.* Instead, he was yanked back, for the range of the second rope was markedly shorter than that of the first one. Instantly, he let go and his momentum carried him— barely—to the end of the canyon where he managed to grab hold of shrubberies several feet below the entrance. He waited a short moment to catch his breath, then quickly climbed up to the cave. As he was about to enter, he remembered the additional danger lurking past the entrance of the grotto. *This flight made me forget Baal's men,* he thought. *They may be waiting inside this cave to kill me.* He stayed motionless, preparing for the most dangerous move. Pebbles fell down the opposite side of the cliff. They bounced on a rock and fell to the valley floor. Ahiram looked up and saw someone back off hurriedly. *Arbitrators, most likely. They must be waiting for me to let go of the rope before allowing Hiyam's team to come after me.*

Ahiram inched up, silent as a shadow, and peered inside the cave. It was barely large enough for one man to crouch. Relieved, he climbed in and sat on the sandy ground. *Hiyam and her men will be here soon.* He got up. *Let them come. Three or four more killers will make no difference.*

He turned around and walked briskly along a very narrow path with sharp-edged rocks jutting from either side. Sooner or later, Hiyam and her men would reach the entrance, and the men of Baal would surround him from all directions.

The narrow passage widened and turned onto a broad, flat-walled corridor where no ambush could be mounted. His walk became a jog and then a vigilant sprint. He knew Hiyam had to bring her team to the entrance of the cave, but once they were all there, they would come after him at full speed.

The corridor widened again, and he sped up, maintaining a comfortable rhythm until he reached a three-pronged fork where the right path sloped down and the left turned sharply to the right. The torches lining the middle path indicated this was the one the arbitrators wanted the players to follow. Unhesitatingly, Ahiram followed the left path. Beyond the bend, three flights of stairs led him to a walkway that ran over the main path. Presumably, the miners used the lower path to move carts in one direction and the upper path to move them in the other. Thankfully, enough light from the torches below seeped through vents cut into the wall which allowed him to resume his fast run.

Several hours later, Ahiram reached the Cave of Many Ropes. Standing on a ridge four feet wide, he could hear the river gushing through the deep canyon six hundred feet below. The cave was a huge echo chamber that amplified the rush of the water into a roar that prevented two people standing side-by-side from hearing each other.

Above him, a series of nets and ropes, which the miners had used in the past to cross the abyss dangled from the high ceiling. Supposedly, men and dwarfs stood on these nets to mine the meyroon from the ceiling. No one had ever seen meyroon, much less mined it. However, the story handed down through the ages affirmed that men mighty and strong, alongside gifted dwarfs, were able to stand on these nets and mine above the abyss. They were called Meyroon Abaliim On-Nayiir, which meant "the flying miners of meyroon." Some fell into the rushing water that carried them to the Eye of Death, a gaping hole through which the river went underground before emerging in the open, several miles down at the edge of the forest. Only one miner was known to have survived this fall. Maril, an exceptionally gifted man who fell into the river, survived the Eye of Death, reached the forest, and founded the Kingdom of Sencher-Mendal, northwest of Tanniin which eventually was broken into the two neighboring kingdoms of Oronoque and Togofalk.

Like the miners of yore, the players were required to move from one net to another in order to cross the gaping hole splitting the large cave in two. Ahiram inspected these nets with a critical eye.

"If I were a High Rider," he muttered, "I would loosen one of these nets and make it look like an accident."

He reached into his belt, selected a grappling dart, attached a rope to it, and held it in his hand. He crossed the length of the ledge and leaped onto the first net, which swayed under his weight but held firm. Swiftly, the Silent began hopping easily from one net to the other. Midway through, a net tore along its full length, and Ahiram fell headlong. Instantly, he threw the dart. It caught the next net. As he suspected, the High Riders had not tampered with the next net, thinking one would do the trick. *Good thing they don't know what Silent are trained to do*, he thought as he climbed quickly. He freed his dart and resumed his halting progression from one net to another, moving as swiftly as prudence allowed. He did not want to confront Hiyam and her team while hanging from a net.

Thankfully, the rest of the crossing was uneventful. Ahiram reached the opposite side of the river, where one of the most difficult segments of this Game began. Facing him was a second abyss. Here, a quieter tributary of the main river flowed two thousand feet below. The cliff was steep, and the ceiling, as high as in the previous part, sloped down gently. Thirty-two consecutive ropes ran the distance from these heights to the river below. Both ends of each rope were bolted to the ceiling with iron pegs. Known as the Flying Stairs, they were used to carry or transfer buckets down from these heights, but how the contents were transferred from the end of one rope to the start of the next was a mystery.

Near the first rope, a cluster of handles hung from a hook. Each handle was shaped like two bull horns joined with an iron coupling. The coupling doubled as the axis of a grooved, wooden wheel, made to roll on the ropes.

The competitors were required to use these rolling handles to descend the flying stairs by placing the wheel on the rope and gliding down as they held the handles. At the end of each rope, the participants had to grab the next rope, transfer the handle over, and glide down again until they reached the ground.

"You will be tempted to forego the handles and use your hands and feet to go down. Do not do it." Tanios' voice rang clearly in Ahiram's mind. "Due to the constant humidity in these caves, the ropes are very slippery. Every player who tried this strategy ended up either burning his hands or falling into the river. Use the handles. Imagine you are running away from a fire. Do not think, and do not hesitate. This is one situation where concentrating solely on the act, and not worrying about anything else, will get you through. Nothing else will."

"It is a dance, Ahiram," he could almost imagine his sister now speaking to him as if he was still a child in Baher-Ghafé and she was consoling him: "Dance with the wind, dance on the ropes, dance joyfully. Your movement must be beautiful. Dance for Hoda." Ahiram smiled as the face of Hoda faded away. Ahiram climbed up, took a handle, and secured it to the rope. He opened the little pouch that Habael had given him, sprinkled the white powder on his hands, and rubbed them.

"What is it?" he had asked the old man. "A magical concoction?" Habael had gazed at him with eyes that burned with an ancient fire. It nearly scared him. "Do not speak of magic so lightly, young man," Habael had said with a voice he barely recognized. The old man's features had quickly softened, and he was once more his usual self. "Flour and salt," he had said evenly. "It keeps your hands dry for a firmer grip."

Ahiram held the horns and jumped. The speed surprised him, and he nearly knocked his head against the stalactites as he whizzed by. He reached the end of the first rope abruptly and was almost thrown down, but before the handle slid back, Ahiram managed to grab the next rope and transfer the handle over. This time, the speed of the descent was even greater than before. Ahiram braced himself for the jarring stop, which came all too quickly. He gripped the handle hard as he swayed forward and barely managed to avoid slamming into the ceiling. The handle rolled back a few feet before stopping and putting the next rope out of his reach. He was beginning to understand the real challenge of this crossing. *There are thirty remaining ropes to go through*, he thought. He wiggled forward, held the rope with one hand, swung ahead, and caught the next rope. Quickly, he placed the wheel on the rope and sped along.

The strain on his arms and legs increased with every crossing. His grip started to slip with the sweat and humidity, and he locked his legs even harder. Midway through, he reached for the pouch of flour and salt, and rubbed his hands again with the powder, hanging by his feet. When he tried to put the pouch back in place, he let go of it a little too soon and it dropped from his grasp. Ahiram winced as he saw the precious powder dissipate in the air. *I'll have to finish without it.*

Still hanging from his feet, he swung back up, caught the rope with his left hand without letting go of his feet, and laid on top of it. He inspected the next rope. Water seeped from the ceiling above and it was soaked with icy-cold water. *My hands are dry now and I'd like to keep them that way.*

His shoulder began to throb, for it had not yet fully healed from the injury sustained in the Game of Bronze. He slithered forward as far as the rope would allow, reached with his right arm, and placed the wheel on the next rope without touching it or the ceiling. He tried to grab the second handle with his left hand, but it was out of reach.

I could gain a few inches if my back was not stuck against the ceiling, he thought. Quickly, he switched around and hung beneath the rope, facing the ceiling. The next rope was now behind him, so he moved back as far as the rope would allow. He reached out, placed the handle on the wet rope, and managed to grab it with both hands. He let go of his feet and zipped down backward.

"Not good," he said arching his neck trying to see behind him. In the blink of an eye, he let go of the handles, turned around, and caught them before they escaped out of reach. Just then, the ceiling became flat. The wheel's speed decreased until it stopped moving.

"This rope is a lot longer than I thought," mumbled Ahiram.

He was one hundred feet high and could see that the remaining seven ropes did not lead to the ground, as he had originally thought, but to a platform accessible by stairs. He swayed forward and backward to move the wheel, until he reached the end of the rope where he resumed his descent.

Ahiram reached the end of the twenty-ninth rope and had only three more to cross when he heard a terrified scream behind him. He looked back and saw nothing, but he knew that one of the participants had not made it. He turned around as an arrow grazed his left cheek and hit the ceiling, drawing a spark from the rock before falling down. The archer stood up on the platform. He leaned on his long bow, a murderous grin on his face. He watched Ahiram hanging from the rope.

"Zat wos a worning shot," he said with the thick accent of the northern land of Bar Tan, famed for its archers, "but I lioke ployin with my torget foirst." He grinned once more as he slowly pulled an arrow from his quiver, clearly savoring the moment. But before he notched the arrow, Ahiram let go of the handle, held the rope, and lay on top of it without losing his balance.

"Troyin to hoide I see," said the archer amused. "No proiblem. I'll kill you slowly."

In the few seconds it took the archer to speak, Ahiram took one of his crossbows and clipped the end of his longest rope to its shaft. He positioned the dart, drew the bow and released.

The archer shot his arrow. Ahiram fell.

The archer moved to the edge of the platform and looked down. He frowned.

"Where did he go?" he asked. "He should be floating in the woiter, I shot him. Nobody told me the Soilent use moigic."

"We don't," said a voice behind him.

He turned around and faced Ahiram's soles rushing at him. A wave of pain hit him like a brick, then all went black. The Silent held the man by his arm to prevent him from falling to his death. He took the archer's tunic and helmet and snatched his crossbow and quiver. *This is not the best disguise, but it will help,* he thought. He descended the stairs, and after some effort, managed to pry the dart free from the wood beam behind the platform.

He stowed the dart and the rope back in his belt, then continued down the stairs, silent as a cat, and landed on the dry spot of a stone slab that was mostly submerged beneath cascading streams of fresh water. He had entered the *Meipoor* (the waters of purification). There, in a basin of pure gold, rocks were purified, and supposedly, the meyroon extracted.

The basin of pure gold was a short distance away. Ahiram opened his eyes wide. In the basin, a pair of crystalline-blue wings, the presumed color of meyroon, floated. He had managed to locate one of the two pairs of wings, and it was his for the taking.

$$\succ \text{❁❁❁} \prec$$

The men of Baal manning the Lone Tower were getting bored. These mercenaries came from the north, the dreaded Kingdom of Bar Tan, the western steps of Thermodon, and the icy mountains of Varkun. They were paid by the Temple to maintain a threatening presence in Tanniin. Used to action, these rough and uncomplicated men were uncomfortable in confined spaces such as these.

In a surprise move, the King had asked their garrison to guard the castle. The idea seemed pleasant at first, but to the dozen soldiers stuck in the staircase of the Lone Tower, it quickly became unbearable. The staircase was hot and stifling, and there was nothing to do other than count each other's nose hairs. Only strict discipline and the fear of the high priestess kept them in check.

One of them, Obyj the Varkunian, saw someone come up the stairs. He whistled, and all the men stood to attention. Seeing that it was Bahiya, he felt his throat constrict and began to sweat. These were hardened criminals who could kill anyone without pity when ordered to do so, but none of them wanted to be in a room alone with High Priestess Bahiya. As soldiers of the Temple, they had seen some of their companions suddenly disappear and knew they were the victims of the dreaded Kerta Priests of Baal.

Bahiya belonged to a different order of Baal known as the Methodicals. Whereas the Kerta priests focused on the human mind and sought to subdue the will of man to the whiles of the priests. The Methodicals mastered the magical arts of sowing and evading curses. The Kerta priests penetrated the minds of their victims and worked from within. A Methodical's curse was second to none, and there were no walls strong enough to keep them out.

But these differences were lost on the mercenaries, who feared Bahiya as if she were the goddess Mot in the flesh and believed she could send them to her abode, the Pit of the Dead, with a simple touch.

A High Rider walked behind her. *Probably her personal guard,* thought Obyj. He glanced at the young man, shut his eyes, and nearly bit his tongue as he clamped his jaws together to prevent his teeth from clattering.

The man walking behind the priestess was as pale as a ghost. Obyj did not care to know if the young man was on his way to the Pit or if he was some otherworldly creature that came from there. He wished he was somewhere else, like that good-for-nothing Shlick who was sent to the mines to shoot down the slave. *Shlick, you dirty scum,* thought Obyj, *if I hear you brag about it, I'll make you eat the next beer mug you touch and—*

Bahiya's voice shattered his daydream, "I have been informed by the commander of the Silent Corps that someone performed forbidden acts of magic in this tower." Her voice was as cold as steel. At the mention of magic, the men's courage failed them.

We're dead, thought Obyj. *We're all dead.*

"I have come to investigate," continued the high priestess. "I do not wish to be disturbed. You will go back downstairs and guard the tower. Do not allow anyone to come up until I call for you. Have I made myself clear?"

"Yes, Your Honor," replied the men. They could not believe their luck.

When Bahiya spoke of magic, they thought she wanted to use them in her experiments the way the Kerta priests did with their comrades. They thought they were dead, or worse, turned into monsters. Instead, she was sending them down to guard the tower. They clambered down the stairs as quickly as their wobbling feet would take them.

"Wait for my signal," she repeated.

Obyj and his companions stood guard around the Tower. They waited for the signal, hoping it would never come.

An eerie silence permeated the wide corridors of the royal floor, as if the living had deserted Taniir-The-Strong Castle.

"The spirits of the dead are here," whispered one of the soldiers.

"Ghosts condemned to an everlasting winter of sorrow and pain," added another.

Obyj's knuckles were hurting him. He glanced around and felt a wave of relief wash over him when he saw the commander of the Silent walking toward them.

"Come up quickly," shouted Bahiya. "Come and see."

Reluctantly, they returned up the stairs and were awed by what they saw through the Star Room's windows.

340

17. QUEEN RAMEL

"From their youth, the daughters of the high priests of Babylon were exposed to the wiles of that court. The Adorant wooed them to join their lot, while the priestesses of the Temple of Baal thought to win their confidence and esteem; and men of various royal houses lavished extravagant gifts on them.
When these shenanigans are added to the merciless ploys of any high court, it produces young women whose chief vice is a refined form of selfishness.

"Soon, this egotism flowers, buds, and produces tyrannical souls bent on the merciless subjugation of others to satisfy their petty desires. Thus, Babylon, their mother, molds them in her own image.

"This city, the favored daughter of the gods, has grown conceited and pitiless. O, glittering Babylon, wonder of the gods, your downfall shall be great on the day of your visitation. Lo, these daughters of yours cry out from the Pit, and their cries reach the gate of heaven."

—Sayings of Jehdi, Great Priest of the Temple of Baal.

High up in the Lone Tower, Garu and Ibromaliöm were sitting on the floor of the Star Room looking dejectedly at each other. The strange door handle Master Habael and Jedarc had examined earlier lay on the floor, inside a triangular area between three black candles. Behind a veil of feigned bonhomie, the two men disliked each other intensely. They would have strangled the other had the refined mannerisms of the court not turned into a rigid cast preventing strangulation. The court considered such means of being rid of an importunate acquaintance to be uncouth. A dose of poison over a quaint supper, a discrete dagger while in Whisper Grove, or a clean kidnapping were some of the polite ways the nobility used to resolve an enduring disagreement.

Garu looked at Ibromaliöm and could not help but imagine him writhing in pain, bitten by a thousand snakes. Ibromaliöm yawned, shattering Garu's daydream, transforming the fleeting pleasure into shame. The head judge looked away. As much as he hated Ibromaliöm, he was glad to have him around. In a twisted way, Garu had grown attached to his dislike of Ibromaliöm. It gave meaning to his existence, which he believed to be an empty void. Though he did not admit it, Garu was jealous of Ibromaliöm on account of the Queen.

Until the arrival of Queen Ramel, Garu's existence had been peaceful. He had spent his time taking walks and studying plants and trees; subjects he loved to discuss with Master Habael. Life at the castle was pleasant, and his duties as a royal tutor were light and enjoyable. He taught history and languages, and was often involved in diplomatic missions.

The day Queen Ramel came to the castle, some years back, was etched in his mind. This indelible mark would remain there, he believed, until the day he died.

He remembered the first time he met the Queen and his mind brought him back to that very day, that very moment, and he relived it as if it were an eternal present.

He had been on his way back from one of his long walks when he first laid eyes on her, and he was awestruck. His heart became inflamed with a passion he had not known. He had believed, perhaps naively, that by serving her and fulfilling her every whim, she would, over time, develop similar feelings for him. Thus, Garu had become Ramel's slave, living in constant torment. He dreaded seeing her, yet despaired when he did not. He watched her every move, jealous of any man whom she would look at—except for the King, whom he knew she despised. He hated being far from her and yet did not know how to approach her. His days had fallen sway to the changing seasons of her mood, and the beating of his heart was regulated by her caprices. If, during a chance encounter, the Queen bestowed on him her tender gaze, Garu would be transported to the summit of joy. But if instead, she passed him by without a glance, he would be plunged into a raging sea of despair. In short order, he had changed from a quaint scholar, to a prisoner of his inchoate love for the Queen. Led by his imagination in a frenzied gallop, he had become unable to resist her wishes, ready to go to extremes for her. In his feverish mind, there was one major obstacle between the Queen and himself: Ibromaliöm.

Garu had known Ibromaliöm was a former *Tajèr*, a money man, as they were vulgarly called by the common folk. In principle, Garu had nothing against the lesser known organization of the Tajéruun. A Zakiir was a memory man: his job was to retain faithfully whatever he was told for a hefty sum of money. Ever since Baal forbade writing, the Zakiruun became the living history of Baal's Empire, faithfully consigning all transactions to memory. The Zakiruun were hand-picked men, chosen and trained for this task since their earliest youth. The Order of the Zakiruun became the keeper of every man's secrets, good or evil. Mostly, the Zakiruun memorized mundane business transactions. In cases of dispute, their faithful recitation of the contract was binding. Collectively, the order knew who sold what to whom, who owed how much for how long, and at what interest rate.

Two and a half centuries ago, Tajèr, a rich Zakiir, had met with a small group of wealthy colleagues. He had told them that many of his clients were hampered by the lack of short-term loans, preventing them from completing lucrative transactions. "These merchants trust us with their secrets. We remember the details of every transaction they make. We know them better than they know themselves," he had observed. "If we can loan them the funds for a reasonable fee, they will accept it."

He had prevailed on six other Zakiruun, and together they pooled a portion of their sizeable wealth into a common lending fund for low interest loans. So successful had their wager been that in a short span of years, their individual fortunes tripled, then doubled, and doubled again, until it rivaled that of many priests and monarchs. To avoid attracting unnecessary attention, they had shrouded their operation in a veil of secrecy, becoming an invisible order within the already mysterious order of the Zakiruun. Tajèr's little group had grown steadily until it numbered 144, a magical number according to Tajèr. After his passing, his followers became known as the Tajéruun. A mere one hundred years later, Sulariöm became the first Tajèr elected as overseer of the entire order of the Zakiruun, and ever since, every elected overseer has been a Tajèr. Garu was well acquainted with Galliöm, the current overseer of the Zakiruun: a mighty Tajèr, wealthy beyond imagining. Ibromaliöm, a well-to-do Tajèr in his own right, used to work with Galliöm, but left after a harsh dispute—the details of which he shared with no one.

As the niece of Sharr, the high priest of Babylon who oversaw the entire order of Baal, Ramel was of higher rank and might than Ibromaliöm. Yet, she never rebuked the former Tajèr, even when he would speak contemptuously to her. This baffled Garu and pained him profoundly.

Why would she allow Ibromaliöm to treat her so contemptuously? Was she not aware of Ibromaliöm's sarcasm? Surely everyone in the castle must have noticed his lack of respect. Garu interpreted the Queen's lax response as a diplomatic maneuver meant to keep peace with King Jamiir—who supposedly had bestowed his protective mantle on

Ibromaliöm. Whether this protection was real or imagined, Garu never bothered to check. He needed an explanation and had found one.

Despite his loathing for the Tajèr, Garu could not help but admire the nonchalant attitude Ibromaliöm displayed before the Queen. Garu tried on several occasions to assert his authority over Ramel, but a charming smile, pout, or gentle rebuke from her would melt his resolution away. He then equated freedom from his passion for the Queen with betrayal, and smothered the slightest inkling of freedom in a pool of dark remorse. To assuage the wave of regret that would follow, he had resolved to be ever faithful to the Queen. This he found consoling, and he would often wrap his renewed faithfulness around him like a child wraps himself with a blanket to ward off the bitter cold of the night.

"Are you sure you found it?"

Ibromaliöm's voice startled Garu.

"Yes, I told you," he replied gruffly. "I saw the door. I saw it. I know how to get there."

"I went down the secret stairs and followed your directions. They dead end deep into the ground. There is no passage."

"Of course there is no passage there," snapped Garu. "A cloak hides this passage from view; you knew that, so what did you expect? A flashing sign to point you in the right direction? Speaking of a flashing sign, Habael and a young Silent caught sight of you as you were coming up the stairs, but they could not find you. I convinced them you were not here, but it was not easy."

Ibromaliöm ignored the remark and continued. "How will you know how to open that door and deflect the curse?"

Garu shrugged his shoulders, "We will see when we get there."

"You had better, my friend, because I will not be falling under the curse," shrieked Ibromaliöm. "You are the slave of that woman, not I."

Garu sighed, put his face in his hands, and rubbed his eyes. He suddenly looked old and tired. He let his hand drop on his chest and gazed around him. The room was desolate with its burned candles and the dirty pools of dried, black wax marring the elaborate tiled floor. *Like leprosy eating away a beautiful face*, thought Garu, shuddering. He eyed Ibromaliöm, and envy surged in his soul once more. He wanted to despise this man, yet he felt only envy, and he hated himself for it. How did he get tangled with the Queen and Ibromaliöm in this machination?

Images from the past flashed before his eyes anew; a not too distant past when he had been content to take short walks up the mountain, reflecting on the natural beauty and enjoying the easy life in the castle. It had been during one of these outings that he happened to cross paths with Ramel. He had stood to the side and bowed. She had lightly touched his shoulder, and when he looked up, she smiled. Her smile had taken his breath away, and her gaze had ravished his heart. He did not remember what she had told him then, but he knew his heart had been enflamed with passion for her.

In the months that followed, he tried to understand why he had fallen in love with her. What was it that had touched him so deeply? Was it her smile when she stopped to greet him? Was it her eyes when she looked at him? Was it the light touch of her hand on his arm that had ignited fire in his heart? He could not tell anymore, but he still remembered vividly how, in that first encounter, he had been on top of the world, higher than the highest tower, elated beyond measure. Ever since, however, he had lived in crushing anxiety. Slowly his will had crumbled, yielding to the devastating passion that possessed him, until it had turned him into a faithful dog, a slave content to live in her shadow. He could not bear being away from her, yet being in her presence was constant torture. Thus, his life oscillated between the night of her absence and the shining light of her presence when she spoke to him. He lived for crumbs: a passing smile, a polite greeting, an evasive gesture.

His agony perdured until that fateful day when he had been abruptly told to meet the Queen in Whisper Grove just after midnight. He had gone to the meeting an hour and a half early and waited patiently in the cold for Ramel. He could hardly breathe. She had met him wrapped in a mantle of green velvet with a hood framing her lovely face in the moonlight. Her perfume had entranced him, and her words inebriated him. She had held his hand and told him of her high esteem for his work, her admiration for his knowledge, and her appreciation of his fidelity. She had kissed him on the cheek before leaving. He had remained on the bench, oblivious of time and space. Eventually, the cold had gnawed at his flesh, and he retired to his room with an everlasting feeling of love.

These meetings had become more frequent and lasted longer. Ramel's physical traits hypnotized him. He drank every one of her words, and they had fallen on his parched soul like rain in the desert. Her words had become a divine elixir that kept him coming back for more. Spring had turned into fall, and golden leaves danced in the wind like Garu's soul in the sea of love.

Then, abruptly, and for no apparent reason, Ramel had withdrawn from him. Life became an eclipse, his soul the playground of titanic forces. Anxiety had exploded in volcanoes of shame and self-recrimination. Bitter flows of burning lava had consumed his hope and exhilaration, leaving behind a scorched desert where winds of despair toyed with him and doubt tore him apart like an earthquake shatters the face of the earth. He nearly went mad and had tried to kill himself with a mixture of hemlock, thickened duck blood, and stale well water. Instead, he had ended up with a stubborn stomachache that no remedy could permanently heal.

Eventually, his strength gave out, and the storm that had ravaged his heart subsided. A dull emptiness had taken its place. Garu had felt thin and hollow, nearly nonexistent: a mere wraith, a shadow haunting deserted corridors like a ghost. Servants had laughed at him behind his back, even to his face, yet he did not care. His only hope, his only aspiration, had been to glimpse the Queen, even if fleetingly. Soon, he had lost his appetite and spent most of his nights awake, unable to sleep. He could barely speak, and whenever he would chance upon her walking with her retinue, she would glance indifferently at him as though he were a fly on the wall. These encounters had left him breathless and afflicted him day and night.

Soon, Garu's haggard face haunted the castle and had become the butt of the court's jokes. If Ramel overheard a nobleman deride Garu, she did nothing to stop it; instead, she laughed gaily at the inferred compliment. This behavior had not endeared her to the commander of the Silent Corps, who informed the King that Master Garu had lost his countenance and was an embarrassment to the royal court. All along, Jamiir had known that a daughter of Babylon, well versed in Baal's art of seduction, could drive a man to madness. He had rebuked his wife and met with the scholar to assess the situation. Garu could no longer carry a conversation. He would remain silent for long periods of time, downcast and oblivious to his surroundings. The King had resolved to send him to his summerhouse in the mountains for rest. Garu had been relieved.

No sooner had he arrived at the summerhouse than an unexpected visitor was at the door: Ramel. He had nearly fainted. She had entered and was her former warm and joyful self. She had spent most of the afternoon with Garu, and when night came, had asked him to swear an oath of complete obedience to her, under the curse of Baal. He agreed, even though he knew Baal's curses were of the worst kind. It was sheer folly, he knew, but he could not resist Ramel's charm. He had willingly accepted to become her slave. She had left him with the command to wait for her instructions.

Weeks went by without any news, until one day, Ibromaliöm came with a Zakiir. It had been the worst day of Garu's life: a day of shame, but a day of reckoning. Ibromaliöm had remained impassive, and told him he was to learn from the Zakiir everything he could possibly learn about spells and counter-spells. "Her Majesty the Queen wants you to learn all you can on the breaking of Baal's spells. This Zakiir is sworn to her Majesty. He will recite the *Libre of Sureï* for you. Learn as much as you can, as quickly as you can. That is all."

Now that the deception had been revealed, Garu felt strangely calm and recollected. He had not become angry; he had not even thought of revenge. Rather, he had felt as though he was regaining his reason—or at least a small part of it. He had been duped. Ramel had overtaken him and had compelled him to put himself under a curse. Still, he knew he had done it willingly for love, and as senseless as it seemed, he would do it again out of love for her.

He had thrown himself into the study of spells and counterspells with such ardor and vigor that he learned far more than the Queen or Ibromaliöm had anticipated. They had simply underestimated his mental capacities. In short order, Garu had learned how to deflect the effects of the curse by a careful use of hexes that required a small, personal item from an unsuspecting victim. Not too long after, Ibromaliöm had come to check on his progress and inadvertently had left a handkerchief on the table. After his departure, Garu had gazed at the object long and hard. He hated Ibromaliöm, suspecting him to be behind this odious ruse. In a fit of madness, he had considered using his newfound knowledge to his advantage. *All I have to do*, he had thought, *is place a few hexes on Ibromaliöm. In time, he will fall into my hands, and I can then use him to coerce Ramel to do my bidding.*

It had been tempting.

But wrong.

Confusedly, Garu had understood that his love for Ramel was pure. True, though she was married to the King, he had wanted her to divorce Jamiir and come live in the depth of the forest with him. He knew this was an impossible dream. Nonetheless, it was an honest dream. He would rather carry this curse like a badge of honor than sully his love for her in another man's blood, even if this man was as wicked as Ibromaliöm. That day, when Garu had thrown the handkerchief into the fire, he knew he had achieved a great victory. He was still the Queen's slave, and the curse hung over him like a cloud of bad dreams, but inside, he refused to harm another man out of love for Ramel—which meant that he was not without hope.

Three months before the start of the Games, the King had called him to Taniir-The-Strong Castle and put him in charge of overseeing the preparations. The Queen then informed him that she had chosen him as head judge. She also picked Ibromaliöm and Hylâz, the Zakiir who had been reciting the book to him as auxiliary judges. None of them were surprised to see Ramany—a local merchant and notorious informer of the Temple—appointed as the fourth judge.

Once more, his heart had become the battleground of intense feelings of self-loathing, burning love for the Queen, and raging hatred for Ibromaliöm. He knew that the curse he was under was gnawing at him, worming its way into his heart and soon would possess him—it was only a question of time.

Despite Hylâz's best attempts to hide the truth from him, Garu managed to piece together the few hints Ramel and Ibromaliöm had carelessly shared with him and guessed what they were after.

The *Libre of Sureï* was broken down into two parts: the first dealt with various curses and countercurses; but Garu understood only the general structure of a curse. Since Sureï had meant for accomplished masters of the spell world to hear this libre, he did not provide details on the creation, deployment, or control of curses.

The second part of the libre dealt with a series of lengthy descriptions of locales and objects that Sureï had cursed. Hylâz could only recite the section concerning the Lone Tower and the ancient castle ruins of Taniir-On-High, which overlooked Taniir-The-Strong Castle.

Garu knew this libre was highly confidential. He had asked Hylâz why he was permitted to recite it to him, a non-member of the Temple. The Zakiir had reminded him that as a priestess of Baal, the Queen was duty-bound to neutralize centers of magic by whatever means necessary.

"Every priest and priestess of Baal is allowed to use acolytes—slaves usually—to help in this task, provided these helpers are under a curse that will kill them in short order or cause them to lose their minds," he had said softly. "Every learned person knows that," he had added with a sarcastic tone.

"I see," Garu had replied softly. "The Queen is performing a good deed, and she has found a fool to do her bidding."

Hylâz had shrugged his shoulders and did not answer.

"This seems to make sense," Garu had continued. "Explain this to me then: why is Ibromaliöm involved?"

The sudden flash of terror in Hylâz's eyes had confirmed Garu's suspicions. "This is a cover-up," he had said, "a story she used to get her uncle, Sharr, to loan her a Zakiir who knew the *Libre of Sureï*. Is that not so? Ibromaliöm has other plans now, does he not, Hylâz?"

"Do not involve me in this madness, Garu," had spat Hylâz contemptuously. "I am a Zakiir bound to recite this book whenever my client asks me to do so. High Priest Sharr is my customer. He instructed me to recite this book to you at the Queen's bidding, and so I did. I am not involved in this scheme, and I have no intention to divine the Queen's plan."

Garu had not pressed this point. Sureï's recitation resumed: "Deep beneath Taniir-The-Strong lay a hidden temple to Tanniin where two sources of great power were intertwined. The first is the *Ithyl Shimea,* a libre of dark power that the Temple cannot control. The second rivals the *Ithyl Shimea* in power and is beyond the reach of mortal men. I laid a curse of destruction on this place. Woe to those who dare enter."

18. A Dark Quest

*"To seek what you do not understand is to misunderstand your
quest. To quest after a shining unknown is to let darkness shine
within you. Like a dying firefly, it will consume your soul, and
turn you into a ghost.*

*"Then again, a ghost is what you may have been seeking all along.
Truth renews you and fills your being with life. Ghosts are the
fruits of ignorance. Indeed, ignorance is to knowledge what a ghost
is to a body; it retains the form and loses the substance."*
–Memoirs of Shalimar the Poet

Garu finally understood that the Lone Tower was never meant to be an
observatory for stargazing. The star readers were questing for the hidden
place, but Baal eliminated their order before they succeeded. And now,
he, Garu, was about to succeed where they had failed. He figured out
that this odd handle was meant to open a hidden door leading to the
strange place. He also knew this place was somewhere beneath the tower
in the depth of the mine. He had had no hopes of unraveling Sureï's
curse, but when Hylâz recited a passage about strange objects called
absorbers, he perked up.

According to Sureï, absorbers were pebbles made from a dark stone
found in the spell world. They had the ability to absorb the effects of a

curse for a short time. "There may be a need for a priest of Baal to momentarily enter a cursed location," Hylâz had recited in his usual, soft voice. "Absorbers will deflect the curse for a few minutes. As they absorb the curse, they will produce a reddish glow, which will die down when they can no longer sustain it. They must be allowed to cool before they are used again. After repeated use, they will grow brittle and break into small particles. If the one carrying the absorbers is within the range of the curse when the absorbers fail, the curse will kill him."

When he told the Queen about the absorbers, she had nodded, and a month later, Ibromaliöm brought him half a dozen of these strange objects. "Courtesy of the Queen," he had told him with a sardonic smile.

"We will have a few minutes to get in, find what you seek, and get out," Garu said.

"No, my friend," Ibromaliöm replied, grinning so widely that Garu felt that the tall man was turning into a shark. "The absorbers will hold the curse back for four, maybe five, minutes, not long enough for the Queen and I to take what we have come for. This is why we need your assistance."

Garu knew what that meant. When the absorbers fail, the curse would be unleashed against their carrier. It would find him, and he would die a horrible death.

Ibromaliöm stirred and sighed irritably. He hated these sessions where he was at the mercy of Garu and his extravagant experiments. He knew the price he could exact from Galliöm in exchange for the *Ithyl Shimea. Let Ramel run after magic and silly incantations,* he thought, grinning. *Gold is my magic.* Still, Ramel had asked him to keep an eye on Garu, and he could not risk irritating her, not now when they were so close. *Soon,* he thought, *soon I shall have my revenge on Galliöm. We shall finally see who will be overseer of the Zakiruun.*

Garu sneezed, shattering Ibromaliöm's daydream.

"Are you certain you can locate the place next time?" he snapped.

Garu sighed. "I already told you: finding the place in the spell world is like searching for an apple in a mound of pears."

"What are you talking about?" cut in Ibromaliöm, with a sharp tone.

Garu shrugged his shoulders. "This is how Taniir-The-Strong Castle appears in the spell world," he said.

"As a mound of pears?" asked Ibromaliöm incredulously.

"Look, I do not make up these things. The room we are searching for is shaped like an apple. So I am searching for an apple in a very large mound of pears which is constantly changing."

"Why?"

"To express the gods' displeasure? I don't know why," growled Garu. "I know which side of the mound the apple is on and during today's session, I got a quick glimpse of it. I need one more session to see it closely. Then, it is a matter of using one of Sureï's simple location spells to find it in the real world."

The conversation died for now. They spoke to each other when necessary or when fits of anger and resentment bubbled up in a heated argument that would last for as long as their expansive appetites for arguments lasted.

Garu pondered Sureï's mysterious warning once more. Clearly, there were two magical objects in the hidden room: the *Ithyl Shimea*, and another that, according to Sureï, "rivaled the *Ithyl Shimea* in power and was beyond the reach of mortals." This he could safely ignore, since Ramel never mentioned it.

The *Ithyl Shimea* frightened him. After hearing Hylâz recite the entire Book of Sureï several times, Garu understood that Sureï, the greatest of all sorcerers, was afraid of it as well. Yet, this was the object Ramel and Ibromaliöm were seeking. An object so powerful, it would consume whomever touched it. Garu was certain of it now.

Oh Ramel, my love, what madness possessed you to desire darkness? Would it have made you happier than the natural fragrance of thyme and parsley, I wonder?

Then there were these murders. Two men had been murdered. One short passage Hylâz read to him recently gave him grave concerns.

"Every spell has a counterspell," Sureï said, "and the counterspell to break the curse I set in major centers of magic is a dangerous procedure known only to the Inner Circle of the Temple. It requires four drops of blood, no less."

Ramel, my love, what have you done? Are you behind these murders? Are you trying to double-cross Ibromaliöm and get to the hidden place on your own? What are you up to?

"How much longer do we have to wait here?" asked Ibromaliöm.

Ibromaliöm's voice startled Garu. Disoriented, he gazed at the room and saw the candles and the wax, and remembered why he was sitting on the floor facing Ibromaliöm. A pang of despair took hold of him for a moment, but he managed to push it away. He swallowed before answering. "We cannot move before the wax cools."

"Are you sure, *absolutely sure*, you know what you are doing?" asked Ibromaliöm scornfully.

"Shall I demonstrate what would happen if we moved now?" replied Garu in a hoarse voice. "It may prove instructive to try it on you and see how this will affect your bearing."

"Stop that," snapped Ibromaliöm.

"Careful, do not move. Remember the wax."

"What happened earlier when you screamed and jumped back? I almost heard someone laughing."

Garu answered slowly, "A raayiil... I do not know what these are precisely: they are part vision, part creature, and part prophecy. Ancient beings of great might that haunt the spell world. It is hard to explain." Garu was not about to reveal to Ibromaliöm what he had glimpsed deep beneath the surface of the earth, a movement that not even the mighty Baal was aware of—something he thought he might use to his advantage.

"What else did you see?"

"Something black and near," replied Garu, shivering. "A creature of power searching, prodding, looking for someone."

"Who?" asked Ibromaliöm patiently. "You? Us?"

Garu shook his head. "No, someone else, there is someone else with a power unlike anything I have seen before."

"Are you sure you are not getting mixed up? I have heard the spell world is confusing, making things that are far apart appear to be next to each other."

Garu shook his head. "We should stop," he pleaded with Ibromaliöm, even though it shamed him. "Please, Ibromaliöm, listen to me. This is much more dangerous than you think. I fear for you... I fear for the Queen."

Ibromaliöm laughed sarcastically. "Worry about your bones, old man, and continue to pine for your petty queen if it pleases you, and let me worry about myself."

Garu slumped against the cold wall and closed his eyes.

"Four drops of blood."

He shivered and glanced at Ibromaliöm. A feeling of impending doom took hold of him, and he could not shake it off. *What are you up to, Ibromaliöm?* he thought. *Everyone knows that a drop of blood means a sacrifice, and two men are dead already. Are you practicing magic in secret?*

Ibromaliöm and Ramel had refused to listen to his feeble pleas. They were determined to see this adventure through, and nothing would stop them, save death. *And there are worse things than death,* thought Garu, shuddering, *much worse.*

"Did you create this raayiil?" asked Ibromaliöm.

"Created a raayiil?" Garu nearly choked to death laughing. He calmed himself and looked at Ibromaliöm. "I had forgotten how little you know about these things. No, I cannot create a raayiil; it reveals its existence to those channeled along its path. It expresses the will of the gods.

Something else is happening that I do not control."

"But was it because of you?"

"No. I told you. I cannot bring a raayiil into existence. Do I need to repeat it more than once before it gets through your thick skull?"

"Speak to me like this one more time and I will..."

"Careful, the wax," Garu's voice was toneless. "What we have done here—this little dabble in the magic of Baal as I try to figure out where this door handle will lead us—all of this is beginner's babble next to the magic in the spell world. I do not know how to deal with higher forms of magic," he lied. "So, believe me when I say that something is happening outside of our control."

Ibromaliöm sighed, exasperated. He understood the reason why they were locked up here, but he did not like it. "And to think I agreed to join in your little show," he spat on the floor. "You showed me nothing."

"You saw what I saw: a set of stairs, a huge door," replied Garu evenly. "One more session and I will use the handle to open the door."

"But you have not shown me the *Ithy*..."

"Do not pronounce the name of that libre," commanded Garu speaking with a strong voice. "You are a fool if you think that the spell world will not take notice of you."

Ibromaliöm gritted his teeth in irritation.

"The wax has hardened; we can leave," Garu added, rising to his feet. He sounded withdrawn and unconcerned, and attributed his state to the after effect of the incantation. He welcomed the respite from his habitual emotional agony. He glanced at Ibromaliöm and thought, *She admires and respects him, but right now, I do not care.* He took pride in this thought. For once, he was able to look at this man without envy or rage. Ibromaliöm opened the door and jumped back, nearly falling on Garu. They were both startled to see Commander Tanios framing the door.

"Gentlemen, glad to find both of you here—" started Tanios.

"I have pressing matters to attend to," cut in Ibromaliöm.

"Master Ibromaliöm, the murderer struck again. We found a dead man in the Silent's quarters this time." The commander's tone was measured and focused. "What do you have to say about this?"

"A third?" whispered Garu, "Oh no..."

"Not again," moaned Ibromaliöm. "When are you going to stop the killing? It annoys me to no end. Get the murderer to commit his murders elsewhere. We have no time for this distraction. We are busy."

Tanios entered the room, forcing Ibromaliöm to back up. Garu stood and leaned against the wall. Unconsciously, he wiped his sweaty palms on the cold stone.

"What in the name of Tanniin, are you two doing here?" asked the commander, baffled by the sight. He went to the table and reached for the door handle.

"Do not touch it!" screamed Garu.

Tanios kept his hand over the object and stared at Garu, waiting for an explanation.

"It is very hot. It will burn you."

Tanios looked thoughtfully at the handle and moved his hand away.

"So what are you doing here? What is all this?"

"Commander Tanios, are you interrogating us? Do you suspect that we may be the murderers?" asked Ibromaliöm in his usual jarring style.

The commander was not impressed. "You are the one speaking of suspicion. I was merely interested in what is going on here, given what Queen Ramel told me this morning."

"What did she tell you?" asked Garu, a bit too eagerly. Tanios glanced at him and looked at Ibromaliöm, who kept his gaze firmly locked on the tips of his shoes.

"She told me that you are seeking El-Windiir's sarcophagus."

"She—" began Garu, with his eyes wide open.

"Commander," interrupted Ibromaliöm. "Your behavior is shocking. I am a member of the royal court, and, unless you have an injunction from the King for my arrest, I demand to leave this place immediately."

"Well, Master Ibromaliöm, you are welcome to leave. However, I have strict orders to protect all members of the court from the murderer. Two Silent will watch over you at all times."

"This is unacceptable. I protest," screamed Ibromaliöm.

"Screaming will worsen your case," replied Tanios imperturbably. "There are no exceptions to this rule. You may leave now."

"You are placing us under house arrest?" replied Ibromaliöm, gritting his teeth. "I shall appeal to the King."

"No need, Master Ibromaliöm. His Majesty is waiting for my full report. I will be sure to mention what the two of you have been up to."

"And what is that?" asked Garu.

Tanios glanced at Garu and smiled. "Master Garu, do you think the commander of the Silent is so ignorant of the ways of Baal? You are performing magical incantations to discover how to use this handle, and you are doing it on castle grounds. Wait until the high priestess hears this. She is going to take a great interest in your activities."

"Fine, fine," grumbled Ibromaliöm, "I will take your escort."

"Wise choice, Master Ibromaliöm," replied Tanios. "Your escort will walk you back to the plaza to witness the end of the Game of Gold."

"Garu, are you coming?"

"You go ahead, Master Ibromaliöm," cut in the commander. "Master Garu and I are going to have a little chat," and before Ibromaliöm could reply, the commander shut the door.

Seething with rage, the tall judge went down the stairs, flanked by two Silent.

Inside the Star Room, Garu felt trapped like a rat. Beads of sweat covered his forehead that he did not dare to wipe. The commander walked around the table, careful to stay outside the circle of wax.

"Master Garu," he said, after an insufferably long time, "now that we have taken care of our dear friend, Ibromaliöm, I would like you to tell me slowly, and in detail, what happened here."

Garu tensed his muscles and looked inadvertently at the door. Tanios turned around and looked at the door as well, and opened it. Two Silent stood guard just outside.

"Now that we have taken care of that little detail, tell me, what were you doing here with Master Ibromaliöm? You are looking for the tomb of El-Windiir, are you not?"

"Well, the Queen had expressed a passing interest in the subject, so I did some research for her." Garu was sweating.

"And you used magic to find the tomb?"

Garu's mind was racing. He needed a cover-up. "It's Ibromaliöm... he hates the team of Baal, and so, he convinced me to use certain incantations to make that team lose."

"And you know how to do that?" asked Tanios, unconvinced.

"I know a little magic, yes? An erudite, such as myself, comes across forgotten paintings deep within the mines. I got to know people from all walks of life, who shared with me what they know..."

The commander's keen eyes rested on him, and in the muted silence of the tower, Tanios' quiet gaze became intolerable.

"You are playing a dangerous game, my friend," said the commander at last. "The King is bound to see that you have managed to get the Queen involved in your little research, and I doubt he will be very pleased. The Queen is young and admires your knowledge. She can be easily swayed to give you access to Babylonian knowledge that you should not be privy to. Beware, Master Garu. Magic has a way to exact a heavy price—much too heavy at times."

The bitter tone of this last sentence surprised Garu. "I don't... I mean... it was Ibromaliöm who asked me." Garu knew he was speaking the truth, even though it was only the partial truth.

"And how did he convince you?"

"He offered to waive all outstanding debts I had with him." Garu could see that Tanios was processing what he had just told him.

"You may go, but stay with your escort. There is a murderer in these corridors, and we do not know when he will strike again."

"Thank you, Commander Tanios, for your solicitude." He added with a hushed voice, "If I were you, I would keep a close eye on Ibromaliöm. His hatred for the men of Baal knows no bounds."

"I shall remember this, my dear Garu, now go in peace."

Garu walked to the table and looked at Tanios. He picked up the door handle and left the room quickly.

Tanios stayed in the room a little longer, pacing. He looked at the place where the handle sat a moment ago, wondering why Garu was lying. When he placed his hand above the knob, he did not feel any heat dissipating. The handle was cold. Tanios knew enough about magic rituals to know that the current arrangement was an incantation for Baal. It would be foolish to ask Baal to act against its own, especially against members of the sacred Temple of Baal. Ibromaliöm knew better than to ask that from Baal. Evidently, Garu was lying, but why?

He could have placed both of them under arrest, but then the King would have been forced to reveal to Bahiya that magic was being performed in his castle, which would spell the doom of the kingdom. Instead, the King would order the immediate release of the two judges. Better to escort and keep an eye on them, rather than risk a useless confrontation with His Majesty.

He wondered if he was looking for two murderers instead of one.

Only time would tell.

19. The Finish Line

"I have said it before and it bears repeating: hope is our greatest enemy, the scourge of the human heart, a cruel ploy of the Pit to lure man into the depth of darkness. Hope is an illusion, for the gods have decreed the fate of man to be what it is: a painful trek into oblivion. All we can do is avoid a worse fate by falling into the Pit, and this is precisely where hope will lead us.
"Every priest of Baal is a sworn enemy of hope."
−From the Teaching of Oreg, High Priest of Baal

Night had fallen; cold and damp. Thick clouds brooded over the unlit plaza while a dense fog blanketed the lake and valley. The crowd, twenty thousand strong by now, huddled on three large wooden structures that slaves had erected  hastily that morning. Intermittently, a *hookah* (water pipe) would light up; an ephemeral bright spot swallowed all too quickly by the muted darkness.

Up ahead, burning torches lined both sides of the western road from the spot where Ahiram had climbed during the Game of Bronze, back to the plaza—a two-hundred-yard stretch. As the evening grew old, the fog crept up, swallowing a few torches. They sputtered and blinked in the whitish swirl like the pupils of a phantasmagorical dragon. All eyes were trained on that spot, waiting for the athletes to burst into their final sprint to the finish line.

The disaffected merchants stood by their empty carts, having sold out as early as noon. No one had expected the crowd to swell up the way it did. A tall, burly merchant, wearing an open shirt—revealing a chest so hairy a gorilla would have been jealous—stood staring at the lit path. To relieve his boredom, he took a silver coin stamped with the effigy of the King and began tossing it up, catching it with great ease. He tossed the coin once more, sneezed, and the coin fell to the ground. It bounced on the stony surface, and the ringing sound it produced jarred the night, startling the nearby spectators. It bounced again and landed on its edge, spinning as it followed a semi-circle. The coin hit a tiny pebble that tipped it forward. It wobbled for a moment, then fell into a muddy puddle, face down.

As if on cue, a pack of coyotes deep within the forbidden forest howled, shattering the quiet. A young girl, not yet ten, buried her head in her father's chest beneath the thick blanket that kept her warm. Her younger brother sitting next to her—still holding the bell he had rung two days ago—scolded her, "Stop it, Misty, Ahiram is fighting for us. Show courage." The merchant blushed, picked up the coin and wiped Jamiir's muddied face. He then stuffed the silver piece in his pocket and stood still next to his cart.

Two days ago, a smaller crowd derided and jeered the Silent, thinking his participation a cruel joke at their expense—yet another attempt by the Temple to crush their fighting spirit. Tonight they began to believe in the impossible. His victory meant the difference between freedom and slavery, life or death for the Kingdom of Tanniin. Their glimmer of hope born when Ahiram won the first Game had now grown into a fierce flame fueled by their thirst for freedom.

The arbitrators had told the crowd about this morning's earthquake.

Since no one outside felt it, persistent rumors convinced the crowd that the high priestess had used Baal's dark sorcery to cause the earthquake in an attempt to kill the slave. A few hours later, another rumor began circulating: the King had consented to the death of their hero. Hot anger simmered behind the stoic faces, anger directed at the King and the Temple. Whispers of three men of Baal turning into monsters which stalked the castle seeped through the crowd. Bahiya did this to three of her own men, the story went, but Commander Tanios and his Silent killed the monsters. These rumors were music to Soloron's ears who grinned beneath his cowl. *Everything is proceeding as planned*, he thought, satisfied. *Soon, Taniir-The-Strong Castle will be ours.*

Meanwhile, the four judges stood by the finish line waiting for the athletes. "Look at all these people," whispered Ramany in Hylâz's ear. He was visibly afraid. "They are so quiet. Do you feel the muted anger hovering over them like a dark cloud?"

Hylâz looked up. "Well, there are no clouds hovering over them. I am not certain that was a good choice as far as metaphors go."

"Spare me your sarcasm, Hylâz," snapped Ramany. "This is serious. There are at least twenty thousand people here, and they are angry."

Hylâz pointed to the hills west of the plaza, which the fog had spared. "Can you count the number of pit fires on that hill?" he said softly.

"By Tanniin's horns, there are hundreds of them," whispered Ramany.

"More," said Ramany in a halting voice. "Thousands. I'd wager there are at least forty thousand people waiting over there."

"What? Forty thousand more?" gasped Ramany, "You mean we're surrounded by a mob sixty thousand strong?"

"Calm down," snapped Hylâz. He then whispered, "do not speak of being surrounded. Pray the slave wins this Game."

Ramany shivered. Even though the air was cold and wet, he was sweating. He dabbed his forehead with a handkerchief. "You're right. The slave had better win these Games now," he said, as he glanced fearfully at the crowd, expecting it to rise any moment now and savagely rush toward them. Slowly, he turned his back to the plaza and focused on the empty road. The torches' flames were swaying in the wind, threatening to go out, but the arbitrators kept a close watch.

"What happens if no one wins tonight?" he asked, after a while. "I mean, what happens if none of them can get out of the mines?"

"The rules are binding," whispered Garu in their ears, causing them to jump from fright. "Calm yourselves," he snapped. "I repeat: the rules are binding. No team can be declared a winner unless they cross this line. We have no other choice but to wait."

"How long do we have to wait before we declare forfeiture?" asked Ibromaliöm, matter-of-factly.

"If no team comes forth by the stroke of the third watch of the night," recited Hylâz, "then, and only then, judges are authorized to declare forfeiture provided there is unanimous consent and all other avenues have been duly examined and declared null and void."

A quick glance at the giant hourglass standing nearby told them there was still a half hour to go.

Despite the late hour and their tiredness, they kept staring at the road. Ramany could not stop shivering. He refused to consider what would happen to him if Ahiram did not win this round. Nearby, the entrance to the Cave of Bronze stood like a gaping wound in the side of the mountain. The caves were shrouded in a deafening silence that the moan of the westerly wind broke intermittently, like a mourner lamenting the fate of the departed.

Time stretched lazily and still no team came forth. Garu stood apart, brooding while Ibromaliöm paced with a deliberate slowness, lost in thought, unconcerned by the current events. Hylâz and Ramany stepped away from the two other judges.

Hylâz, glanced behind his back to check that Garu was not eavesdropping, "What if... how shall I say this... what if all teams have been incapacitated, what would happen then?" He glanced nervously at the crowd.

"Well, you heard the head judge. I suppose we would have an incapacitated winner," replied Ramany.

"But that would be dreadful," said the judge in a squeal.

"I will go further," added Ramany. "It would be most dreadful."

"Are all Games this..." Hylâz seemed at a loss for words to describe the current Games. This was his first participation as a judge.

"Eventful?" suggested Ramany.

"Yes, I suppose this is the word I was looking for. 'Eventful' would describe these Games rather aptly, would you not say?"

Ramany closed his eyes and rubbed them gently. "I would go further. I don't remember another Game that was this eventful, except perhaps when a group of commoners managed to fool the judges by pretending to represent the Kingdom of Oronoque. They took part in the Games, only to meet their fate."

"They all died?" gasped Hylâz.

"All of them," replied Ramany somberly.

"What happened then? How did the crowd react?"

"The crowd rioted against the Temple and nearly stoned the judges to death. In the end, to keep the peace, the King exiled all four judges."

"When did this happen?"

"During the Game of Gold."

The wind blew forcefully, and the moaning from the cave intensified. Hylâz looked reproachfully at Ramany who shrugged his shoulders and rolled his eyes.

In the far distance, a shout tore through the silence like a knife cutting through ice. The crowd stood as one man, and all eyes were now on the empty road wondering what this shout meant.

They heard the shout again, and the silence settled in once more like a heavy blanket. A low rumble filled the plaza as the crowd began to question the meaning of these shouts. Small groups formed in animated discussions. Garu did not seem to pay heed to the shout, but Ibromaliöm stopped pacing and was looking toward the mountain.

"Ibromaliöm woke up," whispered Hylâz, but Ramany shrugged his shoulders in irritation.

Ibromaliöm's evasive behavior displeased Hylâz profoundly, and Garu's seeming disinterest in the Games disappointed him. He was convinced that most of the events of the past few days could have been prevented had the judges been better prepared. Mostly, he blamed Garu's lack of leadership. Had he been leading effectively, the slave would have been humming a different ballad by now, but what is done is done.

"Look, someone is coming," shouted a man from the crowd, pointing in the direction of the path that the procession had taken this morning.

Hylâz and Ibromaliöm looked and saw four members of the Silent carrying a dead man. Carefully, they laid the body on the ground, then the leader of the patrol approached the four judges.

"Greetings, Your Honors."

"Greetings to you, young man," replied Garu. "What tidings do you bring us tonight?"

"Sad, I am afraid, Master Garu. We have found the body of this worthy contestant in the lake."

"And to what team did he belong?" asked Ramany.

"The Team of Baal, Your Honor."

"You went through the walls of fire to retrieve the dead man?" asked Hylâz. "I am impressed."

The Silent blushed with embarrassment.

"Actually, my dear Hylâz," interjected Ibromaliöm sarcastically, "I most certainly need not remind you that these so called 'Walls of Fire' are entirely under the control of the arbitrators. As you must know, they are lit for the Games and extinguished once the last contestant has gone through them."

"My dear Ibromaliöm," snapped Ramany, "I am blinded by the dazzling light of your tact."

"Gentlemen," intervened Garu with a tired voice, "do I have to remind you of the seriousness of the matter at hand? Can we let this fine young man explain to us how he found the dead body?"

"Your Honor, we have received orders from Commander Tanios to scout the mines in order to determine whether the contestants were able to survive the earthquake or not. Upon entering the mines, we followed their trails to the lake where we found the body of this man on the shore. We could not proceed further into the mines."

"Why was that?" asked Ibromaliöm abruptly.

The Silent hesitated before answering, "The lake prevented us."

"What do you mean?" asked Ramany.

"I mean that every time we tried to get into the water, we were thrown back onto the shore by surging waves. We attempted the crossing several times, and each time we were forced to go back to the shore."

"To what do you attribute this behavior?" asked Hylâz.

"I do not know, Your Honor. All I know is that we were not able to cross, so we came back, bringing with us the body of this man. Now, if you would excuse us, we must report to Commander Tanios." With a curt bow, the leader and his men were gone.

Having a knack for regulations and details, Hylâz asked, "Why did Tanios order these Silent to enter the mines during the Game?"

"Because I asked him to help us," answered Garu. "The arbitrators could not report properly on the status of the participants, and I felt it important to engage the Silent to determine their whereabouts."

"Why were we not briefed of your decision?" asked Ibromaliöm.

"Because, my dear Ibromaliöm, I was convinced that all three of you would have supported my decision. Is it not the case?" Hylâz and Ramany nodded their approval. Ibromaliöm and Garu stared at each other, locked in a battle of wills. After a painfully long time, Ibromaliöm lowered his gaze and nodded affirmatively. He turned around abruptly and resumed his nervous pacing.

"This brings the total count of young men who have died since the beginning of these Games to four," sighed Hylâz.

"Four?" asked Ramany.

"Yes, one from Prince Olothe's team and three from Baal's team."

"Three? You mean two, do you not?"

"No, I mean three. The man from Olothe's team was found murdered in the storage area on the first floor, remember? This is when Tanios interrogated us, and I woke you with my snoring."

"Yes, I am aware of the two murders."

"Well, now you can add to your count this unfortunate young man who drowned in the lake."

"Assuming this is a murder, then when we add the victim found in the Queen's Ballroom, we end up with three deaths. Who is the fourth?"

"You may not have been briefed, my dear Ramany, but this morning a man belonging to Hiyam's team did not show up. Early this afternoon, the Silent found the unfortunate man dead."

"He was dead?"

"Yes. Murdered like the other two. And you know where they found him?" added Hylâz in a conspiratorial tone.

"No, where?"

"In the Silent's quarters, no less. Right there, under the commander's nose. This murderer is amazing, I tell you."

"Tanios must be *very* angry now," said Ramany shuddering.

"*Very*," said Hylâz, nodding. "Very, very angry."

"How unfortunate," added Hylâz heaving a deep sigh. "My, my, these Games are rather eventful."

The crowd, by now, had become agitated. They had seen the four Silent come forth carrying a dead man. They had witnessed the quick exchange between the leader of the Silent and the judges, as well as the departure of the four young men with the body. They wanted updates and felt the judges were concealing important information. Garu turned around and raised his hands. The crowd quieted expectantly.

"Dear friends, it pains me to inform you that one of our worthy contestants has lost his life during the Game of Gold. It would seem that this fine young man, owing to undetermined circumstances, drowned in the lake. As you are well aware, death is no stranger to these Games. It is not uncommon to see young men and women come to the Games full of life, vibrant with hope and expectations, only to meet their ultimate fate. These Games are indeed unparalleled in all the territories of Baal and bestow upon their winner the highest honors. They also exact the highest price from some of those who take part in them. Such are the laws of the great Games of the Mines. As for the remaining participants, they have been delayed due to the earthquake, which sealed the main exit. However, there are many other pathways that one may take to leave the mines. Rest assured that as we speak, most, if not all the teams, must be close to one exit or another. I would ask you to keep calm and honor these participants by waiting with us a little longer. Tomorrow is another day, and by tomorrow, all these unfortunate events will be behind us. On behalf of Their Majesties, the King and Queen, and my most honorable colleagues, I thank you for your understanding."

Garu bowed and the crowd applauded mechanically. The applause started low and polite, and abruptly turned into a roar. Garu who was still bowing, lifted his head and was startled. He was receiving a standing ovation and the arbitrators were running toward him. *I know my speech was good, but I did not think it was that good,* he thought. He walked toward the arbitrators running in his direction to reassure them that he could handle the crowd without their protection, but they passed him and continued running up the road behind him.

He turned around and saw Ahiram and Hiyam sprinting down the path. They were running toe-to-toe and crossed the finish line together.

Hylâz smacked his head with his hand. "Not again," he moaned. "What are we to do? The rules do not make provisions for a slave as a co-winner of a Game. Did he lose or did he win this Game?"

"Let us verify the artifacts, shall we?" snapped Garu.

Ahiram raised a mask of gold. The crowd surged like a mighty wave, and the judges were nearly trampled underfoot, but the angry shouts of the trumpets broke the surge and quieted everyone. Garu elbowed his way through the human forest and had to use his full authority to reach Ahiram and Hiyam, who now stood side-by-side. The three other judges joined him.

"Well, young man, what have you to say for yourself?" Garu spoke with a gruff voice. Despite appearances, he was impressed that this slave had won single handedly The Game of Gold was no small feat.

"Here is the mask, Master Garu," replied Ahiram with a weary smile.

"Yes, yes, indeed, it is the mask of gold. Do you have the shoes of bronze and the belt of silver as well?"

Ahiram exhibited these pieces to the delight of the crowd. To win the Game, it was not enough to find the proper artifact at each step; Ahiram had to keep them until the last Game was over. This is why the Game of Meyroon was the most dangerous. In the past, stalling and pouncing became a widespread tactic that various teams used to try to win the Games. They would intentionally trail the winner in the first three Games to conserve their strength, then pounce on their exhausted prey during the fourth Game, and steal the shoes, belt, and mask. The judges modified the rules a few years back to disqualify all but the top four teams from participation in the Game of Meyroon.

"Yes, yes, there is no doubt, young man," continued Garu, who had finished his deliberation with the three other judges, "You have all the artifacts. Now your turn, young lady. Show us the mask, if you please."

Hiyam handed them a mask of gold. The judges inspected it and confirmed its authenticity.

"Very well, now please show us the remaining artifacts," asked Garu.

Hiyam blanched. She was the fastest runner on her team, and when she had seen Ahiram ahead of her on the road, she had snatched the mask of gold from one of her teammates, but she had forgotten the shoes of bronze and the belt of silver.

"They are with the rest of my team," she stuttered. "We have them."

"Unfortunately, my dear lady, the rules are very specific," said Garu. "No team can be declared a winner of the Game of Gold unless they exhibit all three artifacts. As such, I declare the slave Ahiram the uncontested winner of the Game of Gold. Congratulations."

The euphoria of the crowd knew no bounds. A dream once thought lost was now becoming reality. It had taken shape and now had a face. The city of Taniir-The-Strong was swelling with visitors attracted by the ancient prophecy. The flow of people did not give any sign of abating. The garrison of Baalites was on full alert and reinforcements were being sent from the two southern ports of Mitreel and Aramin.

The elation of the crowd was so strong that the arrival of Hiyam's team was hardly noticed. Standing before the judges, her discomfiture turned to shame when no team member could produce the shoes of bronze. In the mayhem and confusion of the geyser, she had forgotten that the dead High Rider was carrying them. Ramany, wanting to sooth her pain, told her that the other teams were missing the mask. She nodded and closed her eyes.

"Aha," exclaimed Hylâz, "since none of these good teams have all three artifacts, we have a winner." Garu rolled his eyes and sighed. "For the rules are clear: 'if at any stage after the Game of Bronze, only one team has in its possession all constituent parts deemed valid, then this team is to be declared winner, and the Games are over.'"

"Wait, what did you just say, Hylâz?" asked Garu.

"Huh? What did tiny one say?" asked Frajil. He was talking to his older brother, Soloron, as they stood a mere three rows away from

Ahiram and could clearly hear what was being said.

"He said that Ahiram has all three artifacts, and no other team does, so Ahiram wins."

"Huh?" answered Frajil.

"Listen Frajil," said Soloron patiently. "Ahiram has the shoes, belt, and mask, right?"

"Yes."

"No other team has the shoes, belt, and mask, right?"

"Yes."

"Ahiram wins. That's what the tiny fella over there said."

"Huh?"

"However," said Ibromaliöm, "the rules stipulate that the Games must take place under normal and reasonable circumstances. I would venture that this particular Game does not satisfy either category, in which case such a Game ought to be annulled."

"Correct as usual, my dear Ibromaliöm," continued Garu pensively. He motioned for the other three judges to follow him and moved away from the crowd. The judges lowered their voices in order not to be overheard by anyone. "But if we were to annul the Game of Gold, does it then follow that one may win the Games without the mask of gold?"

"According to the rules," replied Hylâz, "no team is worthy of winning that did not gather all four elements."

"I see," replied Garu, "we are throwing the slave as bait to the other teams. He enters the Mine of Meyroon, and the teams missing an artifact will converge on him to steal his items. I wonder who makes a final decision in this matter. According to the regulations, that is?"

"This one is easy," said Ramany. "His Majesty the King is the supreme judge of the Games."

"To the King then," exclaimed Garu, who was relieved to know that for once, he did not have to make a difficult decision. They broke off their consultation and went back to the middle of the circle. "My dear people, after this superb victory of our young friend here, a number of legislative issues have been brought to our attention regarding the proper interpretation of the rules and their relevance to the Game at hand. Therefore, in strict observance of the rules, we shall defer all judgments to His Majesty the King who will be able to instruct us in these matters so that all is done in strict conformity to the rules, which are properly prescribed and ordained for the benefit of all. With these glad tidings, I wish all of you who were faithful through and through, a quiet and restful night. I hope to see you tomorrow for the glorious conclusion of these Games, so unlike any other event in the annals of the kingdom. Long live the King!"

The crowd answered, "Long live the King," mechanically and resumed their rejoicing. Eventually, after mingling with the crowd, Ahiram went back to the royal castle, flanked by Banimelek and Jedarc. Abiil, the man who met with Soloron and Frajil at the tavern a few days back, gave them a slight nod. Soloron smiled as he left the plaza with his giant of a brother in tow.

"Tomorrow, we roast the chicken," he said softly.

"Chicken? Where?" exclaimed Frajil. "Show me chicken. We could roast it tonight."

"My dear Frajil, you will have to wait until tomorrow when the chicken is delivered into our hands."

"Oh, yes, yes, I forgot all about it," said Frajil.

"About what?" asked Soloron wondering if, for once, Frajil understood what was implied by these words.

"The marketplace is already closed. We cannot buy a chicken before tomorrow morning."

Soloron sighed and went back toward the horses. *Tomorrow will be a busy day*, he thought.

"Gentlemen, this has been a rather busy night, far too busy for my taste. I shall give my decision in the morning. For now, I wish all of you a good and restful night."

Everyone rose as the King left for his private apartments. Upon entering, King Jamiir III was surprised to find Queen Ramel waiting for him.

"My dear Ramel, have the events at hand disturbed your sleep?"

"What is His Majesty's decision?"

"Since when has the Queen shown any interest in the governance of the kingdom?"

"There have been three murders in this castle since the start of the Games. I do not feel safe while these Games are in progress."

"I trust that Commander Tanios will resolve this matter. He is a capable man. As far as the Games are concerned, the King will let his decision be known tomorrow morning."

"I trust His Majesty considered the impact that his decision will have on his servants throughout the kingdom. My servants informed me there was only one golden mask in the race and that pursuing the Games means almost certainly a death warrant for the slave, whom many consider to be a hero. If His Majesty were to authorize this last Game, it may be interpreted by the people of Tannin as an act of treason."

"An act of treason?"

"May the King live forever," said Ramel, bowing. "Surely His Majesty knows that the servants of the King see in this slave the fulfillment of the prophecy concerning the rise of Tanniin?"

"Yes, yes, I know," said Jamiir with a tired voice, "I know all about their dreams and aspirations. But what can dreams do in the face of the harsh reality of Baal? The high priestess told me the Temple is sending reinforcements. This will be the last time these Games will take place. The forces of Baal are preparing to take over the castle at the end of the Games, and they are thinking of dismantling the Silent Corps. I am not even certain the kingdom will be preserved." The King fell silent for a while and Ramel waited.

"I have striven to protect the crown of Tanniin from a complete takeover by Baal, and I thought I had succeeded by authorizing the construction of a temple to Baal in this city and by appearing there in person. This slave has brought years of efforts to naught. Baal will be taking over, and we will most likely be exiled. Oh, do not fear, my dove, since you are the niece of one of the greatest priests of Babylon, the exile will be comfortable, if not pleasurable, and I owe this to your person."

Jamiir bowed before the Queen. She bristled at the implied sarcasm. "Now, my dear Ramel, what should the King do? Excite Baal's wrath even more by declaring this slave the winner and allow an insurrection to take place? Bahiya was very clear: any insurrection will be crushed without mercy by the Baalites and many will die. The Games will go on tomorrow, and the slave will die. I believe the King has no other choice. If Your Majesty will excuse the King, he is tired."

Ramel bowed before her husband and withdrew to her private apartments. She could hardly control herself. From the start, she had despised Jamiir for the weakness she perceived in him. He was indecisive, she thought, lacked any will to resist and above all, had fallen under the priestess' charm. Her marriage encroached on her sense of honor: she, the niece of a high priest of Baal from the eternal city of Babylon, was married to a coward and this at the instigation of the high priestess of Baalbeck. Ramel clenched her fists as she dismissed all her servants. She went out onto her balcony where three candles were burning. She took one of them and lit a fourth. Her features hardened, and had the King been present, he may not have recognized the quiet, soft-spoken Ramel in the woman standing on the balcony. In this obscure twilight of the four flickering candles, Queen Ramel looked like a warrior before battle.

≻✪✪✪≺

"You surprise me, Daughter. Why these feelings toward the slave now that you know he will die tomorrow?"

Hiyam had just learned from her mother the decision of the Temple of Baal to dispose of Ahiram in the Mine of Meyroon. She lost her composure and stood stricken with grief; her heart plunged in a bitter sea of sadness. It was more than she could bear, and she dropped into her seat, crying.

"What is it, Daughter?" asked Bahiya, even though she already knew the answer.

"I have always admired the men of Baal for their courage and loyalty. But courage and strength such as this, I have never seen. Since the start of these Games, we have used force and deception to break him—a slave. Shame on us. Had we given him a chance to defend himself, I would have felt the honor of Baal would have been upheld, but killing him like a rat? His blood will spill on Baal's face and on my memory."

"This is no matter for discussion," replied Bahiya sternly. "These orders came to us directly from Babylon. Neither you nor I, nor the King, nor anyone else has a choice. It is settled."

Bahiya stood up and turned her back to her daughter. Hiyam bowed her head. The high priestess continued in a softer tone of voice. "You should go and rest, Daughter. Tomorrow will be a long day for you, and remember, you will be crowned winner of the Games. You will have to behave as a true daughter of Baal. I expect nothing less from you."

"Mother, why does he have to die? Would it not be better to capture him and bring him as a slave to Baalbeck?"

"And keep him chained between four walls? If he were to escape and come back, the Temple would be shamed." Bahiya's voice, which was normally taut as a bow, quivered and fell. Hiyam looked up, surprised, but the weakness, if it ever existed, was now gone. "We cannot allow this to happen. Only death will make him truly silent. Know this, my daughter, the Temple of Baal does not resort to these extreme measures if other options are available. In this case, we cannot see how to avoid bloodshed while keeping him alive. If it is any consolation to you, know that the twelve men of Baal who will be waiting for him in the cave are expert warriors, and his death will be as swift and as painless as possible."

"Yes Mother, like thieves in the night."

Before Bahiya could reply, Hiyam left. She wiped her tears and walked toward her room. Unconsciously, Hiyam attributed the weakness in her protective shield and the failure of her magical powers to Ahiram himself. Even though her mother reassured her that this slave could not have access to such high magic and that he suffered, like everyone else, from the geyser this morning, Hiyam could not shake off the idea that somehow, Ahiram was stronger than she. This feeling had turned into respect bordering on awe. She considered him to be a worthy foe, not a mere slave, not a mere nuisance to be rid of. She understood her mother's decision and that of the Temple's, but she could not help feeling as if she was murdering an outstanding opponent, and in so doing, dishonoring her name and that of the High Riders. She went into her room, closed the door, and wished that she were miles and miles away by the fountain of the Temple in the cool breeze of the sunset when the grapes are golden ripe and the water is fresh like the laughter of a child. For the first time in her life, Hiyam felt lonely.

Yet, had she seen her mother's composure after she left, she may have been surprised.

Bahiya was pacing back and forth, her hands on her stomach as if in pain. She was moaning as her tears dripped onto the floor before her. "Be strong, be strong," she said in a soft voice. "Do what you must." Finally, unable to contain her sorrow any longer, she collapsed on her bed, burying her head in the soft pillows to muffle her sobs.

"Give up the Games, Ahiram. It is over." Tanios' voice resonated in the nearly empty Room of Meetings in the quarters of the Silent. Ahiram was sitting on a chair. Tanios was pacing. Banimelek, Jedarc, and Habael were standing behind Ahiram. "They are going to kill you tomorrow, I am convinced of it," continued Tanios. "They will most likely do it in the Mine of Meyroon, and make it look like an accident."

"I can defend myself—"

"Against a patrol or two, maybe, but against thirty or forty hardened High Riders? It would be suicide." Tanios sighed. "I have arranged for you to hide in the caves beneath the ruins of Taniir-On-High Castle. There is a colony of dwarfs who live there, and they can keep you safe long enough for the entire matter to subside. Once Baal relaxes his surveillance, we will slip you out and away to the northernmost part of the kingdom. In a few years, you would be able to move around like a free man."

"*Like* a free man?" Ahiram looked at his master, who stopped pacing and looked back. Ahiram stood up. "Commander Tanios, where I come from, there is a saying: 'Hold a shark captive and it will bind your honor to its cage.' So it is with me. I cannot give up the Games and hide, for if I do, I would be giving up my honor, and worse, the honor of my family. I knew all along that I might die in these Games, but at least my death would be honorable and meaningful. For what does it mean if a man is forced to live in the shadows, turning his face from the sun that gives him life? He is no more alive than a withered tree still standing in fear of falling down. I will go tomorrow to these Games as I have done today, come what may. If I must die, I entrust you with a message for my father: 'He was worthy of your trust, and he died upholding your honor.' Now Commander, with your permission, I should like to retire. I need a good night sleep."

Ahiram bowed deeply and left the room. Tanios sighed.

"Did you expect anything else, Commander Tanios?" asked Habael.

"No. His stubbornness is as strong as his love for his family."

"Yes, I know. That is what makes him endearing to us all."

"He speaks like a free man," exclaimed Jedarc.

"He has always been free in his mind. He is not one who can be turned into a slave," replied Tanios gruffly.

"So, what are our options?" asked Banimelek who was growing impatient. He was a man of action, not of discourse.

"My orders are clear: no interventions on our part under severe punishment. I trust I do not need to repeat myself."

"No, Commander Tanios," replied both Jedarc and Banimelek.

"Good. Now gentlemen, why do you not accompany Master Habael back to his quarters? It has been a long day."

"It has indeed," replied Habael, "and who knows what tomorrow will bear?" With that, the three men bowed before Tanios and left.

"Tell me, my dear Banimelek," asked Habael, "what do you make of this third dead man in your quarters?"

"I'd like to meet the killer face-to-face," replied Banimelek angrily.

"Yes, indeed," replied Master Habael, smiling. "Does the location strike you as peculiar?"

"I have not given it much thought, Master Habael," replied Banimelek, who was a warrior, a strategist, and an exceptional athlete, but was not one to ponder mysteries to uncover their deeper meaning.

"What about you, my dear Jedarc?" asked Habael.

"It does," said Jedarc softly. "If I wanted to kill a hornet, I would certainly not do it in a beehive."

"Well said," replied Master Habael. "Well said, indeed."

They walked silently until they reached Habael's modest quarters in the servants' area on the first floor. As Banimelek and Jedarc bowed to bid him good night, Habael touched their shoulders lightly.

"Earlier on," he said, "I spoke with Commander Tanios, and you might be interested to know that 'severe punishment' means a temporary relocation to the northeastern Fortress of Hardeen."

Banimelek and Jedarc looked at each other and then at Habael.

"That would be dreadful, Master Habael," said Banimelek, grinning.

"Most dreadful, indeed," echoed Jedarc.

"My thought exactly," replied Habael. "Well gentlemen, good night. I trust this is going to be a rather busy night for you. What with the surveillance of the castle and all other matters, is it not so?"

"Very busy, indeed," replied Banimelek. They bowed and left. On their way back to their quarters, Banimelek looked at his friend.

"Well, Jedarc, how do you like the northeastern breeze?"

"I love it, I simply do. The sun, the sea, and the Empyreans. I don't know if they are prettier than Hiyam, but I would not want to miss out on the wedding."

"The wedding? What wedding?" asked Banimelek.

Jedarc stood before his friend and bowed. "The wedding of Banimelek to a ravishing and beautiful Empyrean princess."

Banimelek put his arm around his friend's shoulder, and the two of them traveled down the halls whistling an old song about war, glory, and bravery—and about the wedding of an Empyrean and a hero.

Meanwhile, somewhere in the castle, a secret pathway closed silently behind a nocturnal shadowy figure stalking the dark corridors of Taniir-The-Strong.

20. ECLIPSE

"The sun is the seat of Baal's power. There, the god of the heavens issues his edicts—to bless the human race with fertility and peace or to rain on them the fire of his wrath. Understand then: the occlusion of the sun is the Pit stirring and the birth of a new order."
–Introduction to the Book of Knowledge, Ussamiah the Togofalkian

"Eclipse this, eclipse that, of what use is an eclipse to me? I wish someone could eclipse that matronly Togofalkian over there. She is about to pilfer the grilled chicken. Now that would be useful. It would fill my belly and let me sleep at night. But alas! That plump woman is the royal cook who prepares the chicken."
–Soliloquy of Zuzu the Hip, Jester of the Royal Court of Tanniin

Earlier that morning and shortly after the last athlete leaped into the canyon, the King and his retinue made their way back to Taniir-the-Strong along a road that overlooked the dense forest of the castle's surroundings.

The sky was of a deep azure without the slightest cloud, and a clean breeze carried a bouquet of refreshing scents as if the mountain wanted to rejoice in the last days of summer.

"Isn't the forest gorgeous, my dear Bahiya?" asked the King.

Bahiya gazed admiringly at the sea of trees surrounding them. Baalbeck lay in a flat plain where trees were sparse. Since she and Tanios had walked into the Sondarion, the greatest of all forests, she had been attracted by the silent mystery that hung like a shadow in the depth of the forest. A longing suddenly came upon her, and she wished she could leave the path and wander beneath the lush, green canopy. The strength of this whimsical desire surprised and overwhelmed her, filling her mind with dazzling scenes from the forest; places she knew she would never see. She pictured herself standing in a quiet clearing beneath trees whose girth took her breath away. She saw herself gently floating up to the treetops, and then still higher in the air, until the forest gleamed like an emerald. She was vaguely aware of Jamiir's presence, but his frame dissolved slowly until she could see him no more. In her vision, she was flying over the trees as they flowed down rolling hills to the edge of a two-mile-high abyss.

"Bahiya, beware. Beware, Bahiya."

The voice was distant, weak, and she knew she was in danger, but it was already too late. The trap had closed shut, and she was a prisoner. Still, she tried to fight the flood of images pounding her with greater intensity as she hovered uncertainly at the edge of the chasm. Something crashed through the trees behind her. She wanted to ignore it, knowing it was an illusion, but her hair stood on end when she felt its presence behind her.

In the split second that her fear surged, the power that had brought her into the spell world yanked the entire cliff forward. She fell with the trees into the void as the green avalanche rolled and exploded into a giant wave that carried her forward at terrifying speed. The landscape around her was of Tanniin, but while her body stood next to the King, her mind had been pulled into the spell world. This was a magical kidnapping that required skills beyond most mortals. Once this visual spell had overtaken the mind and forced it to focus on these images, the victim could not break free without external intervention.

The source of this magic is in the northwest, she thought. This meant that in real life, the perpetrator was physically located in the northwestern region of Tanniin. Bahiya watched the forest surge forward, heading north by northwest, and she was powerless to stop it. She reached the edge of the main road that ran the length of the kingdom from north to south. *The forest,* she thought, aghast, gazing at the trees to the east, *they are turning gray.*

Her kidnapper let her hover over the road for ten hours. In the spell world, the passing of time was omnipresent and accurate. *He wants me to focus on the road. The monotony of the same image repeating itself will increase his control over me.* She gritted her teeth but could not resist. Eventually, he forced her to fly over the road, and the forest to her right became a green blur while the trees to her left turned into a gray fog and the road ahead a dirty yellow strip. "When the images become solid bands of color, the prey is moments away from meeting its predator." She was quoting Sureï the Sorcerer, and knew her will was about to fall prey to her predator. She would become a puppet in his hands and do his bidding. Magdala, the forbidden forest, came into full view east of the road, when she heard a voice speak a word of command. "Let the link be broken."

A blinding, white flash shattered the image. She heard a distant scream of rage and anger, and her mind became blissfully dark. When she opened her eyes, she was still standing next to the King. He was looking ahead, lost in his thoughts, and had not taken notice of her. At first she feared he had been captured by the same attacker, but when he blinked, she knew this was not so. The assault had been directed at her and her alone.

The King looked at her and she smiled. Bahiya's steely eyes did not flinch, nor did she let her demeanor betray her inner turmoil. She was experienced enough with the harrowing pain of magical acts to conceal her suffering. Traveling in and out of the spell world was a punishing experience, and the slow passage of time was integral to the suffering. *A minute here can be several days over there.* She reminded herself that a ten-hour visit was a mere thirty seconds, no more. She was exhausted, as if she had physically endured a ten-hour-long trial, but she kept her composure.

"Yes, Your Majesty, I agree that the forest is gorgeous," she replied with a faint smile.

They resumed their walk in silence.

Up ahead, the Lone Tower surged over the forest, its diamond-shaped Star Room glittering in the morning sun despite the shutters marring its arched windows. Bahiya profited from the silence to raise a protective cloak around her mind. *They will find it a lot harder to pull me in the next time around,* she thought. She felt a surge of gratitude to her anonymous savior. *Could it have been...?* She stopped short before saying a name for fear of exposing a deeply held secret.

"Lovely day, isn't it?" asked the King, grinning.

She had to agree. It was a lovely morning, fresh and breezy on this Sin, Tébêt 7, 1197. Most farmers knew that a massive storm hid behind the exceptional weather they were enjoying now. Storms during the month of Tébêt were as violent as they were rare. The locals called them *Baraak Sil Tanniin* (Tannin's Wrath).

Bahiya focused her attention on the attack. Someone had managed to bring her into the spell world by exploiting a mere whim she had. A consummate Kerta priest would need hours to accomplish this feat, yet her attacker did it in seconds. *There are three people with that kind of power: High Priest Sharr of Babylon, Sarand the Soloist, head of the Adorant, and Galliöm, Master of the Tajéruun. But what would any one of them be doing in the northern region of Tanniin?*

>✦✦✦≺

Baal was known by many names. Majaar was his title as Lord of the Plenty; and the Temple of Baal Majaar in Babylon was a microcosm, a miniature replica of the universe. In size, it was two hundred and ten *sîzu* long (a sacred measure of roughly two-thirds of a foot, used only inside the Temple) and 143 sîzu wide. These measurements encompassed the first seven prime numbers representing the seven planets the priests saw from their Star Room: the seven heavens of the gods.

Set atop *Ishtar Elis*—Ishtar's Hill—opposite the suspended garden, the temple dominated the sprawling city of Babylon, for no other building was allowed to exceed its height. The outer walls were of a deep topaz, etched with golden *Karubiim* (winged lions—the charioteers of Baal). They stood with outstretched wings, shining beneath the gleaming sun. Its thirty-foot-tall bronze cupola rose still higher. Cast from a singular mold by skilled dwarfs, it symbolized the sun, the center of the universe, and the god Baal, ruler of the world.

Inside the rectangular building, thirty giant pillars held the thirty-foot-high, gold-plated roof. Roughly twenty feet from the walls, a marble egg-shaped platform rose to a height of ten feet. Accessible by golden stairs, this was the Outer Circle reserved for the priests and the chanters. Two choirs of fifty singers each stood along its eastern and western rims, separated by fifty hooded drummers kneeling behind their instruments. A mosaic of a glittering mantis adorned it center—a tribute to Mirandu, the goddess of fertility. Behind the mosaic rose was a second raised platform. Made of silver, it carried the massive golden altar of Baal accessible only to the priests of the Inner Circle.

A gong reverberated in the temple, and High Priest Sharr walked from behind the altar followed by his assistant, Kalibaal, priest of the Inner Circle. The midday ritual was about to begin. The high priest wore a gilded, ruby-studded coat with wide short sleeves over a long, white gown embroidered with golden thread. A high-pointed, rigid bonnet hid his balding head. The left side of the bonnet featured the god Baal holding a scepter, while the right side showed Baal standing with a thunderbolt raised aloft. He bowed several times before the large, black stone altar, then took the seven-branched acacia censer to incense the massive gold statue of the celestial god crossing the rainbow driven by winged lions. The chariot was at the zenith, and the god standing erect was blessing the whole world with his scepter. Beneath his chariot, a thunderbolt hung ominously, reminding man of Baal's wrath.

"Eternal Prince, lord of all being, guide in a straight path the Temple whom thou loveth... Thou hast raised us, entrusting us with dominion over all people. By thy command, merciful Baal, may thy Temple, which I have built, endure for all time... From the horizon of heaven to its zenith, may it have no enemies."

Kalibaal stood behind Sharr, holding a velvet pillow where three seals of jasper and carnelian lay encased in gold crevices. He was wearing a gown similar to Sharr's, under a simpler silver coat and no headdress.

"May thy enemies be smitten, O lord, and may thy Temple's day be resplendent," he replied in a tremulous voice. He picked up one of the seals—commonly known as *scarabs* in Babylon—with a gold pincher and placed it on the surface of the water inside a large blue marble bowl sitting on the altar. Four pyramidal mountains etched in gold graced the bowl's rim.

A cow with a suckling calf occupied the main part of the seal, which had a hatched exergue standing for the celestial mountain of the god.

"From your servants, accept this offering, O Lord," intoned Sharr.

The choir to the right of Sharr was composed of fifty priests, many of whom were women. They began humming a single word, "Baal," continuously. They wore white tunics, and unlike the two priests of the Inner Circle who wore ornamented, closed shoes, these priests of the Outer Circle stood barefoot. The drummers, all male priests of the

Outer Circle, maintained a slow, steady beat, symbolizing the living heart of the god.

The second choir standing to the right of Sharr was composed of twenty-four Adorant, the dreaded all-female charmers of the Temple. Unlike a priest, an Adorant did not use spells or curses outwardly against her prey, but would use them inwardly, making herself so appealing that her victim would capitulate and would will to do the mistress' bidding. The Adorant clashed often with the Kerta priests. The leader of the Adorant, Sarand the Soloist, was said to possess powers rivaling those of Sharr. Had she been there for this ceremony, she would have been standing with Sharr in the Inner Circle. As to the secretive order of the Kerta priests, they worshiped Baal Essaaru—The Lord of Death—in a separate, underground temple.

The Adorant sang a four-part canon to entreat the god on behalf of the earth mother and her children. They wore light-green, sleeveless tunics and leather sandals with laces reaching just below their knees. An almond-shaped ruby held by a golden chain graced their foreheads. Their headdress formed complex geometric figures which were powerful incantations the women used to capture the hearts of many and turn them into willing slaves of Baal.

"Baal Shamaïm," intoned Sharr, calling on Baal as the god of the seas.

"Bless our ships and may their light soothe Anat and tame Yem," replied Kalibaal, dropping a second amulet in the bowl. This one represented a double-finned shark surrounded by waves.

Sharr then began whispering a seemingly nonsensical incantation, which was the heart of the daily ceremony. His voice did not carry over, but the Priests of the Inner Circle were all accomplished magicians and could hear him by other means. The high priest was obligated to recite it and was also required not to share it with anyone under pains of death. To meet both aims, he lengthened the recitation by including random words and curses against anyone who would try to decipher it. The

Temple expected a few ambitious priests of the Inner Circle to try. If they were found out, the high priest would make an example of them by delivering them into the hands of the Kerta priests. If one succeeded, he would become the next high priest. Sharr would then have to drink a deadly poison before being exiled to the spell world, where his slow, agonizing death would last centuries. In this way, the Temple was guaranteed that the priest or priestess with the strongest magical powers reigned supreme and governed the affairs of men.

Sharr's entreaty lasted half an hour, during which everyone else lay prostrate on the ground.

"Baal Malaage," sung Sharr, signaling the end of the prayer, "Lord of the Plenty, may you bless our plains with good grain and strong men."

Everyone stood up, and the drummers resumed their music.

"Fill our granaries with plenty and sustain the reign of your Temple," responded Kalibaal, carefully dropping the third scarab depicting a serpent surrounded by fire.

"Baal Adiir," continued Sharr, "omnipotent Lord of the Heavens, who has no equal among all the gods, let the Pit be sealed, let your Temple reign in peace and tranquility. Give us length of days, power, and the strength to endure for the sake of your name."

The Adorant's voices rose in a long psalmody that would rob the hearts of mere mortals from their senses. Only those priests who had mastered the test of the Adorant were admitted into the Outer Circle.

"Hear us, Adonaï," replied Kalibaal.

"Adonaï Baal etéru," sung the men. "Lord Baal save us."

"Lead us to your celestial abode," replied the Adorant.

"Do not feed us to the roaring flames of the Pit," intoned the men and the women, their voices rising to a high pitch as the drums reached a frenzied beat.

"So may it be," shouted Kalibaal.

"So it is," responded Sharr.

All present, except Kalibaal and Sharr, clapped their hands three times and fell prostrate once more.

The water in the bowl became troubled. A bright, white flame appeared on its surface, rising higher and higher. None dared look, believing Baal himself had come down to accept their offering. The water fizzed, steam fogged the entire altar and slowly dissipated, and still no one moved. After a long interval, Sharr stirred and arose. Kalibaal followed him. Together, they bowed before the altar then walked behind it, opened a hatch, and disappeared down a flight of stairs to a bare, circular room beneath the temple. Kalibaal closed the hatch behind them. When the men and women heard the hatch close, they rose silently, bowed to the altar, and left the temple. Silence fell once more on the large, dimly lit space.

Beneath the Temple, the two men stood in the Inner Circle's antechamber. Just ahead, behind a simple cloth curtain, the gateway to the spell world stood shimmering. Both priests removed their shoes and walked on the icy-cold stone to the edge of the gateway. They had learned long ago to endure the paralyzing pain that shot up their spines whenever they drew close to the gateway. The pain was so intense it would have driven the uninitiated to madness. The two men peered at the dark, swirling water inside a three-legged, large onyx bowl. Seven golden horns protruded from the bowl's rim, and the three legs of burnished bronze were patterned after those of the Karubiim, the winged lions of Baal. Their claws were of hardened steel tipped in rose gold. The knees were of jasper studded with bdellium.

"The north stirs," whispered Kalibaal. "Once unleashed, it will be difficult to contain."

An invisible wind was moving the surface of the water. Sharr waved a hand over it, and it became rigid like ice, but without freezing. Thin silver threads appeared below the surface. They flailed, their tips sinking into the bowl, and when they reappeared, they clasped a flower. As they dragged the flower to the center, a blinding flash of light cut through the darkness. The silver web was broken, the image disappeared, and the water became still.

"What just happened?" asked Kalibaal, fear seeping through his words. "What was that light?"

"The Urkuun lashed out at the priestess. The meaning of this action escapes me."

Kalibaal was dumbfounded. In the twenty-seven years he had served as priest, he had never once heard the high priest admit ignorance.

"Perhaps it was trying to attack the King and it missed?"

"An Urkuun does not miss," chided Sharr. "What is most troubling is the blinding flash of light. Another power is awakening. The Seer must be close to his quarry."

"What does it mean, My Lord?" asked Kalibaal, holding his breath.

Sharr faced Kalibaal, his piercing eyes burrowing into the younger priest's soul. "It means, my dear Kalibaal, that your reign as a high priest will be heavy indeed. The Second Age of Blood is upon us."

>✪✪✪<

Jamiir loved to walk, a privilege few monarchs outside his kingdom possessed. No king of Tanniin could govern unless he could walk on his own two feet around Taniir-The-Strong. A ruler would be carried in a dragon-shaped palanquin only on rare and solemn days: birth, presentation to the winged god on his third year, his wedding, and when he was too sick to move or on his deathbed. Customarily, a small company of twelve Silent guarded the royal procession; the reputation of this elite corps did the rest. Presently, Sondra led the Silent. She walked in front of the King while two teammates scouted ahead and two more closed the royal ranks. The remaining seven formed a fluid and discrete circle around the King, who took no notice of them. Jamiir smelled the scent of fresh pine and marjoram. It invigorated him.

"Beautiful day, is it not, my dear Bahiya?" repeated the King.

"That it is, Your Majesty," replied the priestess wistfully.

"Few notice the beauty of our forest," said the King, pointing at the nearby trees. "Here, poplar, chestnut, beech, oak, and pine grow in judicious harmony. Deeper in the forest, there are majestic yew, ash, and maple trees, whose girth and size are unknown elsewhere. Look over there," he said, pointing to his left. "Isn't this bougainvillea bush in full bloom next to this cluster of wild orchids magnificent? And down below, do you see the timid hydrangeas swaying gently, as if lulled to sleep by the breeze?"

"I see the terraced benches of rhododendrons," said the priestess.

"The hydrangeas are below the second terrace. These flowers grow beneath our trees freely," he added. "Aren't they beautiful?"

"His Majesty has a keen eye and a great love for gardening, I see," replied the priestess politely.

They resumed their walk.

"Master Habael's knowledge of the forest is astounding," said the King. "I enjoy my walks with him. He will make a gardener of me."

"Babylon's gardens are a true jewel," said Bahiya softly. "When Your Majesty visits the royal city of Baal, I hope His Majesty will find the time to tour the suspended garden."

Jamiir did not reply, but the meaning was clear. If the priestess appreciated his allusions to freedom, she was not moved and made it amply clear he that would be visiting Babylon soon. *So it is decided*, he thought, *and the death of the slave, which I approved, will not soften the blow.* He smiled, closed his eyes, and breathed the forest's fresh air.

"Halt," ordered Sondra. "Your Majesty, we must clear the road."

Ahead, where the path met Royal Road, a large group of townsfolk had sealed off the access that led to the King's castle.

Sondra reached them quickly and faced them alone. She pulled her cowl away, revealing the distinct Silent's green and black uniform.

"Please, make way for the King." She spoke casually to avoid any provocation.

"What about Ahiram?" asked a middle-aged man with a burnished face. "Me thinks these nasty rumors ain't right."

"They're true, though, like blue's blue," said a short, burly woman.

"They don't make us happy," added a young man holding a pitchfork. "It ain't right. We only want what's right."

"Tell'em white owls to stay out of it," hollered a tall woman from the side. "We don't need their meddling noses in our Games." The people of Tanniin referred to the men of Baal as "white owls" because of the gray tunics they wore. In the legends of Tanniin, the owl betrayed the god Tanniin by guiding Baal to the dragon's secret lair in the dead of night. A white owl was a renegade, a traitor, and a cheat.

A chorus of "yeah" and "white owls out" rose through the crowd.

Sondra lifted a commanding hand. "The best way to help Ahiram is to let the King pass," she urged in a soft but commanding voice. "Making His Majesty wait will make matters worse."

"Traiteh," yelled a man hidden from view. "Murdereh. You're no king of Tanniin!"

"Enough," ordered Sondra, her voice raising a notch. "Let Ahiram's friends leave now and let his foes stand." She knew her team's crossbows were at the ready, but she was unconcerned. This crowd was not murderous, only angry and frustrated, but without ill-intent.

Slowly, the crowd disbanded. The Silent met and held every man and woman's gaze. She needed them to know who was in control. She shared their pain and anguish, but she was a Silent, committed to protecting the King and obeying the commander, whom she trusted wholeheartedly. She waited until the last of them had gone before giving the signal to move forward.

"If I may say so, Your Majesty," whispered Bahiya, "you might consider asking Baal's barracks to protect the castle. Who knows what this mob will do next?"

≻✵✵✵≺

When the King reached the castle, he followed the high priestess' advice and called the men of Baal to secure the castle. Tanios tried to dissuade him to no avail. Within a few hours, the men of Baal were deployed in the castle, and the Silent were asked to stay in their quarters. *Is this the beginning of the end?* wondered Tanios.

Still, the royal castle's security was Tanios' responsibility. He inspected the first and second floors and saw to it that the men of Baal were covering the vast castle suitably. "Baal's soldiers are trained for the battleground," he muttered, "not for stealth and enclosed spaces." Why Jamiir confined the Silent to their quarters confounded him.

As soon as the soldiers saw Tanios, they stood at attention, saluting him as if he were their leader. His fame had spread far and wide—something that always surprised him. He had just reached the third floor and was walking toward the Lone Tower when he heard someone calling from the Star Room: "Come and see. Come and see." Tanios leaped forward. A soldier shouted, "Make way for the commander." The Star Room was filled with soldiers gazing through the window.

"What is the matter?" asked Tanios.

The men in the tower were surprised to see him but answered to the authoritative voice. "Look, the sun is hiding its face."

Tanios knew what they meant before looking out the window. Darkness had fallen on the land: Tholma, "the black sun". Tanios sighed, "It must be an omen." The sun was the judgment seat of Baal, the god of the air. Tholma was a powerful omen of upheaval and war, indicating the heavenly order had been shaken as if a celestial tremor, akin to an earthquake, had disturbed the seven heavens. Something was about to happen. He turned and looked at the men behind him. He wanted to reassure them and call on their sense of discipline when one of them leaped, jostled Tanios, and jumped out of the window. At first, Tanios took it for a case of suicidal madness as he had seen Tholma cause in the past, but then a soldier collapsed in a pool of blood. He was dead.

Tanios recognized the victim as one of the Junior High Riders.

On the floor, in front of the victim, lay a triple silver dart. *The fourth drop of blood*, thought Tanios, as he leaned over the ledge, trying to see the body of the fleeing murderer on the tiles of the castle's roof, but he saw no one. A rope was swaying two feet away from the window. He leaned over and yanked. It held, presumably tied to the tower's rooftop. *What is the murderer trying to do? There is no exit up there*, thought the commander. Ignoring the commotion in the room, he quickly climbed up. The narrow circular slab was empty. He walked around the edge, looking for any sign of the murderer, but saw nothing, as if the murderer had vanished. How could the murderer climb back down with his bare hands? Supposing he had jumped and run away, he would be intercepted by the soldiers stationed at every door. This made no sense.

Below, Obyj, who had watched the man collapse, leaned against the wall, white as a sheet. Unable to control his fears any longer, he shrieked, pointing at the dead man with a trembling finger. "The Pit, the Pit is opened. It will swallow us." Dropping his spear, he forced his way through the men around him and ran down the stairs screaming.

Pandemonium ensued. The leader of the patrol, a stocky bearded man, who believed only in blood, ale, and gold, slapped his men on their heads to restore order. Tanios leaped back through the window. Immediately, hands seized him and angry voices filled his ears. When the men realized they had not caught the murderer, they released him with muttered excuses and embarrassed looks.

"He is dead."

Bahiya was kneeling by the victim. Seeing her in their midst, three men blanched. The rest swallowed hard and stood to attention, wishing they had run away with Obyj. The high priestess was visibly angry. Who knew what she would do to them now.

Tanios noted, absentmindedly, that the door of the Star Room was ajar and the strange handle was missing. Someone had removed the wood planks that blocked the windows. Most likely the priestess wanted more light in here to better see what Garu had been up to.

"He is dead," she said, seething with anger as she faced Tanios. He did not flinch, but met her gaze calmly. The men were simply awed. "Yes, my dear Tanios, he is dead, and you failed."

"Shall I remind you, Priestess," he snapped back, "that it was *your* idea to bring these men here."

"It was His Majesty's order," cut in Bahiya.

Tanios ignored her. "You know they are not fit for watching over confined spaces like these. You have only yourself to blame."

"This castle is not safe," she replied tersely. "Baal will permanently take over the castle's security. Tonight, we *will* celebrate my daughter's victory and her team. I do not wish to see any other man of Baal die before our eyes, while nothing is being done about it."

She stormed through the door. The men looked at Tanios, uncertain what to do next. "Wait for me at the bottom of the stairs. I want to ask you a few questions," said Tanios.

The men complied, filing out of the room. Tanios remained alone with the dead man.

"You do not have to worry, my dear Bahiya, this was the last one," he whispered.

He looked out the window and watched the end of the eclipse. "And now, I wonder what is to happen next. Nothing will ever be the same."

≻✦✦✦≺

Ahiram drew near the pair of wings, cautious not to step in the Pool of

Purification. He moved slowly at first, then sped up as the prospect of winning excited him. He was so close.

"They are beautiful; they look like the wings of a Zaril Andali, the bird of the blue sky."

Ahiram conceived the image in his mind and froze instantly, his senses heightened. He remembered Habael's dream, the dream the old man had recounted four days ago while they were in the kitchen at breakfast. He could hear Habael word for word.

"You know, lad, the other night I had a dream. I was crossing a suspended bridge, and I looked down into the water. Lo and behold, I saw a bird: a big, beautiful, crystal bluebird. But when I drew closer, I realized the bird was dead and decaying."

Thank you, Master Habael, thought Ahiram. "A crystal bluebird in the waters and a big disappointment," he muttered. He stepped aside, walked back to the platform, and peered into the water. He picked up a smooth, palm-sized rock. Standing on the stairs of the platform, he threw the rock. It arced in the air and hit the wings sideways, jerking them out of place. Nothing happened. *So they're not trying to kill me with a boulder or fire*, thought the Silent as he walked back toward the wings. He leaned over and examined the upturned wings carefully and found what he was looking for: the wings were tied to a thin thread, nearly invisible in the water.

Ahiram followed it until he reached the back of the cave where the water trickled down moss-covered, smooth stones from somewhere above. The thread disappeared inside a crevice. Ahiram stood back, crouched, and yanked it. He heard the twang of crossbows being released and saw a volley of arrows shoot out from a concealed opening.

The arrows soared overhead and were lost, deep within the cave.

Ahiram shuddered. "Had I picked up the wings, these arrows would have found their mark."

An arrow whizzed by. Four men of Baal attacked from the riverside.

Two of them had bows in their hands, the third a spear, and the fourth a sword. "The Joyful Four," whispered the Silent as he leaped forward. The Joyful Four was a popular song about four drunkards who tried, but failed, to share a lone bottle they found while in the desert, and ended up dying of thirst instead. By extension, a group of clumsy men was often given this dubious sobriquet.

A second arrow whizzed by him and rebounded harmlessly off the walls. Thankfully, the path ahead was a narrow, winding passage slanting upward away from the water. Ahiram ran quickly, dodging the arrows. Soon, the sandy ground gave way to stairs hewn in the rock. They were made of large, irregular slabs of dissimilar height. The Silent bounded up the stairs, and as they turned slightly to the left, he stopped in his tracks. At the top of the stairs, seven men of Baal were waiting for him with spears and swords. His pursuers were fast approaching. Ahiram was trapped.

21. Ithyl Shimea

"Woe to him who tastes the bitter chalice of a curse. His eyes will turn into lakes of fire, his ears will shed blood, and he will wither away faster than the leaves of fall, until, at last, nothing shall be left of him but an eternal scream of horror."
—**Teaching of Oreg, High Priest of Baal**

"Taxes, meetings, and curses—they are real, you know. You can't avoid taxes, but their effect is temporary. You must avoid curses, for they are permanent. As for meetings, let's just say they cannot be avoided, and their debilitating effect is permanent."
—**Diplomatic Notes of Uziguzi, First Adviser to Her Majesty Aylul Meir Pen, Empress of the Empyreans**

"Open this door," snapped Ramel, unable to contain her excitement. "I can hardly wait."

Two weeks before the Games, Garu had found the secret passage at the base of the Lone Tower. This led down steep, spiraling stairs to the Pool of Purification in the Mine of Meyroon, where two hours earlier, Ahiram had been cornered by his adversaries. Now, Garu finally discovered the second secret door—the one he had been looking for while in the Star Room: a simple, stone slab standing to the left of the stairs Ahiram had climbed when running away from the soldiers. This hidden door opened onto a slanted path that meandered downward a long way and ended in a huge cave. Garu and Ibromaliöm presently lit the dozen torches they brought with them. Not surprisingly, they found sconces on the walls to hang them. They had correctly reasoned that the room they were seeking must have been part of a larger hidden complex.

As the torches lit, they were startled by two gold dragons standing on bronze pedestals opposite each other. The statues towered overhead fully erect, their wings jutting forward and touching in the center, forming a bronze canopy.

"It's a temple to the god Tanniin," whispered Ramel.

Two smaller statues stood farther back, where the door to the temple lay. The huge door had been sealed off by rocks and dirt. The back wall bulged in several places under the ground pressure, and the ground was littered with rocks and debris of smashed vases. A marble statue lay on the ground, having lost its head, and two silver platters, mangled by the rocks, lay next to it. A jar offering made of stone lay smashed; its silver coins scattered. They gleamed gently in the light.

"Someone went to great lengths to seal the main passage," observed Ibromaliöm.

"And then the temple was forgotten," added Ramel, in a sad voice.

"Your Majesty," called Garu, "you should see this."

Ramel and Ibromaliöm walked to the front of the temple where the main altar stood inside a sanctuary nearly sixty feet in diameter. Behind a wide stone altar stood a statue of Tanniin, unlike any they had seen before: the god was perched on a chariot from which Baal was missing. His wings overextended, the dragon crooned in a shout of glory.

"Tanniin overthrowing Baal from his heavenly chariot," explained Ramel, speaking softly. "Never before have I seen this."

"This temple is old," observed Ibromaliöm, as he refrained a sudden shiver. The cold and damp air did nothing to comfort him.

"Very old," confirmed Ramel, her voice quivering with excitement, "predating the coming of Baal to Tanniin. It may have been commissioned by El-Windiir himself."

They gazed at the altar silently, their breath streaking the air.

"So this is it, then." said Ramel, breaking the mood. "This is where the secret chamber must be."

"Yes, Your Majesty," replied Garu, pointing to a spot close to the door they had come through. "It must be over there."

"How would you know that?"

"Look, Your Majesty; the handle on that panel and the one from the tower are made of the same magical substance."

They drew closer to the door. Ibromaliöm noticed a side altar he had not seen before and froze.

"This temple may be old, but someone has been here recently," he whispered, pointing to an offering of dried fruits and a jar of honey.

Ramel gasped. "A votive offering? Here? Now? This is truly amazing. There is no priest to receive these offerings and perform the necessary sacrifice."

They crossed over and drew closer to the altar. A mosaic depicted Tanniin in mid-flight, raining the fire of life on grassy lands below. Those who worshiped him believed his fire to be sacred, rejuvenating, and a source of life.

"Look," Garu pointed at two candleholders. "These candles are new. There is no dust on them, and they have barely been used."

"The priestly order of Tanniin has survived?" asked the Queen incredulously. "Did you two know about it and not tell me?"

The two men shook their heads: Ibromaliöm condescendingly and Garu vehemently.

"You may wish to ask the commander," said Ibromaliöm, amused. "He might have an answer for you."

"This may or may not be a priest of Tanniin," said Garu, examining the offerings closely. "This is not a votive offering," he said after a short while. "Look at the fruit. They are partially spoiled. See the discoloration on the figs? And the apricots are no longer ripe. And—"

"Spare us your erudition, Garu," said Ibromaliöm, sharply, "and get to the point."

"The point, my dear friend," replied Garu, "is that this basket is much older than this jar over here, and if I am not mistaken..." Carefully, Garu removed the oil-soaked rag stuffed into the neck of the jar, which was customarily used as a sealant for short periods. He smelled the content and backed away quickly.

"As I suspected, this is not honey. It's blood."

"Blood?" exclaimed his companions.

"Yes, blood. The fruit is an older offering. The blood is a recent offering." He looked furtively around, trying to discern if someone else was present.

"I think the murderer has been here."

"The murderer?" asked Ramel, disbelieving her ears, "but how could he have found this place before you? Unless of course—"

"Oh please, Your Majesty," cut in Ibromaliöm, "Garu may be many things, but he is not a murderer. The fat fool does not have it in him to kill a fly."

Ramel's tremulous laughter cut Garu like a knife. She was relieved, knowing the murderer was not in their company. "Perhaps, my dear Ibromaliöm. But you, on the other hand, could and may kill."

Ibromaliöm held her gaze, smiling. "Indeed, Your Majesty, I would but for the right price or the right cause. What profit is there for me in these murders? Come now, let us not speculate, but tend to the business at hand."

"But if the murderer is neither one of us," asked Garu, "how did he manage to find this place before us?"

"We will have time to delve into this mystery once we have collected what we have come for," replied Ibromaliöm, exasperated. "Hylâz and Ramany must be wondering about us. A word from them to that pesky commander and—"

"Your Majesty, are you certain you want to do this?" asked Garu.

"Do you question my motives, Garu?" snapped the Queen.

"Fine then," he replied with shoulders sagging. "Let's do it."

Garu strolled ahead as they followed. In the dim light of the torches, the Queen could not make out the details of the ceiling. Still, she could see that the wide, blue marble tiles ended abruptly right before the two statues. Beyond, the ragged dome of the cave shone faintly in the light. Several of the slabs had fallen, and their shards littered the ground.

"You could almost feel El-Windiir's desperation as Baal drew closer," whispered Ramel. "This was to be a major temple, but he was forced to abandon it."

One of Ibromaliöm's steely boots screeched ominously, dragging a pebble with it. The tall man kicked it irritably.

"Let's get on with it, Garu," he snapped. "This place is filled with dead things. Dead things we should not have seen or touched."

Garu did not pay heed to Ibromaliöm's comment. His sense of foreboding was growing heavier by the minute. He wished he could take Ramel far away from this place to a small cottage deep in the forest, but he knew she would never agree to it. His shoulders sagged as they approached the massive panel. In comparison, the door they had come through felt like a mouse hole.

"At long last," said Ramel, breathing a sigh of relief in front of the wide panel. "We have found you."

The door was fifteen feet high and ten feet wide. Encased in a triple silver frame, its two panels were made of burnished bronze and were held in place by six massive, gold hinges. Its handle was of gold as well and shaped like a dragon with a missing tail. A pair of black wings in a ten-foot ellipse was the only carving on its surface. The chiseling was exquisite, for they could see the contour and relief of each scale. Four crystal spheres, cast into the door, framed the ellipse.

"If these wings are made of meyroon," said the Queen in a dreamy voice, "their worth would exceed that of the kingdom."

"What do we do now?" asked the ever-practical Ibromaliöm.

Garu raised the handle from the Lone Tower and pointed to the door's handle. "These two are but one handle. I need to break the spell that keeps them apart. Once the handle is whole, the door will open."

"I am growing impatient," snapped the Queen. "Open the door."

He looked at her and smiled. What Ibromaliöm saw as greed and intemperance, Garu saw as joy and innocence. "Your Majesty," he said, soothingly, "this is not a simple soldering job. I cannot melt these two handles and create a new one. This is magic, so please be patient and have no fear; this door will open for you."

"And to think we are the first ones to see El-Windiir's tomb," said Ramel, clasping her hands. Unable to resist anymore, as if entranced by what lay behind the door, Ramel tried to touch it. She staggered, screaming in pain.

"Your Majesty," pleaded Garu, straining under the effort of his magical spell, "the door is protected by a powerful spell. Please do not touch it again."

"Then open the door," she snapped, unable to contain her excitement. "I can hardly wait."

Evidently, the door was ancient dwarfish handiwork and could only be opened with its handle. After several failed attempts, Garu sighed and wiped his forehead.

"I am not having much success in getting the two pieces to fuse together."

"You told us," said Ibromaliöm, his voice barely a whisper, "the black sun weakens the power of the Pit. You said on a day such as this, Tanniin loses his power, Baal is restrained, and the curse of El-Windiir can be broken. You said the curse of Alissaar Ben Nadam could then be avoided. So why is it—"

"I don't know," interrupted Garu, exasperated. "I am doing the best I can. Would you like to try?" he growled, brandishing the handle, but Ibromaliöm backed away. "Afraid, I see?" snickered Garu. Clenching his teeth, he strained once more to fuse the pieces together.

"Open the—" repeated Ramel, but was cut off by the impatient gesturing of Garu.

Holding the small handle firmly against the larger one, he muttered a few words and waited, half expecting a flash of light to bind them together. He released the small handle. To his dismay, it fell duly to the ground. Her Majesty was barely able to control her anger.

Garu squatted, closed his eyes, and paid no heed to the Queen or his companion. Ibromaliöm took to pacing, and the Queen, her hands behind her back, tried to distract herself by admiring the ceiling. She was about to tell Garu to open the door one more time when he sprang to his feet, picked up the small handle, and looked at it intently, as if he were seeing it for the first time. He took a couple of steps back, breathed deeply, and holding the handle, he stretched his arm forward and spoke in a loud voice:

"Indili Amiralim Ilil Aftal Tanniin!" The handle flew from his hand, nearly breaking his fingers. It snapped to the back of the larger handle while, simultaneously, a bright, green light flashed, fusing them together. When they opened their eyes, the handle was whole.

"How did you do it?" exclaimed Ramel, who was genuinely impressed for once. She looked like a child before a great present.

Garu blushed. "I looked at the handle and I saw these horns. They had bothered me all along. Why should a dragon's tail have two horns? I remembered then the ancient poem—"

"The one about the bull and the dragon?" asked Ramel, who

understood where this was going.

"Exactly, Your Majesty," replied Garu affably. "The bull, it is said, is the only animal to ride on the back of Tanniin."

"Because," continued Ramel, "by working the soil, it distributes Tannin's fertility to all. So, as a reward, Tanniin gave the lowly bull a heavenly vision."

Garu nodded. "So, I simply said the refrain of the poem, 'Let the bull ride Tanniin.'"

She looked at him, and he saw admiration in her eyes. He thought how lovely her eyes were.

Ibromaliöm was showing signs of impatience. "Your Majesty, we should enter now."

"Garu, open the door," commanded the Queen.

Garu obeyed. He grabbed the handle and pushed. The two panels pivoted silently on their hinges, revealing a rectangular room, save for one corner that was cut by a wall of the Lone Tower.

"Garu," ordered Ramel, handing him her torch, "light up this room."

Garu obeyed, and moments later, six burning torches hung on golden sconces.

"The walls..." said Ramel, "they are covered with gold. The floor, the ceiling as well, and here... this silver altar," said the Queen, clasping her hands. "Could it be?"

"Yes," replied Ibromaliöm, running his hand on the altar's gleaming surface. "El-Windiir's altar of sacrifice. Powerful magic must have been performed on its surface."

"Do not touch it!" shouted Garu. "This room reeks of magic. Do not touch anything. We should leave now."

They ignored him.

"Look, Your Majesty," whispered Ibromaliöm, "the back wall, there's a second door."

"Ibromaliöm," said Garu with an altered voice. "Your hand, the one that touched the altar; it's bleeding."

The tall judge watched as drops of blood fell from his hand onto the altar. "It's nothing," he said in a casual, dreamy voice. "Nothing at all."

Horrified, Garu watched the drops of blood seep through the surface of the altar, disappearing entirely. He was beginning to understand why Sureï had cursed this place, and he wished he had never set foot in int. *El, help us*, he prayed silently. *El, please help us.*

The second door was shorter and narrower than the one they had come through. It was richly decorated with gold, silver, and bronze. Atop the door sat the sculpted head of a dragon in gold. Its eyes were of the darkest metal they had ever seen, yet the strange, dark pupils sparkled like midnight-blue crystal.

"I cannot believe what I am seeing," whispered Ramel. "Look at those eyes," she continued, her voice rising in excitement. "It's meyroon!"

They stood staring at the two pairs of eyes. Even Garu was mesmerized by the meyroon. Overwhelmed by what they had managed to do, they remained speechless, gazing at the extraordinary eyes, knowing they were standing where no one had stood in centuries. They were certain that beyond the second door lay the tomb of El-Windiir.

Suddenly and without warning, a gray jet of light shot up from the altar. Garu felt the walls liquefy and lose their consistency. The altar's surface boiled, and gray thorns grew from it. One of the thorns shot out, hit Ibromaliöm in the forehead, sinking deep inside his skull. Garu screamed and covered his eyes, and when he opened them, the room's appearance was as before: gold walls, the silver altar, the Queen, and Ibromaliöm standing in front of the door.

"Garu," snapped Ramel. "You fool, get up. This is not the time to be scared. Open this door, now."

Garu was disoriented. He felt lost and powerless. "What just happened?"

"You slipped, my friend," said Ibromaliöm, in a sleepy voice that sent a chill up Garu's spine.

"Open the door, Garu. I am certain the tomb of El-Windiir is there."

"It is," said Ibromaliöm, who stood mesmerized by an object lying on a cloth in the center of the altar.

"What is this?" asked Garu, gripped by a sickening feeling. "Where did this libre come from? It wasn't there before."

"This is true," said Ramel, with an altered voice. "It wasn't here."

"Ramel, please listen to me," Garu said. "I implore you; we should leave now before something terrible happens. This place reeks of magic. Look, no dust anywhere. Only magic can do that."

Indeed, the room was immaculate with not a wisp of dust or cobwebs, as if all living things, as well as wind and dust, stayed away.

"How could that be?" asked the Queen.

"I am not certain," replied Garu, "but I think," he said, trying to control his fear, "we are not seeing this room as it exists in the real world—we are seeing it in the spell world."

"The spell world?" replied the Queen aghast. "Are you certain?"

"I don't know. I don't know," replied Garu, his teeth chattering, "but we must get out of here as quickly as possible. We should not be here."

"How are you not yet dead?" complained Ibromaliöm, without taking his eyes from the book. "The absorbers should have shielded you from the curse of breaking into this sanctuary for a few short minutes only. We are long past that time, so how come you are still alive?"

"The absorbers," gasped Garu. He fumbled in his pockets, and his face grew deathly pale. "I don't have them. I forgot them. How could I have done such a thing?"

"More importantly," cut in Ibromaliöm, "how are you still alive and well enough to complain?"

Ramel clapped her hands with irritation. "Who cares? The curse is broken. Maybe he broke it when he opened the door. Open this door, Garu. I want El-Windiir's shoes and belt. I want to fly like him."

"Forget El-Windiir and his artifacts," replied Ibromaliöm with a low voice. "They are childish pranks compared to the libre on this table. This is the Shimea. A libre of power so great it can..." Ibromaliöm did not complete his sentence. Garu, who was still trembling with fear, lifted his gaze and barely contained a scream.

"The Ith..." he could not continue. "It's not... It's not..." He wanted to say that it was not supposed to be here. This was far worse than his worst nightmare, as if the Pit had wormed its malice past the lid that was supposed to lock it in the depth of the earth. This malice was now here, or rather, they were in it.

A murderous glint lit Ibromaliöm's eyes as he looked at them. "It is mine," he said softly. "Mine alone."

"Ibromaliöm," chided the Queen, who had not noticed the change in the tall man, "don't be a spoil. Show some patience. After all, we have agreed to share the treasure together. You promised."

"Indeed, I did," replied the tall man, who was getting closer to the book. "And Ibromaliöm keeps his promises."

Seeing the change in Ibromaliöm, Ramel thought to exploit it. She smiled and whispered in an alluring, taunting voice, "Open the libre, Ibromaliöm. Go ahead, open it."

"No!" screamed Garu. He pushed her back and stood between her and the book. "Your Majesty, Ibromaliöm, listen to me. This libre must not be opened. It must not be touched. The curse to enter here has been broken, but there is a deep malice about this libre. It is not for mortal men to peer into."

Without warning, an earthquake hit. Garu saw the ground beneath them suddenly liquefy and turn into a green ooze; but it reverted to its normal state so suddenly that he thought he must have been hallucinating. The Queen lost her balance and fell backward. Ibromaliöm fell forward onto the silver altar and screamed an inhuman scream of pain. He flailed his arms wildly and flung the book off the altar. It fell, bounced, and lay open just when Ramel rolled onto her side and came face-to-face with the book.

Its pages were blank. Dazed, she glanced at them just as a short sequence of words appeared on the surface of the right page. Ramel felt compelled to read. How she was able to read she did not know, but the meaning was clear: "The libre *Shimea*—an instruction in the ways of the *Ithyl Shimea*."

Suddenly, the Queen's vision dimmed and darkness replaced light at the onset of a curse. Searing pain dug into her flesh like thousands of tiny blades, and she screamed in unbearable pain.

"No," moaned Garu, as he struggled to his feet, but Ibromaliöm was quicker. He rushed forward, snatched the cloth still on the altar, and threw it on top of the book. Leaning over, he shut the book, wrapped it in the cloth, looked at the Queen, then at Garu with the eyes of a madman, and bounded out of the room. The earthquake stopped then, as abruptly as it had started.

Garu looked at Ramel and recoiled in horror. A deep scar disfigured her face. Starting from the top right side of her forehead, it curved down covering her eyes then slanted through the midsection of her left cheek and into her neck. Ramel was blind. Garu drew closer to his Queen, held her in his arms, and began to cry uncontrollably, but in the depths of the mines of Tanniin, there was no one to hear him.

>✸✸✸<

Ahiram relaxed his muscles in preparation for what he was about to do. The deadly circle of men was closing in on him. Their swords were raised. He knew he had only one chance to act.

Before he moved, four Silent materialized behind the men at the top of the stairs. Banimelek, Jedarc, Elio, and Thurun attacked. They were all Ahiram's classmates, and they were not about to let their friend die at the hands of the High Riders.

Although taken by surprise, the High Riders reacted quickly. "Run, Ahiram, run!" screamed Banimelek. Ahiram threw an escape dart at the feet of the four men who had been tracking him up the stairs. The dart exploded, forcing the soldiers to a hasty retreat. He threw a second one and burst through the four startled soldiers waiting for him, then sped ahead into a corridor. Seeing no one in pursuit, Ahiram wanted to continue looking for the wings, but just then another group of High Riders raced after him, springing from the shadows. He ran faster, leading his pursuers into a section of the mine that he was not familiar with. Pathways followed one another in a blur, and he knew he was lost.

Ahiram did not know where he was going, but he had no time to think. Running was all he could do. At the end of one turn, he ended up on a narrow ledge overlooking the river sixty feet below. The waters rushed furiously toward the Eye of Death. Ten High Riders were blocking the exit. This time there was no way out and no tricks. Death in front, death behind, and nowhere to go.

The men looked at him, grinning. He was now standing at the edge of the cliff. One more move and he would fall.

"Come on, slave, drop the mask, the belt, and the shoes," said their leader. "If you do, I'll kill you swiftly. I promise you won't suffer."

Ahiram removed the shoes, belt, and mask from behind him. They would slow him down during a fight. "Come and get them," said the Silent in low, tense growl that should have alerted the men of Baal, but they were too proud to fear him.

The leader sighed, "Your choice, your pain."

The High Riders attacked. The first man to reach Ahiram did not see the Silent's fist but felt as if a battering ram had hit him in the chest. He was thrown back, hit two other soldiers and the force of the impact was so great, the three men fell unconscious. A blade whizzed by. Ahiram caught it between his open palms, clasped it, and twisted so violently that he broke his attacker's wrist, who fell on his knees holding his injured arm. Then, with a back-kick he threw another High Rider against the wall of the cave. The man crumbled to the floor.

"Five down, five still standing," growled Ahiram, his eyes burning with a strange fire. He pointed at his artifacts and smiled at the leader. "Like I said, High Rider, come and get them."

Just then, the earth shook violently and the ledge where the Silent stood broke off and fell into the void, taking the slave with him. The man with the injured wrist and another soldier followed him screaming. The remaining four scrambled to safety and managed to hold onto the wall long enough for the earthquake to subside. Carefully, they peered over the ledge but could see only the glimmer of the cold water raging through the bottom of the ravine.

"He's gone," said one of them in jubilation, for the high priestess had promised a hefty prize for whomever killed the slave; and fewer men to report back meant a heftier portion of the reward for the survivors.

"How convenient," said another, pointing at the shoes, the belt, and the mask. "He left them right here for us to pick up."

"But what if he is not dead?" asked their leader. "We did not see him die. He could come back."

"Come back from this?" asked the first man, pointing to the sixty-foot plummet into rushing waters. "Come back alive from the Eye of Death? Are you out of your mind? No man who has fallen into these waters has ever been found again."

"Except one," muttered their leader.

"So, what would you have us do? Go down and search for him?"

Their leader scratched his head once more. "I suppose not."

"What do we do with them?" asked a soldier, pointing at their four unconscious companions.

His leader smiled. "Do? Nothing. Absolutely nothing. After all, why split a prize among seven when you can split it between four?" The other three men laughed. "Pick up the artifacts," he ordered as he walked to the tattered edge and peered down. Black, swift waters glittered far below. "Let's go. Lady Hiyam is waiting for us. She needs the mask to win." They left, patting one another on the back, their mission accomplished.

>✸✸✸<

"Come on, Hiyam. We need to move."

Hiyam looked at her team members, who were waiting for her. She was standing in front of a large boulder in the waters of purification. Her heart was heavy, and she had lost all interest in the Games. Notwithstanding, what her mother had told her, she could not bring herself to believe that Ahiram's assassination was carried out for the common good. The boulder seemed light as a feather compared to the weight on her conscience. Her men were not aware of the slave's fate, or if they were, they did not let it worry them. They were still in the Games wanting to win and understandably so. Honor and rewards awaited them, both here and back home.

Hiyam moved away from the boulder toward the staircase. As she climbed, she heard her teammates speaking softly. She knew all too well what they were saying; how she had deliberately slowed their progress when they were trying to enter the cave. How she trailed last and forced them to move at a snail's pace.

None of this matters anymore. I am no longer a High Rider. Ahiram, you won. I will quit and leave Baalbeck.

She dreaded being present when the men of Baal were accomplishing their dark deed. As she moved up the stairs, she hoped to catch up to Ahiram. She hoped to see him in front of her, but it did not happen. Predictably, her team was able to find a pair of wings judiciously placed. Her heart sank low when she saw the mask of gold waiting for her nearby. Her team members picked it up; they knew where it came from.

The day-long crossing of the mine was uneventful. Nothing seemed to stop their impending victory. As they were about to reach the exit, their voices rose and they relaxed. They were already appreciating the sweet taste of victory. *Too much sweet is bitter,* thought Hiyam, as she approached the exit. She braced herself for the hardest part of this Game: the compliments. She wondered if she would be able to listen to them without screaming as they enumerated all her accomplishments.

>❖❖❖<

"So?" asked Hylâz.

"So, what?" replied Ramany, with a tone of voice that attempted to be patient but failed. He knew all too well what was coming.

"What are we to do? We are positively in violation of the rules."

"Which rule?" asked Ramany, hoping against all hope that Hylâz would profess his ignorance.

"Rule 64, first part, second subpart, which states that no winner can be declared without the four judges being present to witness the victory," Hylâz was offended that Ramany would show such lack of appreciation of the crisis at hand. "Neither Garu nor Ibromaliöm have been seen since this morning, and they are nowhere to be found. Hence, it is reasonable to surmise that they will not come any time soon. So, we are in violation of the rule, and I would venture to say that the situation is now serious. I would in fact say that the situation is very, very grave."

"What must we do?"

"The rule on this point is clear: four judges must preside for the declaration of a winner. We are two. Which means we are lacking two."

"Does the rule explicitly mention four distinct judges? Is it possible for two judges to act as four?"

"The rule is not explicit, but if your argument applies, then we could, as a corollary, deduce that one man could act as four judges, and if this be so, then a further reduction would mean that no man can act as four

414

judges. Since this logical conclusion is logically ridiculous, it must follow that the presupposition is ridiculous, logically speaking, that is."

"Why are you speaking in dwarfish?"

"Pardon?"

Ramany sighed. "Never mind. So what do you suggest?"

"This is what I have asked you. You are the senior member now, thus I must defer to you," said Hylâz.

"I know what to do," replied Ramany with a loud voice. He caught himself and continued more quietly. "We shall declare you, my dear Hylâz, the lead judge and defer to you to solve this difficult and important matter." Ramany smiled and stood tall. He was proud of himself for finding such an easy way out.

"I accept the honor," replied Hylâz. A moment of silence followed. Hylâz raised his hand before continuing. "As lead judge, I decree the following in conformance with the rules and regulations of the Games. Given that four judges are requisite for passing a proper judgment, and given that no proper extraneous conditions were set in the choosing of said judges; I solemnly decree that you, Ramany, shall go forth and choose two men worthy of this high office who would replace the deserters in this most important and noble task. Go, henceforth, my dear Judge, and complete this task worthily."

Having said that, Hylâz turned around and walked out of the cave. Ramany was stumped. He thought he got himself out of trouble only to find that he was in deeper trouble. Frustrated by the whole affair, he walked toward the crowd and picked the first two men he saw. "You and you will be judges with us tonight to determine who the winner shall be. Follow me." Frajil looked at Ramany with a dazed expression on his face. The short, fat man standing by his side looked at him and said, "Did he say we are judges now?" Frajil emitted a sound that mimicked the grunt of a gorilla. The short man took it for a "yes." He straightened his posture and followed Ramany. Seeing that Frajil had not moved, he gestured impatiently. Frajil recognized the gesture and followed them while his brain struggled to make sense of what had just happened to him.

"Ah, my dear Ramany, I see that you have carried out your mission with alacrity and zeal. I am proud of you. Now, whom do we have here as judges of the Games of the Mines?"

"I am Birg Zamil, purveyor of pork," answered the short, fat man.

"Well, my dear Birg Zamil, you will assist us in the important task of conferring the palm of victory to the winner. And who do we have here?" continued Hylâz after a slight hesitation. Somehow, he did not feel reassured in the presence of this giant.

"Frajil."

"Well, my dear Frajil, you too are invited to participate in this august mission." Hylâz took a step back when the same gorilla-like grunt came forth from Frajil.

"So, Master Hylâz, what are we supposed to do?" asked Birg Zamil, who took his mission to heart.

"Well, my dear friend, when a team comes out of these caves, we verify that it has in its possession each of the duly authorized and stamped artifacts: a pair of wings, a golden mask, a silver belt, and a pair of bronze shoes. Then, after careful and attentive examination of said artifacts, we convene, confabulate, and decree that the stamped artifacts are indeed authentic; and we have a winner. In the unlikely event that the artifacts are fraudulent, we shall solemnly declare said team disqualified and in a state of dissolution. Is this clear?"

"Amply so, Master Hylâz," answered Birg, who was starting to feel comfortable in his role as judge. For once, he wasn't talking about pork and the various ways to cook it, and this alone procured Birg happiness, even if the words of Hylâz sounded like gibberish to his ears.

Frajil had remained motionless. He was debating whether to hit someone or not. This was his habitual reaction to events he did not understand. Since most events were beyond his grasp, he was in the habit of hitting lots of folks, unless his brother, Soloron, was there to mediate between the world and his brother's mind. Frajil felt at home mostly when dealing with chicken, in battles, and in one-on-one combat. Everything else seemed strange and complicated. Nevertheless, this case was different.

"Tiny man makes noise. Hit tiny man," reasoned the giant. "But tiny man smiled, so no hit tiny man." Given that no one provoked him, and no one shouted his name, Frajil had to admit, reluctantly, that Hylâz was not fighting him. Still, the situation was aggravating and he needed something to soothe his nerves. Frantically, he surveyed the area in search of someone to hit, but found no one besides Hylâz in close proximity. And so, Frajil remained in an unsteady state, oscillating between wanting to hit Hylâz and not wanting to hit him.

At last, a team surged from the mine. The crowd stood up like one man. It was Hiyam and her men. The expectant crowd hushed immediately, its spirit sinking like a shipwreck being swallowed by dark waters. One-by-one, the proud folks of Tanniin walked away. Hiyam wished she could shut her ears for their silence was dreadful. The sun slipped below the mountains, bloodying the sky, and beneath that fiery red of this late summer day, the crowd processed as if in a funeral. They passed her by with sullen, empty faces. She looked down and clenched her fists. Hylâz came forward and asked to see the complete set of artifacts, and received them from one of her teammates. Hiyam was so grieved she failed to notice the new judges.

"Gentlemen," said Hylâz, exhibiting the artifacts to the three other judges, "I have examined each of these objects, and they all bear the stamp of this year's Game. I am proud to declare that the team of Baal has won. What say you?"

"I agree," answered Ramany. He did not like the crowd's behavior and wanted the whole thing done and over with as quickly as possible.

"I agree," echoed Birg, trying to imitate Ramany's authoritarian tone.

The three men waited for Frajil, who seemed lost in deep thought.

"Well, my dear friend, what do you say? Do we have a winner?"

Now, "winner" is a word Frajil understood all too well, but it was never put to him in an interrogative mode. That threw him off and kept him undecided. He grunted prudently. Hylâz took it for a "yes."

"We have a winner," he declared.

He went back to the team of Baal and congratulated Hiyam, declaring her champion of the Games. Her teammates lifted her onto their shoulders despite her protests and carried her to the King's castle. Shortly thereafter, the team from Quibanxe came out with a pair of wings, and Hylâz conferred upon them second place.

Ramany sighed. He was relieved. It was done. They could go back to the castle and forget about the entire matter. Tonight there would be rejoicing and much food, and tomorrow he would be able to return to his hometown and his peaceful life.

Long after everyone left, Frajil remained motionless in the deserted place. By not hitting anyone, he felt he had accomplished a great thing. Suddenly hungry, he went to the taverns in search of something to eat.

➤✪✪✪✦

The plaza stood abandoned. Slowly, darkness overtook sky, moon and stars, and in this foreboding silence, a man walked out of the cave. He stopped and feverishly inspected the package he was carrying.

"I have it," he whispered. "I *own* the libre. Those who will read the *Shimea* shall number by the thousands. They shall read and be cursed; they will die a horrible death. But no matter. Bit by bit, they will uncover the content of the *Shimea* for me, and I, I alone shall wield the power of the *Ithyl Shimea* to break asunder the bonds of Baal."

He laughed a wiry, maddening laugh, then leaping forward, he sprinted away leaving behind him a thin trail of blood.

22. WINGS OF FIRE

"Magic is complex. Young apprentices believe their magic to be self-contained and self-sufficient; its beginning and end under their control. Their elation would be amusing, and their joy bearable, if the truth was less tragic.

"A modicum of experience teaches them that magic is a thread in a complex web spun by the god they have entreated. Those foolish enough to believe in magic without the gods put others in mortal danger. Magic is a dialogue with the god who, ultimately, controls the magician.

"Sureï said: 'Magic begets magic. To obtain what he seeks, a magician must play the gods against one another. If he fails, his magic will start a chain reaction that is almost always tragic.'

"A great magician uses magic reluctantly."

–Teaching of Oreg, High Priest of Baal

Ahiram fell headlong into the river. He felt his breath driven from him and nearly lost consciousness, but his training kicked in and stayed the initial panic. He avoided thrashing and focused on orientation. A short moment later, he burst through the surface gasping for air. The water was freezing, and he knew it would be even colder once it flowed underground. Behind him, the two men of Baal were doing all they could to keep their heads above the raging flow. He could see they were terrified. Soon, the water would swallow them all, drowning them in the Eye of Death, the underground pass through which the water surges before emerging in the open on its way to the northern forests of Tanniin.

Ahiram looked around, but there was little he could do. The strong current kept him away from the walls, and his fingers were numb. He could barely keep his head above water and was inexorably dragged toward the submerged passage. The current's power grew, and he could feel the rushing waters around him gathering strength, ready to entomb him in the darkness of the pit. He tried frantically to do something to move away from the Eye of Death. He wanted to swim against the current but could barely move. He was getting closer and closer to the pit, and he was terrified. By now, the water's pull was so great he could barely keep himself afloat. He looked ahead and saw the end of the flow. He took a deep breath and sunk beneath the surface.

$$\succ \bullet \bullet \bullet \prec$$

The men of Baal who had seen Ahiram's plunge were at the bar in the Shining Tavern, oblivious of their surroundings. The high priestess did not receive them when they came back to announce that the slave was dead. As far as they were concerned, killing a slave was nothing to fuss about, but the reward gladdened their hearts: three gold libna each, which was enough to purchase fifty young slaves. This was far beyond what they had expected. They drank to her health, their health, and the health of every dead slave they had ever known.

"Celebrations are in order," yelled one of them.

They had been celebrating rather loudly for the past hour. Sitting alone at a dimly lit table was Frajil, eating a whole chicken. He was trying to think, and the noise these men were making was not helping. It reminded him of *The Ballad of the Tajéruun*, a song Soloron loved to hum. "Bom, bom, bom, the Tajéruun." Frajil muttered the last part of the song's chorus absent-mindedly, then shook his head. He needed to concentrate. Somehow, he was not sure that eating a chicken in a tavern was what Soloron meant when he said, "Tonight we roast the chicken." It did not occur to him that he should rejoin his brother's camp and ask him. Once Frajil focused on a problem, he did not know how to stop until it was resolved; whether the resolution made any sense was an altogether different matter.

So there he was, convinced he had roasted a chicken. The cook did the roasting, but this was not a detail that would stop Frajil, for he had no concept of cooking, or payment for that matter. Thankfully, Soloron arranged to pay Tika, a Togofalkian with a shady past and the owner of the Shining Tavern, for whatever Frajil ordered. To Tika's relief, this giant of a man had been a well-behaved customer, who drank mostly water, ate whole chickens, and said "please" and "thank you." Soloron had been true to his word, paying for Frajil's meals regularly.

The men from Baal laughed loudly, and one of them threw his goblet overhead. It bounced off a table where two farmers sat and crashed to the floor. No one complained or much less glanced at them. If they did, a swift death would be their lot.

Some wine had splashed Frajil and jolted him, breaking his concentration. He was nowhere near solving the riddle of the roasted chicken. He wiped his face and tried one more time. *Tonight we roast the chicken. What chicken? There are many chickens*, thought Frajil. He gazed at the pile of bones left from his poultry. *Frajil eating roasted chicken but there are more, so...* An idea, vague and wordless, began to form when another goblet came crashing down, splashing Frajil in the eye. This was more than the giant could bear. He yelled at the men. "Little ones, stop talking. Frajil trying to think about roasted chicken."

The entire tavern froze. Tika hid his face with his hands and cowered under the counter. Frajil smiled blissfully, for the tavern was now completely quiet. He could think now. "If there are many chickens," he said for all to hear, "then which one Frajil goes after?"

The men of Baal drew near his table.

"What is it that you said?" asked the one closest to the table. Had he been sober he may have kept his distance from the giant, but tonight he felt he could conquer the world. Frajil was so busy concentrating that he did not hear what the man said, nor did he see him standing next to him. This strenuous effort gave him a headache; something Frajil rarely had.

The man of Baal took Frajil's goblet, poured its contents onto the giant's head, and laughed loudly. His companions laughed with him. Frajil felt the cool liquid go down his face and looked up to see three men laughing. He thought the situation funny and started laughing as well. They thought he was laughing at them and did not think the situation funny anymore; instead, they felt insulted.

The man closest to Frajil drew a dagger.

Now this was a gesture Frajil fully understood. He was relieved because he did not have to worry about the roasted chicken anymore. He had only to act. In a matter of seconds, the three trained High Riders lay on the floor amid shards of broken wood, smashed goblets, and strewn chicken bones.

"Tika, another table, please. Frajil need to think again."

The customers could scarcely believe their eyes. Most of them had been following the Games and knew of the slave trying to win his freedom. The news of Ahiram's death dealt a crushing blow to their dreams of freedom. Unwittingly, Frajil, by his action, had rekindled their dying hope.

"This Tanniinite," whispered one of them, "he wasn't afraid of the white owls."

"He's a giant," explained a second.

"Yeah, but they're three," chimed in a third.

"He'd done 'em in all by himself," said a fourth. "He did."

The giant gazed at the scattered mess on the floor. This reminded him of something... Yes, a conversation here with Soloron... He could see himself pointing at a smashed goblet and yelling, "The King." The chicken, the King... the chicken, the King... In a flash, Frajil concluded, "roasting the chicken" meant storming the castle. He was not supposed to eat the chicken here but be at the castle with Soloron and his men.

"King has best chicken," he concluded with a wide grin. "Soloron deserves best chicken." Oblivious of his surroundings and the men watching his every move, he stood up and yelled, mostly to rouse himself, "To the castle!"

His war cry ignited a fire. It crystallized the repressed anger and resentment of those who had hoped the slave would win the Games. True, his victory would not have changed their daily lives—Baal would still tax them, and his High Riders would steal and murder unfettered—but it would have let the world know that hope endured in their hearts. These soldiers mercilessly had dashed that hope when they killed Ahiram. But now, the murderers lay on the floor, and this giant man gave them a goal to reach, an action to channel their pent-up frustrations. The King was a traitor; he should not be allowed to live.

"To the castle," they shouted back.

Their voices startled Frajil. He looked at them and yelled "Tonight we roast the chicken."

"We roast the chicken," they shouted back.

Frajil smiled, trying to mimic Soloron when he gave orders. Even though the giant was not sure why he was giving orders, these men looked like they were waiting for one, so he gave it to them.

"To the castle," he shouted louder, unsheathing his two double-blade swords as he stormed through the door. "We roast the chicken."

The men ran after him shouting, "To the castle." The war rally fanned like wildfire throughout the city of Taniir-The-Strong, igniting the hearts of its citizens and propelling them into action. Without any warning, the peaceful city of Taniir-The-Strong saw this small group turn into a mob. Frajil reached the castle's perimeter with an armed multitude rushing behind him. The insurrection had begun.

The servants were making ready for the ceremony of the Games. The Royal Hall was being festooned with the colors of Baal. Clusters of slaves busily moved through the open doors carrying all the necessities for the feast. The musicians were rehearsing in a corner, and the banquet tables were readied.

King Jamiir III was in a mixed mood. He was relieved that the Games had ended and satisfied that the slave has been disposed of quietly and swiftly. Nonetheless, his wife's absence annoyed him, and the commander, who had searched for her discreetly, had not found her. To make matters worse, the master of the Silent Corps had asked to be excused from the ball tonight, as did Master Habael, Garu, and Ibromaliöm. To top it off, the high priestess, who should be celebrating the victory of Baal, sent word informing the King she would not attend due to a sudden illness.

If I did not know better, I would think I am facing a mutiny, thought the King. He looked around him and saw the sullen face of Hiyam, who was slumped in her chair. *What is the matter with her?* he wondered, irritated. *After all we have gone through to assure her victory, the least she could do is be grateful.* He closed his eyes trying to think of something pleasant, but could not.

The Silent were devastated, though none were more crushed than Banimelek and Jedarc. After disposing of the men of Baal with the help of Elio and Thurun, they searched for Ahiram in vain. They could not bring themselves to say what they were both thinking. Ahiram may not have survived. The sequestering of the Silent in their quarters while the King feasted with Baal did not help matters. The High Riders were now in charge of the castle.

Banimelek's thoughts went back to his friend. He imagined Ahiram dying alone in the mines, killed treacherously by Baal. He lifted his eyes and looked at Jedarc, almost pleading for an answer. His friend looked at him with eyes filled with sadness. He had nothing to say. Banimelek spoke out loud what they were thinking in their hearts: "We should have protected him. We could have saved him."

Ahiram was tossed and turned in utter darkness by the furious maelstrom. His head hit the ceiling of the siphon he was rushed through. The water jerked him closer to the ceiling. Instinctively, he raised his left arm and felt his wrist rap against something spongy, yet so sharp it seemed to draw blood. He yanked his hand away and slammed it against the rough edge of an opening. Frantically, he searched for something to hold on to, and somehow, his fingers landed on a hard surface. He gripped and pulled. The object did not budge. His right hand found the other end of the opening, and he managed to haul himself up. To his surprise, he broke through the water. There was air. He could breathe. His right hand slid and he nearly fell into the raging current once more, but he steadied himself with his legs and rolled onto a wet, flat rock, panting in the dark. He nearly drowned again when a gush of water filled the space for a short moment before receding. He coughed, spitting water out, as he thought of the two men of Baal dying in the dark. This was a death he would not wish on his worst enemy.

Ahiram tried to stand but hit his head against a low ceiling. He crawled on all fours in the dark, trying to find his way, not knowing where to go. He placed one hand on the walls searching for a path, but there was none. Eventually, he reached a dead end and went back to the hole he had climbed through. The roar of the powerful rush beneath him was deafening. He continued moving forward, feeling the wet, cold walls around him, searching for another exit, but it was in vain. He reached a second dead end and panicked. *What if there is no exit? What if the water is the only exit?*

Walls surrounded him on all sides, and the water filled the cave regularly before receding. He sat down, leaning his back against the wall, not knowing what to do. The darkness was so complete that he could not even see his hands. He was drenched and began to shiver in the cold draft. The habits gained from years of training took over, staying his fears. Ahiram quoted from the *Book of Siril*, chapter 4, verse 12: '*Trials renew the Silent. He never gives up.*' He heard a loud popping sound and the cold draft suddenly became even colder. *Not now*, he thought, *I could do without the cold air.* He jolted up but remembered the low ceiling in time to avert bruising his skull yet again.

His heart was pounding.

"A draft." *If there is a draft, then there must be a passage somewhere. Drafts do not occur in enclosed spaces.* He tried to follow it back to its source, moving at a snail's pace and forcing his hands to examine every nook, however small. His persistence paid off and he found it, right above the water; a hole, barely large enough to let him through.

No wonder I had a difficult time finding it, thought the Silent. *It's directly above the hole through which the water comes in.*

Ahiram felt the borders of the opening to create a mental image. The water filled the hole once more, and he waited until it receded. When the water came back, he started counting slowly until it receded again, doing his best to ignore the mind-numbing cold jabbing at him. He repeated this little exercise until he was certain that he knew when the water came, and when it left. He squatted at the edge of the hole, and just when the water came rushing in, Ahiram stepped forward and let it carry him. He clasped the ragged edge of the gap and pushed up. His upper body was now inside the hole and he managed to hold on by the tips of his fingers. He waited for the water to come back, and when it did, he kicked his legs and thrust himself up. When the third surge came, he managed to slide completely inside the narrow passage. He rested precariously against the walls and then inched his way up, not knowing whether this gap would lead him to freedom, or to another dead end.

≻✦✦✦≺

"He did what?" Soloron could not believe his ears. "That oaf is storming the castle on his own?" Frajil had thrown away Soloron's carefully crafted plan and was forcing him into action. "Wait until I lay my hands on him; I will teach him a lesson he will never forget."

He looked at the messenger who was standing before him.

"Are you absolutely sure that Frajil is storming the castle? This is very important. Are you absolutely sure?"

The messenger took a step back. "Yes, master, I am sure. I saw Frajil going up Royal Road followed by a large band of men with sticks, swords and torches. Many of them were yelling, 'Death to the King. Death to the traitor.' Frajil was shouting, 'To the castle, tonight we roast the chicken,' which I personally found odd, but many of Frajil's utterances are mysteries. This is when I ran to inform you."

"Mysterious, indeed. Fine. Frajil wants to roast the chicken. We shall join him. Sound the alarm. We move now."

≻✦✦✦≺

King Jamiir surveyed the hall where they were supping. It was half empty. Outside, a brooding storm was giving signs of imminent rain. Lightning, increasing in frequency, filled the night. When the black sun appeared today, almost all the participating teams had asked to take an early leave to return home. Hiyam and her surviving teammates—now a team of five—were the only ones that stayed. The royal court was present, but the King could feel they were here mostly out of duty. The black sun was a bad omen. Tanios was sitting at the royal table but had hardly touched his food. The King had changed his mind and requested his presence, even though Tanios had asked to be excused. The commander obliged. Suddenly, they heard a commotion outside the halls, followed by screams and tumbled dishes. A man came running into the hall holding an empty bowl, the content of which was now dripping onto his clothes. "An insurrection! An insurrection, Your Majesty. Men are storming the castle. We are being attacked." Tanios stood up, but the King prevented him from taking another step.

"Tanios, do not worry about this. I will personally take care of it. To you and your Silent, I entrust the safety of the high priestess and her daughter. If anything happens to them, there is no telling what Babylon will do. Take them to the port of Mitriil and do not leave them until they are safely on a boat sailing toward Baalbeck. This is an order. Go."

Tanios looked at the King as though wanting to say something. Then he turned abruptly and went over to Hiyam. "You and your men, follow me. Now." They got up and followed him out of the hall, walking quickly until they reached Bahiya's quarters. Tanios was surprised to see her dressed in black with a sullen face and tired features. He could have sworn she had been crying. *With women such as these, one cannot tell where the truth ends and the deception begins*, he thought.

"The castle is besieged. By order of His Majesty the King, I am to escort you, your suite, your daughter and her men to the port of Mitriil. I ask that you follow me at once."

Bahiya nodded imperceptibly and left the room, her silver box in hand. Tanios saw that she was ready for travel. Her maidservants had already packed. He wanted to ask her how she knew but refrained from doing so. At this point, he was executing the King's order. He escorted them down the Lone Tower to the second floor and into his quarters.

"Master Habael, you are here. I was getting worried."

"I came up to check on the Silent. What is the cause of your worry, my friend?"

"The castle is besieged; we are facing an insurrection."

"What is she doing here?" Tanios had barely the time to stop a raging Banimelek from laying his hands on Hiyam. "Have you betrayed us also, Commander Tanios, that you bring these vipers to laugh at our sorrow?"

Jedarc tried to stop his friend by saying, "She was following orders," but Banimelek shoved him away and ran toward Hiyam and met his commander, who sent him tumbling through the air. Quick as a cat, he adjusted his posture, landing gracefully on his feet. Tanios drew near the Silent, raised his hand to slap him, but stopped at the last minute. Lightning filled the air and powerful thunder shattered the night. The rain came pouring down.

"By order of the King," he said, looking at the Silent, "we are to escort the high priestess, her daughter, and their suite to Mitriil. We must guarantee their safety. Is this clear?" No one answered. "Master Habael, you are coming with us. Banimelek, Jedarc, Sondra, and Thurun, you will scout ahead via the Garden Tower, then through the soldiers' garden into the stable. Everyone else, take as many horses as you can, go down into the horses' run, then walk your steed to the narrow gate. You are the Silent. The insurgents are our people. If they are manning the gate, they will listen to you. We ride through the night and take shelter beyond the great pass. Have I made myself clear? Move, we have not a moment to lose."

How long had Ahiram been climbing? He could not remember. He had lost track of time. Only his stamina and his will to live prodded him, forcing him to continue his arduous ascent. He blindfolded himself to stop his weary eyes from straining to see in the complete darkness. The passage was still narrow, and at times, had threatened to close in on him. There were moments when he thought he was trapped underground, left there to die slowly as though buried alive. Yet, by patiently applying all that he had learned from Commander Tanios, he escaped the stony grip and kept moving with the stubborn assurance that this serpentine passage would eventually lead back to the mine. The passage turned and twisted so many times that he could no longer tell if he was traveling up or down. Dragging himself into this narrow space was difficult regardless of the direction. Could it be that this crack in the depths of the earth would lead him back to the river? *No,* thought Ahiram, *air is coming through this passage. It must lead somewhere. I'm going up... I'm going up...* These last words became a litany that he repeated regularly to give himself courage.

Suddenly, a shadow leaped before him. He recoiled. *What was that?* the Silent thought. *How is it that I can see? What happened to my blindfold?* Ahiram felt his face and did not feel the cloth. *It must have fallen off and I didn't even notice. Am I losing my mind? Was that a shadow?*

The shadow was gone. He looked again and there it was. Ahiram waited, wondering if a beast haunted this wretched place, but no; there was no one else. Cautiously, he inched along and felt the passage turning left. Emerging from the turn, he saw the shadow again, but it was not a shadow. It was an area that, although dark, was a shade lighter than his immediate surroundings. *I am getting closer to a source of light.*

This thought galvanized him, and he moved forward with renewed energy. He dragged himself through the narrow passage and continued without interruption. He could see something ahead; he must have been nearing the exit. Now he could see his left hand gripping the rock ahead of him. The difference between shadow and light sharpened further, and the contour of the exit appeared: a ragged circle beyond which light flickered. He drew closer and finally managed to push through, landing on a smooth, flat surface.

To his left he saw a wall whose wide door had been condemned by rocks, standing precariously. He looked to his right and would have jumped from fright if he could, for a dragon, jaws wide-open, was inches away from him. Ahiram retreated inside the hole so quickly that he scraped his elbows against the rocks. He expected the mighty beast to roar and scorch him to death, but nothing happened.

What is it doing? he wondered, as he waited for the fiery breath. *Why is Tanniin not...* then a thought hit him. *What is Tanniin doing here in the first place? Have I reached the abode of the god?*

This thought struck him as incongruous, for the rocks around him looked and felt like ordinary rocks. Cautiously, he moved forward and glanced at the face of the beast. It had not moved. *A statue. It's a statue of Tanniin.* Relieved, Ahiram chuckled silently and derided his own gullibility.

He wiggled out of the underground passage one more time. He tried to stand, but his aching muscles would not obey. He lay on his back not knowing who to thank for his incredible fortune. He could not shake the feeling that someone was watching over him.

The dragon's face belonged to a statue of bronze. The dragon was crouching on the marble face of a plinth, while his elongated neck dove down, curling completely around the pedestal so that the head lay on the ground. Oddly, the extended wings were too short for the huge body.

I have not been in this part of the mines before, thought Ahiram.

He felt something poking him in the back, touched it, and smiled. *Master Habael*, he thought unbuckling his belt, *I cannot thank you enough for what you have done for me.* Wearily, Ahiram managed to sit down and examined his belt. The pockets had weathered the water rather well. He remembered dropping the pouch of flour and salt Master Habael had given him during the Game of Meyroon, but the two vials were still with him, and they were intact.

So that's what was pushing against my back, he thought as he pulled them out of the snug pocket. He drank the content of the first one, and the special mixture of assin and timrand rejuvenated him. The second contained a dark, thick liquid. He took some and rubbed it on his aching shoulder. Soon, he felt his strength come back. He rose and forced himself to pace. As he did so, his eyes caught sight of a monumental door left ajar. A flickering light was seeping through.

There are burning torches here, he thought as his mind cleared. *I must not be alone.*

Quickly, Ahiram locked his belt in place, and staying in the shadow of the wall, moved forward. As he examined the cave with renewed attention, he realized that he was standing in an underground temple dedicated to Tanniin. The statue he had seen faced an identical statue across what must have been the main body of the sanctuary. As he walked toward the massive door, he reached a second set of statues, much bigger than the first two, and he saw a side altar with a basket and an open jar.

Someone worships here, he thought, shocked. He realized then that the Temple of Baal had not managed to eradicate the worship of other gods, and he wondered if this was something unique to Tanniin, or widespread across the land.

As he drew closer to the door, he saw four red blotches on the four corners of the door and he knew it was blood. *Someone performed a blood offering here?* he thought, dumbfounded. *Who, and for what purpose?*

As he crossed between the statues, he saw a smaller open door. He peered inside, but saw only the beginning of a path slanting upward. He inspected the ground and noticed that the door had rapped against the tiles, pushing back the dust.

This door has been opened very recently. So, whoever made this offering must have come through this passage, and since this door is still open, they have not left.

Silently, Ahiram reached the large door. The handle was shaped in the form of a dragon with two bullhorns sticking out of its tail. Something throbbed inside the room; something that made his heart beat a little faster. He peeked inside, and seeing no one, walked into a hallway hewn out of the rock and left unfinished. Six burning torches lit the narrow passage. The walls were jagged and coarse, and the floor was partially covered with slabs. Otherwise, the hallway was bare. Seeing footsteps, he knelt to examine them.

Two men, one with a heavy gait were here, and a woman. These imprints could only have been made by shoes worn by a member of the royal court. She fell, and I can't make out what else happened here. He backtracked, chiding himself for walking over the footsteps. Still, he figured out that one of them left in a hurry, and the other carried the woman away. He stepped back out and examined the ground around the smaller door. *They left the way they came. Wait, what are those?* Bending a knee, he examined a fourth set of imprints he had noticed before. *Judging from their position, this fourth person did not come with the group. I don't recognize this pattern, but they belong to either a woman or a small man.*

Ahiram stood up and surveyed the large, empty temple. *Is it plain coincidence that all of this is happening on the fourth day of the Game? What are all these people doing here and what's behind that door, anyway?*

Only the oppressive silence answered. Deep within the earth, nothing lived, and nothing moved. The two statues of Tanniin glittered in the dim light as if they were trying to come alive. *I need to get out of here*, he thought. A loud popping noise coming from the two statues shattered the silence and startled him. Instinctively, he jumped back inside the hallway just when an arc of dark light shot up from the temple's ground and hit the spot where he had been standing a moment ago. A powerful gust of air hit him like a mighty fist and sent him tumbling inside the room. The door slammed shut and the light went out. Laying on the ground in the darkness, Ahiram heard a high-pitched screech drowned by a stronger roar as if two warriors, tall as mountains, had just been awakened. Afraid and confused, he crawled backward until he slammed into the back wall. The raging screams outside had turned into a verbal duel. Words of power were being spoken in a language he did not know, nor did he care to learn: the words were like blades meant to subdue and kill. Something slammed against the door. Ahiram felt the ground shake and rose to his feet. The deafening roar reached a new pitch. Ahiram covered his ears just as a blinding light flashed in the temple outside. It lit the outline of the door and in that brief moment Ahiram saw that the door was smoldering. Suddenly, the light went out and with it the uproar, as if the eternal silence of the mountains, patient like a spider, had once more swallowed the living.

What is happening? wondered the shaken Silent, *There is some high magic at work here.* He recalled the words he had heard during the Game of Silver, "I am the Urkuun of the Ninth Order. Soon, you will know me as your master." *If this Urkuun fired that bolt, then who is he fighting with? Tanniin?* Standing motionless, he waited, wondering if the door would shatter under a renewed attack. Time went by and the silence became once more oppressive. Ahiram closed his eyes, and relaxing his stance, he leaned his back against the wall and let his hands run softly against the cool surface of the rock. When he opened his eyes, he jumped away from the wall: the room was now illuminated by a soft, yellowish glow streaming from a spot high above the wall he had been leaning against. Fearing an attack inside the small room, he tried to open the door, but it would not budge. Turning slowly, the Silent expected another blast, but instead, the gentle light began to throb like a star shining in the dark. *There are no stars beneath the surface of the Earth.* The shining object hovered high above him. Ahiram squinted but could not make out the contour of the mysterious artifact. Tired of looking up, he lowered his gaze, then closed his eyes to rub them. In that moment, an image formed in his mind: the clear image of a symbol. He knew he had to call to it, even though he did not know why. Seeing the symbol, he knew its name as if it had been a long forgotten word he should have known all along. Extending his arm, he said, "Taw."

A blinding flash, a wave of heat. The light went out. Then nothing.

He felt something cold in his open palm. Immediately, the object glowed softly, and Ahiram saw that he was holding a gold tile. It was an inch wide by three inches long and could not have been more than a quarter of an inch thick. The symbol † was etched on it. The back of the tile was smooth with no markings.

Is this a taw? he wondered. *What's a taw anyway?* Dazed and in shock, as if in a dream, Ahiram looked at the symbol intently, and he saw himself back at the beach with Hoda on that fateful day when Yem took him away from home. There had been a flash, and then... *I have seen this symbol before,* he thought. *But when exactly?* He had forgotten what had happened on the beach that day, and had forgotten that Hoda had been with him.

"What are you?" he asked the object, "and why did you come to me?" A long, mournful, creaking sound responded just as the entire back wall came crashing down, taking with it most of the hall and leaving only a thin ledge where Ahiram stood, mere inches from the main door which was still very hot. He waited in silence, half expecting the Urkuun, or some other unnamed creature, to leap forward, but nothing happened. The ledge where he stood was now over sixty feet above the ground of a large cave.

"Master Sharr, Master Sharr!"

Kalibaal was running. The Inner Circle had not seen a priest run for as long as the Temple of Baal Majaar had stood.

"I have seen it, Kalibaal," said Sharr, opening his eyes. He stepped away from the swirling pool. "The Seer has found the first Letter of Power."

"Is this the end, master?" asked Kalibaal, wide-eyed. "Can he defeat the Urkuun?"

"If he knows how to use the Letter, he might," replied Sharr. "The Letters are powerful, but they are useless if he does not know how to handle them. Now that he has the first Letter in his possession, the Béghôm will find him in short order, and no man can withstand the crushing power of this beast. But even if he does, the Urkuun will kill him. The Seer is most likely inexperienced. He will not survive."

"What if he does?" asked Kalibaal. "What then?"

"Then, may Baal help us, for we would have to unleash the unthinkable."

Kalibaal bowed down and quickly left the icy Inner Room. He needed time to think, to reflect. He stepped outside and found a quiet spot between two palm trees behind the temple. The moon was now rising, casting a pale light on the suspended gardens of Babylon.

"All of this," he said, speaking haltingly, "all of this doomed to…"

He did not finish his sentence. Despite Sharr's forceful words, he felt he was living in the last days: that soon, the heavens would be rolled back, and the Seer would scorch the earth, turning it into a land of unbearable desolation.

>❂❂❂<

Jethro could not believe his eyes. He did not want to believe what he was seeing. His back against the cold, smooth wall of the Library, the warden could not tear his gaze away from the medallion. Like a thief in a treasure-filled cave who was caught by a guardian spirit, he stood mesmerized by the Merilian that had just turned bright red, as if it were the eye of an invisible beast about to devour him. The color intensified and turned to bright white. Jethro moaned, recalling the fate of Rahaak, the high priest, who six years ago, nearly to the day, dared to defy Sureï's curse and was killed by a white beam from the medallion.

"The gods be cursed," spat the frail, old man, "I am not going to die here, I *will not* die here."

Slowly, carefully, his back to the wall like a slug before a frog, he slid along the wall, keeping his eye on the bright source of light, he inched his way toward the exit and just as he was about to leave, the white light died down. Startled, Jethro stopped and watched breathlessly, dreading the moment when a high-pitched scream and beam of light would fill the Library, as it had done before.

Unable to move, he glanced quickly at the open door, a mere three feet away. Fear pinned him to the wall like an insect to a spider's web, and he could not get his legs to obey him. Time passed and the face of the Merilian had assumed once more its unremarkable, dull and dark appearance. *Like a dragon who just closed his eyes,* thought the warden of the Office of the Librarian, *but who is ready to pounce without notice.*

"Jethro," called a woman, "are you alright?"

The warden swallowed with great difficulty and whispered, "Help me, please." As the woman helped him leave the library, Jethro knew he would live to see another day, and for this, he was grateful.

➤✸✸✸❮

About the same time, five thousand miles northeast of the Library, a small, plain wooden box began shaking and rattling as if it were a miniaturized earthquake. Ashod quickly looked up from his study and watched it with great attention.

The Merilian Hoda brought with her is awakening. So, the Seer is alive, and he has managed to find a Letter of Power. Did he survive Sureï's curse?

Could he have found one of the few letters which were not cursed?

The box stopped abruptly. Ashod kept looking at it, trying to make sense of what had just taken place. *Is he dead? Or was the Merilian trying to send a signal we do not know how to interpret?* He sighed. *It all begins now. Everything is about to change. May the gods have pity on us.*

What now? wondered Ahiram, "Is there an end to this?" His voice echoed in the cave.

An awful noise answered him; the smashing, grinding, breaking cacophony that rock and wood make just before a collapse, and Ahiram knew that the door behind him was about to shatter. He jumped over the ledge, landing on a small platform below where he found a series of uneven stairs. He bounded down the steps, reached the bottom, and hid behind a large boulder when the keystone holding the hallway's roof shattered. The noise was deafening, and the avalanche of rocks that followed filled the cave with dust and debris.

Coughing and sneezing in the cloud of dust, he stumbled forward, feeling his way in the ambient darkness, for he could see very little. He knew the hallway was gone and wondered if the temple survived or whether the entire structure had been flattened. He thought about the narrow passage he had climbed through and shuddered. *This avalanche may have slammed it shut,* he thought.

Slowly, he began to recognize various shapes. For a faint light suffused the entire cave, seeping from somewhere high above. After a while, the dust settled and the air cleared. The bare cave was circular with a thirty-foot-wide wrought iron gate that closed a side alcove, which alone was bathed in light. On a bronze platform, four silver dragons carried a gold sarcophagus. Ahiram gasped. Here, before him, in this lost corner of the mines, was El-Windiir's resting place, the place where the founder of the kingdom slept, undisturbed for close to three thousand years.

"If the legend is true," whispered Ahiram, still unable to believe what he was seeing, "then his weapons may still be there... inside the sarcophagus." Ahiram forgot his weariness, his fear, and his anguish. With renewed hope, he approached the tomb.

"All along," he said as if speaking to the dead king, "for all this time, your shoes of bronze, the real shoes, and your belt of silver, the gold mask, and the wings of meyroon have been here, under the city. And here I am, a slave, like you were, El-Windiir, and I found them. It's as if you wanted me to find them." He spoke softly as he slid the gold tile into his pocket. Slowly, he climbed a short flight of stairs, seven steps in total, and stood before the massive gate. Fortunately, it had no locks and despite its antiquity, it pivoted on its hinges with a grating sound. He entered the alcove and drew closer to the sarcophagus. The long side facing him depicted an army fighting a tall monster which Ahiram did not recognize. The leader of the army stood next to a slain standard bearer, while arrows flew overhead. A gleaming sword in hand, he was pointing to the monster as he looked back at his men. Ahiram walked around with deliberate slowness. On the shorter side, he saw a gold mask whose features vaguely resembled that of a dragon. On the second long panel, Ahiram saw the leader, who faced the monster, kneeling before a woman holding a cup. Behind them, a group of women stood holding the man's sword.

The last panel had three pairs of wings on it.

Ahiram lay a trembling hand on its cold surface and recollected himself. Resolutely and aware of what he was about to do, he climbed onto the bronze platform between two of the silver statues. He leaned on the sarcophagus' lid and pushed strenuously, expecting it to resist. To his surprise, it moved along hidden rails, producing a screeching sound. He pushed once more, revealing its contents.

He peered inside and saw the skeletal remains of the mighty warrior in full military attire. His sword had slid and fallen to his side. The skull was covered with a mask of gold, the waist had a belt made of silver, and the feet still wore shoes of bronze.

"The tomb of El-Windiir," he whispered. "Could it be true?" He wished his friends were with him to share in the excitement. *They must think I am dead by now*, he thought. *Well, they're in for a surprise.*

Deeply moved by the remains of the man who had been an anchor of hope for him, he leaned over, and careful not to disturb the peace of the legendary hero, brought the sword out of the tomb. Something shot up swiftly in a trail of dazzling colors. Ahiram looked up and beheld a pair of wings floating gently in the air. They were made of the darkest material he had ever seen, and radiated a blue light, clear as the day.

Claiming the sword, he let out a shout of triumph, "I, Ahiram, heir to El-Windiir, will be victorious before the King tonight. I will descend on the Royal Hall from the skies and show everyone the power of El-Windiir. Let the bell ring anew; let the flag of Tanniin be raised on high."

Overwhelmed, Ahiram genuflected.

"Tonight, I regain my freedom, and tomorrow I will leave for Baher-Ghafé, and return to my family. I will stand before my father and tell him I have kept his name: I have honored him. Then, I will come back to Tanniin, and woe to those who stand against me: they shall taste the fury of El-Windiir."

His voice echoed in the great hall. He knew with an absolute certainty that a new day had dawned; a great power had been awakened.

Ahiram stood up.

Had Kalibaal seen the fierce storm brewing in the young man's eyes, he would have recoiled in fear.

The Age of the Seer had begun.

To Be Continued…

EPIC OF AHIRAM

୫ଔ

Book Two

Wrath of the Urkuun

GLOSSARY

Dates in the manuscript follow the American convention of month, day, year. For instance, Tébêt 7, 1197. The majority of the kingdoms used the Babylonian Calendar instituted by the Temple of Baal. A year was three hundred and sixty days in length, subdivided into twelve lunar months of thirty days each. A month had four weeks of seven days named after the seven abodes of the gods the Babylonian magi had seen. The first day of the week was Sin. Tébêt was the tenth month of the year. When adjusted to our solar calendar, Tébêt 7, 1197 fell on Sunday, August 10, 1181, of the Age of the Temple.

Most names have been transliterated from the Common Tongue of the Age of the Temple into English. There are marked differences in pronunciations, indicated below. Two of these bear further explanations. As a rule, the Common Tongue places the emphasis on the last syllable. For instance, an English reader will stress the first 'A' in the name A-hi-ram, but in the Common Tongue, the stress is on the last syllable, "am," a-hee-RAM.

Nouns in the Common Tongue are gendered. A month is masculine, a mountain is feminine, the moon is feminine, and the sun is masculine, etc. I have occulted these gender differences in the English to avoid unnecessary distractions except in dwarfish speech and in proper names.

The gender of a name in the Common Tongue is embedded in the last syllable and I have striven to preserve this in English, particularly with names whose last syllable contains "ii," "ee," "uu" and "oo." A double "e" and a double "i" are both pronounced like the double *ee* in words such as *sheet* or *meet*. The double "e" is used in feminine names as in Noraldeen and Layaleen, whereas the "ii" is used in masculine names as in "Tanniin" and "Jamiir."

Both "uu" and "oo" should be pronounced as in *moon*, the former in masculine names, such as Urkuun and Aramuun, and the latter in feminine names, such as Foosh and meyroon.

The double "aa" is an exception. The Common Tongue uses it to represent both feminine and masculine names. I have chosen, somewhat arbitrarily, to reserve the "aa" for masculine names, such as Arfaad, and used the accented "â," for feminine names such as Silbarâd. There is no difference in pronunciation between the double "a" and the accented "a."

In certain names of Empyrean, Togofalkian, or Zemorian origins, the "i," "o," or "y" modify the pronunciation of a preceding vowel. In those cases, I have represented these letters with an umlaut because the phonetic transliteration is too unwieldy. For instance, the name of the Empyrean Empress Gaëla Meïr Pen would have been approximately written as "Gahyela Mehyeer Pen."

a	In the table of pronunciation and the glossary, whenever an "a" is pronounced "ah" as in "apple," it will be spelled ǎ. When it is pronounced as "James" or "May," it will be written ā. For instance, the name *Arfaad* will be phonetically notated as Ǎrfǎǎd.
aa, â	Pronounced as a stressed "aah."
ai	Pronounced as in "bray" or "fray."

an	Unless otherwise indicated, "an" in the middle of a proper name is pronounced as in "ant," or the French word "enfant," and not as in "Anna" or "Anne".
e	In almost all cases, it is pronounced as in the French article "le" or as the "u" in "burger".
ë	Appears after a vowel only. Pronounced "yeh" as in "yellow" where the "y" is stressed.
ei	Pronounced as in "vein" or "main."
g	Pronounced in all cases as in "group."
gh	No English equivalent. The best we can do is to pronounce it as in the word "ghoul."
h	The "h" is always soft as in "hello."
i	Pronounced as in "he" or "she" and not as in the personal pronoun "I."
ï	Appears after a vowel only. Pronounced as "yee" where the y is stressed.
ii	Stressed "ee" sound.
j	Pronounced as the "s" in "treasure" and not as in "just." In what follows, we use "ĵ" to remind the reader of this alternate pronunciation.
kh	No equivalent in English. It is a harder version of the "gh" in "ghoul."
ö	Appears after a vowel only. Pronounced as "yoh" where the y is stressed.
on	Pronounced as in "monsoon" or "monsieur."
oo	Pronounced as in "cool" or "pool." (Appears in feminine names.)
u	Pronounced as in "pure."
uu	Pronounced as the "oo" in "moon" or "soon." (Appears in masculine names.)

A

Abaliim	Ah-bah-**leem**	Meyroon Abaliim On-Nayiir; the flying miners of meyroon. Dwarfs who mined the meyroon down shafts were so deep that they were never seen again.
Abiil	Ah-b-**eel**	A servant of the castle of Taniir-The-Strong.
Adorant	Ah-do-**rant**	A special order of priestesses of the Temple of Baal, whose voices can drive man to madness, despair, or slavery, becoming puppets in the hands of the priestesses.
Adulaan	Ah-du-**laan**	A river that runs outside the walls of Taniir-The-Strong.
Aharof	Ah-ha-**roff**	Means "letters."
Ahiram	Ah-hee-**raam**	Son of Jabbar and Hayat from the town of Baher-Ghafé. A member of the Silent.
Alissaar	Ah-lee-**saar**	Alissaar Ben Nadam is an alias for Sureï. See Sureï.

Alkiniöm	Ah-l-kee-nee-**yom**	A famed minstrel who lived toward the end of the Troubled Peace, some fifteen hundred years before the birth of Ahiram.
Alviad	Ah-l-vee-**yad**	A Silent.
Amalein	Ah-mah-**lein**	*Lantern of Hope*; the name of a star.
Amalseer	Ah-mal-**seer**	Undying Hope; the name of a star.
Amsheet	Ah-m-**sheet**	The city fortress of Tanniin guarding the northeastern boundary.
Andaluzian	An-dah-**lu**-zian	A title given to women of exceptional beauty.
Andaxil	An-dah-**xeel**	The legendary cave of the southern dwarfish realm, where the greatest treasures of the seven tribes are buried. Lost during a major war. Cursed by Sureï.
Aramuun	Ah-rah-**moon**	One of the highest peaks of the eastern Tangorian range in Tanniin. The Aramuun soars, above nineteen thousand feet. Although 'mountain' is feminine in the Common Tongue, a

		'peak' is actually masculine.
Arfaad	Ar-**faad**	Captain of the High Riders in the Temple of Baalbeck.
Assin	Ah-**seen**	This Togofalkian idiom means 'bitter health'. Togofalkians tend to avoid hard sounds and will typically replace the 's' with a 'z'.
Atlant	Ah-t-**lant**	The city of legends famed for its treasures and great knowledge.
Aylul	Eye-**lool**	The first name of the Empyrean Empress, Aylul Meïr Pen. The last syllable is always stressed and never shortened. Aylul can be translated as *youthful fall*, indicating someone who is young yet wise.

B

Baal Adiir	Baal Ah-**deer**	Highlights the power and omnipotence of Baal.
Baal Adonaï	Baal Ah-do-**ny**	Baal, my Lord.
Baal Essaru	Baal Eh-**ss-ah**-ru	Baal, Lord of the Dead.

Baal Majaar	Baal Mah-ĵ-aar	Baal, Lord of the Plenty.
Baal Shamaïm	Baal sh-ah-may-ee-m	Baal, Lord of the Seas.
Baalat Jubeil	Baal-ah-tĵ-u-b-eil	Lady of Byblos. A deity worshiped in Fineekia.
Baher-Ghafé	Bah-hair Gh-ah-ff-eh	Coastal village of Fineekia. Ahiram's birthplace.
Bahiya	Bah-hee-y-ah	High Priestess of the Temple of Baalbeck. The name means 'comely' and 'beautiful'.
Balid	Bah-leed	Carpet merchant. Husband of Foosh, friend of Kwadil. His name means 'slow moving'.
Banimelek	Bah-nee-meh-leck	Silent. Friend of Ahiram. His name means 'son of king'.
Bayrul	Bai-rule	Great judge of the Games of the Mines who established the modern rules regulating the Games when Ahiram participated.
Beit-Windiir	Bey-t when-deer	'The House of Windiir'. Southern coastal city of Tanniin.
Béghôm	Bay-Gh-ohm	Creature of the Arayat.

Bragafâr	Brah-gah-**faar**	Coastal city along the northwestern tip of the southern kingdom of Indolan. Famous for its strange frozen whale.

C

꓄

Chesbân	Ch-eh-s-**ban**	Second month of the year. Corresponds roughly to the month of May.
Corialynn	Cor-yah-**leen**	A Silent.
Corintus	Co-**rin**-tus	A Silent of incredible talent that disappeared mysteriously.

F

Y

Fineekia	Fee-**nee**-k-yah	Land of Fineekia, from where Ahiram hails.
Foosh	F-**oo**-sh	Wife of Balid. Her name means 'to overflow'.
Frajil	Frah- ĵ-**ee**-l	A giant of a man. Warrior. Soloron's brother.

G

꓄

Gaëla Meïr Pen	Gah-**yell**-ah Mey-**yeer** Pen	Daughter of the Empyrean Empress. Heir to the throne.

Galliöm	**Gah**-lee-yom	Head of the Tajéruun.
Garu	**Gah**-roo	Principal judge of the Games.

H

Habael	**Hah-bah**-yell	Gardner at Taniir-The-Strong.
Haialeen	Hah-yah-**leen**	Primordial pool of life filled with Water of Blessing.
Hawâl	Hah-**waal**	The heart of the Pit where the Lords of the Deep are locked.
Hayat	Hah-yah-tt	Ahiram's mother. Her name means 'life'.
Hiyam	Hee-**yam**	Daughter of Bahiya, leader of the team of Baal during the Games of the Mines. Her name means "lost in love."
Hoda	Ho-dah	Ahiram's sister. Her name means 'she who shows the way'.
Hylâz	Hee-**laa-z**	Judge of the Games of the Mines. His name means 'Pensive'.

I

Ibromaliöm	Ee-bro-**mah**-lium	A judge for the Games of the Mines. Former

		Tajèr. His name means 'The one who buries poverty'.
Ithyl Shimea	Ee-**thee**-l She-meh-**yah**	A libre of power the Temple cannot control.

J

ᚼ

Jabbar	ĵ-ah-bb-**aar**	Ahiram's father. His name means 'mighty'.
Jamiir	ĵ-ah-m**eer**	King of Tanniin. His name means 'burning coal'.
Jedarc	Ĵ-eh-dark	A silent and a friend of Ahiram.

K

ᛉ

Kalibaal	Kah-lee-**baal**	Priest of Baal. Member of the Inner Circle in Babylon. Sharr's right hand man.
Kanmar	**Cahn**-maar	The Lord of the Deep in Indolan. He is Yem, the god of the sea according to the Temple of Baal.
Kwadil	Kwah-d**eel**	Dwarf. Wealthy merchant. Friend of Balid.

L

Layaléa	Lah-yah-leh-yah	Corintus' wife. Her name means 'lovely night'.
Layaleen	Lah-yah-**leen**	The wife of the El-Windiir. Her name means 'starry night'.

M

Malikuun	Mah-lee-**kuun**	Plural of Malku. The Lords of Light.
Meyroon	Mey-**roon**	Meyroon is lighter than a feather, harder than the hardest steel, and cannot be cursed, nor melted by fire or shattered by the coldest ice.

N

Noraldeen	No-rah-l-**deen**	Silent. Friend of Ahiram. Her name means 'shining light'.

R

Raayiil	Raa-**yeel**	A creature of the spell world. It appears as a composite of a dream, a vision and a prophecy,

		and takes complete control of the human mind.
Ramany	Rah-mah-nee	A judge for the Games of the Mines.
Ramel	Rah-mel	Queen of Tanniin. Sharr's niece.

S   W

Sharr	Sh-ah-**rr**	High Priest of the Temple of Babylon and the ultimate authority of the entire Temple order of Baal. His name means 'fire'.
Sureï	Su-ray	The greatest sorcerer the Temple has known.

T   †

Tajèr	**Tah**-jeh-r	The name of the first Zakir, who thought to profit from the accumulated knowledge. His name came to mean 'merchant'.
Tajéruun	Tah-jeh-**ruun**	Plural of Tajèr.
Taniir	Tah-**neer**	The name of the legendary castle in Tanniin built by El-Windiir (Taniir-On-High) and the name of the city where,

		currently, King Jamiir reigns. The name means 'To light'.
Tanios	Tah-nios	Commander of the Silent
Tanniin Ashod	Tah-**neen** Ah-**shod**	The greatest of all dragons, known as Daron Ashod among the dwarfs and as Black Dragon by the Empyreans.
Tébêt	Teh-bet	Lunar month corresponding roughly to the month of January.

U

Y

Urkuun	Ur-**kuun**		Creature of the spell world of incredible power. Cannot be defeated by natural means.
Uziguzi Aor Jar	Uz-ee-gu-zee wor ĵ -ar	A-	Councilor to the Empyrean Empress Aylul Meïr Pen.

Z

Z

Zakiir	Zah-**keer**	A man whose sole purpose in life is to consign to memory the secrets of others.

Zakiruun	**Zah**-kee-**ruun**	Plural of Zakir.
Zaril Andali	**Zah**-**reel** An-dah-**lee**	A mythical bird in Tanniin whose blue wings were the source of every blue sky. Its feast is celebrated at the winter equinox to ward off the bad spirits of the night.

About the Author

Michael Joseph Murano is the author's pen name. Michael began writing at the age of sixteen and never stopped since. The curious fact that he delayed the publication of his first novel until now is a story too long to tell. Suffice it to say that Michael has written the ten books of the Epic of Ahiram over a period of fourteen years, with the initial intention to enchant his seven children by reading to them evening after evening.

Michael has written, in French and English, numerous plays, children's books, a collection of poems for his wife, and a series of audio stories he continues to record for his two youngest daughters.

Michael's blog, www.epicofahiram.com is a portal unto the rich world of Ahiram. He invites you to join him there and discover the epic of the slave, born to be a hero.

Made in the USA
San Bernardino, CA
04 October 2014